New York Times bestselling author Penny Jordan has been writing contemporary women's fiction for more than ten years. She has a string of international bestsellers to her name, including *Power Play, The Hidden Years* and *For Better For Worse*. Penny has sold over fifty million copies of her books worldwide, with translations into twenty-six languages. Born in Lancashire, England, she now lives with her husband in a beautiful fourteenth-century home in rural Cheshire.

Penny's previous novels include:
LOVE'S CHOICES
STRONGER THAN YEARNING
POWER PLAY
SILVER
THE HIDDEN YEARS
LINGERING SHADOWS
FOR BETTER FOR WORSE
CRUEL LEGACY

Penny Jordan

POWER GAMES

MIRA BOOKS

ISBN 1-55166-126-8

POWER GAMES

Copyright © 1995 by Penny Jordan.

Printed in U.S.A.

Prologue

The room was badly lit and uninviting. It smelled of stale disinfectant and there was a thin film of dust over the tops of the metal filing cabinets. The frosted-glass window overlooked the hospital car park, cars and their drivers dim, obscure shapes moving ceaselessly to and fro.

The girl seated in the chair watched them dully, while the older woman across the desk from her exchanged looks over her head with the man standing awkwardly in the doorway.

The room was small. It had originally been a storeroom. Beyond the open door they could hear the normal everyday sounds of the hospital, the muted voices of the nurses, the whir of trolley and bed wheels, the high-pitched cries of the newborn and the murmurs of their mothers. . . .

The girl spoke, her voice low and filled with exhaustion, betraying, like her drawn white face and the fragility of her too thin body, the strain she had been under.

'And you're sure that no one will ever know . . . that no one—' She paused, catching her trembling bottom lip between her teeth. She was young, acknowledged the woman, barely nineteen, and in many ways she looked younger—in others she looked immeasurably older.

'—that no one will ever be able to find out.'

'No one,' the woman assured her quietly.

A nurse carrying a baby walked past the half-open door. The girl winced as she watched her.

'Where . . . where do I have to sign?' she asked, her voice cracking slightly.

The woman showed her, instructing as she was bound to do, 'You are quite sure that you know what this involves, aren't you? That once this document is signed there can be no going back . . . that it won't be possible for you to change your mind. . . .' She looked towards the man standing by the door, who nodded his head slightly.

'Yes. Yes, I do know that,' the girl confirmed. Her words rustled as dryly as the dying autumn leaves outside.

Her hand was shaking as she leaned over the table and started to sign her name.

The older woman felt for her, but there was nothing she could do.

'It will be for the best,' she told the girl gently, when she had finished her signature and lifted her head to stare blindly towards the window.

'You will see. You will be able to make a new life for yourself, start afresh.... Forget ...'

'Forget?' Again the girl's voice betrayed emotion. 'I can never forget,' she whispered passionately. 'Never ... Never. I don't deserve to forget.'

'It's over now,' the woman told her firmly.

'Over?'

The girl focused on her. 'How can it ever be over? It can't. For me it can never be over... *never!*'

1

'Have you read my report on the approach we've had from the Japanese?'

Bram Soames looked away from his office window, which fronted on to the private enclosed garden of a London square, and turned towards his son.

Outwardly father and son were very similar in appearance, both tall and broad-shouldered, with athletes' tough, well-muscled physiques, thick brown-black hair, ice-green eyes and subtly aristocratic profiles inherited—so Bram's paternal grandmother had always maintained—from a pre-Victorian liaison between his great-great-grandmother and the peer to whom her father owed his living.

It had been, according to his grandmother, the classic tale of the innocent vicar's daughter seduced by the notoriously rakish earl.

Privately Bram was inclined to suspect the features could just as easily have been inherited from some poor relation, but because it was an intrinsic part of his nature to allow others their vulnerabilities and vanities, he had never publicly questioned his grandmother's version of the story.

It was also a family tradition that the eldest son always received one of his notorious progenitor's names; in Bram's case he had been triply gifted—or cursed—in being christened Brampton Vernon Piers.

In Jay's case, of course, things had been decidedly different, but then . . .

Outsiders always imagined they must be brothers rather than father and son and typically Bram was tolerant of their assumption, while Jay was invariably irritated by it and often actively hostile towards the person voicing it.

After all, with only fifteen years between them it was only natural that people should make that mistake.

Now, as Jay waited for his response, Bram acknowledged that his son wasn't going to like what he had to say. 'I'm sorry, Jay,' he said steadily, 'but it just isn't on. We're a small specialist company and to go in for the kind of expansion this scheme involves—' He paused. 'We simply don't have the resources to man that kind of project. I'm a technician and this business is run from that standpoint. This Japanese scheme would potentially involve us in handing over to lawyers and accountants.

'*Potentially* it could take this business right to the forefront of modern computer technology,' Jay broke in angrily. 'Right now we're a small British-based outfit in the third league. With this Japanese backing—'

'We're a market leader, Jay,' his father stated with quiet firmness. 'If we weren't, the Japanese wouldn't be approaching us.'

'But we need to expand!' Jay exploded. 'To get into the American market. *That's* where the future lies—the mass market. The specialist stuff we do is all very well, but the real market isn't there. Just look at—'

Bram interrupted, 'There *is* a definite market for our products. We've built our name and our reputation on what we're good at.'

'On what *you're* good at,' Jay retorted furiously. 'And that's exactly what this is all about, isn't it? Oh, you're happy enough to give me my own office and my own title, even a directorship, but when it comes to giving me any *real* power, any *real* support.' The green eyes hardened with a bitter contempt that Bram's could never have reflected, causing the older man's heart to ache with a familiar mixture of exasperation and sadness.

Power, control, recognition—they mattered so much to Jay, and they always had done. The turbulent child whose deliberate and wilful manipulation of Bram's guilt and pain had caused Bram's friends to suggest it might be wiser, for his own sake, to distance himself from the possessive demands of his child, had turned into an equally turbulent and dissatisfied adult.

But to suggest to Jay that his intense need for power and control had its roots in the traumatic days of his childhood was like tempting a wild bird of prey with fresh-killed meat.

Jay would swoop on the suggestion with all of his considerable power and force, take it and worry at it and savage it with an avid blood-thirst and single-mindedness that left delicate stomached onlookers nauseated and Bram himself feeling compassion and guilt.

But in this instance he could not, as he had so often done with the much younger Jay, give in. Not to keep the peace, but in the hope that in doing so he would be giving Jay the reassurance he knew his son so desperately craved and equally desperately refused to acknowledge.

'No, Jay. I'm sorry,' Bram repeated firmly, ignoring his son's aggressive and untruthful assertion that his role in the business was that of a cipher only—a job Bram had created simply to keep his son in a demeaning and subservient position.

In fact, if the truth were known, in some ways Bram wished that Jay had chosen a different kind of career rather than joined him in the business.

He was wryly aware that, along with all the physical characteristics, Jay had also inherited the skills that had made him one of the most innovative and skilled computer-program writers of his generation.

But typically Jay had wanted more. Taking his MBA at Harvard had, Bram knew, been a form of one-upmanship on him.

While Bram still felt the most important role he had was to create the programs on which the company's success was founded, Jay believed that the future lay in expansion and mass marketing.

'You're sorry,' Jay snapped bitterly. 'I've put weeks of work into this project. I'm due to fly to New York tonight to meet with the Japanese and the Americans. How the hell do you think it's going to make me look when I have to turn round and tell them we're not interested?'

Now they were getting down to the nub of the matter. It was his pride that Jay was most concerned with, his potential loss of face. Not that Bram hadn't already guessed that.

'I shouldn't worry too much,' he told his son now with the quiet steadiness that had always deceived the unperceptive into mistaking his apparent lack of aggression for weakness. 'If I'm any judge, you'll probably find they'll assume you're trying on a bit of brinkmanship. The Japanese, in particular, are very skilled in that particular field.'

Jay frowned. His father was probably right, he acknowledged, and he certainly wasn't ready to give up his plans for the future of the business, no matter what his father said.

The mood of savage resentment which had swept over him when he realised his father was not going to accept his plans eased, softened by the thought that he could still find a way of changing his father's mind, of proving that he was right.

As a child he had been aware of the vulnerability of his position in his father's life, hostile and aggressively suspicious of anyone else's influence over his father, and those feelings had carried into his adult life. At twenty-seven he was old enough, mature enough to be far more skilful at concealing those feelings and the cause of them, from himself as well as from others, than he had been as a child; just as he was equally adept at denying that his powerful need to gain ascendancy and control over his father sprang from those same deep-rooted feelings of fear.

It was obviously farcical to try to claim to himself or anyone else that his father, at forty-two, might be losing his grip on the company and that he, Jay, had for his father's own sake, somehow to wrest control from him.

But the computer industry was notorious for its appetite for young supple minds, its hunger for progress and innovation. The future of their business lay with the young, not, as his father insisted, with the traditional markets.

Nor with this latest scheme in which his father had got involved creating programs for improving the quality of life of those who were, in various ways, mentally or physically disabled—'mentally or physically challenged,' as his father had mildly corrected him during Jay's recent furious tirade against the potential expense involved if his father went ahead with such a venture.

'No, I realise there won't be any profit in it in the immediate future,' his father had agreed. 'But shouldn't we offer to help those who would otherwise live life on the sidelines? And if we *are* successful there could be considerable profits involved— through patents alone.'

'And that's why you're doing it, is it, Father?' Jay had challenged him sardonically, 'Because you're looking ahead to future profits?

'Balls,' he had contradicted flatly. 'You're doing it because you're a soft touch and everyone knows it. Don't try telling me that Anthony Palliser approached you because he wanted to offer you an opportunity to make money. No, he approached you because he knew no one else in the business would even look at a deal that virtually involves giving away programs we don't even know if we can write yet. Programs which will have to be individually tailored for each person who uses them.'

'Programs which will give people who would otherwise not be able to do so, the ability to communicate,' Bram had told him. 'Think what that means, Jay.'

'I am. It's a complete waste of time and money,' Jay had insisted.

'*My* time and *my* money,' Bram had reminded him gently.

His father's time, his father's money. They ran through Jay's life in a twisted skein that rubbed continuously against his soul, chafing and scarring it.

One of his earliest memories of life with his father had been of a woman's voice, cool and remote, saying impatiently, 'Bram, for goodness' sake, think. The last thing you've got time for now is the responsibility of a child. We're on the brink of getting our first real break, of finally making some money, and God knows we need it.'

He had hated that woman then and he still hated her now. A feeling which he knew, for all her cool distance and remoteness, Helena fully returned.

'What time is your flight to New York?' he heard his father asking now.

'Six-thirty this evening.' He added suspiciously, 'why?'

'No reason,' Bram responded. 'It's just that I've got a meeting with Anthony at four-thirty—he's looked out some research material he thought I'd like to study—and I thought you might like to join us.'

'What for?' Jay challenged him sourly. 'Like you said, it's your time you're putting on the line—and your money.'

'Jay—' Bram started to protest, but the younger man was already turning to leave the office. Despite Jay's six-foot-two height and the powerful male strength barely cloaked by the conventional dark business suit, Bram was achingly reminded of a much younger but equally surly Jay turning his back on him and stalking off in stubbornness, his shoulders stiff with anger, the power of his emotions making his then much smaller body virtually vibrate with their intensity.

'He's manipulating you and you're letting him get away with it.' Helena had warned him in exasperation. And of course she had been right—in a sense—but how did you tell a small, furiously angry and bitterly resentful child who still sometimes, two years after their deaths, cried out in the night for his mother and grandparents—a child who you knew used his aggression and manipulation to mask his terrified fear that you, too, might desert him—how did you convince such a child that he had absolutely nothing to fear? How could you deliberately strip away from him the comfort blanket of his stubborn pride by revealing to him that you knew, far from hating you as he claimed, just how much he actually craved your love? How did you tell him that the arms he stubbornly resisted and rejected were, in reality, only too ready to close around him and hold him protectively, safe from the rest of the world and all its hurts?

It had made Bram ache with a throat-closing pity to watch as Jay fiercely rejected any attempt on his father's part to be physically close with him. To Bram, a very tactile man who had no problems in expressing the emotional side of his nature, Jay's rejection of the kisses and cuddles he so obviously craved made Bram want to weep.

'You don't have anything to feel guilty about,' Helena had protested when he had tried to explain.

'Oh, but I do,' Bram had corrected her softly. 'After all, I fathered him.'

'You were fourteen,' Helena had reminded him. 'A boy... a child still, yourself.'

'Yes,' Bram had agreed steadily. 'But while that might be an excuse, Helena, it is Jay who pays the price for my immaturity. No child of fourteen can be a parent... a father, in any real sense of the word. In being responsible for Jay's conception, I have robbed him of his right to a real parent, of being born into a relationship where he was wanted and loved, of having a father who *could* protect him . . . give him the security he needs.'

'You have given him security,' Helena had insisted. 'You've given him a home, abandoned your own life, your own plans, your own friends because of him. He should be grateful to you instead of . . . of trying to completely destroy your life.'

'Helena, no child should ever feel he needs to be grateful to a parent for being loved and wanted. No human being should ever have to grow up under that weight of emotional hunger. I know Jay can be difficult. . . .'

'Difficult! He's impossible, Bram. He's ruining your life. You should put him in a home—have him fostered—for his sake as well as your own. . . .'

What Bram could still see in his adult son and what other people could not see was the fear of a child who believes that he has to earn his parent's love. What he, as a father, could never forgive himself for was causing that fear.

He had hoped that as Jay matured he would come to recognise for himself what motivated him and see that his fear was needless, that the angry possessive grasp he insisted on keeping over both their lives deprived them both; that allowing other people into their lives could only enrich them both. But this had simply not happened.

And just as Jay had so jealously guarded his relationship with his father and been fiercely antagonistic to anyone else coming into their lives, so now he guarded his own privacy. Bram knew from the brief scraps of gossip that percolated through the office grapevine that Jay was a highly sexed man whom women found dangerously attractive, until they realised that sex was all he wanted from them, and all they were going to get from him.

Inadvertently listening in on a conversation at a dinner party between one of his son's ex-lovers and her friend, he had heard her say dryly, 'Physically, Jay is just about the best lover I've ever had. He knows all the right moves, all the right buttons to press, but after a while you start to realise that this is all he is doing. It's as though he's written a program for sexual success—it's cold and clinical. I pity the woman he eventually marries. He's the type who'll go for some fresh, virginal, up-market aristocratic girl, long on pedigree and short on savvy. He'll seduce her, marry her, pack her óff to a house in the country as soon as he's got her pregnant and then go back to the real business of his life.'

'Which is?' her friend had asked, eyebrows raised. 'Or need I ask?'

'Oh, it's not sex,' she had been told. 'No, Jay's real purpose in life, his real consuming passion, is his relationship with his father . . . making sure that nothing and no one comes between them.'

'Because he's afraid of losing the business, you mean,' the friend had suggested.

'I'm not sure. I remember once, though, when he was supposed to be taking me out to dinner and I happened to mention that Bram was going to spend the weekend with my cousin. She was just newly divorced then, and she and Bram have always been good friends. Jay cancelled the dinner date without any proper apology and my cousin rang me a few days later, very aggrieved, to complain that less than a couple of hours after Bram had arrived, Jay turned up, insisting he needed to see his father on some vital company business, and he stayed on almost all weekend.'

'Well, I suppose if Bram did marry again Jay could lose out to any children of that marriage, and let's face it, Bram might not have the same kind of stud reputation as Jay, but there's no doubt about it, he is a very, very sexy man. . . .'

'Very,' the other woman had agreed.

Bram hadn't waited to listen to any more. Hearing himself described as a very sexy man had made him feel more wryly amused than flattered.

His sexual relationships had, over the years, been few and far between, and conducted with the kind of cloak-and-dagger secrecy which some men might have found sexually exciting but which he had simply found inhibiting and depressing.

Inevitably the woman involved would grow impatient and resentful of the way their relationship had to be kept hidden from Jay, and when Bram had ignored his own misgivings and brought their relationship out into the open, Jay had inevitably sabotaged it with such single-minded vindictiveness and passion that Bram had not been surprised when his lover had retreated.

'I love you, Bram,' one of them had told him emotionally. 'You're everything I've ever wanted in a man—and more. Being with you permanently would be heaven on earth. Having Jay in that life would be sheer purgatory.'

'Why can't you send him away somewhere . . . boarding school . . . or Borstal?' another had gritted at him furiously. But while he sympathised with her, Bram had shaken his head.

He had already damaged Jay enough. Punishing him wasn't the answer. Instead, Bram had tried to show him that he had nothing to fear; that nothing he could do would destroy Bram's love for him; that loving someone else would not diminish his love for Jay. But in the end Bram had been forced to acknowledge that Jay was never going to believe him; that in many ways he didn't want to believe him, because he didn't want to relinquish the hold he thought he had over his father.

Perhaps it would have been different if Bram had met someone he had felt intensely passionate about, but he never had. His own emotional and physical desires were something he had learned to put on hold while Jay was young. When, he wondered now, had the necessity become a habit it was easier to keep than to give up?

He wasn't a cynical man, but he couldn't help but be aware that often the women who actively sought him out were not necessarily doing so because they wanted him as a man. The fact that he was a millionaire several times over was no secret, thanks to the financial and popular press.

He had originally set up the business while he was still at Cambridge, ignoring the warnings of his friends that he would be better advised to follow their example and get himself a regular job and, even more important, a regular salary with one of the many computer firms head-hunting the pick of the crop of the university's graduates.

Bram hadn't been able to wait to be head-hunted. He needed to earn money immediately to support himself and Jay. Instead he had opted for freelance work, which brought in a smaller income perhaps, but allowed him to be at home.

It was Helena, a friend from his university days, who had first suggested he set up his own company. She had always had a shrewd head for business.

Unlike Plum—or Plum's father.

Helena had christened her daughter Victoria, but Flyte MacDonald, her first husband—the big powerful redheaded, vehemently left-wing Scotsman she had fallen in love with and married all within the space of a month and totally against her parents' wishes—had immediately nicknamed their baby Plum, and the name had stuck.

Flyte had been and still was a sculptor, an unknown one then, but a highly acclaimed one now. Bram thought that Plum's name rather suited her. There was undoubtedly something ripe and sweet about her, luscious, a sweet juicy allure which went with her hedonistically sensual nature.

Helena had divorced Flyte when Plum was three years old and had later married her second husband, James, with whom she had had two more children. Neither of whom was anything like Plum.

Shortly after her sixteenth birthday, Plum had announced that she was leaving school and going to live with her father.

Normally controlled and calm in everything she did and said, Helena had been white-faced with anger and disbelief when she had related their quarrel to Bram.

'Flyte's to blame for all this, of course. He's the one who's encouraging her to ruin her life like this. James is furious.

'She's always been rebellious...difficult....' She had frowned and looked away, unable to look directly at him as she admitted, 'There have been problems . . . at school . . . boys, that kind of thing, but James persuaded them to let her stay on.... And this is how she repays us.

'Can you imagine what people are going to say...to think, when they learn that she's moved in with her father? Everyone knows the kind of life Flyte leads . . . his reputation is notorious. He—'

'He is her father, Helena,' Bram had said, trying to placate her.

Privately he suspected that Plum would soon get tired of living with her father. Flyte's work as a sculptor might be highly acclaimed, but there was no denying the fact that his lifestyle was as brash and unconventional as the man himself.

He lived in a small mews house on the fringes of Chelsea, which he had bought years before when property prices and the area itself reflected the bohemian lifestyle of its inhabitants.

Now things had changed and so had the neighbourhood, conventional middle-class couples replacing the original inhabitants. But Flyte had not changed along with them—much to the chagrin of his neighbours, who did not enjoy the fallout from the frequent and noisy quarrels Flyte enjoyed with the succession of equally uninhibited lovers and models who passed through his life.

The Porsche-owning city broker who lived next door had complained that his impressionable children could be affected by Flyte's lifestyle. Also, he added, he did not enjoy the constant interruptions from the sculptor's visitors, who weren't sure which house was his.

The neighbour was not pleased by Flyte's response. As an apology, or so he said, Flyte had given him a statue—of a pair of naked lovers enjoying a form of physical intimacy which duplicated the number of the broker's house. The faces of the lovers in the statue had an uncanny resemblance to those of the broker and his wife.

'You could put it in your front garden,' Flyte had explained innocently. 'That way there won't be any danger of anyone mistaking my house for yours.'

Somehow or other the incident had been picked up by the papers, much to the fury of the broker. Matters were not helped, from the broker's point of view at least, by his comment, quoted in the press, that he had never participated in such an activity with his wife, never mind modelled for the sculpture.

As Bram had prophesied, Plum did not stay long with her father, who, to his credit, had refused to allow her to leave school.

She was now back living with Helena and James, 'when she bothered to come home, that is,' Helena had complained bitterly to Bram, several weeks earlier.

'I know that things are different now from when we were young, but—' she had bitten her lip '—James says if she can't behave properly and decently then she will have to live somewhere else. He's concerned about the effect her behaviour will have on our other two,' Helena had explained. 'He believes that if they think we're condoning what she's doing, they might . . . What else can we do, Bram? I just can't get through to her. She's always been so difficult . . . so very much more Flyte's child than mine. I really feel as though I don't have anything in common with her. She's so emotional, so . . . so uncontrolled.'

So sexual, she might have said, Bram recognised, but she didn't.

Plum herself, however, appeared impervious to her mother's icy disgust at her high sexual profile, her sexual exploits and the widespread reputation she had gained.

Bram was inclined to feel sorry for Plum more than anything else, despite the fact that—

The shrill ring of a telephone in a neighbouring office cut across his private thoughts. He glanced at his watch. He would have to leave soon if he was going to keep his appointment with Anthony on time.

He had known Anthony, or rather *Sir* Anthony now, since their university days and they had remained in contact, even though their career paths had widely diverged; his into his own business and Anthony's through work as a student with the voluntary overseas service into the post he now held as the head of a large charity.

'I've got a proposal to put to you and a challenge,' Anthony had told him several months earlier, and when he had explained what he wanted, Bram had laughed and agreed.

'You're right, it is a challenge.'

'And one you don't want?' Anthony had asked him.

'Leave it with me,' Bram had responded. 'Let me think about it. . . .'

Now Bram hurried into the corridor having suddenly remembered something. 'Jay,' he called out as he entered his son's office.

'Yes.'

Ignoring Jay's curt hostility, Bram reminded him, 'You haven't forgotten about Plum's eighteenth-birthday party, have you? You'll need to get her a present.'

Bram winced inwardly as he saw the look in Jay's eyes. His son had never particularly liked Plum.

'What have you got in mind? The way I see it, it's either a chastity belt or a copy of the *Kama Sutra*, although I suspect that the latter would be superfluous since, according to gossip, she's already run through every position in it and invented a few more of her own into the bargain. And as for the former—' he gave his father a wintry, slightly malicious smile '—it would be rather a case of shutting the stable door after the horse has bolted, wouldn't it?

'Still, it's good to know that even the supposedly infallible Helena isn't quite the perfect mother she would like us to think.'

Bram listened to his son in silence. If anything, Jay disliked Helena even more than he did her daughter.

'Plum's a child still, Jay,' Bram said eventually in defence of his godchild. 'She's . . .'

'She's a slut,' Jay supplied brutally.

As he walked past his son's office half an hour later on his way out of the building, Bram noticed that the door was open and the office empty, Jay's desk cleared.

Jay wouldn't let his proposal of expanding the company end where it had today, Bram knew. But on this issue he intended to stand firm, not as Jay had so bitterly accused him, because he wanted to humiliate him and withhold authority and control from him, but because he genuinely believed that the kind of expansion Jay had in mind was too big a risk.

The receptionist, seeing him appear in the front reception area, gave him a startled look and asked him if he wanted her to page his chauffeur.

Bram smiled at her and shook his head. It was a pleasant, sunny afternoon and he didn't consider himself too decrepit to walk the mile or so across the city to the charity's head offices.

When he stepped outside and tasted the dust-ridden, polluted air of the capital, he acknowledged that it was at times like this that he most missed the wide-open spaces of Cambridge's flat fenlands.

The decision to move his business to London had been forced upon him by a variety of circumstances—the need to be based somewhere central to his growing band of worldwide customers; the need to provide Jay with a more stimulating environment than that of a remote, run-down fenland cottage, as well as with the right kind of schooling—but privately he had never stopped missing the silent stillness of the fens.

It was typical of Anthony that he had managed to persuade the owners of the magnificent Georgian building which housed the charity's headquarters to lease it at a peppercorn rent.

'It never pays to be too humble,' he had told Bram when Bram had once commented on the magnificence of the building, which included a mirror-hung ballroom where the cream of society gladly paid a small fortune to rub shoulders with one another and, with any luck, get their photographs on the pages of *Tatler* in the process.

Bram still wasn't sure if he was going to be able to provide the help Anthony wanted. He would like to, though, he would like to very much, he acknowledged as he recalled the video Anthony had shown him of a young man, previously almost totally unable to communicate, who through the medium of a specially adapted computer was now actually able to speak.

If he could write programs which would help others in a similar way, it would—what? Offset his burden of guilt at having achieved so much in a material sense while having done so little when it came to his son?

No, but it *would* give him an immense sense of satisfaction. Communication was a vital part of life, and to be able to help to give others that gift . . .

Once during his early days in Cambridge he had been exploring the city and had wandered into what he had assumed to be an empty church, just as its choir had started to sing. The sound of their voices raised in an anthem that would probably now be considered too old-fashioned and robust, had briefly moved him to tears.

Unable to sing himself, he had been deeply moved to come so unexpectedly across such a joyously and full-blooded paean of praise.

It saddened him that Jay, who had a very good voice, refused to enjoy his gift. His own gift, if it could be called that, was far more mundane, but if through it he could help others to make their own special sound of joy. . .

His mouth curled into a faintly self-deprecatory smile. How Jay would have mocked him if he could have read his thoughts.

The young receptionist, who had watched Bram walk into the building, suddenly discovered what it was that made some older men so swooningly sexy. The thought of those heavy-lidded eyes looking deeply into hers, that gorgeously sexy mouth kissing hers, made a delicious shiver of sensual pleasure run through her body.

She bet he'd be terrific in bed as well. Older men were; they took their time, knew what to do, and this one, even though he looked well into his late thirties, also looked as though under that dull city suit he had the kind of lean hard body she had always secretly yearned after. Her boyfriend lifted weights and couldn't understand that she found his overdeveloped muscles more of a turn-off than a turn-on.

'Brampton Soames,' Bram announced himself to the girl, giving her a smile which he would have been surprised to know made her curl her toes in her shoes beneath her desk.

This was Brampton Soames, the multimillionaire. Her face flushed slightly as, with a startled look, she told him, 'Sir Anthony has had to go out.'

'Thank you, Jane, I'll deal with Mr Soames . . .'

Disappointed, the receptionist watched as Sir Anthony's secretary walked firmly over to their visitor, drawing him away from her desk and towards the lift.

'I'm sorry, Mr Soames,' she was apologising to him, 'I intended to be here when you arrived. Unfortunately though, I got delayed . . . a phone call.'

'That's all right,' Bram told her. 'I understand that Sir Anthony has had to go out.'

'Yes. A meeting with our patron. He left his apologies.'

'I was only calling to collect some papers,' Bram told her. 'Perhaps . . .'

'Yes, he has arranged for the head of our Research and Records Department to provide you with the information you requested. He did suggest that if you had time you might find it worthwhile to have a talk with her. She's been with the charity for almost twenty years as an archivist, and Sir Anthony thought she would be far more able to supply the kind of information you would need than he could.'

'I'm sure she can,' Bram agreed.

'I'll take you up to her office,' the secretary told him. 'Her name is Taylor Fielding.'

'Taylor... Is she an American?' Bram enquired curiously.

'I don't think so. Her accent certainly isn't American, but perhaps she has American connections. She's a very private person. Although I've worked here for nearly eight years myself, I know very little about her.'

Bram didn't pursue the subject. It was part of his nature to be interested in other people, curious about them, but never in any kind of intrusive way. He was sensitive enough, though, to pick up on the reticence in the secretary's voice and to wonder at the cause of it. Women working together were normally far more open and forthcoming with one another than men. While it would cause no particular comment for two men to work together for eight years without revealing any personal details of themselves, for two women to do so . . .

Unless, of course, there was some kind of antipathy between them, but the secretary's tone hadn't suggested so.

Which meant that Taylor Fielding, whatever else she might or might not be, was obviously an extremely private person. With an English accent and an American name. Interesting.

As the secretary guided him through the maze of corridors and stairs in the part of the building not yet modernised, he allowed his imagination the luxury of free flow.

Taylor Fielding. Perhaps she would be a little, neat, timid brown mouse of a person, a female version of Beatrix Potter's industrious Tailor of Gloucester. The workings of his own imagination made his mouth curl in warm amusement with that same smile that the receptionist downstairs was still daydreaming over.

And that was how Taylor first saw him when she opened her door to Sir Anthony's secretary's knock.

2

She was nothing like Beatrix Potter's tailor, nothing at all, Bram acknowledged as he stared in amused appreciation at the woman coming towards him. She was tall, tall with a body so gently and erotically voluptuous that the sight of it forced into the straight jacket and prim high-necked white blouse she wore with a dowdy navy pleated skirt, left him torn between laughter and tears.

Laughter at the total incongruity of such a magnificent body so inappropriately clothed. She should have been wearing something French or Italian in a soft subtle natural shade to highlight her delicate colouring, not that appallingly harsh combination of navy and white which all but doused and drowned it. And tears because his intuition, that streak of intense awareness of other people's feelings, relayed to him her own loathing and terror of a body so lushly feminine that just to look at her made him want to reach out and stroke her—not out of lust but out of reverence. This woman was no American, not with that pale skin untouched by the sun, and those light, almost luminous blue-grey eyes and dark red hair, hair that was criminally confined in a bun.

The knowledge that totally unexpectedly he had become physically aroused by her, added to the fact that from the look of freezing anger she was giving him, she was also aware of it, made him grimace to himself and call his body firmly to order.

The recognition that the sight of her had given him what in his early teenage days had been universally graphically described by his peers as a 'hard-on', coupled with the knowledge that he couldn't even remember the last time he had experienced such an uncontrollable, intensely physical, response to any woman, left him caught between irritation at his body's immaturity and a rueful awareness of exactly what Miss Taylor Fielding would no doubt be thinking of him.

He knew she was a Miss because he had seen the name printed on her door.

'Taylor, this is Mr Soames,' the secretary announced.

'Bram.' Bram introduced himself, stretching out his hand. The look of icy hauteur he received in return was deliberately contrived, a just punishment no doubt for his body's flagrant breaking of the rules, but the way her body flinched away from him wasn't. That reaction was far more basic and instinctive.

'I've extracted the information from the records that Sir Anthony asked me to obtain for you,' she was saying to him as the secretary left. 'Here it is....'

At any other time Bram would merely have been gently amused and perhaps a little saddened for her at the way she pushed the file towards him, removing her hand from it as though she feared he might somehow make an attempt to touch her. But for some reason on this occasion, and with this woman, her reaction hurt him personally, not for her sake, for his own.

'I understand that you've worked for the charity for almost twenty years.' Was he imagining the sharp flicker of fear beneath the ice that wintered her eyes? He didn't think so. So what then was she so afraid of, so afraid that her fear generated an anger with herself that he could almost feel? Him? His question? Both?

Intrigued as much by her contrasting emotions as by the cause of them, Bram found himself wanting to know more about her — much more. He wanted to protect her, and at the same time he also had a very male and far less altruistic desire to unwrap her poor punished body from its cruel constrictions and watch as the anger and coldness were banished from her eyes by warmth and laughter.

Somewhere? Where? His arms... his bed... his ...

Whoa ... hold on, he warned himself firmly. Didn't he have enough complications already in his life without adding any more? And besides, hadn't she already made it plain that there was no way she was going to reciprocate the kind of thoughts he was having?

'Your file,' he heard her say coldly, her voice sharp with irritation.

Why was he looking at her like that, watching her like that? Taylor wondered angrily. As though...as though... Hurriedly she looked away from him, feeling both angry and defensive. She didn't like people, men, watching her so closely. It made her feel nervous...angry...edgy, sending alarm bells clanging through her nervous system. What was it about that kind of look in a man's eyes—sexually curious, sexually interested, sexually predatory—that once seen, you never forgot, never failed to recognise? It infuriated her that he was looking at her like that. She had done nothing to encourage his interest after all, far from it.

'Will you have dinner with me?'

The quiet question shocked her, fear and anger leaping through her body like two choke-chained guard dogs taught to respond to threat.

Bram had known what her answer would be even before he asked the question and as he measured her hostility and rejection he wondered if he had totally taken leave of his senses. There were women, plenty of them, who would have moved heaven and earth to be invited out by him, but this woman would never be one of them.

'No.'

There was nothing restrained or polite about her sharp refusal. The small word was explosive with anger and resentment and spiked with her fear. She threw it at him as though it were a hand grenade, a weapon she wanted to use to destroy him completely. It was too late now to tell her that from the moment he had walked into her office, his behaviour had been so completely out of character that even he had been surprised by it. He doubted she would believe him and knew that she would not want to believe him—him or any man who dared to overstep the boundaries she had set around herself.

Bram had come across women who were genuine man-haters, but they had been nothing like this woman. Their feelings had sprung from cold dispassionate contempt. Hers had been formed in far hotter and more painful fires. He wondered if she knew how vulnerable she seemed and how much that vulnerability made him ache for her—in every sense, the emotional and the physical.

He was just about to say he was sorry and attempt to soothe her when her office door opened and another woman came in, apologising for interrupting, after a quick and femininely appreciative glance in Bram's direction. Watching the dismissive way Taylor turned her back on him to attend to the other woman's query, Bram mentally shrugged as he headed towards the door. And then stopped, some impulse he hadn't known he possessed making him pause and murmur softly to her before he left. 'I'll be in touch. I haven't given up.'

The white-faced look of concentrated panic she threw at him made him wince. Not for himself but for her. It obviously hadn't been the right thing to say, and what was worse, he had actually known that before he opened his mouth. What the hell was the matter with him? He wasn't normally so gauche, far from it; but then the truth was that normally when it came to women, he had had more practice using his powers of tact and subtlety to fend them off, not draw them on.

'Wow,' Taylor's companion commented after Bram had gone. 'Now that's what I call a sexy man and a half. Who was he?'

'Brampton Soames, the head of Soames Computac.'

'What!' The other woman's eyes widened even further. 'All that and money, too. I'd have thought he'd be much older. Hasn't he got an adult son?'

'I really don't know,' Taylor responded dismissively in a voice which warned that Bram Soames, his sex appeal and his adult son were subjects in which she had absolutely no interest whatsoever. Which wasn't completely true. She had an interest all right, but it wasn't the same one as her colleague, who was now bemoaning the fact that she hadn't arrived just that little bit earlier before Bram had been about to leave.

Taylor's interest had nothing to do with his sexy good looks, his charismatic personality or his reputed millionaire status; her interest centred solely on the fact that he was a man and that as such she wanted nothing whatever to do with him.

'What is it with her?' she had once overheard one of her younger female colleagues demanding, unaware that she was actually within earshot. 'She acts and dresses like some old-fashioned spinster from a pre-war film. I know she's got virgin written all over her, but if she just made a bit of an effort, dressed herself up a bit more, changed her hairstyle, she could probably still get herself a man.'

Get herself a man. Taylor had had to bite down hard on the inside of her mouth to prevent herself from screaming out aloud that a man was the last thing she wanted, the very last thing.

'She's obviously got some kind of hang-up about sex,' the girl had continued blithely.

A hang-up about *sex.* Taylor's body had shaken with silent mirthless laughter. Her colleague was still enthusing about Brampton Soames. Taylor looked pointedly at her watch. It had been a present from her parents, a reward for passing her A levels.

She had been terrified during that final year at school that she would disappoint them, that she wouldn't achieve the high grades they expected of her, that she would let them down. Her elder sister had left Bristol University with first class honours and had then gone on to achieve the highest marks in her year in her postgraduate course.

Caroline had wanted to become a surgeon but their father had dissuaded her. 'It would have been different were she a boy,' he had explained dispassionately, 'but as a woman she'll be better off with a career which allows her to combine it more easily with a family.'

Their father wasn't the kind of man who wanted his daughters to be token men; he wanted their scholastic achievements to reflect his own brilliance. As one of the country's leading research biologists, he was well aware of the importance of inherited gene patterns for preserving excellence, but he was a very male man as well. His critical approval of her as she grew up had always been important to Taylor. A frowning look at her across the breakfast table in her early teenage years, the small comment that he didn't care for her new hairstyle, or that she seemed to be putting on a little weight could cast a dark shadow over the whole day, while her father's approving smile could leave her basking in warmth and sunshine.

Her mother had equally high standards. She'd trained as a pathologist but had only worked part-time after the birth of her daughters. Like Taylor's father, her family too had a long history in medicine, combined with a very solid upper middle class county background. Both girls had been sent to private schools where the emphasis was equally divided between academic success and social grooming.

Without anything specific ever having been said Taylor knew her parents had very high expectations of her. Caroline had once been well on her way to fulfilling those expectations. When she returned from her year off in Australia, visiting distant relations who owned and ran a huge outback sheep station, she had been going to study law—a choice of career thoroughly approved of by their father. Quite naturally, since it had been, in effect, his choice.

As she reflected on the traumas of that long-ago summer, Taylor felt her throat close up on the hot acid burn of emotion.

Damn Brampton Soames. This was his fault, making her feel like this, making her remember....

She didn't see her sister any more. Her parents had disowned Caroline after she had broken all the rules and married a trainee manager she had met and fallen in love with on the Australian sheep station. Taylor could still remember her parents' shock, their outrage and disgust at what she had done. They had cut her out of their lives and warned Taylor that she must do the same, and she had complied with their demands. Taylor had become doubly anxious not to fail them—in any way.

She planned to leave her office slightly early this evening; there was a library book to collect and she had some shopping to do. She didn't like being out when it was dark if she could avoid it. Winter evenings were an exception, of course, and she had had to develop various coping strategies to deal with them—like unobtrusively falling into step beside another woman in the street, not travelling by public transport unless it was absolutely necessary. Instead she used a small private-hire taxi firm which specialised in supplying only female drivers.

It was an expensive luxury, but one she was prepared to make other sacrifices to afford. Still, she was always glad when the dark nights started to lighten. The dark always made her feel uncomfortable, wary...afraid. She always slept with all the lights on in her flat, including the lamp in her bedroom, if you could call it sleeping. She had trained herself to wake at the slightest noise—her body stiff and alert as her anxious glance probed her room, her ears strained for sound.

She doubted that Bram Soames slept like that. No, he would sleep deeply and confidently, his big powerful body spread across the bed. And if he had a woman there beside him, no doubt he would keep her chained possessively to his side with that way some men had of throwing an imprisoning arm or leg over their partner.

Bram Soames. She hadn't given much thought to what kind of man he might be when Sir Anthony had mentioned his visit and asked her to give him the file. All she knew about him was that he had agreed to work on a computer program to help people with speech difficulties to communicate. An ambitious project and very praiseworthy—if he could do it. If not? Well, no doubt it would gain him and his company a good deal of free publicity, she'd decided sourly. No, she hadn't given much thought to what kind of man he might be, but she knew now that he was the complete antithesis of all that she might have imagined had she done so.

That strong physical sexual presence that had invaded her office, making her feel nervous and afraid; that unashamed uninhibited sexual arousal of his body which he had made no attempt to conceal. Over the years she had come across men far more predatory sexually, but somehow they had not unnerved her in the way that he had. Perhaps because *they* hadn't seemed to invite her to share the amusement, his *bemusement*, almost, at his own reaction to her—as though it had caught him off guard as much as it had her.

But that was impossible, of course. A man of his age . . . of his experience. Well, he was wasting his time with her.

'I haven't given up,' he had warned her.

Her body shook suddenly, her teeth chattering. Shock, that was all it was, shock. Odd that such a stupid unimportant thing should do that to her when . . .

'I'm sorry,' Taylor told her colleague, who she realised was watching her curiously. 'I have to go. Can we sort this out in the morning?'

The first thing Jay did once he had checked into the Pierre, his hotel in New York, was to ring his secretary in London.

'Is my father around?' he asked, once he had discovered there were no important messages waiting for him.

'I don't think so,' she told him. 'But I'll check for you.'

Irritably Jay stared out of his bedroom at the view of Manhattan beneath him. He had flown Concorde, using the time to go over his strategy for negotiating with the Japanese, and had decided that it still might be easier to pressure his father to change his mind and agree to the deal. Having mentally rehearsed his arguments and how he would block his father's attempts to counter them, he was not very pleased to be told Bram had left the building and that no one seemed to know where he had gone.

Jay cursed as he replaced the receiver. He was tempted to take the risk of lying to the Japanese, hoping that he could persuade his father to change his mind.... No, that was too much of a risk, Jay acknowledged.

He hadn't told his father that he planned to be away for two full weeks. Jay had friends, contacts he had made at Harvard whom he planned to see while he was in New York. Many of them now held extremely influential positions, and if his father could be fooled into believing that Jay was contemplating crossing the Atlantic and joining forces with one of them, driven to do so by his own father's lack of faith in him . . . Jay smiled cynically to himself, reached for his Filofax and checked through the list of appointments.

There was no way he was ready to give up on the Japanese deal, and if he had to use some subtle manipulation to force his father to give way, then so be it. He would.

Yes, in many ways his stay in New York could turn out to be a highly profitable one, not least because . . . A faintly cruel smile curled his mouth as he reached into his luggage and removed a small package.

There was nothing particularly remarkable about the very ordinary unmarked video it contained—unless, of course, you happened to know what was on the video.

His father had reminded him about Plum's birthday. He started to laugh. He only hoped that Plum would appreciate, enjoy, get as much pleasure from receiving her gift as he was going to get from giving it to her. He suspected that she certainly wouldn't appreciate just how much effort he had put into getting it for her.

Ten minutes later as he stepped outside the hotel and gave the driver an address in SoHo, he glanced frowningly at his watch. He had a dinner engagement later on with an ex-girlfriend who was now based in the city, but with any luck his appointment shouldn't take too long. His destination was one of the large loft-conversion apartments which had once been the home of the city's artists. The woman who owned the loft and worked from it was an artist, too, in her own way. Jay had found out about her through a friend of a friend who had heard about the kind of work she did.

He got the cabbie to drop him off on the corner and then walked down the street, pausing to examine the small discreet brass plate outside the address he wanted. It proclaimed that the building was owned by Aphrodite Films Ltd. The woman Jay had come to see *was* Aphrodite Films and Aphrodite Films was . . .

Well, what was Aphrodite Films? First and foremost it was in a class of its own, fulfilling and satisfying a market which it had created, a market which had nothing to do with Hollywood and also nothing to do with the shadowy pornographic cousins on the other side of the industry; or so Bonnie Howlett always soothingly reassured her clients.

Clients came to her because they could be assured of two things. The first was that they would get what they wanted and the second was that Bonnie guaranteed absolutely, completely and for ever, that their business with her was confidential. As she always told them, with the fees she charged, she could make far more money from what she was doing with the guarantee of complete confidentiality she gave them, than she could from blackmailing them.

And Bonnie's clients believed her. They believed her, they trusted her, and they told their friends about her. And in all the years she had been giving those guarantees, Bonnie had never broken one. No one other than herself and the client ever saw the finished product, of which there was always only one copy. What the client then chose to do with that copy was her business and hers alone.

Bonnie had had women come to her who confessed they
would rather kill themselves than have anyone else know what
they were doing, and others who admitted just as openly that
what they were planning was to be a special surprise for a boyfriend or lover.

Bonnie had long ago ceased to be shocked or surprised by the
desires and needs of human nature. Sometimes she did feel sadness and pity, but she kept these emotions strictly to herself. It
was not, after all, her job to feel emotion for her clients, simply
to see that they got what they wanted.

Now as she let Jay into her office, she looked at him warily. It
was very unusual for her to be approached by a male client, and
if he hadn't been so insistent that what he wanted was simply to
have a small tape tidied up a little, to look more professional, she
would probably have refused to see him altogether. Her business was to supply women, her own sex, with the kind of visual
sexual stimulation they wanted, specific visual stimulation, in
which normally they themselves featured, generally in their own
individual fantasy.

If necessary, she could and did provide these women with the
partner or partners of their choice—partners who came with a
strictly monitored clean bill of health. Mostly young out-of-
work actors who were only too glad of the confidentiality clauses
she insisted on them signing, and the fact that no one else would
ever see what they had done. Working on the pornographic side
of the industry was still a big no-no on the legit side of the business—it did not do to get found out. No one who worked for
Bonnie ever got found out and she paid well. Or rather her clients did. A woman wanted to have herself videotaped enjoying
the sexual attention of two different men? No problem, Bonnie
could arrange it.

That she might also want these same men dressed up in the
clothes of the eighteenth century, with one of them posing as a
highwayman, seducing her inside the coach he had stopped on
some quiet rural stretch of road, was also no problem. Bonnie
knew just the right location...just the right coach...just the right
place to get the dress.

Now as she watched Jay, Bonnie was mentally assessing him.
She already knew that the video he had handed her would not

contain any frames of him. He was far too guarded, too wary, too suspicious to involve himself in anything which might be used to harm him. And too controlled. Much too controlled for a man so obviously sexually attractive, and she suspected, totally heterosexual.

'What exactly is it you want me to do with this?' she asked Jay as she took the tape from him.

'Professionalise it,' he told her promptly.

'Professionalise.' Her eyebrows rose, the bastardised word having sounded odd delivered in his cool very crisp British voice. 'I'll have to look at it first,' she warned him.

'How long will that take?' he asked, flicking back his cuff to glance at his watch. A plain utilitarian Rolex, which she noticed looked as though he had owned it for a long time. He was, she recognised, very arrogant, self-assured...perhaps too much so.

She didn't allow herself to smile as she told him calmly, 'Normally two weeks, but at the moment I'm very busy, so it could be three if things go well. I'll have to check it out first.'

'I don't have three weeks. I'm only in New York for a fortnight.' He stopped and gave her a penetrating look.

Arrogant, yes, but perhaps not totally without some instinct for other people's reactions, Bonnie acknowledged.

'It's a birthday present,' he told her, changing tack. 'My father's...a very close friend...'

His father's what? Bonnie wondered thoughtfully.

'How long before you can let me know?'

'You can ring me in three days' time to find out if I can actually do anything with it.'

He wasn't pleased, Bonnie recognised, and he would have tried to pressure her to give him precedence, had she not intimated that he had no option but to accept what he was being told.

Jay was already regretting the impulse that had led him to telephone Nadia from London, asking her out to dinner. They had originally met at university and had become lovers after an aggressive and lengthy pursuit on his part, not as she had once accused him, because he had particularly wanted her, but because everyone else did. Their romance had already been over then, ended by Nadia, who had told him calmly that in bed he was too good, and out of it, nowhere near good enough.

Jay hadn't been unduly concerned about the ending of their relationship, Nadia's razor-sharp brain, coupled with her healthy feminine intuition, had begun to make him irritably wary. She asked too many questions, and drew too many conclusions. She had a top-flight job now with a New York firm of brokers, and it had crossed Jay's mind when he originally got in touch with her that she might be able to provide an angle on the people he was negotiating with. But now his father's firm rejection of his plans had soured his mood. And the mocking amusement in Bonnie Howlett's eyes as she told him how long he would have to wait to get his video hadn't improved it. He wasn't quite sure yet how he intended to give Plum her 'present,' publicly or privately. Privately would probably be best—not that he had the slightest compunction about staging a public viewing of it. After all, if she was stupid enough to make the damn thing in the first place, and then leave it where it could so easily be found . . .

It irritated the hell out of him the way his father constantly made excuses for her. And, of course, he knew why. Christ, his father even let her get away with claiming that she loved him and that she thought Bram was just about the sexiest, most gorgeous man that ever was.

'It's a lovely thought, but truthfully, little one, I'm far too old for you,' Bram had told her the first time she propositioned him.

Jay knew this because Plum had told him about it herself, crying that her heart was broken because his father had rejected her.

'And I know I could make it good for him,' she had told Jay earnestly. She might love his father, but that certainly didn't stop her from being sexually promiscuous on a scale that caused those who knew about her reputation to view her with either approval or contempt depending upon their outlook. What irked Jay most of all was that despite it all, she still somehow managed to preserve an almost dewy-eyed look of innocent freshness and to hang on to her place in his father's affections—a place higher up the scale than his own? Right now, though, he needed to decide what to do about dinner with Nadia. The last thing he needed was that incisively sharp brain of hers latching on to his mood and then questioning it. He'd move his dinner date with her to another evening, he decided, when he would be in a better frame of mind to handle her.

In Jay's experience, the best and easiest way to silence a woman's questions was to take her to bed. But the thrill of sexual conquest wasn't one that motivated him any more. In his teens and at university, yes, he had gone through a phase of equating manhood with sexual conquest.

'You like being in control too much,' Nadia had accused him just before she ended their relationship. 'In fact, you don't just like it, you need it. Well, I'm tired of being "given" my orgasm, like a child given a sweet, and if you must know, I'd get a lot more pleasure from going to bed with a man who genuinely wanted me. The only pleasure you get from having sex with me is that of knowing you're in control. Well, not any more.'

Since then he'd never repeated the mistake of allowing any woman to get to know him as well as Nadia had done—in bed or out of it.

3

In London Bram was going out for the evening—not *à deux* with an ex-lover, but rather more formally at the invitation of the Foreign Secretary, who was hosting a small reception.

Bram knew, or was acquainted with, many of the other guests. There had been a suggestion the previous year that he might be nominated for an honour in the New Year's Honours list until he had very firmly let it be known that, gratified though he was, he did not wish to be considered. He did not believe that, in the present economic climate, the amassing of a large personal fortune merited such a nomination—no matter how honestly earned or through how much hard work and even taking into consideration the concurrent input into the exchequer via the Inland Revenue.

'You give as much to charity, and probably more, than most of the others being nominated, and you can be sure they won't be turning their honours down,' Jay had pointed out cynically.

'I give a small percentage of my income, but I *do* nothing,' had been Bram's response.

Worldly ambition, wealth had never really motivated him. He had simply been in the right place at the right time and with the right kind of skills. His business success had, to his mind, been founded on chance and luck. The small empire which had developed from it, the people he employed who were dependent upon it, they *were* his responsibility and he took that responsibility seriously, as he had tried to explain to Jay. He suspected that Jay had not understood his desire to protect their employees and preferred, instead, to believe that his father was deliberately thwarting him.

It had perhaps been unwise, Bram acknowledged, to remind Jay of Plum's forthcoming birthday. Jay was so hostile towards her. Because he couldn't see the similarities between the childhood traumas which had led to the adult emotional problems of them both, or because he could?

Did Jay recognise that the roots of Plum's promiscuity, her intense need for male love and approval, lay just as surely in her childhood as the roots of Jay's need for total control over everything and everyone did in his?

He must do. He was far too intelligent not to recognise this, Bram decided. Was there any modern parent who did not grieve for all the ways in which they had failed their child? Helena might mask her feelings of guilt by distancing herself from Plum and claiming in public that she was too much her father's child, but no doubt there were times when she, like him, wondered in despair how it was possible to love a child so much and yet still fail them so badly.

When Jay returned from New York he would have to talk to him again about his reasons for turning down his expansion plans.

It had never been Bram's desire to become so successful. In the early days all he had wanted to do was to earn a decent living. Not even to his closest friends could he confide how much life had begun to pall, how heavy he sometimes found the burden of his success. It seemed so ungrateful not to take more pleasure in what he had achieved.

And what was he doing to Jay by condemning him to the role of heir in waiting? Jay's business acumen was far sharper than his own. He was more than qualified to take control of the business, and under his guardianship its profits would undoubtedly grow. But what about its people—would they, too, thrive under Jay's management?

Jay—had there been a week, a day, an hour even, in the years that he had taken full responsibility for his son that Jay had not dominated his thoughts and in many ways his actions as well?

But it was not Jay he was thinking of later in the evening as he joined the other guests at the Foreign Secretary's reception.

It was Taylor.

And not just because Sir Anthony and his wife were among the guests.

It was the kind of occasion at which the British excelled, Bram reflected as he refused a champagne cocktail and studied the other guests. It might not have the stiff formality which hallmarked similar occasions at the embassies in Paris, nor the

expensive trappings and attention to detail which glittered
through even the lowliest Washington dinner party; but the
slightly shabby elegance of the rooms, the relaxed mood of the
guests, that indefinable and inimitable air of ease and perma-
nence, of tradition, which is so very British, overlay the whole
proceedings like the fine patina on a piece of richly polished antique furniture. The signs of age and familiarity of usage deceived only ignorant eyes.

'Bram, how are you?'

Bram turned, smiling warmly as he heard the familiar voice
of another guest.

'Have you seen Helena recently?' she asked him. 'I really must
get in touch with her.'

Olivia Carstairs and Helena had been at Roedean together.
They had kept in touch over the years and it was through Helena that Bram knew Olivia.

'We received an invitation to Plum's eighteenth, but unfortunately Gerald is due to go to Russia the day before. It's such a
pity about Plum. I really feel for poor Helena. But then teenage
girls can be so difficult.'

Her voice held the confidence of being the mother of four sons,
Bram noticed wryly.

'And of course, the problem is,' Olivia continued, 'by the time
she does come to her senses, the poor girl will have gained such
a dreadful reputation. I remember when I was at—' She broke
off, apologising. 'Oh dear, I'd better go. Gerald looks as though
he's in trouble. The problem with these affairs is that one never
has the time to talk to the people one really wishes to converse
with. You will give Helena my love?'

'I shall,' Bram assured her.

Her comments about his goddaughter hadn't been motivated
by malice but, even so, they made him frown. In other circumstances he would have been tempted to talk to Plum himself, to
try gently to help her understand that she could not and would
not find the emotional security she was seeking by trying to
purchase it with sex. However, he was acutely aware that Plum
considered herself to be in love with him—how could he not be
when she had earnestly and forthrightly told him so on more
than one occasion?

Two years ago, when she was still not quite sixteen, he had let himself into his apartment one night to find her waiting in his bed for him. His fortieth-birthday present.

The combination of her too adult sexuality and her too youthful body and face had filled him with a mixture of despair and distaste. How could he explain to her that his love for her was that of an adult for a child, and that to him the thought of knowingly being sexually stirred by *any* fifteen-year-old girl was acutely repugnant. Her straight coltish limbs, her high small breasts, which she was displaying to him with such terrifying insouciance, were those of a child, not a woman.

In the end he had had to leave her in possession of his bed and spend the night in a hotel. Since then she might not have gone so far as invading his bed, but she certainly still insisted that she loved him.

On the other side of the room Anthony was talking to the aide of one of the charity's royal patrons. Bram made his way over to join them.

'Ah, Bram.' Anthony welcomed him with a smile, introducing him to his companion. 'I was just telling Charles here about you. I'm sorry I had to break our appointment this afternoon, by the way, but no doubt Taylor was able to help you.'

'Very much so,' Bram agreed, as the royal aide turned away to speak to someone else. 'But . . .'

'But?' Anthony repeated, frowning as he picked up on the hesitation in Bram's voice. 'Was there a problem?'

'Not with your archivist,' Bram assured him. 'Far from it. But I have to admit I just wasn't prepared for the amount of material she gave me. I haven't had time to look at it properly yet, but I doubt that I'm going to be able to extract the statistics I need without some very knowledgeable assistance.'

'Well, that needn't be a problem,' his friend assured him. 'In fact, the person in the best position to help you is Taylor herself. She's been with the charity for a long time and the new information-collating system we put in last year was very much her baby.'

'Well, if you're sure she can spare the time,' Bram responded reluctantly. 'I must admit she would seem to be the ideal choice, especially if, as you say, she's familiar with your own computer system.'

While Anthony was assuring him that some satisfactory arrangement could be reached, Bram was inwardly marvelling at his own hitherto unsuspected capacity for duplicity and manipulation. He had never before in his life imagined, or needed to imagine, employing the kind of deceitful sleight of hand he was using now. He had simply never had the need . . . or the desire.

He had a gut-deep feeling that working alongside Taylor was not going to be a good idea—either for his libido or his emotions. But the attractive proposition of another chance to get close to Taylor far outweighed any possible doubts.

'I imagine she must have come to you straight from university,' he heard himself saying to Anthony further compounding his deceit.

'No. She did actually go to university, but she left without taking her degree. I'm not sure why.' He started to frown. 'She's an extremely private person who doesn't encourage personal questions, although I do know that she eventually obtained her degree via the Open University system. She's got a first-rate brain. And a good sense of humour, too, when she allows it to surface. Sometimes, though, it's almost as though she's afraid of laughing, as though she's afraid of . . . '

'Living,' Bram suggested quietly.

'How high do you rate your chances of being able to come up with something for us?' Anthony asked.

'It's hard to say,' Bram responded honestly. 'Especially since I need to break down all the reference material and collate it properly.

'What I'm hoping to do is to establish some common ground between the different degrees of communication problems and to use that as the base for a general program which can then, hopefully, be adapted to meet the needs of the individual user. But as yet we're a long, long way from that stage.'

'Well, having Taylor seconded to you should help.'

'Oh, it will,' Bram told him truthfully. 'It will.'

'I'll speak to her first thing in the morning. It shouldn't be too much of a problem. She was complaining only the other week that since we've put in this new computer system, she's finding she has time on her hands.

'I was discussing this project with our patron this afternoon,' Anthony continued. 'He was very enthusiastic about it. It's going to make one hell of a difference if you can pull it off. Commercially for you as well as for us.'

'Potentially, yes.' Bram agreed cautiously, aware that he was now voicing the same doubts which Jay had expressed earlier — but from a very different standpoint.

It was almost one o'clock when he eventually left the reception and made his way back home.

He did not, however, retire straight to bed. Instead, he went into his study, a square room to the rear of the house, with windows which overlooked a surprisingly large garden. With the heavy antique damask curtains closed, shutting out the sounds of the city, it was almost possible for him to imagine he was back on the fens.

Almost . . . A wry smile curled his mouth as he contrasted the expensive elegance of his present surroundings with the small, shabby cottage he had rented there. The two places, the two lifestyles, were worlds apart, but he was still the same man.

No, not the same, he acknowledged. He had changed the moment he had walked into Taylor's office. She intrigued him, interested him, aroused his curiosity, his compassion—and his desire! And if he did desire her, was that so very wrong? Not wrong, perhaps, but certainly foolhardy—surely he had learned enough about life to realise the stupidity of wanting a woman who did not want him?

He picked up the file. He hadn't lied when he told Anthony he was going to need help collating the information she had given him . . . Well, not totally, although he suspected she would take convincing of that fact.

And if she chose not to be convinced, if she refused to work with him? To work with him—was that all he wanted? Would he be able to stop at merely working with her? He was more than forty, he reminded himself, well capable of controlling whatever inappropriate physical or emotional desire Taylor aroused in him. As he had done the first time they met? His body tensed a little uncomfortably as he looked down and saw what he had doodled on the edge of the file. A small and extraordinarily feisty-looking little mouse.

4

Down below, to the left of Jay's bedroom window, Fifth Avenue lay under a haze of car exhaust fumes and heat. To the right the trees in Central Park were just beginning to lose the bright, fresh greenness of early spring. The temperature was rising, and with the approach of summer came an energetic and collective shedding of layers of clothing from women's bodies, which should have rejoiced the heart of any red-blooded male, Jay acknowledged as his glance lingered briefly on the slim, golden limbs of a girl crossing the street below him.

Perhaps if he had been able to make his father see reason, bring him round to his point of view, he might have felt more inclined to join the general rush to welcome summer.

As it was . . . New Yorkers obviously had conveniently short memories, he decided cynically. In another six weeks' time they would be moaning about the stifling heat of their city. In another six weeks . . .

On the surface his meeting with the Japanese had gone well enough; they had seemed to accept his careful noncommittal statement that he and his father both felt they needed more time before coming to a final decision about such a very important step. On the surface . . . Oh, they had been polite enough, but there had been that firm reminder that they would not wait for ever, that resources for investment were finite and there were other small companies in which they were interested. Like Jay they had other business in New York, and their comment had somehow sounded more like a warning than general conversation.

Another meeting had been set up for six weeks' time. Six weeks—would that be long enough to bring his father around to his point of view? To make him see sense? To make him realise how very, very vulnerable they were, and how much they needed the kind of partnership the Japanese were offering?

Jay frowned impatiently as he continued to stare out of the window. What was his father doing—thinking—was he regretting not agreeing with him?

The familiar edginess and anger he always felt when he and his father were apart, when others were in a better position to influence him than he was himself, were beginning to make him wish he hadn't committed to a two-week stay in New York. Damn. Jay silently cursed himself—and Plum. Still, it would be worth the wait just to see her face when he gave her her 'present.' Hers and everyone else's, once they realised just what it was.

He was already regretting rearranging his dinner date with Nadia, but she had wanted to see him, or so she'd said.

Their affair had ended more than six years ago, and although he continued to hear, through mutual acquaintances, about her almost meteoric career progress, they had not kept in touch on a personal basis.

He glanced at the phone, wondering if it was too late to ring her and cancel their date for the second time, but then, if he did, he was grimly aware of the conclusions she was likely to draw.

'If there's one thing I can't stand, it's a man who sulks,' she had once told him pithily, after they had quarrelled.

'I do not sulk,' he had countered angrily, but she had raised her eyebrows and mocked.

'Oh no? If you believe that, then you're nowhere near as intelligent as you like to pretend to be, Jay. When it comes to handing out the silent withdrawal treatment you're an expert. And they say that *women* are manipulative! The moment a situation comes along where you think you might not win, you don't want to be involved. You back off and retreat into that cosy, safe little world of yours and you bar the door behind you.'

That had been just one of the quarrels which had ultimately led to the collapse of their relationship. In personality they were poles apart. Nadia was the great-granddaughter of Russian immigrants who had fled to London at the time of the revolution; her nature was passionate and volatile, and when she believed in something, she believed in it utterly and completely—and expected those close to her to believe in it as well.

When Jay had refused to do so she had denounced him as being too cold, too clinical, too good at using logic to deny real feelings.

But Nadia had had a logic of her own, a logic which had ultimately led to her ending their relationship. She'd told Jay that,
although sexually he was a very good lover, the cost of main-
taining their relationship was an investment she was not prepared to make. 'Think of our relationship as a bank,' she had told
him fiercely. 'I am the one who does all the emotional paying in,
Jay. You are the one who is always drawing out, who makes no
contribution emotionally.

'I have too much respect for myself, too many things I want to
do with my life, to burden myself with that kind of debt. I am
not like your father, endlessly prepared to fund your emotional
poverty. I have a need to make withdrawals of my own . . . to re-
quire my own support. Fucking you is heaven, but loving you
would be hell.'

No, he mused, theirs had not been the kind of relationship
which would allow them now to sit down comfortably together
and reminisce over their shared past.

Not that Nadia had ever been the type to waste time reminiscing about the past. She lived in the present and worked for
the future. Even while at London University she had been very
clear-minded about what she wanted, where she was going. . . .

'I am a citizen of the world,' she had been fond of saying. 'The
fate which has denied me the right to a country of my own has
also freed me to live without any hampering emotional attach-
ments to any particular country. My great-grandparents might
have settled here in Britain, but they were always treated as outsiders. I owe no more loyalty to Britain than I do to anywhere
else.'

'But it's Britain, the British people, who have given you your
security, your education . . . your freedom.' Jay had challenged
her.

'No,' Nadia had countered fiercely. 'These are things I have
taken for myself . . . worked for myself. . . . I do not owe anyone
anything.'

She had never made any secret of her ambitions, and now, by
all accounts, she was well on the way to fulfilling them.

Half an hour later as Jay stood under the shower letting the
spray hammer his flesh, he found himself thinking about her
again.

She had been his first really serious lover, challenging and mocking him in the days before she finally allowed him to catch her, and continuing to do so even afterwards.

He had never discovered just how or with whom she had learned the sexual expertise which had made her such a skilled lover. Now, with hindsight, he suspected it had been with an older man—or men. She had certainly been confident enough to tell him quite clearly and firmly when he didn't please or satisfy her as she wanted.

She had been the first woman, the only woman, when he thought about it, who had made it clear that she considered the act of cunnilingus one that she not only had every right to expect from him as a regular part of their lovemaking, but also one by which she judged the manner of a man.

'Only a man who is ignorant of the true pleasure of sex thinks that all he has to do to give a woman satisfaction is to penetrate her,' Nadia had declared scornfully after listening to a fellow male undergraduate boasting about the number of times he had "fucked" his partner in one twenty-four-hour period.

'For a woman, penetration is nothing. It is the way a man savours and relishes the scent and taste of her, the way he lingers over every tiny lick and suck. There is nothing . . . nothing more erotic than having a man beg to be allowed to go down on you. Nothing.'

Jay had learned since that she had been both right and wrong. There *were* women to whom cunnilingus was everything, the *only* orgasmic pleasure, and there were also women who did not feel sexually satisfied unless they had been physically penetrated—and there were women who filled the distance between the two by desiring and enjoying an infinite variety of intimacies.

In his experience sex was not so much a mutual pleasure as a mutual trade-off; it wasn't just the New Age seriousness of the dawning of the nineties, trailing its ghoulish warnings about promiscuity and AIDS, which was making sex something that people felt more inclined to hang back from rather than rush into. It was a general feeling of cynicism about the motivations behind the act, a disinclination to believe that it was done, ultimately, for anything more than personally selfish motives.

'Time was when a guy who stayed at home and gave himself a hand job was considered a maladjusted weirdo . . . pathetic,' Jay had overheard one man telling another in the changing rooms at his gym. 'Now a guy's only got to say in public that he prefers to take responsibility for his own sexual release and he's got every woman in the place convinced he's Mr Sensitive New Man.'

He, personally, might not have taken things that far, Jay admitted, but his sex drive had certainly diminished over the past few years.

Beauty without brains had never appealed to him, even when he was younger, but now... When had he first begun to feel that there was something empty about his relationships, something lacking?

He moved uncomfortably across the room, irritated by his thoughts. He had Nadia to blame for this emotional introspection.

Nadia paused in the act of smoothing the fine black wool crêpe of her dress over her thirty-three-inch hips, frowning as she moved a little closer to the mirror to study her reflection critically.

There came a point when a woman was approaching her thirtieth birthday where being enviably slim could suddenly change to being unenviably thin—scraggy, in fact, with brittle chicken-stick bones and skin that, without the healthy satin gleam of youth, could appear far less appealing to male eyes than the plumper flesh of more rounded women. Treading the fine line between slender suppleness and that ageing, desiccated thinness was an art. So far she had more than mastered it. The warm silken flesh of her bare arms contrasted perfectly with the fabric and colour of her dress. Her legs, clad in the sheerest of sheer stockings, were exactly the same colour as her discreetly tanned arms—just enough to give a healthy glow rather than a winter pallor, but never, ever enough to mimic the overtanned look of an older generation, who had learned too late of the damaging effects of the sun, which they had embraced with such passionate adoration.

Her dress was simple but elegant, and it fitted perfectly, emphasising the narrowness of her waist and the slenderness of her hips, the delicate swell of her breasts—and if a man was discerning enough, and Jay would be—the fact that beneath it her breasts were bare, small enough and firm enough to allow them to be so.

All that would change if she married Alaric.

He would want children and soon and, of course, there would be pressure on her to conform to the stereotype of WASP wife and motherhood.

If she married him. Was there really any doubt? He would be the perfect husband for her in every way. She couldn't put off her decision much longer. Her frown deepened.

Had Jay appeared in the Big Apple at just the right moment?

It was often said that a woman never forgot her first lover, and while Jay had not been that, he had certainly been the first man to touch her emotions, the first man she had loved.

It was six years since they had last met . . . since they had parted. What would Jay see tonight when he looked at her? A desirable woman? An older version of the ex-lover he had walked away from without any apparent regrets? A successful career woman who had made a name for herself in one of the toughest career arenas in the world? Life was tough enough on Wall Street when you were a man; when you were a woman . . .

It was seven-thirty, time for her to leave. She picked up her wrap.

Nadia saw Jay before he saw her. She had purposefully arrived at the restaurant early and gone straight to the table he'd booked.

She could see him now, pausing to survey the occupants of the dimly lit room, standing a good six inches above the *maître d'* and drawing every pair of female eyes in the place to him, Nadia observed wryly.

And no wonder. While to her his features had been instantly recognisable—they were, after all, carved on her memory, her senses for all time—her femininity marvelled at the subtlety with which nature had transformed a young man—a very good-looking young man—into an adult male, a predator, a hunter at the full height of his power. His young male frame with its long rangy bones had become subtly more muscular, harder, sexier, all the soft flesh of youth stripped away, replaced by a much harder and far more masculine covering that revealed the true magnificence of his bone structure.

Given the chance, the entire female population of the restaurant would have gladly given voice to a long, verbal orgasm just watching him, Nadia reflected cynically, and didn't he just know it.

He had seen her now, the green eyes meeting hers briefly before disengaging as he strode purposefully towards her.

'Nadia . . .'

Even his voice had become more masculine, deeper, more positive, sending a small electric frisson of sensual awareness zigzagging down her spine.

Very impressive, Nadia acknowledged, as he sat down opposite her. But she was determined not to let him know what she was thinking, to make sure that *she* was the one who kept control of the situation.

'Drink?' she asked him, adding gently, 'I hear things didn't go too well with the Japanese. . . .'

Jay's eyebrows rose, his eyes calm, slightly surprised. 'Oh?' He gave a small dismissive shrug. 'I thought they went rather well, but then I suppose it all depends on your point of view.'

'You weren't able to give them any real commitment,' Nadia told him.

'I didn't want to give them any firm commitment,' Jay corrected her. 'Their offer is only one of several options we're considering at the moment.'

'We?' Nadia pounced. 'Ah . . . of course . . . your father. His is the final decision, isn't it?'

'Why exactly did you want to have dinner with me, Nadia? Not to talk business, surely.'

She had rattled him, even though he was fighting hard not to show it, Nadia exulted. She wondered what he would say if he knew that she also had dealings with his Japanese contacts, and that for the first time in her professional life she had broken one of her golden rules. She had kept back from her clients a piece of important information by not telling them that no matter what Jay might say to them, it was his father and not he whose decision would be final. What she was even more reluctant to dwell on was why she had kept that information to herself.

'No...not just to talk business,' she agreed with a smile. 'We're old friends,' she went on. 'It's a long time since we last met....'

'Old friends?' Jay queried. 'You and I were *never* friends, Nadia. Lovers...yes...*friends*, no.

'I understand you're getting married.'

If he had expected to catch her off guard, he was disappointed.

'It's a possibility, yes,' Nadia allowed, pausing to accept the drink the waiter had brought her.

'A possibility,' Jay mocked. 'How very romantic...'

'Marriage should never be about romance,' Nadia told him firmly. 'Romance is...'

'For lovers?' Jay suggested. He was enjoying baiting her, enjoying using her to relieve the tension of the past few days, he acknowledged savagely as he watched the anger flare briefly in her eyes before she controlled her reaction.

'Romance is an illusion, is what I was going to say. Temptingly sweet at first, but it can soon become unpleasantly cloying.'

'So there is to be no romance in this marriage of yours.... But there will, I trust, be love.'

He was treading on very dangerous ground, Jay recognised, dangerous for himself as well as for her.

'Yes, there will be love,' Nadia confirmed, but she didn't add that the love would be Alaric's for her rather than the other way around.

'How is your father, by the way?' she asked with deliberate mock innocence. Talking about his father had always been a good way of goading Jay in the old days.

'He's fine,' Jay responded tersely. 'Look, Nadia—'

'And still unmarried,' Nadia hazarded, ignoring the keep-off signs he was posting. 'What a waste. Do you know, Jay, it's a pity that you and I met when I was so young. If we were to meet now and you were to introduce me to your father...I suspect that he'd be the one I'd want and not you.'

It was, Nadia recognised with an odd spurt of surprise, the truth. She had been twenty-one when she met Jay; he had been just that little bit younger and she had been tired of older men, older lovers. She had met Jay's father a couple of times when he visited Jay at university, and on both occasions Jay had been angrily reluctant to introduce her to his father, who had arrived unexpectedly.

The first time she had naïvely assumed Jay's reluctance sprang from his possessive streak and that he was afraid that she might prefer his father to him.

She had been right about the possessiveness but wrong, oh, so wrong, about the focus of it. The reason he had wanted to exclude her had not been because he was afraid she might prefer his father's company, but because he had been afraid that his father might prefer hers.

She had taunted him mercilessly with that fact once she had discovered it, unable to understand then as she did so clearly now that she had been equally jealous and resentful of the fact that Jay so obviously preferred his father's company to hers . . . that his father was more important to him than her.

'Still not outgrown our daddy complex, I see, Jay,' she murmured dulcetly. 'But then he *is* quite a man, isn't he . . . your father. Not that you'd ever allow any woman to get close enough to find out just how much of a man. You know, I feel very sorry for your father. It can't be easy, having a son like you, possessive, obsessive. . . .'

She tensed as he half made to stand up, his eyes dark with anger. Inwardly she cursed herself. He was going to walk out on her.

Her relief when she realised that he was simply summoning the waiter left her feeling sick and angry. This wasn't how it was supposed to be. She was the one in control here, not Jay. But she could see from his expression that he had guessed what she was thinking.

'What do you want from this meeting, Nadia?' he asked her softly. 'If it's to use me to get rid of the aggression you can't vent on your tame, docile, neutered husband-to-be, then you should have found somewhere more private to do it. Mind you, I'm sure our fellow diners would be enthralled by one of your virtuoso performances—they, after all, haven't seen one before. I, on the other hand, have—and if it's another kind of appetite you wanted to satisfy. . . well, the same thing applies. Sex in public places never turned me on—you should have remembered that.'

Nadia fought to control her urge to scream at him. She could feel the blood receding from her skin and then flooding hotly back over it. She had forgotten just how clever and quick he could be. . . how cruelly scalpel-like the words which he used with such skin-stripping precision. He was better informed about her than she had imagined. Someone had drawn him a very accurate picture of Alaric's character. Foolish of her not to have anticipated that.

'Well,' he prompted.

'Well what,' Nadia responded. 'You're wrong, Jay. I don't want either to argue with you or go to bed with you.'

'Liar. Oh, come on, Nadia,' he demanded when she remained silent, 'why the hell else would you agree to see me? After all, what else did we ever do other than fight or fuck?'

What else had they done? They had laughed, loved, argued, played.

'Good in bed, is he, this fiancé of yours?'

'He loves me,' Nadia responded obliquely. The waiter had brought their food. She looked at it with distaste. Jay, on the other hand, was eating his with apparent relish.

'He loves you.' Jay laughed, causing every other woman in the place to focus on him with hungry appreciation.

'He might love you, Nadia, but that wasn't what I asked. Does he make you scream in ecstasy when he touches you? Does he make you plead with him to hold you, stroke you, lick you, suck you until . . .'

'Stop it. . . stop it,' Nadia demanded fiercely. Her appetite had gone completely now.

'Still the same old Nadia,' Jay mocked her, confident that he had got the upper hand now.

'Oh, go to hell,' Nadia cursed him.

He laughed again. 'I thought you always claimed that was where our relationship took you. What exactly is it you're hoping to get from me, Nadia?'

'Nothing. I've already got what I wanted,' she told him fiercely, and it was true. 'You see, the reason I agreed to have dinner with you wasn't because I wanted to relive old memories by going to bed with you.' She gave him a cold smile. 'It was simply because I wanted to remind myself of all the reasons why I'm glad that it's a man like Alaric I'm going to marry, and not a man like you.'

Jay's eyebrows rose.

'You mean you needed reminding?' His smile wasn't a kind one. 'Is that all you wanted to remind yourself of, Nadia? Are you sure?'

'Positive,' she told him firmly. 'And besides, I want a man who is completely mine, completely adult . . . not one who's so obsessed with his father that he can hardly bear to let him out of his sight. No, I pity the woman you marry, Jay . . . *if* you ever marry. She'll always come a poor second to your obsession with your father.

'What would you do, by the way, if he ever *did* remarry? He isn't like you. *He* is capable of love . . . real love.'

'My father won't marry.'

Several of the other diners looked up as Jay's harsh denial rang out across the quiet room.

'You mean, *you* won't let him,' Nadia retaliated. 'But how could you stop him if that was what he wanted to do? He's still a relatively young man, Jay. Only in his mid-forties . . . if that. Plenty young enough to father a family . . . a second son. It's a well-known fact that older men tend to dote on their children, especially when they're their second family . . . to give them the time they didn't give their first children. How will you like that, Jay?'

'My father will not marry. The last thing he wants is another child, another son!'

'Oh, really? Has he told you that? Is he afraid that he might turn out like you?'

Nadia was on a roll now, confident that she had got Jay on the run, that her sharp little darts were reaching the vulnerable tender heart of him.

What he couldn't know was that they were piercing her heart as well, reminding her of the pain she had experienced when she first realised that with Jay she could never come first. His father held that place in his emotions; she did not even come a poor second.

Thank God for Alaric, with whom she would always come first. Alaric, who adored and worshipped her. Alaric, who shrugged off his family's dislike and disapproval of her. Alaric, who would move mountains for her if she wished it. Alaric, whose methodical, earnest lovemaking might satisfy her physically but could never, ever transport her to the intense emotional heights to which Jay's touch had once taken her. And could take her again.

Immediately she shut down on the thought. She had made her decision...her choice. And even if Jay had wanted her...loved her...

The thought of Jay loving anyone, abandoning himself to such a need of anyone, made her smile bitterly to herself.

'He doesn't need to tell me,' Jay exploded, ignoring the second part of her taunt. 'It goes without saying that a man of his age...'

He stopped speaking as Nadia started to laugh.

'A man of his age... Oh, come on, Jay. How old is he exactly?'

'Forty-two,' Jay told her brusquely, his dislike of her questions on the subject colouring his voice.

Nadia could vividly remember his reluctance, his anger the first time she had questioned him about his father, his reluctance to reveal the small age gap between them, his obvious insecurity about his whole relationship with his father.

'Forty-two—that's nothing,' Nadia taunted.

'More than old enough for him to have married well before now, had he wanted to do so,' Jay retaliated.

'Could he have done that, Jay?' she asked softly. 'Could he have married...? Or would you have found some way of preventing him from doing so?'

'My father lives his own life and—'

'Does he? Or does he live the life you've restricted him to?'

'He's an adult...mature...the founder of a multimillion-pound business. He makes his own decisions, Nadia.'

'Oh, I'm not questioning your father's abilities nor his intelligence. They're obvious for anyone to see. Nor am I suggesting that he's the kind of man who's too weak to control his own life. I have met him, remember, Jay. I know exactly how much of a man your father is—and how much of a father, a very compassionate father.... If I was a woman looking for a man to be a good father to my children, your father would be the kind of man I'd choose...that *any* woman would choose. But then you already know that, don't you, and that's one of the reasons you're so possessive about him. You don't want the competition of sharing him with any little half-brother or -sister, you don't—'

'You don't know what the hell you're talking about,' Jay interrupted her furiously, pushing back his chair and standing up.

He *was* going to walk out on her, Nadia recognised, stunned, shocked as he removed some money from his wallet and flung it down on the table.

There was a tight white line of anger around his compressed mouth, the bones in his face starkly sharp beneath his skin as he fought for self-control. As he turned on his heel and left her, Nadia acknowledged that there had never been anything in their relationship, intensely physical and passionate though it had been, that had come anywhere near matching the inferno of white-hot emotions his relationship with his father provoked.

Would any woman ever be allowed to produce that kind of emotional reaction in him? If one did, it certainly wouldn't be her, Nadia acknowledged mentally as the waiter came up to the table.

'My friend had to leave,' Nadia told him crisply, firmly making sure that the calm eye contact she exchanged with him reinforced her statement.

Half an hour later, on her way back to her apartment, she acknowledged that this was not precisely how she had envisaged ending her evening.

So what *had* she wanted...? Sex...a final fling before she settled down? A nostalgic trip back into the past to a world when her whole universe had been bound by Jay's arms, when all she had wanted or needed was her love for him...? *Her* whole world... Not his...never his—which was why she had ended their relationship in the first place.

Why would any woman ever be stupid enough to love such a man...? Why...? Because she was a woman, and because Jay, for all his faults, possessed that dangerous brand of masculinity and maleness that women, even grown-up, adult, mature, intelligent women like her had been programmed to ache for in a way they could never ache for a nice, kind, worthwhile man like Alaric.

Damn Jay. Damn him. Damn him, damn him . . . ! She was, Nadia recognised, crying.

As Jay strode out of the restaurant a cruising taxi pulled to a halt alongside the kerb, but Jay dismissed it with a curt shake of his head.

Human company or conversation, no matter how mundane, was the last thing he felt like, right now. He was not a physically violent man, and certainly had never felt even remotely tempted to strike a woman, but if he had stayed in that restaurant much longer, listening to Nadia's taunts . . . She had always been good at getting under his skin, trying to dig too deeply into his most personal thoughts and feelings. What the hell had she meant, suggesting that his father might want to marry, have children?

Just for a moment he closed his eyes, the noise of the traffic becoming a muted, distant roar as he was swept back into the past, to a memory of his seven-year-old self saying angrily to his father, 'You don't love me.'

'Of course I love you, Jay,' had been his father's calm, gentle response.

'But you didn't want me. You never wanted me to be born,' Jay had insisted, recalling the cruel comments his grandparents had often made about his conception.

And Bram, of course, with his belief in honesty, had not been able to refute his accusation.

His father marrying, conceiving children, whose birth was something wanted, planned, children whom he would welcome and love, and not have foisted on him the way that Jay had been. Children who would believe it when Bram told them that he loved them, children who would have no idea of what it meant to doubt their right to their father's love. Unlike him.

But then, long, long before Bram had even come into his life Jay had known the truth about his own conception.

Bram's parents and Jay's mother's parents had been neighbours in the small, exclusive, upper-middle-class area of the town with its large detached houses each set in its own grounds.

Jay's mother's father held a high-ranking local government position at county level. Jay's mother had been an only child. Bram's father had been an architect, the senior partner in a prestigious local practice. Bram, too, had been an only child. Neither wife had worked; both sets of parents had socialised together occasionally; both men had played golf and both women had given their time to the same local charities. So it was inevitable that Bram and Jay's mother should have known each other, even though they were at separate, single-sex schools and she had been two years Bram's senior.

Jay's earliest memories of his mother were of someone pretty and loving, but also someone lacking in any real authority or power. It was his grandparents, and especially his grandfather, who decided how they all lived their lives.

His mother pouted, wheedled and manipulated her father into buying her new clothes and paying for expensive holidays. But when it came to her son... Jay had quickly learned that her quick, almost frightened, look at her father meant that he, Jay, had done something to displease his grandfather and that, for his mother's sake, he must not do it again.

As he grew older, it sometimes seemed to him that he was making his grandfather angry just by being there. Despite all the attention his grandparents lavished on him whenever other people were around, when he was on his own it was obvious they didn't really like him at all. His grandfather often got very cross and talked angrily about 'that bastard who caused us all this trouble.'

It was when he started playschool that Jay first realised he didn't have something that other children had—or rather, someone.

He could still vividly remember another boy coming up to him and saying importantly, 'My daddy's a doctor. What does your daddy do?'

Nonplussed, Jay had stared at him, but when he got home he had asked his mother, 'Where's my daddy?'

She had burst into tears and cried so much that his grandmother had come to see what all the fuss was about. His mother's tears and his grandmother's consequent anger frightened Jay so much that when his grandmother had insisted he repeat his question for his grandfather when he came home later, he had stammered so badly he had hardly been able to get the question out.

'Where's your daddy...? A father is something you haven't got. Your father doesn't give a damn about you or about anyone just so long as he—'

'Daddy, please...' Jay's mother had intervened, but his grandfather had overruled her.

'No. If he's old enough to ask questions then he's old enough to learn the truth. To be told how his precious father ruined our lives.'

It was years later when Jay learned the complete truth. After one of his quarrels with Helena, she had turned on him and told him fiercely, 'You ought to be damn glad you've got a father like Bram. When I think... He was fourteen when you were conceived. Fourteen. Under age still, while your mother... well, of course Bram's far too much of a gentleman to say so, but it's obvious that she must have been the one to...

'Your grandfather, her father, wanted her to have a termination when he found out she was pregnant, but it was too late. Bram's parents offered to adopt you, but her parents wouldn't hear of it. No. Bram was to agree to have nothing whatsoever to do with either her or you, ever again, and in return for that they'd actually allow Bram's parents to give their precious daughter ten thousand pounds to help to bring you up.

'If you want my opinion,' Helena had added viciously, 'the chances are that Bram isn't really your father at all. Your mother had been involved in a relationship with someone else, and it was when that ended that she turned to your father for consolation. That was when you were conceived, according to her. Personally, I would be surprised if...'

Jay hadn't wanted to hear any more. He had walked away from her in the same way he had walked away from Nadia tonight. He had been thirteen then. Now he was twenty-seven— old enough to know that walking away from a problem never solved it.

No one else had ever suggested to him that Bram might not be his father, least of all Bram himself, and physically they were so much alike. Knowing Helena, her comment was probably something she had made up on the spur of the moment, driven by the frustration of her resentment of him and her belief that he came between her and his father.

She would undoubtedly have denied it, but Jay knew that her feelings for his father went far deeper than those of mere friendship, and while she might have forgotten the taunt she had thrown at him in the heat of the moment, Jay himself had not.

The sharp, angry blare of a car horn brought him out of his reverie. He wasn't a child any more, but an adult male; it had been a stupid piece of self-betrayal to let Nadia get so deeply under his skin.

'You're too hard on Nadia, Jay,' his father had once rebuked him gently after witnessing them quarrelling. 'Can't you see how much she loves you?'

Love . . . what was it? Jay wasn't sure that he knew—or that he wanted to.

As he waited for the lights to change at the intersection, he was frowning, suddenly anxious to get back to his hotel and ring his father.

5

'You're seconding me to work with Bram Soames? But what about my work here?' Taylor asked sharply, her forehead pleating in a frown as she confronted Sir Anthony across his desk, and fought to conceal from him the shock his announcement had given her.

'You've said yourself that since we installed this new computer system you've got time on your hands,' Sir Anthony reminded her.

'To a point, but there are things . . . surely someone else . . .' Someone else, anyone else, Taylor thought as she fought to control her panic. It had never occurred to her when her boss had asked her to spare him a few minutes, what he intended to say to her. The very thought of working closely with an unknown man filled her with anxiety. Her fear of anyone guessing what she was feeling was almost as strong as the anxiety itself.

'There isn't anyone else,' Sir Anthony was saying now. 'At least no one with your experience. I appreciate that what I'm asking falls outside your normal field of operation, but if Bram can produce a viable working program—' He gave a small lift of his shoulders.

'*If* he can produce a working program,' Taylor countered. 'It's been tried before without any real success.'

'Yes, I know that and so does Bram, but since he's prepared to give up his time free of charge—'

'Free of charge? There's no such thing as a free lunch,' Taylor commented cynically. 'He must be expecting to get something out of it.'

'Not Bram,' Sir Anthony denied.

'Why? What makes *him* so different?' Taylor asked the question almost reluctantly, unwilling to be drawn into discussing a man she had already decided she didn't want to like.

'Well, Jay, for a start,' he told her, explaining when he saw her frown.

'Jay is his son. Bram had to take full responsibility for him when his mother was killed in a car accident. He was still at university at the time. Bram's parents did offer to adopt the boy, but Bram wouldn't hear of it. He said that Jay was his son. His responsibility. A lot of men would have let them go ahead, ducked out. . . . Bram's tutors did their best to dissuade him. They were forecasting a brilliant future for him. He had a first-class brain. But he wouldn't listen. Jay came first.'

'And that makes him a candidate for sainthood?' Taylor asked sharply. 'Women . . . girls in their thousands make that kind of sacrifice every day of the week without getting any praise for it. Far from it.'

'Maybe so,' Sir Anthony allowed, 'but it's their choice to become mothers. Bram had no choice. No say in whether or not he became a father.'

'Rubbish,' Taylor retorted angrily. 'He had every choice. Presumably his son's mother didn't tie him to the bed and force him to impregnate her.'

Taylor could tell from Sir Anthony's expression that her sudden forthrightness had surprised him. It had surprised her as well. Any kind of discussion that touched upon sexual matters, even in the mildest way, was normally something she avoided like the plague, but her boss's comments, his attitude, had angered her so much that she had felt impelled to speak out.

'Bram was only fourteen when Jay was conceived,' Sir Anthony told her quietly. 'It isn't a subject that he ever liked discussing. . . .'

'But he made sure, all the same, that everyone knew he wasn't to blame,' Taylor remarked bitterly.

She knew she was overreacting, but she just couldn't withhold the words or control the emotions that lay behind them, even though she knew she would regret her outburst later.

'It wasn't actually Bram who told us,' Sir Anthony answered her. 'It was his father. He was very bitter about the way the girl's family had treated Bram, and about the way he felt Bram's life had been blighted by what happened. Bram has always put others' needs before his own.'

Taylor realised that she was wasting her time continuing to protest about being seconded to work with Bram, little though she liked the idea.

Little though she liked it? Loathing was a closer description
to what she was actually feeling. Loathing, fear, panic, anger,
but most of all fear... Fear at the thought of working closely with
a man she did not know. Fear at the thought of being subjected
to his will, his domination, fear at the thought of having to be
alone with him, fear at its most basic and damaging level, fear
in its most humiliating and degrading form; fear of a woman for
a man simply because he was a man.

But, of course, there was no way she could explain those feelings to Sir Anthony, no way she could explain them to anyone.

When she read articles in magazines about people who had
contracted the HIV virus and were afraid of the consequences,
of making their vulnerability public, Taylor knew exactly what
they were suffering. She had suffered like that for twenty years,
albeit on a different plane. She knew exactly what it felt like, the
fear, the pain, the isolation, the feeling of being apart, different
from the rest of the human race. She knew exactly what it was
like to have to guard her every comment in case she unwittingly
betrayed herself; to remove herself from any kind of physical or
emotional contact with other people; to protect *them* from the
consequences of any kind of intimacy with her at the same time
as she protected herself.

The past, her past, was always with her, a constant reminder,
and a constant warning. . . .

'Look, I can see you're not keen on the idea of working with
Bram,' Sir Anthony acknowledged, 'but—'

'No. I'm not,' Taylor agreed, interrupting him to snatch at the
escape route he was unwittingly offering to her.

There was no point in trying to explain to him that it wasn't
just Bram Soames she didn't want to work closely with, it was
any and every man.

It had taken almost two years before she had finally conquered her anxiety enough to feel comfortable working with Sir
Anthony, before her brain and her emotions finally caught up
with what her instincts were telling her—that her boss was the
happily married man he purported to be and that his kindness
towards the female members of his staff sprang from a genuine,
slightly old-fashioned avuncular and protective attitude towards the female sex as a whole, rather than from some hidden,

ulterior motive. However, to feel comfortable working with Sir Anthony was one thing. Bram Soames was something—*someone*—altogether different.

'If it's any consolation to you, I suspect that Bram is as reluctant to work with you as you are with him,' Sir Anthony told her.

'You *suspect?*' Taylor questioned him sharply, stifling the unexpected stab of feminine chagrin his comment gave her. Why should she feel annoyed because Bram Soames didn't want to work with her? For years she had trained herself not to be in any way responsive to men, to treat them as though they simply did not exist. It was easier that way . . . safer . . . for her, for them.

'Bram is rather better at concealing his feelings than you are,' Sir Anthony answered her dryly.

'Try looking at the fact that I want you to work alongside him as a compliment rather than a punishment,' he coaxed. 'Because that is what it is. I know how you feel about your work, Taylor. After all, I've tried hard enough in the past to prise you away from your precious archives and to get you to play a far more active role on the public relations side of things. You've got the brain for it and the expertise and you've got a very special gift for being able to put your point across—when you choose to use it.

'Now that we've put in that new computer system and you've got spare time on your hands . . .'

Taylor could feel the panic starting to explode inside her. Public relations work, anything that brought her into the public eye in any way at all, terrified her. At least, if she was working with Bram Soames her contact would be limited to him and conducted in circumstances over which she would have some control.

'No one knows the history of the society as well as you do,' Sir Anthony was saying persuasively, 'which is why I want you to work alongside Bram. This project is too important to allow personal feelings to prejudice it. I appreciate that the two of you might not exactly become kindred spirits, but . . .'

'But for the sake of the cause, I should be prepared to sacrifice myself,' Taylor suggested wryly, her mouth twisting slightly.

'Actually, that wasn't what I was going to say,' Sir Anthony rebuked her mildly. 'I was simply going to point out that you're not being very fair to Bram. He's a very likeable chap, you know. Kind. Well-intentioned. Most women—' he began and then stopped, as though he realised that he was treading on very dangerous ground.

'Most women would what?' Taylor demanded. 'Most women would welcome the chance to work so closely with a handsome, rich, available, heterosexual man?'

How could she explain to her boss that those very attributes that in his eyes made Bram Soames so attractive to the majority of her sex, only served to increase her own fear and revulsion, because the one thing he had not mentioned in that brief catalogue, which as far as she was concerned was the most important, was the word *power*; no man could possess all the attributes Sir Anthony had just listed and not be conscious of the power they gave him. Power over her sex, power over her, and, as she had good cause to know, power could be abused.

'So, it's agreed then,' she heard Sir Anthony say firmly. 'I've suggested to Bram that I leave it to him to liaise with you. I know you'll do your best to help him.'

He stood, leaving Taylor with no option but to follow suit and to allow him to shepherd her towards his office door.

Later on in the safety of her own office she could feel the shock starting to sink in. She ought to have taken a firmer stand, to have refused outright to work with Bram Soames. But how could she have done so? By giving up her job? She wasn't financially independent enough to do that; jobs like hers weren't easy to come by. And besides, she liked her job. She liked its solitude, its security and safety. She liked the reassurance of the routine she had established. The thought of leaving and trying to make a fresh start somewhere else filled her with even greater panic.

Damn Bram Soames! Damn him and his precious program! And yet, even as she cursed him mentally, Taylor acknowledged that she was being selfish and unfair. If he *could* succeed in writing such a program it would transform the lives of so many people.

Perhaps, if she could just focus on that fact and hold fast to it, it might help to make the unbearable somehow bearable, she decided sombrely.

Her office was situated at the top of the building, its narrow, barred window the only source of natural daylight. Some time ago it had been suggested that she move to a lower floor and a larger office with a much bigger window, but she had refused.

It was pointless trying to explain to other people that the narrowness of her existing office window, its thick, almost opaque glass and steel bars, were infinitely preferable to her than something larger, which someone might look or step through. Just thinking about such a possibility made her shudder. How could she ever give up her job here and go somewhere else? Here, in surroundings where she had worked for years, her small eccentricities—as others thought of them—were tolerated; in a different environment . . . a new environment . . .

She closed her eyes and then opened them abruptly as her telephone rang.

Some sixth sense warned her who the caller would be, but it was still a shock to hear Bram Soames's unmistakable warm male voice on the other end of the line.

'I hope I'm not pre-empting things by telephoning you so soon,' she heard him saying after he had identified himself. 'But Anthony did promise he would speak to you as soon as he could about the possibility of our working together, and I was wondering if he—'

'Yes,' Taylor interposed tersely. 'Yes, he's told me.' The palm of the hand gripping the receiver was already damp with anxiety, the forefinger of her other hand curling nervously in and out of the plastic-covered coil linking the receiver to the base unit.

Bram could hear the tension in her voice and hoped that she wasn't equally able to hear the reluctance in his. There was, he reminded himself firmly, absolutely no reason whatsoever why he should not work with her. No logical reason at all.

So, why then, this gut feeling that he would be far safer to retreat?

The silence from Taylor's end of the line was slightly unnerving. If it hadn't been for the slightly erratic sound of her breathing he might almost have thought she'd hung up on him.

Firmly pushing his personal thoughts to the back of his mind, he said calmly, 'I think before we can get down to any serious work we need to have a preliminary discussion. I was wondering if you were free tomorrow afternoon?'

In her office Taylor flipped over the page of her diary. It was completely blank.

'No, I'm sorry... I already have an appointment then.' Did her voice sound as betrayingly unconvincing to him as it did to her? She almost hoped he would guess that she was lying and decide to ask Sir Anthony to suggest someone else to help him, and she held her breath as she waited for his response.

'I see.... Well, in that case, I wonder...I'm eager to get started on this project as soon as possible. At the moment I've got some free time, but...'

He paused while Taylor reflected coolly that if he had hoped to impress or bully her by playing the big powerful, dominant, successful businessman he was going to be disappointed.

'I wouldn't normally ask you to work outside office hours, but is there any chance that we could meet tomorrow evening, say about six-thirty?'

Six-thirty—after the rest of the office staff had gone home and only the cleaners were around. Taylor cursed herself inwardly for the trap her fib had built around her.

'I...in the office? I think the building is locked up at six,' she told him quickly. 'I don't think...'

'We could have our discussion here,' Bram told her after a moment's silence. 'I could send a car for you and—'

'No. No...there's no need. I...'

The total panic he could hear in her voice made Bram frown. She had struck him as such a contained, almost over-controlled person, on the surface at least, that he was unprepared for the intensity of emotion he could hear in her voice.

'I...I'll cancel my afternoon appointment,' Taylor told him shakily. 'I...what time did you have in mind?'

'Two-thirty?' Bram suggested diplomatically.

'Yes...very well then...' Taylor agreed. Her throat felt raw with tension, the muscles aching, the sound of her voice unfamiliarly husky.

Her body was drenched in cold sweat and she was starting to shiver. It took her four attempts before she managed to put the receiver down correctly.

If just *talking* to Bram Soames could affect her like this, then what was she going to be like when she was working with him? It was pointless, useless telling herself that a man with his sexual magnetism, his strong blend of power and charisma—a very obviously heterosexual man who had apparently chosen to remain unattached—was hardly likely to express even the remotest interest in her. The knee-jerk sexual male response she had witnessed in his body at their first meeting did not count. The fact that a man like Bram Soames could and no doubt did have his pick of eager women who made a career out of pursuing men like him, was not the point. The point was that he was a man.

As she focused numbly on the small oblong of obscured daylight from her barred window, she acknowledged that in many ways the window was like her life, what to another woman would be restrictive was to her protective. She needed that protection.

She knew there had been whispered speculation among her colleagues about her sexual orientation. The very fact that she shunned male company so determinedly was bound to give rise to it. But Taylor had no sexual or emotional desire for her own sex. A small, bitter smile twisted her mouth. Unbelievable as those who knew her or thought they knew her might find it, there had been a time when she, too, had dreamed of falling in love, getting married, having children; when sexually she had been open and curious.

And if she was honest with herself, there were still times when, deep down, she felt those needs, nights when she lay awake not just tormented by her fears but filled with bitter anger as well.

It was twenty years now. Twenty years, and there had not been a single day during that time when she had not been conscious of the past, when she had not been fearful of its being recreated, when she had not abandoned the habit of stopping, checking . . . watching . . . waiting.

Twenty years. Almost a life sentence, she acknowledged bitterly, but her life was not over yet. She was thirty-nine, that was all.

She could live to be twice that age; both her paternal and her maternal grandparents had. Her parents . . . She swallowed painfully. Neither of her parents had lived to see fifty. Their deaths haunted her still. They always would.

'You must not blame yourself. You are not to blame,' she had been told.

Her head was beginning to ache, the tight knot into which she had pulled her hair dragging on her scalp. It was a luxury at night to let it down and release her neck muscles from the strain of supporting the heavy weight.

Perhaps she ought to wear her hair short. The last time she had done so had been on her sixteenth birthday. The trip to her mother's hairdresser had been a present paid for by her father, a ritual on the path to adulthood.

She could remember how nervously she had watched her reflection in the mirror as the stylist lopped off her heavy, childish braids. The pretty urchin cut had emphasised the delicate bones of her face, made her eyes seem enormous. Her mother had frowned and commented that the style was rather too adult for her, but Taylor had seen in her father's eyes male approval for her transformation. She wasn't a child any more, she was a woman.

She had kept her hair short for several years after that, and just before she had gone to university she had allowed the stylist to experiment with blonde highlights woven into the strands of hair that framed her face.

Her mother had denounced the effect as far too sophisticated and her father hadn't even noticed the change. Both had been preoccupied then over her sister, who had written from Australia breaking the news of her impending marriage.

'We don't want a big fuss, just a quiet ceremony for the two of us . . .' she had written to Taylor. 'And besides, I know our parents don't approve of what I'm doing.'

That had been a gross understatement of their parents' views. It had shocked Taylor to hear her parents say that they wanted nothing to do with her sister until she came to her senses and returned home—alone.

Somewhere at the back of her mind she had always been aware that their love came attached to a price tag, but seeing the actual evidence of that suspicion left her feeling very vulnerable, which was why—

Her telephone rang again, and she reached out to answer it, glad to escape the painful introspection of her thoughts.

The cab driver gave Taylor a brief smile as she stopped outside the small block of apartments where Taylor lived.

She was a fairly new driver for the firm; most of their regular clients were considerably older than Taylor, who she thought looked about her own age, and, as far as she could see, perfectly healthy.

When she asked curiously in the office about her, no one had been able to tell her anything other than the fact that Taylor had been a regular customer for some years.

The block of apartments was set in neat, well-kept gardens, screened from the main road by trees and shrubs. Initially, when she had gone to view the property Taylor had been put off by this aspect; anything designed to screen the property from the road could also provide a screen for someone trying illicitly to enter the apartments. But in the end she had forced herself to overcome her unease and accept that she was unlikely to find anything better.

The apartment did, after all, fulfil all her other criteria. The large detached Victorian house had been carefully converted into six good-sized apartments, all designed to meet the needs of retired couples. The conversions had been advertised as possessing all the latest security features, locking windows and intercoms.

Taylor had also liked the fact that all the other occupants were people who believed in keeping themselves to themselves; quiet retired professional couples or singles who exchanged polite pleasantries if and when they met before retreating thankfully into their own private domains.

Her own apartment was slightly cheaper than the others and slightly larger, since it was in what had originally been the attic.

It had two bedrooms, each with its own bathroom, a large, pleasant sitting room, a small dining room, an even smaller study, which just about housed her desk and bookshelves, and a neat galley kitchen.

Since no one other than herself was ever allowed inside, there was no one to comment about the apartment's lack of homely touches. There were no small pots of herbs on the sunny kitchen windowsill, no leafy green plants in the sitting room, no family mementoes—materially worthless, but sentimentally irreplaceable—marring the elegant perfection of the sitting room, decorated and furnished in a cream colour. Even Taylor's bedroom with its cool eau-de-Nil colour scheme had an almost anonymous feel to it, as though its owner was afraid to leave any personal stamp on the room in case it betrayed her in some way.

Automatically Taylor paused before entering the lift, turning to glance over her shoulder.

The hallway was empty. She stepped quickly into the lift and pressed the button.

Once again, when the lift stopped and the doors opened, she paused to check before stepping out of it, walking quickly across the dove-grey carpeting into the foyer of her apartment.

It took time to unlock the special double lock to her apartment door. Taylor stood sideways as she did so, which made the task more difficult but gave her a clear view both of the lift and of the stairs.

Once inside her apartment she relocked the doors. And then, as she always did, she walked slowly and almost nervously through every room, checking the empty spaces and the locked windows.

Only when this had been done did she allow herself to relax enough to go into her bedroom and close the thick curtains which screened out the light so effectively she had to turn on a lamp before she removed her suit jacket and started to unpin her hair.

As she opened the drawer in her dressing table where she kept her pin box she paused, hesitated and then, so quickly that it was almost as though she was afraid of what she was doing, she reached into the back of the drawer and removed a heavy silver photograph frame. Holding her breath, she turned it over and stared almost greedily at the photograph inside.

A girl's face smiled back at her. She had an open, warm smile; her whole expression one of intelligence and confidence.

Her eyes were blue-grey, her hair a riot of thick, dark red curls. The photograph was only a head and shoulders shot, but it conveyed the impression of someone who would be lithe and quick, a positive dynamo of movement and life. For a teenager, she possessed remarkable composure and self-assurance. It radiated out of her . . . as did her obvious joy in life, her happiness.

As Taylor returned the photograph to the drawer she could feel a burning sensation stinging the back of her eyes. Her throat ached. Fiercely she blinked away her tears. Her emotion was inappropriate and selfish, and it would mean nothing to the girl in the photograph. Why should it?

6

'The Gibbons file is on your desk. Mike Gibbons should be ringing you later this afternoon. His secretary promised she would try to contact him. Oh, and Franklins have been on several times asking for Jay. When they heard he was in New York, they asked if they could speak to you instead.'

'Marcia stop fussing. I'll manage. You get yourself off to the hospital. Richard will take you. The car's waiting downstairs for you.' Bram shook his head as his secretary attempted to interrupt him, and said firmly, 'No arguments. He'll get you there faster than any taxi.'

Although his voice had been calmly reassuring when he spoke to her, Bram was frowning as his secretary hurried out of his office. She had received a call half an hour earlier to say that her husband had been taken to hospital with a suspected heart attack. Quite naturally, she was now in a frantic state. She and her husband were in their forties, their two children at university. Marcia had worked for Bram for almost ten years, knew all his small foibles and, like the very best PAs, made sure that his office routine ran smoothly. She was panicking now, not just about her husband but, in a lesser way, about Bram as well.

Marcia was more than just his secretary; she was in effect his office manager. She knew all their major customers by name, unlike the junior secretary who would have to stand in for her. It was a pity that Louise, Jay's secretary, was on holiday, Bram reflected as he mentally reviewed his diary for the next few days. He would have to cancel or rearrange as many of his outside appointments as he could in order to be on call in his office.

His frown deepened as he realised that one of the appointments that would have to be rearranged was the one he had with Taylor Fielding. Taylor Fielding. What, he wondered, had caused the fear he had heard in her voice when he spoke to her? Surely to God not *him*. She hadn't struck him as the kind of woman who would be awed or intimidated by another human being's worldly position or material possessions. Far from it. If anything, when they had met he had got the impression that she disapproved of him. Her attitude towards him had certainly veered towards the dismissive rather than the adulatory. He drummed his fingertips thoughtfully on the top of his desk. He was half-tempted to cancel his appointment with her. And do what? Ask Anthony to assign someone else to work with him? Abandon the project altogether? No, he could not take either of those evasive courses of action. Unfortunately, and perhaps at his own instigation, he and Taylor Fielding were fated to be on a collision course.

Grimly, Bram walked through to the outer office and asked the woman who had taken over from Marcia to ring through to the charity's headquarters for him.

Taylor was in her office talking with Sir Anthony when the call came through. In such a small enclosed space it was impossible for her boss not to overhear their conversation, even though he had diplomatically walked over to the small window when he had recognised Bram Soames's voice.

Taylor's heart sank as she heard Bram explain that it was impossible for him to leave his office.

'I apologise for having to change things at such short notice, but I was wondering if it is possible after all for you to come to me later this afternoon. I could send a car for you.'

Taylor closed her eyes. How could she refuse to go when Sir Anthony was there? He was bound to hear what she was saying and ultimately query her decision.

Sickly, Taylor nodded her head, and then, realising the idiocy of what she was doing, managed to utter a tortured agreement to the alteration in their original arrangement.

'There was really no need to send a car for me. I am perfectly capable of walking half a mile or so, you know. Or was it supposed to be less an inducement and more a potential threat?' Taylor demanded aggressively as Bram showed her into his office.

Bram had had an exasperating afternoon. The woman sent to take Marcia's place was new to the company and inclined to treat him with a mixture of awe and feminine appraisal, which instead of finding flattering he found extremely irritating. So irritating, in fact, that he reacted with uncharacteristic heat to Taylor's aggression.

'I hardly think that providing you with transport can logically be considered a threat,' he returned as he pulled out a chair for her and waved her into it.

'That all depends on what viewpoint you look at it from,' Taylor told him angrily. 'Sending your driver to collect me could be seen almost as a form of coercion, of kidnap....'

'Kidnap?' Bram stared at her, his frown changing to an amused smile. 'In broad daylight, on a busy London street?'

'It has been known to happen,' Taylor informed him, her face flushing as her eyes darkened with resentment at his amusement and the shadow of memories she still had to fight to suppress.

'I see. Well, please enlighten me then. Having kidnapped you and had you brought here against your will, what is it exactly I'm supposed to do with you? As you can see, this office is hardly the place one would choose for a passionate seduction and—'

Taylor stood, her eyes flashing, her normal control exploded by the force of her fury. How dare he make fun of her like this! He knew quite well that she had not been talking about sex.

'I will not be manipulated by you,' she told him stormily. 'I will not be forced into pandering to your ego or, just because it doesn't suit your opinion of yourself, for you to be the one to come to me, you—'

Bram stared at her. He pushed his hand wearily into his hair.

'Look. You've got this all wrong,' he told her quietly. 'I changed the venue of our appointment simply because my secretary has had a personal emergency—her husband has been admitted to hospital. Naturally she wanted to be with him, which meant that it would have been difficult for me to leave the office.'

Now it was Taylor's turn to stare at him, the angry colour staining her fair skin slowly burning into a deeper flush of embarrassment.

It had disturbed her to be told that Bram Soames had sent a car to collect her; it had reminded her of... Defensively she switched her thoughts away from the past and back to the present, gnawing worriedly at her bottom lip as she acknowledged that she seemed to have made an error of judgement.

'Look, why don't we start again,' Bram suggested firmly. 'I promise you that I had no ulterior motive whatsoever in sending Richard to drive you. I simply thought it would save time— yours as well as mine. It never occurred to me that you'd think I was trying to coerce or bully you, and I apologise for that oversight.'

But not for his sexist remarks following her outburst against his actions, Taylor noted silently.

She looked calmer now, Bram observed, watching Taylor as she digested his comments, calmer and very alert. He suspected that her outburst had shocked her in much the same way that his own sexually verbal response to it had shocked him.

The strain of the latest tussle of wills with Jay coupled with the intensity of his desire to succeed in his mission to write this special program must be affecting him more than he realised.

'Working together isn't going to be easy—for either of us,' he told Taylor quietly, abandoning his initial urge to cravenly ignore the hostility they seemed to generate towards each other in favour of a more responsible approach to the problem.

'But I think I'm right in saying that ultimately we both want the same thing, which is a successful outcome to this project.'

'If there can be one,' Taylor agreed grimly.

'You don't believe there can?'

'It's been tried before without success.'

'Which doesn't mean that we can't succeed.'

Against her better judgment Taylor found herself unexpectedly warming to that unanticipated 'we.' But then he was obviously the kind of man who was good at generating team spirit, at making others feel they were important, she warned herself.

'Still, it's a view you aren't alone in taking,' Bram continued. 'My son, for one, certainly shares it.' He gave her a wry look. 'I shall just have to do my best to prove you both wrong, shan't I. Can I get you a drink, by the way, tea . . . coffee . . .? It will have to be from the machine, I'm afraid.'

Taylor stared at him. Sir Anthony, for all his paternalism, would certainly never have suggested fetching a more junior member of his staff a drink from the office dispensing machines;

nor indeed, Taylor suspected, would he have drunk one himself. Although she searched his face thoroughly, there was no trace of self-consciousness or mockery in Bram's expression as he waited for her response.

Perhaps she had been wrong about him, Taylor acknowledged hesitantly. . . guilty of overreacting, of allowing her own prejudice to overshadow logic and reality.

'I . . . coffee, please,' she requested.

Taylor moved self-consciously in her chair, pressing a quelling hand to her rumbling stomach, as it gurgled protest at its lack of food.

It was almost seven o'clock but the time had passed so quickly she was astonished that it was so late.

Once she had managed to distance herself from her own fears and preconceptions, she had discovered that Bram was unexpectedly well informed about the problems he was likely to face in writing his program. Even more surprisingly, he was genuinely concerned for the plight of the people he was trying to help.

'I'm sorry. I didn't intend to keep you so long,' he was apologising now, as her stomach protested even more volubly. 'I hadn't realised it was getting so late. There's a very good Italian restaurant just round the corner where I frequently eat when I'm working late. Look, why don't you join me for dinner there, and please don't tell me that you're not hungry.'

Taylor grimaced, suppressing the small spurt of panic that his suggestion reactivated. She really had nothing to fear from this man, she told herself. He was not remotely interested in her as a woman; he was merely being polite. If she started to protest, to object, she was bound to arouse his suspicions and make herself look a complete idiot into the bargain. That comment he had made to her earlier when she had complained about him sending a car for her still rankled slightly.

It would be much easier—much safer—to fight down her instinctive reaction to his suggestion and accept.

Common sense, logic, told her that there was no way she would be in danger. He was quite obviously not a sexual predator, and most certainly not one who was so desperate for a woman . . . for sex, that he needed to waste his time attempting to seduce *her*, when no doubt there were countless women more than willing to fall into bed with him.

'We'll have to walk, though, I'm afraid,' he added teasingly, when she thanked him and accepted. 'Richard will have gone home by now.'

Despite her mounting colour Taylor still managed to look him in the eye.

He was just about to open the office door for her when it was thrust inwards, narrowly missing banging into Taylor. A whirlwind of a girl erupted into the room, apparently oblivious to Taylor's presence as she flung herself headlong into Bram's arms and demanded breathlessly, 'Oh, you are still here . . . good . . . Bram, be a darling, will you, and take me out to dinner tonight. I haven't seen you in simply ages, and it would be yummy going out with you. Even more yummy if we forgot about dinner altogether and went to bed instead . . .' she added suggestively, her voice dropping to a throaty purr that made the fine hairs on Taylor's nape rise in sharp reaction.

Bram, Taylor could see, instead of wrapping his arms around the girl as she so plainly wanted and Taylor had plainly expected—after all, she was everything a man could possibly want, startlingly pretty, young, coaxing and extremely sexy—Bram was, in fact, holding her firmly at arm's length, his face registering not pleasure but rather an almost paternal sternness.

'Plum, I'm sorry but I can't. I'm already going out to dinner—'

'What?' For the first time Plum seemed to become aware of Taylor's presence, her mouth drooping slightly as she studied her with keen competitiveness—and then dismissed her, Taylor observed wryly.

'Oh, but—' she started to protest as she turned back to Bram. He stopped her calmly. 'No buts.'

'But, Bram, I need to talk to you.'

'Not now, Plum, I'm afraid. As you can see, I'm busy.'

'But you'll ring me? Take me out to lunch?'

'I'll try.'

'Well, if you're really too busy . . .'

The hostility in the girl's eyes as she turned to look at her made Taylor acutely uncomfortable, but before she could speak, Bram

was ushering Plum out into the corridor and Taylor had to wait
for him to return before she could say quickly, 'Look, you don't
have to give me dinner. I don't want to cause you any problems
with your . . . your friend.'

Try as she might Taylor couldn't help stumbling betrayingly
over the last word of her hastily rehearsed little speech.

It had surprised her how much the other woman's obvious
sexual possessiveness about Bram had affected her. But then it
had been a long time since she had last been in close contact with
such intense sexuality. The girl, whoever she was, seemed to
wear it like a weapon, Taylor decided as she groped mentally for
the right description. A gauntlet, a challenge which she threw
down aggressively in front of Taylor, warning her off.

Not that she had had any need to do so. The last thing . . .

'Plum isn't my friend, and she certainly isn't my lover, if that's
what you're thinking.' She heard Bram interrupting her turbulent thoughts. 'She's my goddaughter.'

'Your goddaughter.'

Taylor couldn't keep the shock out of her voice, and she knew
her expression must have given her away when Bram continued
quietly, 'She's going through a bit of a difficult time, and what
she really needs more than anything is someone she can lean on,
someone she can trust, someone who loves her as a person. It's
a pity that she and Jay don't get on better, because . . .'

'Jay?' Taylor questioned, her curiosity aroused as Bram
opened the office door for her and ushered her out. It wasn't like
her to allow herself to exhibit interest in other people; it involved too much risk, too much danger, and she was irritated
with herself for having done so now. But it was too late. Bram
was already starting to answer her question as he guided her towards the lift.

'Jay is my son. He and Plum have known each other all their
lives, well, at least all Plum's life. Jay's twenty-seven now and
she's only just coming up for eighteen.'

'Twenty-seven.' Despite what Sir Anthony had already told
her, she felt slightly shocked. A brief glance in Bram's direction
as the lift started to descend confirmed what she already knew.
Even under the starkly revealing light of the lift, he looked far,
far too young to be the father of a twenty-seven-year-old. Not

because he had deliberately tried to cultivate a younger image—on the contrary, his suit was sober and traditionally cut, his shirt white and his tie plain.

Just visible when one was standing as close to him as Taylor was now forced to do, were one or two slightly silvered strands of hair lightening the rich darkness of the rest. The fine lines fanning out around his eyes added to rather than detracted from his sexuality, and to judge from the way he moved his body beneath the covering of his suit . . .

Taylor swallowed uncomfortably, her own body suddenly far too hot.

It was years since she had experienced that kind of physical reaction to a man—years since she had allowed herself to experience it.

You were made for this—for love, for sex.

The words escaped from the barriers she had put up against such memories, and like the memory of the man who had spoken them they made her shudder in sick panic.

Bram frowned as he saw the tremor galvanising her body, and the way her face suddenly paled.

Just for a brief moment she had seemed to relax, the unguarded interest in her face when she queried Jay's age such a contrast to her previous wary tension that Bram had surprised himself by wanting to go on talking to her so that he could prolong that interest. It was like watching someone suddenly come to life; seeing them as a whole three-dimensional figure for the first time.

The lift had stopped, and as they walked through the foyer and out into the street Bram paused to watch a young couple on the other side of the road. They had obviously had a quarrel, and the girl was refusing to get into their car. The young man, growing tired of her refusal, suddenly let go of the door he had been holding open and lunged forward, picking the girl up bodily. As he turned to deposit her in the car she tried to escape, wriggling protestingly in his arms.

Taylor, too, had stopped to watch, but when Bram laughed in amusement at their antics, Taylor turned on him, her face bone-white, her eyes so dark with anger and pain that Bram caught his breath at the intensity of emotion in them.

'Of course, you would think it's funny. You're a man,' Taylor told him bitterly. 'And *because* you're a man you think that it's perfectly acceptable for another man to manhandle a woman, to physically force her to do something she doesn't want to do, to use his physical strength to compel her into obeying him, forcing her....'

Taylor was literally shaking now, and Bram was caught between an instinctive desire to defend himself and his compassionate awareness of her distress.

Out of the corner of his eye he saw the young man deposit the girl back on the ground with gentle care, her angry protests dying away as she reached up towards him.

'Look,' Bram commanded Taylor quietly, taking hold of her and firmly turning her round to face the previously warring couple.

The girl's arms were wrapped firmly around her lover, her face tilted up towards his, one hand reaching up to pull his head down towards her own as she started to kiss him with passionate intensity.

Taylor, who had begun to pull away from his restraining hand, stiffened, her body as immobile as a statue, her attention riveted on the couple on the opposite side of the road. An aching, painful longing boiled up inside her, bringing sharp stinging tears to her eyes as emotions she had long thought forgotten and dismissed, suddenly filled her. She wanted desperately to turn away from the sight of that passionate, intense embrace, from the young woman's obvious need for her lover.

Once she had felt like that, ached like that, loved like that, and through those emotions she had betrayed not just herself but had also caused...

The sound she made as she whirled round, pulling frantically against Bram's restraining hand, reminded him of an animal caught in a trap; the low muted sound so riven with agony and fear that his immediate reaction was to reach out and take hold of her, to bind her to him so tightly that he separated her from her pain, protected her from it. Instinctively he fought down his reaction. She was a stranger to him, after all, a woman he barely knew, a woman whom his sense of self-preservation had already told him he would be wiser not to get to know.

Against his hand he could feel the indentation of her waist, so much sharper, so much narrower than her clothes suggested, her bones tiny and fragile beneath her skin. She wasn't thin; the soft swell of her breasts, the curve of her hips, were richly feminine. But her bone structure was very delicate and her body was much lighter than it should have been, her flesh worn down by whatever deep-rooted anxiety it was that caused those shadows in her eyes, that sense he had of her wariness, her fear.

From her reaction to the couple on the other side of the road, her vocal outburst to him, he guessed that at some point in her life there had been a man, a relationship, which had caused her intense pain. The kind of pain that made her intensely suspicious of his sex and very determined to remain aloof and withdrawn from it.

He told himself that he was glad.

Firmly he withdrew from her, his hand dropping to his side. The young couple were now climbing amicably into their car, the small incident over, their quarrel apparently forgotten.

He glanced thoughtfully towards Taylor as she turned her face away from him in an attempt to conceal her expression, calmly falling into step beside her as he waited for her to make some comment, to give him some explanation for her reaction. One glance into Taylor's shuttered face warned him against making any kind of comment.

Shakily, Taylor tried to compose her chaotic emotions. The small incident with the quarrelling couple had upset her more than she wanted to admit, disturbing old ghosts, reactivating feelings, fears she had thought she had long ago brought firmly under control.

The whole episode had left her feeling horribly weak and vulnerable; angry both with herself for being so susceptible to what she had seen and with Bram for witnessing that susceptibility. She knew she ought to be grateful to him for his tactful silence, his lack of uncomfortable curiosity, but instead the knowledge that he was aware enough of the intensity of her reaction to feel that she needed to be treated with caution and compassion only increased her feelings of angry panic.

She didn't want him feeling sorry for her, knowing that she felt vulnerable. She wanted to be able to dislike him, to feel disdain and contempt for him, to dismiss him as someone who possessed the kind of personality traits she most disliked and feared instead of . . . instead of what? Instead of witnessing her reaction to a scene that not only had aroused her deepest fears and most painful memories, but also had resurrected far more dangerous and unwanted emotions and needs.

Watching that young couple embrace with such open passion, feeling the male touch of Bram's fingertips against her waist, her body—

She faltered in midstep, overwhelmed by a sudden compulsion to tell him that she had changed her mind, that she didn't want dinner after all . . . that she couldn't spend any more time with him. But it was already too late; he was already pointing out the restaurant entrance to her, and her own logic was telling her that she had made enough of a fool of herself already.

7

'I'm sorry. I must be boring you.' Bram smiled across the table at Taylor. 'I do tend to get a bit carried away about this project.'

'It's a very challenging project to take on,' Taylor agreed as she forked up another delicious mouthful of carbonara.

She wasn't quite sure what she had expected from the restaurant. A certain degree of up-market exclusivity, a sense of being a little out of place? But she had been totally wrong on both counts. The restaurant was comfortable rather than elegant, and very obviously family owned and run. The glorious taste of the food had instantly transported her back to the last holiday she, her parents and her sister had shared before everything had started to go wrong.

Tuscany had been relatively undiscovered then, and her teenager's developing mind and senses had eagerly absorbed the new experiences the holiday had brought.

She could still remember the hot dry scent of the countryside; her delight in its medieval towns, in history brought sharply into focus. The reality of it was so clear that she'd had only to close her eyes to imagine she was back in the days of the Borgias when Italy had been at the height of its political and financial powers.

And then there had been the food.

Hastily she brought herself back to the present, watching Bram's expression as he responded to her comment.

'Yes, I know. Jay feels we should be concentrating on expansion and not—' Bram broke off. 'He and I are going through a difficult patch at the moment. Our relationship has never been an easy one, which is more my fault than his.'

As he looked directly at her, Taylor tried to mask her curiosity, but it was too late; he had seen it.

'I was fourteen when Jay was conceived,' he told her. 'It was the result of . . . well, let's just say it wasn't exactly planned or wanted by either his mother or myself. And as far as I'm concerned, no child should have to grow up knowing that he wasn't wanted.'

'Fourteen!' Taylor protested, trying and failing to master her shock.

'Yes. I agree. Not an ideal age to become a father,' Bram conceded. 'Not for me and certainly not for Jay. . . .'

'Fourteen,' Taylor repeated, her food forgotten as she tried to remember herself at that age, tried to imagine how she might have felt at the thought of becoming a mother.

'You must have been . . .'

'What?' Bram asked her grimly, without allowing her to finish. 'Oversexed? A coercive bully?' He shook his head. 'No, I wasn't either. It wasn't like that. The whole thing was quite literally an accident, in every sense of the word. . . . Jay's mother was the daughter of our neighbours. We'd grown up together, so to speak. She was older than I was, sixteen to my fourteen. She'd been dating someone, another boy. I didn't know him, but they'd had a quarrel and she turned to me for . . . for a shoulder to cry on and . . . consolation. Only things got slightly out of hand. Neither of us ever intended—it was the first time for me and I remember feeling afterwards rather bewildered and let down, wondering what all the fuss was about.

'I was at an all-boys school, and of course there'd been the usual bragging and young male bravado. The most I'd ever experienced before was a rather clumsy attempt to kiss a girl at a party, but Tara—' he paused, looking away from Taylor abruptly '—her parents were very strict. Too strict, according to mine, and of course in the time-honoured way of young girls she'd rebelled against them. Her boyfriend, the one she'd quarrelled with, was someone her parents didn't approve of. They'd already forbidden her to go on seeing him, but I doubt they had any idea just how far the relationship had gone.

'I must admit to being slightly shocked when Tara told me. There was no one else for her to confide in, I suppose. Like me she was at boarding school without any close girlfriends locally to talk to.'

'When she saw how shocked I was she teased me about it. Asked me if I'd done it yet . . . forced me to confess that I hadn't. She'd always enjoyed teasing me. I can remember how embarrassed I felt, especially when she started boasting to me about her boyfriend's physical attributes.

'I suppose that was what did it really. The need to prove myself, as it were. I doubt, originally, that she'd intended it to go any further than a piece of playful teasing. She could see how my body had reacted to what she was saying, and when she reached for my zip, I doubt she'd got anything more in mind than making fun of me for my excitement.

'However, as I said, one thing led to another, and without either of us really intending it to happen, we became lovers....'

Bram's mouth twisted slightly. 'Lovers. In reality that was the last thing we were. In reality Jay's conception was a pathetic, clumsy, mismanaged thing that even now I'm surprised it actually resulted in a child.... I really didn't have much of a clue of what to do, and Tara, for all her boasting, wasn't all that much more experienced.

'I went back to school shortly afterwards. When my parents turned up unexpectedly to visit five months later, the last thing I was expecting to hear was that Tara was pregnant with my child.

'I think that up until then they had been unwilling to believe it, but one look at my face must have betrayed my guilt.

'Of course, there was no question of us marrying, nor indeed of there being a termination. It was much too late for that.

'My parents offered to adopt the baby, but her parents refused. However, the only way her father would allow her to keep her child was if she promised never to see me again, and if I promised never to attempt to see my child. They said that I'd done enough, caused enough misery to their daughter and to them—'

'They blamed you?' Taylor interjected, unable to hold back the question or conceal her disbelief.

'I was to blame,' Bram told her. 'Jay was...is my son.... I didn't know then that my agreement would lead Jay to believe that I had refused to acknowledge him, or that his grandparents were going to use the circumstances of his birth to make him feel—' Bram shook his head '—I'm sorry, I must be boring you.'

'No. No, you aren't,' Taylor told him honestly. It was something totally outside her previous experience, to have a man be so totally open with her. Her father had always somehow distanced himself from both her and her sister, and the only other man she had really been close to . . . She closed her eyes, trying hard to resist the memories lurking in the shadows of her mind, waiting to stalk and terrify her as once . . .

'Sir Anthony told me that you had brought your son up alone, but I hadn't realised. You must be very close to each other.'

As she saw the way his expression changed, Taylor knew she had hit a nerve. Unexpectedly, instead of feeling triumph that she had found some vulnerability in a man who, in all other respects, had seemed to her to be totally invulnerable, what she actually felt was an unfamiliar sense of sympathy.

'In some ways, yes,' Bram agreed. 'In others . . .' He paused and looked across the table. It was unlike him to talk so openly about himself on such a very short acquaintance.

He had never been someone who felt it necessary to conceal certain aspects of his personality or his life, withholding information to boost his own sense of power or control, but neither was he given to instant intimacy or confidence sharing.

'Jay was six years old when he came to live with me. He had been brought up to believe that I didn't want him, that I had rejected him. He was very, very insecure. He refused to believe that I did love him, that I wasn't lying to him when I told him that he had no need to fear that I would abandon him. Subconsciously, I suspect, he blamed me for the unhappiness of his early years — with good reason. As a child he was very possessive about me . . . about our relationship.'

Again he stopped speaking. He rarely discussed his real feelings about Jay's possessiveness towards him.

Possessive. Taylor shuddered openly as she silently repeated the word.

'What's wrong?' Bram asked her, as she pushed her food away from her, her face suddenly pale and strained. 'Don't you like it? I can—'

'No. No . . . I'm just not hungry any more,' Taylor told him huskily. 'That . . . that must have been very hard to deal with . . . your son being . . . possessive about you.'

Taylor knew she was walking on dangerous ground, but she seemed drawn compulsively to it, like a child knowingly taking the risk of walking on ice in spite of warnings that it was too thin, thrilling to the sense of danger the action brought, even while terrified by it.

'It hasn't always been easy,' Bram allowed, but he was still frowning as he looked at her plate of half-eaten food. Taylor sensed that he was regretting having confided in her, and that he was deliberately trying to focus both his own and her attention in other directions.

Silently she gave in. After all, she knew well enough what it felt like not to want to talk . . . to explain . . . to feel threatened by another person's curiosity and interest.

'What about you?' Bram asked her. 'Your family—'

'I don't have one,' Taylor told him quickly. 'They're all . . . my parents were killed in . . . in an accident when . . . some years ago. . . .'

'When you were at university,' Bram hazarded, remembering what Anthony had told him about her leaving university.

The look of shock and fear on her face was so intense that it made Bram wonder what on earth he had said to cause it.

'How . . . how did you know about that?' she demanded hoarsely. 'About my leaving university. How did you know when . . . when the accident happened.'

'I didn't,' Bram told her, giving her a puzzled look. 'I just guessed that it could have happened then, because Anthony mentioned that you left before getting your degree.'

'I take it you were an only child. Their deaths must have been very painful for you.' Her frozen intentness, her wary hostility marked such a dramatic change from her earlier manner when they had been discussing Jay that it caught Bram totally off guard. Why had his mentioning the fact that she had left university early caused such a dramatic reaction? Not surely simply because she felt embarrassed about not completing her degree.

While Bram tried to puzzle out what was wrong, Taylor had started to reach for her handbag. 'I . . . I have to go,' she told him when he looked at her. 'I . . .'

'But you haven't finished your meal,' Bram protested.

'I . . . I'm not very hungry,' he heard Taylor reply. 'And besides, it's . . . it's getting dark and . . .'

Had she been another woman, a different woman, he might have been tempted to tease her a little about her reaction—an overreaction—but because he could sense how genuinely agitated and upset she was, Bram held his tongue.

'Let me at least get you a taxi,' he offered quietly. 'As you say, it is getting dark. My fault, I'm afraid. I was enjoying the self-indulgence of talking about myself so much that I hadn't realised the time. You're a very good listener,' he added warmly.

'I . . . I really must go.'

She was avoiding looking directly at him, Bram recognised.

'And . . . I prefer to use my own taxi firm, if you don't mind. The drivers are all women . . . and . . . '

It was obvious to Bram that she didn't like having to disclose even little pieces of personal information. But why? Did she feel that he would mock her, make fun of her for her obvious fear? Did she really think he was that kind of man, so crass and insensitive?

Of course, he could understand how any woman might feel wary of entrusting herself to an unknown man. You only had to listen to the news, read the papers. . . .

But Taylor's fear was more specific than that, he was sure of it. It wasn't the tentative unknowing fear of a sexually naïve, inexperienced woman, the old-fashioned 'spinster' beloved of satirists of another age. No, Taylor's fear was more specific, more acute than that.

'Well, let me at least get the *maître d'* to call the taxi firm for you,' Bram suggested gently.

Reluctantly Taylor gave him the number. She knew that he was only trying to be kind . . . to be helpful; that with Bram, in Bram, she had nothing to fear. But old habits die hard and old fears even harder.

She had let her guard down much too far when she had been listening to him talking about his life. She had been unprepared for his question about the fact that she had left university with her course unfinished.

'It must have been very hard for you, losing your parents like that,' he was saying to her now as he walked with her towards the door. 'I know how badly the deaths of his mother and grandparents affected Jay, although, of course, he was—'

'Only a child, while I was practically an adult,' Taylor supplied harshly for him.

'None of us is ever so mature that we don't suffer when we lose people we love,' Bram contradicted her gently. 'And if you had no other close family to turn to, to share your grief with, then—'

'I don't want to talk about it.'

Bram could hear the panic in her voice, feel it in her tense body as she stood by the door, scanning the traffic for her taxi, desperate to escape from him.

'You might enjoy dwelling on the past,' she added fiercely, 'but I don't. Nothing can change what happened. Nothing.'

She was perilously close to tears, Bram recognised in concern. He reached out his hand to touch her, to assure her that the last thing he had intended to do was to upset her, but she was already stepping away from him, exclaiming in patent relief, 'My taxi's here . . . I must go. . . .'

A little later, as he made his own way home, Bram pondered on the events of the evening. He hadn't been lying or exaggerating when he had said to Taylor that she was easy to talk to. She was. When she allowed herself to drop her guard and relax, there was something about her, an air of gentleness, of tranquillity, that invited confidences.

He only wished that he had been able to make her feel as secure and content in his company as he had felt in hers.

Careful, he warned himself. The pendulum that hung so delicately between his sexual desire for her and his emotions, was beginning to swing way, way too far into the emotional sector.

Desiring Taylor physically was something he could control and contain. Loving her. . .loving her? He started to frown. Now where had that idea . . . that word with all its connotations come from? He'd have to be a fool to go and let himself do something like loving Taylor. And he wasn't that . . . was he?

'Oh, no. Bram, come and take a look at this. Isn't it the most garish display you've ever seen? Who on earth would ever want to plant anything like that?' Helena demanded as she drew Bram's attention to a brilliantly coloured, tightly planted bed of modern annuals.

'It's certainly rather colourful,' Bram agreed mildly.

It had become an annual event, this visit of his and Helena's to the Chelsea Flower Show, something they had done together ever since their first years as friends. Neither of Helena's husbands had been interested in horticulture, unlike Bram, who had thoroughly enjoyed the opportunity his fen cottage garden had given him to have a vegetable and salad plot.

Neither the size of his London garden nor the size of his commitment to his business, permitted him that kind of self-indulgence any longer, but he still enjoyed his annual pilgrimage to the mecca, the Holy Grail as it were, of all things horticultural—although, unlike Helena, he chose not to slavishly follow the gardening fads touted by the more up-market papers and magazines.

He had seen gardens filled to the brim with clashing, brilliant colours which had pleased the eye and gladdened the soul in their own ways, just as much as a garden laid out on all the meticulous principles of planting and taste. It all depended upon how you looked at it, Bram mused. On whether one saw the miraculous bounty of a living, growing plant as just that, or felt and saw it as something that had to be rigidly selected and sited. Or whether it was simply nature's design that filled one with pleasure, or one's own.

However, he was far too kind to say as much to Helena, who seemed to take it as a personal insult if any of the exhibitors failed to meet her rigorous standards of what was and what was not good taste.

Bram watched her affectionately as she moved forward to examine one of the exhibits more closely, and then, out of the corner of his eye, a familiar face caught his attention. His voice warmed with pleasure and something else that made Helena turn her head and focus in surprise on him as he exclaimed, 'Taylor!' Then, 'Excuse me a moment, would you, Helena, I've just seen someone I know.'

Following him as he made his way through the crowd to the tall, red-haired woman who was standing alone, transfixed almost, the expression in her eyes both guarded and anxious as she watched him, Helena started to frown as she realised that Bram's quarry must be the woman Plum had described to her.

'She's far too old for Bram,' Plum had protested, 'and not at all pretty.'

Her daughter had been wrong on both counts, Helena recognised, although pretty was perhaps not the best word to describe Taylor. It didn't do her justice, for one thing. She was beautiful, Helena thought, or rather she had the potential to be, and there was no doubt what Bram thought about her. His pleasure in seeing her was there for all to notice.

After two marriages and a friendship of more than twenty years, Helena had thought that she had finally grown out of her old infatuation with Bram. She *had* grown out of it, she told herself sternly. Bram was her friend, that was all, and if she did feel slightly wary, slightly suspicious and very cross about the woman he was now talking to, her feelings were merely those of a friend, a concerned and very old friend . . . that was all.

As she reached Bram's side, Helena could hear him saying, 'Look, since you're obviously here on your own, why don't you join us. Helena and I were just about to go and have a cup of coffee in the members' enclosure, weren't we, Helena?'

Loyally, Helena confirmed this statement, at the same time wondering why on earth Bram was having to work so hard to get the other woman to join them. Normally her sex was the one issuing invitations to Bram, not the other way around. But while she envied Taylor Bram's obvious interest in her, at the same time she grudgingly approved of the other woman's demeanour.

Whatever the relationship between them, it obviously wasn't Taylor who had been pursuing Bram, Helena acknowledged, as Taylor fell reluctantly into step beside her. Beside her, Helena noticed, and not beside Bram.

'I didn't realise you were a gardener,' Bram told Taylor, outmanoeuvring her tactic to avoid being too close to him by changing direction so that he could walk on the other side of her.

'I'm not,' Taylor responded shortly. 'I just like looking. . . .'

Visiting the show was one of her small, very special treats, an annual event she always looked forward to. As a flat dweller she had no garden, and her parents hadn't been the type to encourage a small child's enjoyment of growing things, disapproving of the disruption and mess it caused.

'Which is your favourite stand?' she heard Bram asking her, his voice taking on a teasing warmth as he coaxed. 'Come on, it's all right, you can tell us. I promise we won't tell if you admit to a predilection for something that isn't socially acceptable and fashionable.'

'He's only saying that because he loves the most appalling displays of overplanted annuals.' Helena sniffed disparagingly.

'While you won't look at anything that isn't filled with dank, dark topiary and insipid white flowers,' Bram teased back.

'I . . . I like the physic garden,' Taylor heard herself admitting, 'and . . . and the herbs . . . they're so . . . so . . . '

'So soothing and healing,' Bram suggested gently for her.

Taylor gave him a wary look.

'Yes. That's part of it . . . but it's also the fact that they've been grown and used for so many centuries. They're timeless, eternal. When you think that people, civilisations, were cultivating and using them hundreds upon hundreds of years ago . . . ' She gave a small expressive shrug.

'Come on, the members' enclosure is just over here,' Bram told them, turning towards Taylor and touching her lightly on the arm as he indicated the direction.

It was the briefest, the most fleeting of touches imaginable, but Helena could see how highly charged with physical and emotional tension it was—both Bram's and Taylor's. They weren't already lovers, she decided intuitively, but if Bram had his way it wouldn't be long before they were. And Taylor . . . did she reciprocate his feelings . . . his desire?

On the surface she might not seem to, but all that wary tension had to have some cause. And besides, what woman in her right mind would turn down a man like Bram?

Despite the fact that the enclosure was busy and full, Bram managed to find them a small table, disappearing in the direction of the bar once he was sure that they were both comfortable.

'Have you known Bram long?' Helena asked Taylor, once they were on their own. She wasn't being inquisitive, she reassured herself. After all, Bram was one of her oldest friends. She had every right to feel protective of him, to want to make sure any new woman who entered his life knew how fortunate she was and appreciated what a very special man, a very special human being, Bram was.

'Not really,' Taylor responded dismissively. 'We're . . . we're business colleagues, that's all. I've been seconded to work with him on a special project.'

Helena frowned slightly. Taylor seemed very determined to deny any personal involvement between herself and Bram, but that hadn't been the impression Bram had just given.

'Oh, I see,' she responded. 'Then you must have met Jay, Bram's son.'

'No, actually I haven't,' Taylor replied.

'But Bram must have told you about him,' Helena insisted.

'A little,' Taylor admitted.

'And knowing Bram, he will, of course, have done his best to show Jay in a good light,' Helena persisted, ignoring Taylor's obvious reluctance to pursue the subject. 'Bram dotes on Jay and can see no fault in him. No matter what Jay does, Bram never blames him, always taking the responsibility himself. Has he told you the history of their relationship?'

'Yes, yes, he has,' Taylor agreed.

Against her better judgement Taylor acknowledged that she was curious to hear what Helena had to say about Bram. It was obvious that the other woman was an old, close friend—and had, perhaps, at one time been more?

'In my opinion Jay has been extremely fortunate, and Bram's been a fool to allow him to have so much influence on his life.' Helena shrugged disdainfully.

'I told Bram years ago, when he first took charge of Jay, that the best thing he could do for both of them was to either find Jay some foster parents or send him to a good boarding school.

'The plain fact of the matter is that Jay always has been and always will be jealous of his father. As an adult he competes incessantly with Bram and at the same time manipulates him so that Bram has no real chance of ever making a life of his own.'

'If that's true, then surely it's up to Bram to do something about it—if he wants to,' Taylor suggested coolly. 'Some people enjoy having others dependent on them. They need the sense of power and control it gives them, even while they deplore and denigrate the one who's dependent on them.'

'Some people may do,' Helena agreed firmly. 'But Bram isn't one of them. He just doesn't possess that kind of character weakness. I've know him a long time. We were friends before Jay's mother and grandparents died and . . . Bram allows Jay to do what he has done, out of guilt . . . because he feels he owes it to Jay to make up for all that he feels he's lost. In reality Jay lost nothing.'

Helena saw Taylor's expression and gave another shrug.

'I'm sorry, but it's true. Jay's mother was on the point of re-marrying, and I doubt that her husband would have been as tolerant of Jay as Bram has been.

'You'll have to be careful when you do meet Jay. He won't be happy about Bram knowing you. Jay has destroyed every relationship Bram has ever tried to have, and he'll destroy yours as well if he can,' Helena warned Taylor heavily.

'Bram and I don't have a relationship,' Taylor denied immedi-ately, her face flushing.

She really ought not to have encouraged Helena. In satisfying her own unwarranted and dangerous curiosity she had given the other woman a totally erroneous impression about the situa-tion.

'Sorry I've been so long,' Bram apologised, smiling warmly at them both as he reappeared with their drinks. 'You wouldn't believe the crush at the bar.'

Half an hour later, when Taylor insisted that she had to go, Helena watched as Bram got up with her.

As she saw the look in his eyes as he stood by the other woman, Helena felt her heart somersault uncomfortably.

Did Bram know yet how dangerously close he was to falling in love with Taylor? Did either of them know it?

Bram in love . . . Helena gave a small shiver and then told her-self fiercely that she was perfectly content with her own life, her own husband. The pain she could feel had nothing to do with any regrets for what might have been. Jay would, if he could, stand between anyone—woman or man—who dared to come too close to his father.

8

Plum was not enjoying herself. She focused gloomily on the now unfrothy and nauseatingly hued remnants of her cocktail, her eyebrows drawing together in disapproval.

A drink should always be a drink, her father always said, and she was beginning to see his point. *Her* drink, despite the claims of the bartender, had done nothing to lift the feelings of gloom which had descended on her since she had last seen Bram.

It wasn't fair, just because he was a few years older...well, all right more than twenty. So what? Men who could give Bram a good decade or more had had no inhibitions about indicating their desire for her. Just because he was one of her mother's friends, Bram seemed to have this ridiculous idea that he had to behave like some kind of uncle towards her, rejecting all her attempts to show him just how good things could be between them.

And they *would* be good. Bram might not wear his sexuality as overtly as Jay, but it was still there. Oh yes, it was very definitely there.

Just thinking about how it would feel if he kissed her was enough to make her go faint with longing.

How *could* he have preferred being with that, that...woman, to being with her? She was old—in her thirties at least. Her figure had been good, Plum admitted grudgingly, and her bone structure and her skin. But her clothes, and her hair, her total lack of any attempt to make herself look attractive... How could Bram possibly prefer her company to Plum's?

Plum scowled darkly, stirring her cocktail with its straw.

There could be only one reason. He must be in love with her.

The thought of Bram being in love sent her stomach plunging giddily downwards. How could he possibly love anyone else, when she loved him so much?

'Hey, Plum, fancy another drink?'

Her frown eased slightly as she recognised the voice of one of her friends.

She and Justin had enjoyed a brief flirtation a few months earlier, a flirtation she herself had ended before it got as far as the bedroom. Although to judge from the way he was looking at her, Justin obviously still had hopes in that direction. Well, why not? she asked herself morosely. Since her darling, delicious Bram had spurned her and given his love to another, she might as well comfort herself with Justin's attentions.

As she nodded in acceptance of his offer, she realised that he had someone else with him—a broad-shouldered, slightly stocky man of just over medium height, five-ten, maybe five-eleven, with rather plain brown hair cut in an equally plain style that matched his blunt weather-beaten features.

'This is The McKenzie by the way, Plum,' Justin informed her in a slurred voice. '*The* McKenzie,' he repeated, heavily emphasising 'the.' 'Head of the Clan McKenzie. A role which I regret to inform you he takes with extreme seriousness. McKenzie, meet Plum. Plum, meet McKenzie. Oh, and by the way, he is also my cousin. Unfortunately for me, since my parents will insist on holding him up to me as an example of the way I should behave.'

'My cousin, The McKenzie, spends virtually all his time in Scotland living with his sheep and doing good works, which is why I've brought him out with me this evening, so that he can have a taste of what real life is all about.'

The McKenzie was none too pleased with Justin's comments, Plum could see. Nor did he look very enthusiastic about being introduced to her.

In fact, if anything, the look in his brown eyes as he focused briefly on her was not so much of disinterest as disapproval. Plum recognised it immediately. After all, she had seen it often enough in her mother's cool, pale blue eyes.

'Gil is down in London for a few days on business,' Justin went on, 'so I offered to show him a bit of night-life. I'll bet you don't have anything like this up in your neck of the woods, do you, old son,' Justin commented patronisingly.

'Nothing,' came back the almost fierce response.

Plum giggled, her own problems forgotten as she studied the solid mass of disapproving maleness standing in front of her.

His clothes were as out of place as his expression—sturdy country tweeds, the kind of clothes her mother approved of.

While Justin ordered their drinks, Plum gave his cousin one of her famous bewitching smiles and asked, 'If you dislike this sort of place so much, why did you come?'

'My aunt asked me to keep an eye on Justin,' he told her bluntly. With a glower at her he added, 'She's very concerned about the type of company he's been keeping lately.'

'Isn't Justin a bit old for that sort of thing?' Plum asked in mock sweetness.

'Not as far as his mother is concerned,' he replied curtly.

'You must think an awful lot of her to play guard dog over Justin,' Plum countered.

'She's my aunt . . . family,' was his stern response.

Family. He said it as though it explained everything. And to Plum it did.

A huge lump suddenly blocked her throat, and she had to turn her head away from him to hide the tears she could feel threatening to flood her eyes.

Where was her family when she needed them? Her mother cared far more about her second family than she had ever done about Plum. Plum was a nuisance, a reminder of the marriage Helena wished she had never made, her father's daughter in every single way, or so she had always been told.

And as for her father . . . That he would ever send some stern guardian to stand over her was impossible to imagine. Her father believed in complete freedom for her and for himself . . . for her and *from* her?

Poor Justin. She would hate to be in his shoes, with this solid, disapproving, boring young man shadowing her every movement, she assured herself quickly.

Poor Justin . . . She reached abruptly for her glass.

'Come on, Gil, it's your round.'

Hazily Plum lifted her head from where she was resting it on Justin's shoulder, to nod in tipsy confirmation of his demand.

'I think *both* of you have already had more than enough to drink. It's getting late and—'

Both of them! Plum sat upright, giving him an indignant, baleful look. He might think he had the right to interfere in Justin's life and tell him what to do, but he didn't have any rights over her.

She opened her mouth to tell him so and then stopped.

At some stage in the evening she must have spilled some of her drink, and now there was a horrible stain right on the front of her new silk shorts.

Her face crumpled as she wailed protestingly, 'Oh no! Just look at that! These shorts cost the earth. They're brand-new, as well, and the stain probably won't come out.'

'Very likely,' Gil McKenzie agreed hardily.

His tone had been so openly disapproving and unsympathetic that Plum immediately demanded suspiciously, 'What does that mean?'

He made no attempt to placate her, a novel experience for Plum, who was used to reducing most men to quivering, sycophantic bundles of panting, raging hormones.

'It means that if you will wear such a ridiculous and obviously fragile, impractical item of clothing and then consume excessive quantities of brightly coloured alcoholic drink, the inevitable is bound to happen.'

'Really? How clever you are.' Plum beamed falsely up at him, giving him her most winning, naughty-little-girl, I'm-so-sexy smile—the one that drove the majority of men crazy with lust. 'But then men are clever like that. It's all those male hormones . . . all that male logic. I'm afraid I'm just no good at anything like that.'

He was looking at her now with open dislike, Plum recognised. Her temper suddenly getting the better of her, she added in a much clearer and crisper tone, 'What a pity you aren't also clever enough to know that women find know-it-all men stuffy and patronising, and what's more, they make us very angry, and inevitably when we are angry we display it,' she told him savagely. 'Like this.'

She stood and deposited what was left in her glass very carefully and thoroughly over the front of his shirt. The feeling of satisfaction the action gave her more than made up for the fuss that followed, including their summary ejection from the bar.

'You are an idiot, Plum,' Justin complained drunkenly when they were outside on the pavement. 'Now we'll never get another drink.'

'Yes, we will,' Plum told him. 'We can have one at my place.'

'Good idea,' Justin agreed. 'Let's find a taxi.'

Plum could see from the look Gil McKenzie was giving her that he could cheerfully have murdered her and no doubt have boiled up her bones to make soup for his horrible sheep.

He did, of course, try to persuade Justin that it would be a much better idea for them to leave Plum and go home, but to her glee, Justin refused.

'You go, if you want to, old man,' Justin urged him. 'No need to worry about me. I can always bed down at Plum's place if necessary, can't I, old girl.'

'Of course,' Plum agreed, adding wickedly, 'there's plenty of room. I've got a double bed.'

She also had a spare room but she was not going to tell Gil McKenzie that.

'Nice place you've got here,' Justin approved in a slurred voice when the taxi had finally decanted them outside Plum's flat and she had opened the door.

'What do you think, Gil?' Plum asked. 'Do you like it?'

'It looks very expensive.'

'It is,' Plum agreed. 'So it's just as well I don't have to pay the bills.'

His look of shocked distaste amused her, and she felt quite cross when Justin agreed enviously, 'Yes, I wish my parents would rent somewhere as decent as this for me. You're a lucky sod, Plum.'

'My stepfather bought the flat as an investment,' she answered carelessly, her eyes suddenly shadowing.

He had also bought it, she was sure, as a means of removing her from the home he shared with her mother and their own children.

Oh, publicly he always made a show of 'loving' her. She had often heard people comment on what a good and caring step-father he was, and certainly she lacked for nothing materially.

But he had never held or cuddled her the way he did her step-sisters. Neither he nor her mother ever smiled at her the way they did at them. But then she wasn't like her stepsisters, was she? They were good, lovable children, and she had always been a bad girl, a difficult child. Even at school they had called her that.... She shrugged the memory aside. Her mother and stepfather might not love her or approve of her, but other people did. Men did . . . well, most men. Gil McKenzie, she suspected, would more than understand and share her nearest and dearest's opinion of her.

'Okay, so what are we going to have to drink?' she asked.

'I don't think either of you should have anything. In fact, both of you have already had more than enough,' Gil McKenzie answered grimly.

'Oh . . . oh, go and boil your head,' Plum told him childishly. 'Come on, Justin,' she instructed her cousin, ignoring Gil. 'The drink's cabinet's over there. Let's go and see what's in it.'

Gil McKenzie surveyed Plum's sitting room. It was three o'clock in the morning. He had a week of important and complicated business meetings ahead of him, and the last thing he had wanted or needed was his aunt asking him to play sheepdog to his damned cousin.

And as for the idiotic, appalling woman Justin had allowed to manipulate him into coming home with her . . .

Gil sighed as he glanced across to where Plum was lying awkwardly in a chair asleep. Woman? She looked more like a girl . . . a child.

But a child could never have driven him to the edge of losing his temper and his self-control the way Plum had tonight; and a child could never have been as openly and brazenly sexual in her speech and actions.

Had Justin slept with her? Were they lovers? He scowled, caught off guard by the sharp sense of bitterness the thought brought him. After all, why should he care one way or the other?

Justin, too, had fallen asleep—on the sofa on which he now lay, snoring loudly.

'You don't have to stand guard over him. He's quite safe.'

Gil's scowl deepened as he realised Plum had woken up and was watching him.

'I'll never get him back to his flat in this state,' he told her curtly.

Plum shrugged, her mouth opening wide in a huge yawn to reveal pretty, small, white teeth.

'So what. Leave him where he is until morning. You can always sleep in the spare room,' she added. 'It's that door, and it's got its own bathroom.... I can even supply you with a pair of pyjamas and a toothbrush,' she added, her smile telling him that she was enjoying taunting him.

'I keep them just in case—' she confirmed his suspicions '—along with anything else that a . . . visitor might need.'

The austere look he gave her showed her he was not impressed.

She was sobering up now, and his obvious lack of interest in her piqued her a little. Not that she was in the least attracted to *him*, she assured herself hastily. There was, after all, only one man she really wanted, she reminded herself mournfully, and if she couldn't have him, then she might as well . . .

Gil was turning away from her and standing up. She eyed him thoughtfully beneath demurely lowered lashes, which concealed the naughty gleam in her eyes.

'Of course, if you're worried that Justin might not be comfortable on the sofa, you could always put him in the spare bed and share my room.'

The arctic look he gave her unnerved her a little. It wasn't the kind of response she was used to getting to her teasing, flirtatious remarks.

'No, thanks, I don't sleep around, and I don't particularly care for the thought of having a one-night stand with someone who does.'

Normally, such a self-righteous comment would have had Plum dissolving into helpless laughter, but for some reason, on this occasion it made her feel close to tears.

'I wasn't offering to have sex with you,' she denied huffily, shrugging. 'Anyway, it was just a joke.'

'A rather dangerous joke,' Gil informed her. 'Have you ever thought of the danger you could be inviting with that kind of comment? There isn't an awful lot of you, and if some man decided to have sex with you against your will . . .' he began severely.

'Rape me, you mean?' Plum asked him. A tiny shadow crossed her face. There had been men who had occasionally been . . . difficult, when she had informed them that they had made a mistake. . . . But she had long ago perfected a way of soothing their damaged egos.

'Only a man who's a pervert or totally sexually frustrated would do something like that,' she told him airily, tossing her head. 'I suppose you must be quite frustrated yourself, if you don't have sex very often. Unless, of course, you're still a virgin. It can't be easy for a man of your age to tell a woman that you haven't had sex before,' she added.

'I am *not* a virgin, nor am I sexually frustrated,' he told her through gritted teeth. 'And now, if you don't mind, I would like to get some sleep, so—'

'You're very moralistic, though, aren't you,' Plum interrupted. 'Is that some kind of religious thing or something—'

'No, it is not,' Gil told her, his irritation very obviously increasing. 'I simply don't sleep around.'

'Oh, you mean you've got a low sex drive. Well, there are things they can do for that,' Plum told him informatively. 'You ought—'

'There's nothing wrong with my sex drive,' Gil told her furiously. 'Although I dare say it comes nowhere near matching up to yours.'

'Oh, but I don't—'

Just in time Plum stopped herself, her mouth forming a startled O of astonishment as she realised she had been about to tell this man, who was being completely horrid to her and whom she did not like one little bit, something that was one of her most closely guarded secrets. Something in fact that most of the time she didn't even like to admit to herself.

'I'm going to bed,' Gil told her.

So he didn't like her. Plum shrugged mentally. He wasn't her type anyway. She liked tall, good-looking, flirtatious men, men who knew how to make a girl feel good about herself. Men who loved her sexuality and who couldn't wait to coax her into bed with them. Men who were only too delighted to abandon their attempts to arouse her and to allow her to please them with the warm, expert caress of her mouth.

It was so much better that way. She had so much more control, so much more power, and there was none of that unpleasant thrusting invasion of her own body.

And afterwards, they were even more delighted with her than they had been before.

Gil McKenzie didn't know what he was missing.

And who cared anyway? She certainly didn't. He was as boringly self-righteous and disapproving as her mother.

Abruptly Plum shivered, wrapping her arms around herself as she stumbled towards her own bedroom, fiercely blinking away the tears that threatened to blur her vision.

Tiredly she undressed and prepared for bed, but she couldn't sleep. Gil McKenzie's dislike of her had reactivated too many uncomfortable old memories.

Automatically she opened the drawer in the cabinet beside her bed, and rummaged around in it until she found what she was looking for.

The vibrator needed new batteries, but there was enough power left in it for what she wanted. She felt so much safer doing it like this, so much less exposed and vulnerable.

The first time her mother had found her masturbating she had been four years old, unable to fully understand her mother's reaction to what she was doing. Touching herself in such a way was something she liked doing. It was comforting. Her mother's icy fury, anger and disgust upset her so much that she needed that comfort even more.

Her mother had pushed her hands away as she told her that she was disgusting and dirty.

Plum hadn't understood what those words meant—then— still, even her mother admitted now that it wasn't her fault that she was oversexed. Plum herself had heard her telling her stepfather years ago that it was something Plum must have inherited from her father.

She closed her eyes, tensing her body as the sensation inside her peaked and the first surge of her orgasm convulsed her.

Calmed and relaxed, she turned over and slid gently into sleep.

Gil opened his eyes. The room was stiflingly hot, his throat and eyes dry and sore. He pushed back the duvet, grimacing as he remembered the events of the previous evening.

He hated cities, hated being away from home at the best of times, but this... Damn Justin. No wonder his aunt was so worried about him. He could just imagine her reaction if Justin were to bring home someone like Plum as a prospective daughter-in-law. Any mother's reaction, for that matter.

It was obvious that Plum didn't have a scrap of common sense, never mind any thoughts of self-preservation. Look at the way she had virtually propositioned him last night. What the hell would she have done if he had taken her up on it?

Didn't she care about the risks she was taking...? Didn't anyone care?

He glanced at his watch. Half past six. He doubted Justin would welcome being woken up, but he was hungry and in need of a change of clothes, and he was damned if he was going to hang around this hothouse of a flat waiting for his cousin to surface from his drunken stupor.

He opened his bedroom door, sighing as he heard his cousin's snores. The door to Plum's bedroom was half-open. From where he stood he could see inside the room to the bed. Plum was lying on it, curled up into a small, childish ball, the duvet kicked to one side. A small childish naked ball.

Gil tried not to look at her as he went to close the door, but she was shivering in her sleep, moving on the bed as though seeking the warmth of the quilt she had discarded—although how anyone could possibly feel cold in this place he did not know. He reacted automatically to her distress and walked over to the quilt, picking it up. As he did so the vibrator fell out of its tangled folds. He eyed it with displeasure before turning round to drop the quilt over Plum's sleeping form.

Only she wasn't sleeping any more....

'Changed your mind,' she purred. 'Mmmm . . . good, early-morning sex is always the best, I think.' Because normally the man in question was eager to get it over and done with and get on his way.

'Come here and let me do something you'll really enjoy,' she invited, patting the empty space beside her.

As she stretched out languorously in front of him, Gil noticed that her body was unexpectedly voluptuous, softly and very femininely fleshed, her skin delicately and prettily pale. She was touching the tip of her tongue to her lips, licking them suggestively while she focused her gaze openly on his crotch.

After the first unexpected and unwanted surge of response, he was so angry with her that he had to take a step back from the bed to stop himself from taking hold of her and shaking her.

'What's wrong?' she asked. 'Don't worry if you're not hard yet. I promise you, you soon will be.'

In the sitting room Justin started to cough. Plum watched as Gil ignored her invitation and left the room.

The man was obviously impotent . . . sexless. So what? That was his problem and not hers. She tossed her head, dismissing the panicky feeling surging through her body. She didn't care— all she cared about was finding a way of making Bram realise how much she loved him.

It had given her a nasty shock seeing him with that woman. Who was she? How long had she known Bram? How serious about her was he? How much of a threat was she? Did Jay know about her?

If she concentrated very hard on thinking about Bram, she could almost block out altogether the sound of voices coming from the other room and the feeling Gil McKenzie's rejection of her had aroused. Almost.

9

'Not interested?' Oliver St Charles asked his daughter sympathetically as she frowned over the letter she had just opened.

'No . . . I mean yes. Brampton Soames has agreed to a preliminary interview, but he wants me to discuss my project in more detail with his PR department first, no doubt so they can veto it if they think I'm going to give him a hard time.'

'And are you?' Oliver asked her in some amusement.

Fate gave him a reproving look. 'That all depends. You know what my goals are for this project, Dad, I want to make an honest report on just exactly how much financial success and power equates to real happiness—not just for those who achieve it but for those who live closely with them, as well.'

'Mmm. Well, in order to do that you're going to have to trust your interviewees answer honestly.'

'Not necessarily. I *am* capable of making my own judgements, you know.'

'And of having those judgements affected by your own prejudices,' her father suggested.

Fate pulled a face at him.

At twenty-one she was an extraordinarily mature young woman whose stability and down-to-earth attitude to life often made the St Charleses the envy of friends whose offspring were not similarly well-adjusted. It had been Fate's own idea to continue living at home while she wrote her final-year university project; not for any financial reasons—Fate was scrupulously insistent on contributing to the household budget—but because she had told her parents sunnily, there was nowhere else and no one else with whom she wanted to live.

They had not been merely lucky, but actually gifted in their only child, Oliver acknowledged. Naturally, as her parents they loved her, but perhaps, more rarely, as a family they actually liked one another as well.

Physically Fate looked nothing like either of her parents, who were both fair-haired. Oliver was tall with a rangy male bone structure, and Caroline was quite petite. Fate, however, was a good eight inches taller than her mother. And while her height might have been inherited from her father, her bone structure— which gave her those delicately feminine wrists and ankles—and her small, classically shaped face had not. Neither had that deep rich, dark red hair, the colour as vibrant and alight with life as Fate herself.

Fate glowed. There really was no other way to describe her that Oliver could easily call to mind. Every time he looked at his daughter he was filled with the most intoxicating mixture of love and pride. Love in her and for her. Pride in the fact that he was her father. Her academic achievements were something else, and naturally it pleased him to know that she had the skills to enrich her life both mentally and materially. But it was her woman-hood, her *self*, which gave him the most joy. And the knowledge that he had not, as she had been growing up, failed her, as he had often feared he might.

He had had a very masculine background and upbringing. To be the father of a daughter when all his life he had been taught that the male sex was superior had made him confront the prejudices within himself. When she was born he had loved her, of course, but she was female and not male. Then he had picked her up and held her in his arms and been filled with such love for her, and such anger against himself, that he had vowed that this female, his daughter, would never, never learn from him to regard herself as second-best.

'I want her to grow up being proud of being a woman,' he had told Caroline the day they had her christened. 'I want her to love herself.'

He was the one who had chosen her name. Caroline had objected a little at first, worrying that Fate might be teased by other children for having such an unusual name. She need not have worried.

Fate had been the kind of child who automatically drew others to her, but even as a child she had not capitalised on that ability; rather it had made her more cautious and choosy about whom she befriended.

Caroline had worried a little bit then about such a strength of purpose, worried that it might, in later life, lead her into manipulating others. But she need not have done so.

There was an independence and a strong sense of self about Fate that some young men seemed to find either off-putting or very challenging. If Caroline had any fears for her daughter's emotional future, they were simply that Fate might, through kind-heartedness, allow herself to become involved in a relationship with someone too needy and dependent, a man who would feed off her emotional strength rather than one who could match it and honour it in her.

Caroline and Oliver had had a very good marriage; their love for each other was still as strong as ever. But then she recognised that they had been very lucky. She wanted Fate to enjoy the same degree of happiness she and Oliver had shared, but she was also glad that Fate wasn't in any rush to settle down. Fate had a wide circle of friends and a very busy social life.

'Why can't people understand how important it is to enjoy life and not just to live it?' she often complained to her parents.

'Perhaps because they're just not as brilliantly perceptive and intelligent as you,' her father teased.

'You don't need to be intelligent to know that life has to have some fun in it,' she had countered. 'If it doesn't, we might as well all live like battery-farmed animals.'

'Some people get their self-esteem out of their work,' Oliver had pointed out to her. 'They feel insecure without it. They need their work to define themselves by, need the status and the sense of purpose it gives them.'

'Yes, I know, but don't you see, that's what's so completely wrong with the present system,' Fate objected fiercely. 'People, children, are taught to value only material progression, outward growth, instead of valuing the inward growth that is really important. That's the basis of my project,' she had told her parents. 'Does material wealth, status . . . success really make people happy. I don't think it does.'

'I doubt you'll get many of your interviewees to agree with you,' Oliver had warned her when she told him what she was planning to do. She had written to more than twenty people who, for one reason or another, were deemed in the eyes of the world to have achieved success and wealth.

So far, five of them had written back refusing to be interviewed. Brampton Soames was the first to agree to see her. Or at least to allow her to talk to his PR department. Was it any wonder she felt slightly pessimistic about her chances of actually interviewing the man himself?

Her mother, of course, took a much more enthusiastic and optimistic view as Fate passed her the letter.

Watching her read it, Fate wondered if her mother would be quite so pleased if she knew of the arguments Fate had had with her tutor over her choice of subject-matter for her project.

'What exactly are you hoping to achieve?' he had questioned her. 'You're planning to undermine the foundations of a world in which you're going to have to live. It won't make you very popular.'

'I don't want to be popular,' Fate had told him. 'I just want...'

'You just want to turn everything upside down, to prove how clever you are,' he had taunted her.

Fate hadn't wasted her time arguing with him. She knew what the root of the problem was. Six months before, he had told her that he wanted to go to bed with her. And she had told him that his desire was not reciprocated. He hadn't tried to pressure her, he wasn't that kind of man but he wasn't used to being turned down and he hadn't liked it.

Fate didn't care. Intellectually she might admire him, but physically he did nothing for her. As she had told her father at the time, 'I'm damned if I'm going to go to bed with him simply to get a better mark.'

Her father, of course, had been appalled and strongly critical of a system that allowed such an abuse of its privileges.

His naïvete had touched Fate. When he and her mother had married her father had had no academic qualifications. During the early years of their marriage, having left Australia because Caroline had wanted to return to England, he had taken on whatever work he could to earn a living, studying at night to obtain his professional qualifications.

It had been while he was labouring on a house conversion that he had fallen into conversation with the owner, who had been so impressed by him that he had offered him a job.

Since the company Henry Lewis owned was based in Oxford, it had been logical that her father, then newly-appointed sales manager and now chief executive, should move to Oxford.

Fate could remember the discussions that move had caused, urgent whispered conversations between her parents late at night when she was supposed to be asleep. She had never really understood why they had been so reluctant to make the move.

It had also rather surprised her that her mother, who had always said how much she would love an older, larger house, should suddenly change her mind and choose to move into a brand-new executive villa on an anonymous development several miles outside the city.

True, the development was on the outskirts of a very pretty village and limited to half a dozen comfortably sized, detached houses, and over the years her mother's home-making skills had ensured that it *was* a home and not just a house. But Fate had often wondered why her mother had not chosen the kind of house she had always claimed she wanted.

Still, it was home now and Fate had enjoyed her days at the local school. Later on when she had gone up to Oxford her fellow students had been inclined to sympathise with her for having to live at home, denied the freedom and independence which was theirs.

Fate had laughed aside their sympathy. Fate liked her parents, she enjoyed being with them, and they respected her independence just as she did theirs. She was perfectly free to take men home with her if she wished. The small conversion her father had built for her over the garage had its own private entrance. One of the things she liked best about her parents was their easy acceptance of sexuality, theirs and hers.

Sex, her mother had told her when they had discussed such things, is a very great pleasure and a very great responsibility. 'And your responsibility,' she had told Fate gently, 'is to yourself.

'Only you can know what is right for you. The worst thing you can do is to be dishonest about your own feelings and your own needs to others, and more importantly, to yourself.

'Nature has given you, through your body and your emotions, a great capacity for enjoyment and happiness. You have every right to both those things. Don't ever allow anyone else to spoil them for you. And a partner who doesn't understand or appreciate your right to them *will* spoil them.

'Never have sex for any other reason than that it's what you want, Fate, and always try to be sure why you want it.'

She had touched Fate's face lovingly. 'What your father and I want more than anything else for you is for you to grow up being proud of the fact that you are a woman, knowing that as a woman you have every right to express and enjoy your sexuality. Unfortunately not everyone shares that view. There are, and always will be, women as well as men who feel so threatened by such sexuality that they feel they have to stifle and control it. As you go through life, you will meet many such people, Fate. People who, for one reason or another, will seek to impose their views and their controls on you. Don't let them.'

It was only now as an adult, a woman, that Fate was truly able to appreciate and marvel not just at the advice her mother had given her, but also at the way both her parents had supported these views.

Fate had friends whose parents were very open about sex, just as she had friends whose parents could hardly bring themselves to acknowledge it existed. But she couldn't think of a single one of her peers whose parents, both father and mother, had so determinedly and fiercely taught them to value themselves and to guard their emotions and their sexuality from any exploitation by others, to have such a strong sense of belief in themselves.

Fate didn't know if, without this, she would have been able to explore her burgeoning sexuality with such appreciative anticipation. She had known long before she had first allowed any boy to go 'all the way' with her, that the experience would be one she was going to enjoy, and it had been.

She and Nick, her first lover, had genuinely cared for each other, loved each other within the limitations of their adolescent ability. In the two years they had been together they had shared sexual heights of mind and body, shivering in ecstasy as well as laughing at bungled uncertain experiments.

Nick had been devastated when she told him gently that it was over. He loved her, he had protested. He wanted to marry her.

That had been four years ago. Fate had bumped into him in Oxford a few months ago. He had just returned from a stint crewing on one of the entrants for the Whitbread Trophy and had been looking enviably tanned as well as a good deal more ruggedly male. The moment he saw her a huge smile had broken out across his face. He had left the people he was with to come loping towards her, wrapping his arms round her in a huge, hard hug as he kissed her affectionately.

They had spent the evening together reminiscing over old times and discussing their plans for their futures.

At the end of the evening he had reached across the table and touched her hand lightly. 'You were right,' he told her softly. 'It was time to end it and let go, so that we could both grow. Funny, though, how once you've had really good, good sex, you seem to lose your appetite for anything that's any less. Don't you agree?'

'Yes, I do.' Fate nodded.

'And our sex was good,' he told her.

'Very.' Fate smiled.

'One more time for old times' sake?' he suggested.

Fate laughed as she shook her head.

'Is there someone else?' Nick asked.

'No,' she told him. There had been someone the previous year, but he had started to crowd her and so she had quietly eased him out of her life. Part of her regretted the loss of the sexual pleasure she knew instinctively he would have given her, but the rest of her acknowledged that she could not have reciprocated the emotional demands.

'Too busy working on your studies, eh,' Nick teased her.

'My studies are important to me,' Fate acknowledged honestly. 'But so are my relationships.'

'You mustn't have met the right man yet, is that it?' There had been a faint shadow in Nick's eyes that had touched her heart. The prospect was tempting, she admitted ruefully. Her body was very well aware of what a physically attractive man he was; her memory knew he was a good lover.

Had he been a stranger seen across a street she would quite probably have lusted after him. Why was it that men thought *they* were the only ones capable of experiencing lust? Or was it that they believed they were the only ones with the right to express those feelings?

'It's all right for men to tell you they want a really good shag,' one of her friends had complained some weeks ago when they were out one evening, 'but just try saying the same thing to them. It terrifies them.'

'It's all down to primeval memory,' Fate had explained to her teasingly.

'Is it . . . how?'

'They can't forget how frightening it felt when the dinosaur turned round and hunted *them*,' Fate had told her.

Their shared laughter had attracted the interest of a group of men nearby. Fate had returned their visual inspection with her own coolly appraising scrutiny.

'What is it exactly you want in a man?' her friend had demanded ruefully later when Fate had refused their offer of a drink. 'The tall one with the fair hair looked gorgeous and he'd got a nice bum.'

Fate had rolled her eyes in mock horror. 'Is that all you want in a man—a nice bum?'

'It's a good starting point,' her friend had defended herself.

'Mmm . . . I suppose,' Fate agreed, narrowing her eyes judiciously as she added, 'but personally . . .'

'Personally what?'

Fate smiled, shaking her head.

'You want the impossible,' her friend grumbled. 'You're a perfectionist. But men aren't like that. They aren't like us, they don't feel the same need that we do to be wanted and approved of.'

'Then perhaps it's time they did—or we didn't,' Fate suggested, withholding the information that the last thing she ever felt in need of was a man's approval.

She had her parents to thank for that, of course.

'It's important to understand,' Caroline had told her, 'that not everyone, not every man you will meet, will feel as you do about things. Sometimes even the most intelligent of girls can fall into the trap of believing just because a man says he needs and loves her, she has a duty to respond to those feelings, that she is in some way responsible for them and for him.' As she'd listened to her mother Fate had seen the slight shadow that darkened her eyes and the way her father had started to frown, and she had puzzled over the sudden emotional tension she could feel in the room. Not surely a past relationship with another man on the part of her mother; as far as she knew, they had never loved or been involved with anyone other than each other.

Given the exceptionally open relationship they all shared, Fate's parents were surprisingly reticent about their own youth, especially her mother. Neither of them had any other family, a fact which Fate assumed brought them even closer together. Both had been orphaned in their early twenties and although Fate sometimes wondered what it would have been like to have had other family, aunts, uncles, cousins, grandparents, she didn't dwell on it. She was, after all, more fortunate than many of her peers in that her parents not only were together but also shared such a mutually loving relationship.

Fate read quickly through her letter again. She'd need to ring and make an appointment for her interview, but she'd do that later in the morning; she didn't want to look too overeager.

'What are you plotting now?' her father asked.

'Nothing,' Fate fibbed, laughing at him.

Wryly, Oliver watched her as she half walked and half danced out of the room.

She possessed a devastating combination of allure and self-confidence, which could only grow stronger with every year. The man she eventually partnered would have to possess some extraordinary qualities to match her, and it wasn't just the doting father in him that made him think so.

There were times when, like any father, he feared for her, feared seeing the precious shining aura of happiness and self-confidence torn from her by pain and loss, but he also realised Fate would have to experience some of these things before she was able to experience the true depth of her emotions.

One day she was going to fall deeply and irrevocably in love, and when she did . . .

He and Caroline had had a good marriage, a loving and very close marriage. He hoped that Fate would know the same happiness. But Fate wasn't like them. Her personality . . .

A door in the house slammed, cutting through his thoughts.

* * *

'What do you mean, the video was too poor quality for you to do anything with?' Jay exploded angrily, as he paced the floor of the studio's reception area.

Nine damn days she had kept him waiting in the end, either not returning his calls at all or making evasive responses to his demands to know whether she could work on the video. And now this!

Outside it was pleasantly warm, not yet the heat of summer in the city when those who could afford it headed to their summer homes in the Hamptons. The studio itself was air-conditioned, of course, but that did not stop the hot, angry blood rushing to Jay's face, leaving the betraying marks of his mood scorching along his cheekbones.

Bonnie remained unmoved. She was enjoying this, Jay sensed savagely. He let his dislike of her glitter briefly in his eyes.

Bonnie saw it and was amused. Good. His reaction to her statement confirmed what she had already decided. No one could be in the kind of business she was in for as long as she had been without getting a certain feel for . . . things.

She had known the moment she replayed the video Jay had handed her that there was no healthy sexual motivation behind Jay's request. In point of fact she had felt a spark of sympathy for the girl, who despite her obvious enjoyment of her self-induced orgasm, still had within her eyes a small shadow of aloneness. What, Bonnie wondered, was his real relationship with the girl? It was pointless asking him, for he was hardly likely to tell her the truth.

'You mean you've kept me waiting for more than a week just to tell me you *haven't* done as I asked—'

'*Couldn't* do as you asked,' Bonnie corrected him mildly. 'These things take time. I had thought originally—' she gave a small shrug '—but the original video was less easy to work with than I thought, and once it had been damaged—'

'Damaged?' Jay demanded, his jaw tensing ominously.

'Unfortunately, it does sometimes happen,' Bonnie said calmly, unaffected by his fury. 'We've patched it together for you as best we can, but—' She gave another dismissive shrug. 'There's always the risk that something like this will happen when you're working with amateur tapes.'

'A risk you neglected to mention when we first discussed my requirements,' Jay reminded her, through gritted teeth.

Bonnie gave him a mocking look. 'So sue me,' she told him dryly.

Jay was still seething ten minutes later when he left the building. He'd been put off and put off by this woman, only to be told that not only had she not done as he had requested, but that apparently she'd as good as ruined the original tape into the bargain.

'These things can happen,' she had told him carelessly by way of explanation. Not to him, they damn well didn't, and he was pretty sure they didn't to her either. But even if she had damaged the tape deliberately, there was nothing he could do about it—and she knew it. His mouth compressed into a bitter line.

First his father's obduracy over the Japanese deal and now this.

His father. He scowled, automatically sidestepping the beggar about to approach him, tensely shaking his head in denial, causing the girl to glare angrily at him and let loose a hail of verbal abuse.

There was nothing to keep him in New York now. He had hoped that his unexplained absence would cause his father enough anxiety to make him want to know what he was doing and when he was coming back.

Jay had learned very young that this ploy worked extremely well. A silent retreat to his bedroom coupled with a refusal to speak to his father or to explain what was bothering him would inevitably result in Bram patiently trying to coax him round.

This time, though, Bram had been curiously unconcerned by his withdrawal.

Perhaps it might be an idea to give him a ring, drop a hint that since he was enjoying himself so much in New York he might well extend his visit. With his precious Plum's eighteenth-birthday celebrations coming up, Bram would be anxious to get him home.

When it came to gamesmanship, he was a past master of the art, Jay congratulated himself, as he headed back to his hotel.

* * *

'What do you mean, Mr Soames, Sr, isn't available?' Jay demanded angrily of the girl on the other end of the line. Who the hell was she anyway? She obviously hadn't recognised his voice, and he certainly hadn't recognised hers. Where was Marcia, his father's secretary?

Jay checked his watch.

'Look, if he's in a meeting you can . . .'

'No, he isn't in a meeting,' the voice replied.

It was five-thirty and she should have left at five. She had a date with her boyfriend at seven and she didn't want to be late. She had no idea who this irate man on the other end of the line was, but she wished he would go away.

'Then where the hell is he?' Jay bellowed impatiently. 'If he's at home, then—'

'No, he isn't at home,' the girl told him. 'Actually he's with Miss Fielding, and he's given strict instructions that he doesn't want to be interrupted with any calls.'

She felt almost guilty at the pleasure she found in giving the arrogant caller this information, her face flushing slightly, because it wasn't like her to enjoy being rude.

For a moment Jay was too taken aback to respond. His father *never* gave instructions that he didn't want to be interrupted. He simply wasn't that kind of man; he didn't run his business that way. And who the hell was Miss Fielding?

Jay could feel himself starting to sweat, the telephone slippery in his too damp hand. But inside he felt chillingly cold and nauseated. A sudden image, a memory of himself as a child standing outside the door and listening to Helena fiercely lecturing his father, swam into his mind.

'You've got to tell him, Bram. He's got to learn that there *are* other people in your life who are important to you, you owe it to yourself. . . .'

Jay blinked and the image was gone, but not the fierce destructive anger which gripped his intestines—that was still there.

'Now you just listen to me and listen good,' he said icily, spacing out his words for maximum effect. 'I want to speak with my father and I want to speak with him *now*. And I don't give a damn what he's said about not being interrupted, nor about who he's with. He can be fucking Miss whatever her name is from here to kingdom come for all I care. I still want to speak to him. Now put me through....'

At the other end of the line, the girl quaked in shocked dismay at this outburst. She had heard quite a lot about Jay during the short time she had worked for the company, but none of it had prepared her for the fury she could feel emanating from the telephone wire.

She was a nice girl, a little too inclined to day-dream perhaps, and an avid reader of romances, addicted to the safe security of their happy endings. Relationships, as she already knew, were not always quite so perfect. But, if she was honest with herself, the brief glimpses she had had of Jay as he strode gloweringly around the offices, all fiercely male and sexual machismo, had inclined her to weave the kind of fantasies around him she would have blushed to disclose to even her closest friend. Now abruptly confronted by reality, she felt her face burn scarlet, not just because of Jay's unwarranted aggression, but because of her own foolishness as well.

And because of that, instead of reacting as she would normally have done, apologising for not realising who he was and immediately putting him through to his father, she said woodenly, superstitiously crossing her fingers at the same time, 'I'm sorry, Mr Soames, but your father did say that he didn't want to be disturbed under *any* circumstances...'

And before Jay could harangue her further she smartly replaced the receiver. She stared at it for several nerve-racking seconds, dreading hearing it ring again.

Well, that's that, she decided fatalistically. She had really burned her boats now and no doubt the first thing Jay would do was report her to his father and get her dismissed.

Still, it would almost be worth it. He had had no right to speak to her like that, and as for what he had implied about his father's relationship with Miss Fielding... Try as she might she couldn't persuade her imagination to stretch far enough to accommodate the picture Jay's coarse words had suggested.

In New York, Jay stared at the telephone receiver he had just replaced. His knuckles were white against the tautness of his closed fist; he could feel the muscle beginning to jerk irritatingly in his clenched jaw.

Stupid bitch, whoever she was. When he got back he'd... Miss Fielding. It wasn't a name he'd ever heard before—in any connection, and he'd certainly have remembered it if he'd heard it linked to his father's. Oh, yes. He'd have remembered—he remembered them all, all the women who'd tried to come between him and his father, who'd tried to push him out of his father's life. None of them had succeeded and this one wouldn't either.

He could picture her now. Some idiotic bimbo who'd attached herself to his father having heard about his wealth. Well, he would pretty soon detach her. And he knew just the way to do it. It shouldn't be too difficult to convince her that he would offer her far more than his father would, out of bed and in it— especially in it.

He was surprised at his father, though. It was years since he had last shown any interest in a woman and at his age...

He heard Nadia's words to him, 'How old is he exactly?' And 'Plenty young enough to father a family...a second son.'

The faint twitching in Jay's jaw became an angry pulse.

He had been away long enough. Too long...

If he flew back on Concorde he could be in London within a matter of hours. He picked up the telephone receiver.

10

'Taylor. Good. You're here. Come and look at this,' Bram demanded, ushering her into his office, not even giving her time to remove her jacket as he caught hold of her arm and rushed her over to his desk.

He looked, Taylor decided as she registered the excitement in his voice and face, like a small boy, all innocent, youthful, shining pleasure in some new discovery. She, in contrast, felt immeasurably old and tired, drained by life of any ability to share in his enthusiasm. If she hadn't already been aware of it, this difference in their most basic attitudes towards life would have starkly underlined the huge, unbridgeable gulf that lay between them.

She might have only known Bram two weeks, but the intense closeness in which they had been obliged to work together had acted like a hothouse, forcing and then forging an intimacy between them which, in other circumstances, would have taken a whole lifetime to develop—if at all.

In these two weeks Taylor had come to recognise—among other things—that Bram possessed an essential sweetness of soul that set him apart from anyone else she had ever known; a generosity of spirit that made her feel inwardly ashamed of her own parsimony—even if it was born of a need for self-preservation and survival. As she listened to him now it wasn't so much the worth of Bram's character that occupied her thoughts as those unpalatable 'other things' the past fortnight had brought to her attention.

'It's a translation of an article that appeared in a German medical magazine,' Bram enthused as he thrust the sheaf of papers under her nose. 'It arrived on Saturday morning from the cutting agency. It supports everything we're working towards, Tay.'

Tay. He had taken to using the abbreviated form of her name towards the end of their first week together. No one had ever called her Tay before. It sounded short and sweet, feminine and lovable . . . intimate and close . . . as though . . .

She forced herself to concentrate on what he was telling her. But it had been a hot day, the heat simmering on the pavement as she travelled from her office to his, and at some stage during the afternoon Bram had loosened his tie and undone the top button of his shirt. She could see the smooth hard column of his throat and the soft sprinkling of fine dark hair edging up towards it.

Her stomach muscles quivered as she automatically tensed them against what she was feeling.

'In fact, after I'd read it I almost drove straight round to show you, but knowing how jealously you guard your privacy. . . Read it,' Bram instructed. 'It validates everything we're working towards.

He was standing so close to her that she could actually feel the heat coming from his body. Again she tried to focus on what he was showing her, but her treacherous attention was far more interested in the man than the journal article he was holding.

'Bram, at least let me get my coat off,' she protested. Her voice, she knew, sounded clipped and repressive, her tone almost that of an old-fashioned prim schoolmarm addressing a grubby, overexuberant schoolboy. Her refusal to share his excitement, that careful distancing of herself from him was just a way of trying to hide what she was really thinking and feeling, a way of trying to control the ache she could feel inside herself.

She had known what was happening to her even before the end of her first week working with Bram. She should have stopped it then, told him that he would have to find someone else to help him, but she had been too weak to do so, and now . . .

Taylor had told herself that it was impossible that after twenty years of rigidly sticking to the rules she had made for herself, she should suddenly, overnight almost, ache so much and so inappropriately for this one particular man that she woke up at night having dreamed of him, her face wet with tears and her body wet with need.

Shock, horror, self-disgust, self-loathing, terror and guilt, she had felt them all in this past week. She had gone to bed every night promising herself that tomorrow she would tell Sir Anthony that she couldn't work with Bram any longer, only to wake in the morning, trembling inwardly with excitement at the knowledge that she was going to see him.

It was like being a teenager all over again. Like being back on that helter-skelter roller coaster of highs and lows, of aching delicious pleasure in the power of her own sexuality and equally intense fear and doubt about what she was feeling.

She tensed aggressively as she saw Bram move towards her, felt his touch on her arm.

Had he guessed what she was feeling? Was he going to—

'Here, let me take your jacket.'

He was smiling at her, his eyes free of any of the darkness that shadowed her own, his touch on her arm completely non-sexual, the pads of his fingertips slightly rough, very masculine . . .

She could feel herself starting to tremble. Only last night she had dreamed of him touching her, of his fingertips caressing her skin, her mouth.

Hurriedly she shrugged off her jacket and then picked up the article which was causing him so much excitement. The words blurred in front of her eyes, her hand shaking slightly.

She read it quickly, barely able to make sense of the words. She couldn't go on like this. Sooner or later she was bound to betray herself. She knew enough about Bram now to know that he would be sympathetic, compassionate, understanding. But his pity was the last thing she wanted. The last thing she deserved.

For years she had convinced herself she had the strength, the will-power, to live her life alone, to shoulder her own burdens, her own guilt, her own fears and that she would never, never be weak enough to inflict them on someone else. And if she had sometimes envied other women their different lives, their lovers, their children, she had always reminded herself of just why she could never be like them.

Although there had been circumstances which had reinforced her loneliness and made her feel envious, there had never once before been a *man* who had made her feel like that, made her ache with longing. Never once until now. Until Bram.

Shockingly, she could feel her throat starting to close up with emotion, with the aching, empty hopelessness of it all.

'Well, what do you think—doesn't it confirm everything we're trying to do?'

'Yes. It does seem to do so.'

Taylor registered Bram's disappointment in her reaction as he heard the flat metallic sound of her voice and misinterpreted the reason for it.

'So, you still feel that what we're doing is a waste of time, that you're only helping me under duress? I'm sorry. I thought . . .'

Taylor couldn't bear any more. She started to turn away from him, stiffening in agonized shock as Bram unexpectedly reached out and clamped his hands on her upper arms, gently forcing her to stand still while he looked at her.

'Taylor, what is it? I know at first you were antagonistic to what I'm trying to do . . . and . . .' And to me, he wanted to add, but intuition stopped him. The trust and rapport he had thought he was beginning to build between them was still far too fragile to carry the weight of his growing personal feelings for her. Oh, she might smile at his jokes, listen quietly while he talked enthusiastically about his hopes for the work he was doing, she might even relax enough sometimes to actually laugh, but she was still inwardly holding him at a distance. And yet every instinct he possessed told him that the very real physical and emotional desire he felt for her was not something he felt alone. All right, so outwardly she might continue to maintain the barriers she had erected against him, but inwardly . . .

Sighing to himself as he felt and saw the way she pulled away from him, refusing to look at him, he said quietly, 'I thought we'd got beyond the stage of playing games with each other, of not being able to be honest with each other . . . to speak our minds . . .'

To be honest with each other. Despairingly, Taylor closed her eyes, clamping down hard on the near-hysterical wave of emotion that washed over her.

Oh, God, if only he knew. She could never be truly honest with any man ever again, not without virtually causing her own destruction, the obliteration of her self-respect, of the person she had so painstakingly spent the past twenty years building.

And yet, not to be honest carried even heavier penalties, which would cast a terrifying dark shadow over any relationship, damaging and eventually totally destroying it. That was one of the reasons she had chosen to live the way she did.

'What's wrong?' he asked her gently.

'Nothing . . . nothing's wrong.' Taylor could hear the panic edging up under her voice and knew that Bram must be able to hear it too, and along with it her deceit.

He had gone too far, pushed her too hard, Bram recognised.

What *was* it that had made her so afraid of any kind of human emotional contact. He had never known anyone whose life was so devoid of any real human relationships.

Could it have something to do with the loss of her parents? He knew, all too well, the traumatic effect something like that could have. Look at Jay, for instance.

Feverishly, Taylor made an effort to compose herself. She mustn't break down in front of Bram, mustn't allow anything personal to creep into their relationship . . . their conversation.

'The German research does seem to bear out your theories,' she began huskily. 'But testing them in laboratory conditions—'

'Does not mean they would work in the real world. I know that,' Bram agreed, recognising that it was pointless now to turn the conversation back into more personal channels.

Taylor hadn't just distanced herself from him mentally, she had distanced herself physically as well. She had moved away from him, putting the length of his desk between them.

His urge to close that gap and to move closer to her was one he was familiar with now. The first time he had experienced it it had shocked him, as had his desire to actually physically touch her. He was constantly having to suppress the desire to tuck back the errant strand of hair from her face, smooth back the cuffs of her shirt so that he could touch the delicate, blue-veined skin of her inner wrist or simply just be close enough to feel her breathing, smell her skin.

What would Taylor do if he told her how he felt, how much he wanted her?

Did he really need to ask himself? He knew exactly what she would do. She would turn and walk away from him just as fast as those deliciously long legs of hers could take her.

'Anyway, it doesn't really matter what the German research proves,' Taylor continued. 'You've said yourself that your own program is nowhere near adequate.'

'It wasn't,' Bram agreed, 'but after I'd read this article . . . I've spent almost the whole weekend working on it, and I think I'm beginning to get somewhere.'

He saw her dubious expression and challenged her. 'You don't believe me? Come home with me and I'll prove it to you.'

Go home with him . . . to his house? A tremor of fearful delight shivered through her. She had backed herself into this trap. If she refused now, Bram would accuse her of dismissing his work unfairly or not having the courage of her own convictions.

'I . . . ' she started to protest, but Bram refused to listen to her.

'It will only take an hour or so, and I'll run you home afterwards.'

Purposefully he started to clear his desk. Taylor's heart missed a beat as she acknowledged she had no choice but to go along with him. It wouldn't be the first time she had been to his home. There had been other evenings when they had worked there together, but tonight she felt very vulnerable, prey to her emotions . . . her physical response to him. Being alone with him would only heighten those feelings.

'I really would like you to see what I've done, Taylor. It's far from perfect or finished, and perhaps I'm fooling myself that I'm working on the right lines. I need an injection of that sturdy scepticism of yours to stop me from getting too carried away.

'I really do appreciate all the help you're giving me, you know. Nothing will ever change my mind about the worth of what I'm doing. But I must confess there are times, many, many times, when I begin to wonder if I'm the right person for such work . . . if I'm just acting out of self-aggrandisement . . . conceit. . . . Jay accused me of wasting my time when I told him what I was doing. Wasting my own time is one thing. Wasting the time and the lives of the people who need the benefits this kind of work can give them is something different again.'

His humility said everything about him there was to be said, Taylor thought. Was it any wonder that she felt the way she did about him? How could any woman not love such a man?

He was walking towards the door, removing her jacket from the hanger, coming towards her with it. Quickly she shook her head.

'No...I... I don't want to wear it,' she told him. If she let him touch her now . . .

'Well, what do you think?'

Bram looked and sounded as anxious and uncertain as a young boy rather than the successful and normally laid-back man she knew him to be.

'I . . . it's good,' she conceded. 'Very good.'

'You think so?' Bram looked surprised and then started to laugh. 'If I didn't know you better I might suspect you were trying to flatter me, Tay. It's certainly a start, but there's one hell of a long way to go yet.

'You're not going to get rid of me that easily, you know,' he warned her, his voice suddenly dropping into husky warmth. 'I'm still going to need your input . . . your help.'

Taylor couldn't help it; she could feel her breathing quicken and her colour start to rise in response to his comment.

'Now I think you're the one trying to flatter me,' she reproved him shakily, trying to sound stern and aloof but suspecting from his expression that she had totally failed.

'Never,' Bram told her. 'I don't play that sort of game, Tay, but even if I did, I doubt you'd ever be taken in by it. You're far too intelligent. So you think we're making some progress then?' he asked her softly. 'You approve of what I'm doing?'

Was she imagining it or was he really very subtly flirting with her? Taylor wondered uncertainly. Was it the shadowed intimacy of his study that reflected tenderness in his eyes as he looked at her, or was she simply deceiving herself?

The original hour he had claimed it would take him to show her the results of his weekend's work had somehow spread into three, though one of them was spent eating the impromptu supper he had insisted on making for them.

'I'm hungry even if you aren't,' he had told her when she initially refused his offer of food. After that, it had seemed churlish to refuse to eat the omelette and salad he had prepared, or to drink the crisp, fruity wine he had poured for them both. She was quite familiar with his house now, or at least the down-stairs. It was much more of a proper home than her own flat, right down to the cat, which Bram told her he had found in the garden shortly after he had moved in and which had adopted him. At first she had felt acutely uncomfortable in such sur-roundings, angered, almost, by the clutter of photographs and mementoes that covered almost every polished surface in the small sitting room, and the pile of books and magazines on the table next to the chair, which instinct told her was the one Bram favoured. It was a deep-cushioned, comfortably shabby-looking chair, which the cat, August, so named after the month in which he had appeared, had also made his own.

In addition to half a dozen or more framed photographs of Jay, from babyhood through gangly, awkward adolescence to brooding adult male magnificence, there were photographs of Bram's parents, of his university friends, of his goddaughter and her parents, and even one of Jay's mother.

From the sitting room, French windows opened into the gar-den. Bram had insisted on showing her round it after they had finished their meal.

'Smell this rose,' he had instructed her. 'I can never under-stand why anyone would ever grow a rose that isn't perfumed. Old-fashioned of me, I suppose.' Privately Taylor had agreed with him. There had been old-fashioned scented Bourbon roses in her parents' garden, but her father had had them taken out and replaced with sharp, spicy specimen plants that had been the fashion that year.

'It's after ten o'clock,' she told Bram now, glancing at her watch. 'I really should go.'

'Yes. I'm sorry. That's my fault. Why is it, I wonder, that time spent with some people seems to drag so heavily and ponder-ously while with others, it rushes past so fast that you want to grab it and stop it, to take hold of the moment and savour it?'

He was looking at her mouth as he spoke, and Taylor found herself fighting the urge to touch her suddenly dry lips with her tongue; a gesture so explicitly revealing and betraying that she might just as well walk right up to him and hold out her arms, lift up her face, implicitly begging for his kiss.

His kiss... She could feel her resolve starting to buckle and fracture beneath the intense pressure of the desire that twisted and coiled so urgently inside her.

Where was her maturity, her self-restraint, her control? Women of her age did not feel like this. Such emotions, such needs, such intensity belonged to one's teenage years.

'I'd better go and get the car. Otherwise...'

As he turned away from her, Bram wondered ruefully if she had any idea just how much he wanted her. Had she any idea just how close he had come to taking hold of her and kissing her senseless? Not a feeling he was in the habit of experiencing. But then, as he was increasingly being forced to admit, Taylor was arousing an awful lot of desires, both emotional and physical, which were unfamiliar to him.

In another man he might have put this down to some kind of middle-aged panic, an anxiety-induced snatching at fading sexuality. But his desire for her, his reaction to her, wasn't just sexual, and when he allowed himself the luxury of day-dreaming about making love with her, it wasn't just her body he wanted to arouse and pleasure, to reach out and touch, it was her. The essence of her, all of her.

Bram was thoughtful as he listened to Taylor's overanimated chatter from the passenger seat. Her voice sounded strained, her whole demeanour nervous and on edge. Because of him? Because she had sensed how he felt and was now afraid because of it?

Normally, her conversation was guarded, her words carefully chosen, something she handled cautiously and warily, as she did everything.

You're getting in too deep, he warned himself as he waited for the lights to change, letting your emotions overrule your common sense. Just because you've fallen head over heels in love with her, that doesn't mean she has to feel the same way.

Maybe not, but there *was* something there. He could sense it, feel it in the charged atmosphere between them. Whatever it was, it wasn't something she wanted to admit to or acknowledge. What she wanted to do was reject it, just as she wanted to reject him.

The dusk in which they had set off had become full darkness by the time he turned the car into the entrance to her apartment. The gates were already open, the parking area floodlit by the headlights of the two police cars parked there. A uniformed police officer stood beside one of them talking with a small, white haired woman.

'That's Mrs Brearton, one of my neighbours,' Taylor told him tensely.

She had stopped chattering now, her whole body straining forward as she stared at the small tableau, her hands curled into anxious fists.

The police officer and Taylor's neighbour had both turned to look at the car as it turned into the car-park. The old lady was nodding her head vigorously and pointing towards the car . . . towards Taylor.

By the time Bram had stopped and switched off the ignition, the police officer was standing by the passenger door.

As he opened it for her, Bram heard him saying formally to Taylor, 'Miss Fielding, I'm afraid there's been a break-in. If you'd just come with me . . .'

'No . . .'

Taylor shrank back into her seat, her face not so much white as parchment-coloured, the colour of fear, Bram recognised as she turned to him, her eyes unfocused, her whole body trembling violently.

'I can't go up there. . . I can't. . . Don't let them make me. . . I can't. . . .'

Her voice had started to rise hysterically, so unexpectedly out of control that Bram was caught completely off guard by it.

She was cowering in her seat, so trapped and locked into her own private terror that Bram doubted she even knew who he was. He could see that she was in the grip of some kind of panic attack.

'It's all right, Taylor,' he told her gently. 'The burglar, whoever he or she was, has long gone now, I'm sure. Isn't that right, officer?' he looked expectantly at the silent policeman.

'Long gone,' the man confirmed. 'We arrived half an hour ago when one of the neighbours rang us. Our detective sergeant is up there now and the other residents are being interviewed. It's quite safe, madam,' he said reassuringly. 'If I could have a word, sir,' he added to Bram, indicating that he wished to speak to him alone.

'What is it, officer?' Bram asked him quickly, walking back to the police car with him, but turning round so that he could watch Taylor.

'The lady's obviously rather highly-strung, sir, and in the circumstances it might not be a good idea for her to be left alone here. At least, not for tonight. Whoever broke into the place has made a bit of a mess of it. Some of them do, especially when it's a woman's flat they break into, if you know what I mean....'

He paused portentously, while Bram frowned at him, his concentration still fixed on Taylor, whose body was now ominously still. Catatonic almost, Bram recognised as the dark staring eyes looked at him and through him.

'No, officer, I'm sorry but I don't know what you mean,' he responded brusquely, and then regretted his impatience as the younger man flushed slightly.

'It's her clothes . . . well, to be exact, her underclothes. Some of them . . . Well, I wouldn't like my missus to come home and find that kind of thing, and she's about as down-to-earth as you can get. We reckon it must have been someone after money for drugs. The whole place is trashed. You don't get that with the professionals. Has she got any friends . . . any family, she could stay with for a few days?'

Bram reacted instinctively and immediately. 'No, she hasn't, but that's not a problem. She can stay with me.'

'Fine, but I'll have to ask you to leave us your name and address, sir, and the detective in charge of the case will probably want to have a word with you. She's upstairs in the apartment.'

Bram paused. Taylor was still seated in his car, still frighteningly immobile. She looked like someone who had gone into a trance. No sign of life or emotion flickered in the empty depths of her eyes.

'I'll stay with Miss Fielding, sir,' the policeman offered, reading and interpreting his reluctance to leave her.

'It affects some people like that . . . the shock, like. It's the shock, especially those like Miss Fielding who've been so careful about their security.'

'How did he get in?' Bram asked him.

'He smashed down her front door with an axe,' the policeman told him. When he saw Bram's expression, he added, 'It does happen, fortunately, not that often. Do you happen to know if she kept a lot of valuables at the flat, sir...cash...jewellery...?'

'I have no idea,' Bram told him shortly. An axe? What if Taylor had been in the flat at the time? What if ...

'Like I said, it was probably someone who was on drugs, most of the violent ones are ... Either that or they've got a grudge against the occupant....'

Five minutes later the unexpectedly petite and slender detective sergeant was saying much the same thing, the quiet matter-of-factness of her voice somehow nerve-judderingly out of place in the carnage inside Taylor's flat.

Cushions, their covers ripped off, their insides obscenely spewing out across the carpet, were lying in a tangled heap in one corner of the room. Beneath his feet Bram could feel shards of broken pottery. The curtains had been ripped from the windows. There were huge marks, gashes in the wall, presumably made with the axe. The bedroom door hung half off its hinges, and beyond it Bram could see a tangle of Taylor's delicate underwear caught up in her sheets.

His stomach heaved and he turned away. Thank God Taylor had not come up.

The police sergeant saw his expression and guessed what he was about to say.

'It happens,' she told him. 'More often than you'd think. Reported in the papers, it causes repugnance and a sense of relief that it's happened to someone else. When you are that someone else, it's a whole different ball game. It isn't always easy for a man to understand just what it does to a woman to know that someone...a man...possibly a pervert, but not always...not necessarily, has defiled her most intimate possessions. It isn't just an act of vandalism and destruction, it's an act of hatred and aggression...almost of rape. There is no male equivalent for this kind of thing.'

She paused as her radio crackled into life, and Bram heard the now familiar voice of the police officer outside, warning her that Taylor was insisting on coming upstairs.

'You can't let her,' Bram protested. 'She mustn't see any of this—'

The detective overruled him. 'She has a right to see it. This is her home.'

'You didn't see her just now in the car,' Bram wanted to tell her. But it was too late. Taylor was already walking into the flat. For a moment she simply stood there staring around as though her surroundings were completely unfamiliar to her. Her face was still pale, her lips almost bloodless, but her eyes were alive now... Too alive, Bram decided as he watched them register shock, disbelief and then fear.

'No,' she moaned softly, her voice rising in volume and pitch as she continued to repeat the word. 'No. No . . . no . . . '

Instinctively, Bram went to her, wrapping her tightly in his arms, using his body as a shield to prevent her from seeing any more, binding her to him, rocking her fiercely in his arms as he tried to soothe her.

'She shouldn't have been allowed to see this,' he protested to the detective. 'No one should have to see anything like this.'

'I understand that she'll be staying with you and that we'll be able to contact her there, sir,' the woman said, ignoring his comment. 'Once we've finished, you'll need to make sure the flat is secured.'

'Yes. Yes, I'll see to all that. She'll need clothes, though.' Bram looked uncertainly towards the bedroom. 'I don't . . . '

'Not those,' the detective advised him, her voice softening slightly. 'We'll need them as evidence, but in any event, I doubt she would ever want to wear them again.'

As she watched Bram gently manoeuvring the shocked woman back outside, the detective felt a momentary pang of envy. It was a long time since anyone in her life had treated her with that kind of tenderness and concern.

She pushed the sofa out of the way and bent down to retrieve the photograph frame that had been underneath it. The glass was cracked. Splintered glass lay all around it, broken by the thief as he tried to prise away the frame, she suspected. The girl in the photograph was smiling through the shattered glass.

Sighing, she placed the photo on the table. They'd had a spate of these burglaries recently. She was thirty-four years old. She felt immeasurably older.

11

‘Tay, are you sure you won't let me call my doctor?'

'No. You mustn't. I—I'm all right . . .' Taylor said emphatically. She looked very far from all right, sitting tensely on the edge of the deep armchair Bram had put her into gently once he had got her inside the house. But at least she was now speaking . . . responding.

Her lack of any kind of reaction, apart from that one brief, almost hysterical outburst when she saw the state of her flat, had disturbed him. He had expected very different behaviour from her. Shock, of course, who wouldn't be shocked? He had felt shocked himself, shocked and sickened by the depraved abuse and violation of another human being's personal possessions by a complete stranger. It spoke of a mind totally out of step with humanity and reality.

But the way she had withdrawn into herself, retreated from what had happened into her private world of terror, seemed totally out of character, even for her.

Not once on the drive back to his house had she spoken. Nor had she objected to the way he had taken control of the situation or to the fact that she would be staying the night with him.

It was as though she had completely abandoned any interest in her own welfare, as though she no longer cared what happened to her. As though life had stopped for her from the moment she learned that her flat had been broken into.

And that, from Taylor, who was normally so guarded, so protective of herself, so determined not to allow anyone else to have any kind of control over her life, worried him even more than her pallor and the rigid tension of her body, its stiffness broken only by the spasmodic fits of shaking that convulsed it.

If she was no better in the morning, he would call his doctor, no matter how much she protested.

If he called him out now, though, the most he would be able to do would be to give her some kind of sleeping tablet, and Bram suspected that she was too deeply traumatised, too heavily in shock to be sedated by that kind of drug.

Helplessly, he watched her. She was aware of him, he knew that, and yet, somehow, it was almost as though she had retreated into another world.

He turned away from her, heading for the door, intending to go upstairs and check on the spare room. It was always kept ready for visitors, but there would be certain things she would need in the morning, including clean clothes. He paused. Marcia was returning to the office the next day. He would have to ring her first thing and ask her to go out and do some shopping for him. Intuitively, he knew that Taylor... the Taylor he knew, would not like the idea of his selecting her underwear—even to the point of refusing it.

The Taylor he knew... but what about this Taylor, the Taylor whose rigid body and blank eyes reminded him disturbingly of television news footage of trauma victims.

'No. Don't leave me.'

Bram turned round. Taylor was watching him, her hands curled into tight fists.

'I'm just going upstairs to check on the spare room,' Bram explained gently. 'You can come with me if you like,' he added, sensing her agitation.

Her behaviour reminded him of a phase Jay had gone through when he had first come to live with him and hadn't wanted to let him out of his sight.

'I...'

He saw the way Taylor was looking around the room, searching for something or someone, her body rigid with defensive dread and guessed what she was thinking.

'It's all right, Taylor. There's no one here but us. You're safe.'

'Safe.'

As she repeated the word, he could see the bitterness in her eyes, and with it a brief resurfacing of the Taylor he knew.

She accompanied him docilely upstairs to the spare bedroom with its own en suite bathroom, shadowing his every movement, standing as close to him as she possibly could but not, he noticed, actually allowing her body to touch his own. That, at least, had not changed.

The bedroom windows overlooked the back of the house, and Bram went to open one of them to let in some fresh air. Taylor immediately protested, shaking her head vehemently, staring at the window as though it had suddenly become a multi-headed hydra.

'It's all right, Taylor,' Bram gently reassured her again. 'No one can get in. The house is fully alarmed, and the garden gates are locked.'

It was true. Bram's insurance company was very insistent on the property being well-secured. 'And even without these safety measures, there's no way that window is large enough for anyone to climb through,' he pointed out.

She said nothing, but Bram could tell from the way her gaze kept returning to the window that he had not fully reassured her.

Ten minutes later, when he had left her with a fresh supply of towels and the assurance that she would be completely safe, he acknowledged that neither of them was likely to get much sleep.

When he had allowed himself the luxury of imagining having Taylor sleeping under his roof—and he had—it had been under far different circumstances from these.

Just now, watching her, knowing her fear, he had ached to reach out and take hold of her, to comfort and reassure her, to tell her that he would always keep her safe.

Her distress had reawakened many emotions he had experienced when he had first taken charge of Jay. Only now they were subtly different. Compassion and the need to succour, to protect were strongly linked with desire. The desire of a man not just for a woman, but for *the* woman—the woman who he knew had the power to irrevocably change his whole life.

He went back upstairs, knocking on the bedroom door before opening it and walking in.

Taylor stood motionless in front of the window, her arms wrapped around her body as though she wasn't merely looking but actually waiting for someone to appear.

'It's late. Why don't you try to get some sleep?' he suggested quietly.

She turned round and looked blankly at him, as though he were someone she didn't know. A stranger, he thought sadly.

There was hostility in her expression, as though she resented his intrusion.

Outside in the street a car backfired and she whirled back to the window, her body tense, defensive.

Ignoring her cry of protest, Bram walked past her and closed the curtains.

'No!' Frantically she sprang past him, desperately wrenching the curtains open again. 'I have to be able to see.'

'To see what, Taylor?' Bram asked gently. 'There is nothing to see, only the garden . . . nothing and no one. Is that what you're afraid of?' he asked quietly. 'That they might come here, who-ever broke into your flat might come here?' He shook his head. 'They won't.'

He didn't bother trying to point out that it was illogical to imagine that whoever had broken into her flat would even know that she was here with him, never mind try to break in. The fear that possessed her was far too primitive to respond to logic.

'You're safe here. No one can get in. You're safe.'

'You can't say that . . . you don't know . . . how . . .' She stopped, her eyes suddenly filling with tears.

Bram couldn't help himself. He went over to her, taking her in his arms, ignoring her protests and her brief struggle to break free of his hold.

'Oh, my poor girl,' Bram comforted her. 'I know how hard all this must be for you, but I promise you everything's going to be all right. You'll see.'

First thing in the morning he intended to go back to her flat to see just how much damage had been done. There was no way he would allow her to move back into it until every trace of what had happened had been removed.

'Come on . . . what you need now is to try and get some sleep.'

He was guiding her towards the bed as he spoke, but she sud-denly refused to move. Staring towards the window, her whole body trembling, she told him thickly, 'I can't. Not . . . not on my own. I can't stay here on my own. . . .'

Bram could hear the panic sharpening her voice.

'You don't have to be alone. I'll stay with you if that's what you want,' he soothed.

'You'll stay with me. Here . . . ? All night?' Her fingers gripped his arm as she spoke, her eyes searching his face as though she suspected that he might be lying to her.

'Yes,' he reassured her. 'All night, every night, for just as long as you want,' he added, knowing as he spoke the words that what he was promising was going to tax his self-control as it had never been taxed before. The very last thing that was motivating her demand for him to stay with her was any kind of desire for him. Bram knew that. Had Taylor been her normal self, he knew the very last thing she would have done would have been to let her guard down enough to make that kind of request, to betray that kind of vulnerability.

'Where are you going?' Taylor demanded anxiously two minutes later, as he gently started to disengage himself from her.

'To lock up and have a shower,' he replied calmly. 'I shan't be long. Why don't you get ready for bed while I'm gone? I can't provide you with any proper nightclothes, but there's a robe in the bathroom.'

He didn't add that it was going to be almost as impossible to find something to wear himself. He disliked wearing anything in bed, and suspected that, like Taylor, he would have to make do with wearing a bathrobe.

And as for where he would sleep . . . He glanced at the room's double bed. In that . . . with Taylor? He might be able to trust himself if he were fully conscious, but asleep, if he should accidentally reach out and touch her . . .

He looked ruefully at the easy chair by the fireplace.

Taylor had withdrawn to the bed, where she stood tensely watching him.

'Ten minutes,' he promised her as he reached for the door handle.

'And you promise you'll stay all night? You won't leave me?'

'I shan't leave you,' he confirmed.

Unexpectedly, when he returned, he discovered that she had done as he had suggested and was now lying beneath the duvet, her gaze fixed on the door. Both bedside lamps were on and the main light as well. Bram saw the agitated movement she made as he switched off the overhead light, but she didn't make any verbal protest.

He saw her eyes widen slightly as she realised that he was carrying a pillow and a duvet.

'I'm rather a restless sleeper,' he told her untruthfully. 'So I thought you'd prefer it if I slept in the chair....'

Normally the last thing he would have needed to do was to make that kind of explanation. But the present situation was far from normal, and Taylor's reactions were more those of a terrified child than an adult. She was innocent of any awareness of what her terror, and the need it induced in her to have him with her, could lead to.

And he owed it to her to respect that innocence. That was his responsibility as a man.

Bram lost count of the number of times during the next hour when, just as he was on the point of sleep, Taylor would call his name in a low, urgent voice, demand to know that he was still awake, to know that he hadn't left her alone with her fear while she slept.

Eventually, though, she started to relax into sleep, each breath she took slowing and deepening while Bram held his, afraid to move or make a sound in case he woke her.

It was almost half an hour before he dared to turn his head and look at her. She was lying on her side facing him, her expression clearly revealed to him by the light of the bedside lamp. The dark sweep of her lashes cast long shadows across her face. The purity of the curve of her jaw and cheekbone were softened by sleep, her lips gently parted.

Even in sleep her body possessed the same careful precision it did in the daytime—her hair neatly braided, no careless abandonment of limbs, or restless movements beneath the duvet to prove that she was human and vulnerable. But she was both; he had seen how much so tonight.... He felt his heart lift against his ribs, his whole body moved by compassion and love.

Fate had handed him an extraordinary opportunity, he mused, as he positioned himself to face her so that if she did waken she could see him. He would be a fool not to use the gift that he had been given.

Once she was over the initial shock of what had happened, she would immediately try to withdraw from him—emotionally and physically. He did not intend to allow that to happen.

Taylor felt as though she was being suffocated. She could feel the heavy weight of something over her head, and the sensation of being powerless, captive, afraid, sending a terrified surge of panic racing through her body, brought her abruptly awake.

The weight on her face was, she discovered, merely the folds of a duvet. Not her duvet, she realised as she pushed it away; her bedding was plain and utilitarian. This was different—fine, silky cotton with some kind of raised embroidery that she could feel with her fingertips. It smelled deliciously of lavender as well. Her grandmother's bed linen had always smelled of lavender.

Her grandmother. It was years since she had thought about her. Since she had allowed herself to think about her, Taylor corrected, as her eyes searched the room with its unfamiliar wallpaper and furniture, the Georgian mouldings of the picture rail and dado, the fireplace.

She froze suddenly, her body turning to ice, her heart pounding frantically with fear as she saw the chair and the man lying in it.

Her eyes measured the distance from the bed to the door. And then she remembered . . . Bram . . . She was in Bram Soames's house. In his bed . . . She closed her eyes and then opened them again, her expression stark as she mentally relived everything that had happened from the moment the police officer had stepped forward.

Angry tears stung her eyes. Furiously she wiped them away. How could she have been so stupid . . . so lacking in self-control? How many other pairs of eyes besides Bram's had witnessed her disintegration? The police. The man who had broken into her flat—and she knew instinctively that it had been a man. Had he been hiding somewhere, watching, gloating? Waiting to repeat his assault on her home . . . on her . . . ?

She could taste her own fear in her mouth. Panic filled her as she clawed wildly at the bedclothes. And then stopped. Where was there to go? To her horror she realised that she was crying audibly now, agonised sobs that tore at her throat and brought

Bram hastily to the bedside, demanding anxiously, 'Taylor, what is it? Are you . . .'

'Go away. Please,' she begged without looking at him. This was the last straw—that on top of everything else he should witness this.

She felt him retreat and heard the bedroom door open and then close again, and only then did she realise how much she had really wanted him to stay. Fresh tears flooded her eyes. What was she crying for? she wondered bitterly. For what? For her home . . . her possessions, for the fear she had experienced and the humiliation. For the shaming, searing loss of self that tore at her and flung her headlong into an abyss far more frightening and enduring than the fear she had always known.

That, at least, had been contained, controlled, locked safely away beyond the steel doors of her will-power.

She mustn't think about the man who had broken into her flat, mustn't allow her imagination to torment her with images of him hiding somewhere . . . watching her . . . waiting. . . .

'Drink this.'

She hadn't heard Bram return, hadn't even realised he was there until she felt his light touch on her arm. She recoiled from it as though it were acid, shaking her head, refusing to take the drink he was offering her.

'It's only tea,' she heard him saying mildly. 'I thought it might help you relax—sleep.'

'Sleep? How can I?'

These bitter, self-pitying words were out before she could silence them. She could feel Bram watching her. What on earth must he think of her? Her skin burned with the dry fever of humiliation as she remembered how she had pleaded with him to stay with her.

'I'm sorry about . . . about what happened . . . about my loss of control earlier,' she apologised curtly. 'I was hysterical.'

'You weren't hysterical. You were in shock,' Bram corrected her calmly. 'And with good reason. Anyone would have reacted in the same way. You were afraid. What woman would not be in such circumstances?'

'Oh, I see. Because I'm a woman I'm allowed to have fear...to be weak and vulnerable. But you, as a man, of course, are above such things. You—'

'That wasn't what I meant,' Bram interrupted her firmly. 'All human beings have the capacity to feel fear.... All human beings, including you. Even if you would prefer to be superhuman, inviolate. There's no need for you to feel ashamed,' he continued.

But Taylor refused to let him go on. 'Isn't there?' Her hands curled into angry fists. 'I'm afraid I don't agree with you.'

She looked past him to the chair where he had been sleeping. Oh God, how could she have been so stupid . . . so weak? Could he see as clearly as she could just what her reactions betrayed?

Overpowering though her terror had been, it wasn't just *that* which had driven her to beg him to stay with her.

'It's almost morning,' she told him tiredly. 'I'll be all right now. There's no need for you to stay.'

'No need on your part, maybe,' Bram told her gravely, 'but every need on mine.'

He put down the cup of tea and took her in his arms, repeating huskily, a breath away from her lips, 'Every need, every desire, every hunger, every emotion I have ever felt or will ever feel.'

He hadn't intended this to happen. He could have sworn that on oath. The last thing in his mind when he went downstairs to get her that drink had been this.

Bram could sense her resistance to him, her shock, her anger, and beneath them, too, he could sense something else. He kissed her slowly at first, lingering over the taste of her lips, sweetly warm and achingly soft, quiescent beneath his touch, apart from a single brief, betraying tremor.

She had tried to stiffen her body against him, but the frantic race of her heart was never induced by fear—or anger. He knew that because it mirrored the excited, aroused yearning of his own.

All he wanted was to show her, with this kiss, all that they could have, all that they could give each other. To show her that he, too, was vulnerable . . . that he, too, could be made to hurt and be afraid.

He had never kissed a woman like this before, nor ever wanted to, savouring every tiny sensation, caressing her mouth as though he had a whole lifetime in which to do so, as though kissing her *was* his whole life.

He could feel her starting to tremble as he held her. His own body was shaking slightly under the combined stress of his aching, loving desire for her and the control he was trying to have over it.

Reluctantly, he started to release her. She was the right woman, the only woman, but this was not the right time nor, perhaps, the right place.

Gently he began to ease his mouth away from hers, tensing as he felt the merest breath of warmth as her lips parted, emitting a sound so soft that he almost missed it. The whisper of his name? A demand to him to stop or a protest not to?

He had never been a risk-taker, least of all with other peoples' lives and emotions. But without even pausing to think of the consequences of his actions, he had already made up his mind what he wanted to believe that soft whisper meant, and acted upon it, one hand cupping her head, the other drawing her even closer to his body as he parted her lips with his mouth, the sound he made against it rough with male satisfaction and desire.

She tasted . . . she tasted of heaven, as sweetly addictive as the most mind-enhancing drug and just as potentially lethal.

The desire for her, which he had been fighting to keep under control virtually from the first moment he had set eyes on her, imploded inside him. The scent, the taste, the feel of her was like drinking a matured brandy on a starved, empty stomach, lethally intoxicating his senses, his whole body reeling under the impact of her.

Bram knew how little it would take to swamp her with his own desire, to use his strength against her weakness. In the heat of their mutual passion she might not protest or object, but how would she feel later about him . . . about herself?

Reluctantly Bram gentled his kiss, lifting his mouth from hers, and then returning to it with a soft groan as she gazed dazedly at him, her lips still parted and moist, her breathing fast and erratic, a small pulse beating betrayingly in her throat. He touched it with his thumb and then bent and pressed his mouth to it. Her body arched involuntarily, her spine taut, her fingers curling into the hard muscles of his arms as she shuddered fiercely.

'I want you so much,' Bram told her gruffly, his hands reaching out to smooth the damp hair back from her face; his touch freed from sexual desire for her now, silently expressing love in its purest form.

'But not now—this is not the right time. It will soon be morning. . . .'

'Yes.'

The docility with which she allowed him to carefully tuck her up beneath the duvet made his throat raw with suppressed emotion.

'Bram . . .'

His heart started thundering against his chest wall. If she asked him to stay with her now . . .   .

But she didn't. Instead she shook her head, her forehead puckering in a frown as though she herself had forgotten whatever it was she had been about to say.

Her eyes were already closing, her breathing slowing and deepening as exhaustion overcame her.

Taylor frowned in her sleep, moving out of the way of the dancing sunlight, trying to tease open her closed eyes.

She didn't want to wake up; she was enjoying her sleepy, dreamy state too much.

In it she was a different Taylor, a Taylor she remembered from a long, long time ago; a Taylor who laughed and teased, her voice and her body bubbling over with passionate joy as she responded to the hoarsely whispered, sensual endearments of the man who held her, touching her skin, stroking her body, telling her how much he wanted and needed her, how much he desired her. When he kissed her throat and the bare curve of her shoulder, delicious little thrills of sensation skittered over her skin.

She sighed voluptuously, allowing herself to sink down into the pleasure of his touch, at the same time teasing him a little by withholding from him her own inner knowledge of just how much he was arousing her, making him wait, making him grow hungry for her, taking pleasure in stretching out each separate sensation of arousal, wanting to savour every single touch, every kiss and caress.

She loved the way he touched her, his hands and then his mouth gentle, tender, reverent almost on her skin, until his own passion overcame him. And even then, all it took was the smallest whispered cry from her to gentle his aroused male suckling of her nipples.

He kissed her stomach, too, light, butterfly kisses which teased and cajoled until she was arching her body up against his mouth, sliding her fingers into the thick strong darkness of his hair as she held him against her and then felt his hands slide down her body, spanning her waist as he lifted her, his tongue rimming the small indentation of her belly button and then moving lower.

It was almost pagan those intimacies they shared. Her face, soft skinned, her flesh sleek and damp, his stronger, bigger, darker as he knelt over her both supplicant and possessor, as he waited for her to acknowledge her need for him . . . her desire.

Slowly, he raised his head and looked at her, searching her face with hungry eagerness, his body poised above hers as he waited for her permission to enter her.

Slowly she smiled at him, a secret, mysterious, deeply female smile of mystique and power as she raised her body exultantly towards that of her lover . . . towards Bram . . .

Bram!

Abruptly Taylor was awake, her body drenched in sweat, her heart pounding not with arousal and excitement but with fear and sick shock.

How many years was it now since she had had that dream? The dream of her powerful secret lover; the man whose body was as well known to her as her own, but whose face, whose identity had always remained a secret.

She knew exactly when she had stopped having the dream and why. It belonged in the past, to a part of her adolescence that was now only a remote, misty memory. A dream lover conjured up by a girl's fevered and immature sexuality.

To dream it again now and to dream that her lover was Bram, a man who . . .

A man who what? A man whom she didn't want . . . didn't hunger for. A man who didn't in the least threaten her self-control or the barriers she had built around herself. Liar, she mocked herself bitterly. Liar! Bram had entered her dreams on previous nights, but never in such an all-consuming way.

Angrily, she pushed the knowledge away. If she had dreamt of anything last night, anyone, it ought to have been of her flat and the man who had desecrated it. Not Bram. Not some silly adolescent dream of lusting for a man's touch, a man's possession . . . a man's love. How could she have let herself . . .

She stopped, her attention suddenly caught by the Marks and Spencer carrier bag placed on the bedside table. There was a note pinned to it in Bram's handwriting. She chewed irritably on her bottom lip as she leaned across to read it.

I checked with the police this morning. It will be some time before you can return to your flat. I rang and explained the position to my secretary and asked her if she could buy some basic replacements to your wardrobe for you.

Taylor knew immediately that whatever was inside the carrier had neither been chosen nor seen by Bram, just as she knew exactly why he had written the note. But instead of feeling relief and gratitude at his thoughtfulness and understanding, she felt a mixture of anger and fear.

For a long time now she had been the one in control of her own life, had believed that she could trust herself to stand alone, and now one shattering event had undermined all those years of hard work, turning her from the woman she had slowly and painfully taught herself to be into someone else—a someone else she loathed and feared—a someone else whom she immediately recognised. And Bram had seen that someone else as well. Had seen her and had reached out to her with gentle compassion and understanding. And desire.

Did he prefer her that way?

Her hand still on the carrier bag, Taylor sat on the side of the bed, taking a deep shaky breath, closing her eyes, tilting her head back. She lifted one hand to her temple, pressing automatically the small pressure point there, seeking release from the tension headache she could already feel building up.

No, Bram wasn't like that. She only wished he were. If he had been, everything would have been so much easier. If he had been she would have known it, recognised it and been easily able to keep him out of her life . . . and her emotions.

As it was . . .

As it was, even without the kiss they had shared, even without last night's dream, she had already known the truth. So why be afraid to give it a name? Would refusing to say it even in the privacy of her own thoughts make it go away? If she refused to allow herself to even silently think the words 'I love him,' would that somehow make her feelings disappear? Was refusing to acknowledge how she felt about him going to stop her heart from flipping over every time she heard his voice on the phone or she saw him walk into a room?

Last night, she had dreamed that she was a girl again and that Bram was her fantasy lover. If only life could be that simple.

To love Bram would be as dangerous and damaging for him as it would be for her. She had no right to allow herself to do so.

If she had the kind of strength, the kind of honesty and integrity she had believed only yesterday that she did possess, she would walk away from him right now.

Walk away to where? Her flat? The shudder of terror that galvanised her body made it jerk as violently as though it had been burned by a high-voltage cable.

No. She couldn't go back there. . . . She could never go back there, not now. So where then? To friends, to family? A self-derisory smile twisted her mouth, her eyes suddenly bleak.

She had neither. Her parents were dead, and as for friends . . .

How could she have friends? Friendship involved trust and honesty. There were things in her life which could never be told to anyone . . . never be shared, secrets which still had the power to haunt and terrify her, a burden of guilt so heavy that she sometimes felt she could almost actually see the shadowy outline of it pressing down against her.

No. There was nowhere for her to go and no one to go to. But if she stayed . . .

If she stayed, she would somehow, from somewhere, have to find the strength to deny her love for Bram, to lie to him, if necessary, when he asked her the question they both knew he was going to ask.

Why did life have to be so unfair? If only she had met him years ago. Before . . .

Shakily she opened the carrier, clumsily tipping the contents onto the bed and then surveying them.

Cream linen trousers, softly styled in her size with a matching waistcoat. A chocolate-brown, washed silk shirt with white linen walking shorts, a black cotton body suit, a patterned silk wrap skirt in chocolate-brown, black and white, and a plain black silk-and-cotton cardigan jacket to go over everything.

There was even a pair of canvas and leather sandals and for good measure a couple of pairs of tights.

Bram's secretary had chosen well, Taylor admitted. The clothes she had selected would work well together, all of them were smart and stylish, the kind of thing Taylor saw other women wearing every day, in the natural fabrics that she loved. All of them eminently wearable, all of them suited in colour and style to her body shape and colouring. And none of them remotely like what she would have chosen to wear for herself.

She picked up the silk shirt. Even without looking at it properly, she knew just how the silk would subtly mould itself to her body in the slightest breeze, the merest opening of a door, the fabric clinging lovingly, sensuously to her skin; the shorts, exactly the right length for sophisticated city living, and for long slim legs. Like the shirt, they were subtly sexy. These were clothes a woman would wear to enhance her sexuality without overstating it. These were clothes that, to the untutored male eye, would appear appealing and attractive, giving their wearer an understated allure that no amount of skin-tight Lycra or cleavage-revealing clothing could ever achieve.

The trousers, she knew, would fit her flatteringly, skimming her body, hinting at the delicate curve of her waist and the soft round shape of her hip. The waistcoat would leave her slenderly bare-armed but would button high enough to conceal the swell of her breasts. The sandals were strong and smart and designed to show off prettily tanned feet and polished nails.

She loved them, Taylor admitted, and already she could see herself in them, see the thoughtful discreet sideways look Bram would give her when he saw her in them, trying not to betray his appreciation of them lest she take umbrage and accuse him of chauvinism and sexually demeaning behaviour towards her.

She could see herself in them, but she could not wear them.

These were clothes that proclaimed she was a woman and proud of being so. She had no right to that kind of pride, she had forfeited it years ago.

Her sense of self as a woman was something she feared and mistrusted. And with good reason. It had already damaged so many people. Hurt them and cast dark shadows across their lives. Because of her...because of her womanhood. Her fingers locked in the chocolate silk as her whole body started to tremble, gently at first and then more violently until her teeth were chattering together and she had gone rigid as she tried to fight off the violent tremor.

Panic attacks had been the doctor's diagnosis. He had offered tranquillisers and counselling, but she had shaken her head and refused. What was the point? Tranquillisers could offer escape only for so long; reality was always there waiting for her and could not be avoided forever. As for counselling...

No amount of counselling could change what had already happened or remove her guilt. There was no absolution for what she had done. The only way she could escape would be through death, and she believed that she did not have the right to allow herself that escape; that her punishment was something she must accept and learn to live with.

A clock ticked steadily in the silence of the bedroom. She looked at it.... It was almost eleven o'clock. She didn't want Bram to come back and find her here still in bed...still vulnerable.

Reluctantly, she picked up the clothes he had bought for her. Her own, like the other contents of her flat, like her flat itself, were something she knew she could never bring herself to look at or touch again.

Bram, she suspected, already instinctively understood that. Would her insurance company be equally understanding?

Taylor had almost reached the bottom stair when the front door opened and Bram walked in. For a moment both of them stood silently watching each other.

To her chagrin, Taylor felt herself flush. Defensively, she rushed into quick, angry speech, gesturing towards the linen trousers and waistcoat she was wearing.

'You needn't have gone to so much trouble—or so much expense. A pair of jeans and a top would have been quite sufficient.' She added ungraciously, 'I've ... I'll reimburse you for them, of course.' Her chin rose aggressively. 'Although I did notice that the price tags had been removed.'

'My fault, I'm afraid,' Bram admitted with a smile. He appeared completely unfazed by her attitude, Taylor noticed unhappily. Because he knew what she was really feeling and why? Did he know as well why she was trying to throw a smokescreen of tough dislike over those feelings? She had a horrid feeling that he did.

'I asked my secretary to let me have the receipts,' he told her. 'You'll need them to present to your insurance company when you file your claim,' he added blandly.

Taylor shot him a suspicious look. 'Yes, I do know that,' she agreed freezingly.

'So I've taken the precaution of getting her to list them and place the list together with the relevant receipts in a file.'

'It didn't occur to you, of course, that that was something I could have done quite adequately for myself,' Taylor challenged him bitingly. 'And while we're on the subject,' she added, without giving him the chance to reply, 'I shall, of course, want to reimburse you for the cost of my stay here and your time.'

Taylor knew that she was being ridiculous, and she half expected Bram to burst out laughing, but to her shock, instead his mouth hardened, his voice cool and distancing, as he demanded, 'Is there anything else I should add to that little list, Taylor? My concern for you, which you have made clear over and over again you don't want? My kiss, perhaps. Am I to charge you for that?'

If he had heard the small betraying gasp of pain she gave, he gave no sign of it, sweeping on coldly, 'And then of course, we mustn't forget the credit side, must we ...? The charges you can make on me for inflicting my presence on your life, for instance. That would attract a pretty hefty level of compensation, I would guess. My refusal to accept that you don't want to allow me into your life—another penalty payment there, I would reckon. Is there anything else . . . ?'

Taylor stared at him, her face ashen with shock as his words hit her like physical blows.

'Oh yes, I nearly forgot. You could charge me for *your* kiss, couldn't you? Or are you going to try to tell me that, like everything else, it was something I forced from you, forced you to endure . . . like my concern, my desire to help you, my need to love you.

'I've been over to your flat this morning. There's no way you can move back in there. I doubt either the police or the insurance company would let you. I had intended to suggest that you stay here—at least for the time being—and to give you my word of honour that I would not try making anything out of the situation. However, in the circumstances, you'd obviously prefer to stay somewhere else. *Anywhere else,*' he added with unexpected savagery, 'just so long as it isn't here with me. Isn't that so?'

Taylor opened her mouth to speak but the words just wouldn't come. Instead, to her humiliation, she felt her eyes fill with scalding tears. They ran silently down her face.

Both physically and emotionally she had no strength left to sustain the level of pain that was now swamping her, flooding her like a full spring tide, finding every smallest crack in her defences and, with its sheer power and volume, forcing itself into them until each crack became a deep fissure and then a huge gorge through which the pain swirled and boiled.

As she lifted her hands to her face in a gesture of agonised supplication and despair, Bram acted.

It had been the shock of coming home and facing her hostility, knowing that she was deliberately working herself up to the point where she could tell him that she wanted to leave, that had fuelled his anger. The last thing he had expected or wanted was to hurt her so badly.

He had never crossed his hallway so fast. His heart was pumping as rapidly as though he had just run up half a dozen flights of stairs. When he took hold of her and wrapped her in his arms, she immediately burrowed closer against him, burying her head against his shoulder, clinging to him while her body trembled and her tears soaked his jacket.

'Tay... Tay... I'm sorry.... I'm so sorry.... I never meant...'

As she turned her face up to look at him, her eyes drowned with tears, he acted instinctively, kissing the damp smoothness of her face as he brushed away her tears, and then, unable to stop himself, kissing her mouth.

It was only meant to be a brief kiss of remorse and apology and, initially, when her mouth quivered under his, he thought it was in rejection. But as soon as he started to lift his mouth from hers, her arms tightened around him, her lips clinging to his parting ones as their trembling increased and spread throughout her whole body.

Never, in his whole life, had Bram experienced such an emotionally charged and intensely passionate meeting of lips, mouths, tongues. He had always known that she would be capable of intense passion, of both giving and wanting the very deepest kind of sensual pleasure and sharing. What he had not expected, though, was the speed with which she had gone from withdrawing herself from him and holding him at a distance to uninhibitedly showing him, allowing him, to see how much she wanted him.

He could feel it in the quivering urgency of her body, see it in her eyes when she opened them and looked directly into his while they kissed, hear it in the small, purring sounds of pleasure she made in her throat, punctuated by a sharp, almost keening sound of need as their mutual passion exploded into a conflagration of uncontrollable desire.

'Take me to bed, Bram.... Make love to me.... I want you so much....' Her voice was husky, and slightly raw, violent shudders running visibly through her body as she whispered the words frantically against his mouth, words Bram had begun to think he was never going to hear.

Take her to bed... Would his physical control hold out that long?

Make love to her!

He shuddered as she pressed her body even closer to his, moving her hips frantically against him. Through the fine linen of her trousers he could feel the jut of her hipbones, the warmth of her skin, the swell of feminine flesh that covered the mound of her pubic bone.

Heat poured through him.

He could feel her hands on his back beneath his jacket. Still kissing her, totally unable to break the physical contact between them, to let go of the sweet sensuality of her mouth, he shrugged it off and felt her tugging his shirt free of his trousers.

He felt her sharp shock of pleasure as she touched his bare skin, and groaned out loud against her mouth. Dear God. What he wouldn't give to be touching her in the same way, absorbing into his very being the smooth warmth of her skin, its texture, its scent, its taste . . . her taste. In his mind's eye he saw himself spreading the smooth paleness of her thighs, lying between them, opening the smooth, plump lips that covered her sex, delicately rimming the sensitive flesh inside them with the tip of his tongue, tasting it and her as his tongue stroked over and over her smaller and more delicately sensitive inner lips until they, too, parted, offering the secret heart of her to him so that he could draw the small, erect crest of her clitoris into his mouth, stroke it, caress it, coax it until . . .

Without taking his mouth from hers, Bram swung Taylor off her feet and up into his arms. He headed for the stairs, while she kept her arms wrapped around him, her mouth fastened to his, her gaze locked on him.

12

It was raining when Jay arrived back at Heathrow, sky and land alike a dull, uniform grey.

By the time he had reclaimed his baggage and found a taxi, his body felt slick with sweat beneath his expensively tailored suit. The anger which had been simmering inside him ever since his aborted telephone call had reached flashpoint several times in the hours since, notably when he had discovered there weren't any seats available on the next three Concorde flights, and that the best the airline could offer him was a standby ticket on a regular flight.

It far too early in the morning to go into the office, as his father didn't normally arrive there until around eight-thirty. Yet it was too late to catch up on the sleep he had lost. The best he could hope for was that a shower would cool off his skin and his temper—emotions he had no intention of recognising as either anxiety or insecurity, but which, instead, he had renamed concern. Just who the hell was this woman who was apparently so important to his father that not even his son was allowed to interrupt his meetings with her? The very thought sent adrenalin coursing through his veins in short, dangerous bursts.

As the taxi made its way through the increasingly heavy early-morning rush-hour traffic, Jay drummed his fingers impatiently on the taxi seat.

'Older men tend to dote on their children, especially when they're their second family. How will you like that Jay?' Nadia's taunt echoed mockingly in his head.

He had denied that any such thing could ever happen. He still denied it—it wouldn't happen. He intended to make sure of that.

This woman, whoever she was, would soon be made to see that there was no place for her in his father's life—or in his father's bed.

The taxi came to a halt outside Jay's apartment building, the driver giving him a sour look as he glanced at Jay's tip.

The place was new and modern—and very exclusive. Among Jay's neighbours were several well-known, top-ranking members of the acting profession, at least one major shareholder in a very successful television company and a novelist whose work had been nominated for the Booker Prize and who had gone on to make both a name and a fortune for himself as a writer of popular fiction. Jay hadn't chosen his apartment because of his neighbours, though. He had bought it because it was a good up-market address and conveniently close to the office. Unlike his father, he had no desire to burden himself with a three-storey house plus garden. Bram was ridiculously conventional that way. To Jay, the apartment was simply a place to sleep—sometimes alone, sometimes not—and eat, occasionally. He felt no sentimental attachment to it. His father, though, was different. To him the place where he lived had to be a home, had to be crammed with family photographs and mementoes. . . .

Jay could still remember the puzzled, sad expression in his father's eyes the day he had walked into Jay's room and found the photograph he had given him of his parents lying face down on the floor, the glass smashed.

'I don't want it,' Jay had told him bitterly. 'Why should I, they never wanted me? They paid my mother to take me away.'

'Jay, that's not true,' his father had protested.

'They gave her money,' Jay had insisted, his eyes defying his father to deny it.

'Yes,' Bram had agreed. 'But not—They did what they thought was best. . . .'

After that Jay had discovered from Helena that it had been his *maternal* grandparents who had *demanded* the money and who had set out the terms whereby Bram was to be denied any contact with his infant son. By then, though, the damage had been done, the fear and bitterness lodged so deeply within him that nothing could exorcise them.

Jay could feel his stomach muscles contracting, an iron band of tension tightening inside his head as he unlocked his door. The cleaning staff had piled his mail neatly on the console table in the marble-floored octagonal hall. He strode through the main living area into his bedroom, dropping his case on the floor. He shrugged off his jacket and unfastened his shirt after rewinding the answer-phone and flicking on the tape.

There were a couple of messages from male acquaintances—Jay preferred acquaintances to close friends—one reminding him of a squash game, the other inviting him to a business dinner; a crisp list of messages from his secretary returned to the office now after her holiday; and a breathy, whispered suggestion from a woman it took him several seconds to call to mind, but whom he eventually remembered meeting at a party and whom he had taken to bed a couple of times, more out of boredom than anything else.

His lip curled slightly in disdain as he fast-forwarded the rest of her message. She had been boring, in bed and out of it, and worst of all, as far as he was concerned, she had even protested when he insisted on wearing a condom.

As he removed the rest of his clothes and walked into the bathroom the tape was still playing. He frowned as he heard someone trying to leave a message without waiting for the beep, his frown deepening when he recognised Plum's voice.

She was saying something about her birthday party.... Stupid bitch... He walked back to the bedroom and was just on the point of fast-forwarding through the rest of her message when he caught his father's name.

His body tensing, he backed up the tape and replayed Plum's message.

'Jay, I've got to talk to you,' Plum began urgently. 'It's Bram. I think... I think he's fallen in love....' The sound of Plum's sobs followed, obliterating the next few words.

'I saw them together...' Plum continued. 'In his office... He was taking her out to dinner and I could tell just from the way he was looking at her. Oh Jay, you've got to do something.... You've *got* to.'

Bram in love... Jay's mouth tightened. This woman, whoever she was, must be clever, he had to give her that. She was obviously making a complete fool out of his father.

Bram in love. Jay refused to allow recognition of the feelings that boiled deep inside him, the real cause of the savage anger that swamped him.

There could be only one reason why this woman had attached herself to his father. Bram was a very rich man, a vulnerable target. Well, Jay would soon strip the rose-tinted illusionary haze from his father's eyes and make him see this woman for what she really was.

He reached for the phone, dialled Plum's number and then stopped. No. It would probably be better if he went round to see her. He glanced at his watch. Eight o'clock. She would, no doubt, still be in bed and probably not alone. Well, too bad. What he wanted to talk to her about was far more important than the sensibilities of her latest conquest.

It amused him sometimes to contemplate the sainted Helena's reaction to the discovery that her daughter was a whore. No, not even that. Whores at least made sure they got paid. Plum didn't even have the sense to do that. She gave it away.

He showered quickly, towelling the moisture off his body before pulling on clean underwear and reaching for a shirt.

He would go straight from Plum's apartment to the office. His father would be in by then and, armed with whatever information he could get from Plum about this mystery woman who appeared to have taken over his father's life, he would be able to make his first assault on her stranglehold.

Jay had to keep his finger pressed on the bell of Plum's apartment for almost five minutes before she came to let him in, still wearing her nightshirt, a bright pink cotton affair that should have clashed revoltingly with her hair, but didn't. Her hair was a messy tangle, last night's make-up leaving dark circles round her eyes.

Her bottom lip quivered in shock as she saw Jay, a mixture of wariness and curiosity in her eyes.

'Jay. . . what do you want?' she demanded uneasily.

'I want to talk to you about this woman my father's seeing,' Jay told her curtly as he walked into the flat and closed the door behind him.

He paused and glanced towards her half-open bedroom door. 'What's wrong?' he demanded, laughing. 'Worried that whoever you've got in there might go off the boil if you leave him for too long?'

'No one's in there,' Plum told him angrily.

'Why so nervous then?' Jay asked, adding unkindly, 'Not, I trust, because you think that I might take advantage of your popular reputation and test just how good your skill at giving a blow job really is.'

Plum went white and then red, angry tears burning in her eyes. 'That's a horrid thing to say,' she said fiercely. 'I would never—'

'Liar,' Jay taunted her. 'You're the original girl who can't say no. Do you think I've forgotten the way you used to come on to me? "Oh please, Jay...let me..."' he whispered, mimicking her voice with cruel ease.

'That wasn't anything to do with sex,' Plum protested furiously. 'That was because—'

'Because what?' Jay jeered.

'Because I wanted us to be friends. Because...because I felt sorry for you,' Plum burst out, her voice rising.

'You felt *sorry* for me?'

For a moment Plum thought he was actually going to grab her. The words fell from his lips like frozen splinters, deadly ice picks, the look he gave her making her tremble from head to toe.

'You felt sorry for me,' he repeated.

Plum could see the colour seeping up under his skin, burning along his cheekbones in livid weals of fury. He gave her a look of such utter loathing that Plum instinctively cringed.

'Do you know what you remind me of, Plum?' he asked her in a cold, deadly voice. 'A tribe of gypsies camped near us in Norfolk. They had a dog with them, a pathetic, cringing, fawning little bitch, who used to crawl on her belly to them for food, the same way you crawl on your belly for sex.

'And you say you felt sorry for me. I wonder what your mother would say if she saw that rather boring little video you made of yourself—'

'It was you...you took it.' Plum exhaled, not even bothering to try to pretend she didn't know what he meant.

'Yes, I took it, and I've still got it. Now tell me about this woman you claim my father's fallen in love with,' Jay demanded, suddenly tiring of tormenting her. She was such a worthless adversary. No matter how cruelly he treated her, how contemptuously, he knew he had only to open his arms, lie to her that he hadn't meant it and she would be clinging to him, crying all over him . . . believing him.

'Her name's Taylor . . . Taylor,' Plum responded quickly. 'I . . . she . . . she's been helping him with some work he's doing.' Her forehead crinkled. 'She works for some charity organisation or other, I think. He really cares about her, Jay. You can see it in his eyes when he looks at her, but she doesn't care about him. She's so cold . . . so hard. And she's old. . . . I hate her,' she added childishly.

'I love him so much and she's going to take him away from me. You've *got* to do something Jay . . . you've got to stop it. . . . You will, won't you?'

She caught hold of his arm imploringly as she spoke and then released it just as quickly, her face flushing hotly under the look he gave her.

'What time is it?' she started to gabble nervously. 'Ma is coming for me at ten. I've got a fitting for my dress . . . for the party.' She pulled a face. 'I wanted something by Lacroix or Valentino but Ma is insisting on going to her boring old dressmaker. You are coming to the party, aren't you?'

Jay didn't answer. He was already striding towards the door. Nine o'clock. Well, at least his father would be in his office by now.

The receptionist watched warily as Jay walked past her, heading for the lift. Once she heard the lift door close she picked up her phone and quickly punched in the number of Jay's secretary.

'Storm warning,' she told the other woman when she answered. 'His lordship is back and in none too good a mood, by the looks of him.'

'Thanks, I owe you one.' Jay's secretary quickly replaced the receiver as she heard Jay's familiar footsteps in the corridor outside.

However, he didn't enter the office. She heard him walking past it, heading for his father's suite.

Marcia looked up calmly when Jay walked in. She had returned to work that day, much to the relief of the woman who had been standing in for her.

'I want to speak to my father,' Jay announced curtly, ignoring her good-morning.

'I'm afraid he isn't here.' As Marcia saw Jay start to frown, she added, 'I think you'll probably find that he's at home. He's—'

Her mouth compressed in irritation as Jay strode out without allowing her to finish what she was saying.

Jay's temper was running dangerously high by the time the taxi dropped him off outside his father's house, his mood a dangerous mix of explosive tension, aggressive anxiety and jet lag. Added to this was the still-festering resentment of his father's refusal to back his expansion plans for the company.

When he realised that he had left his key to his father's house in his apartment he rang the doorbell angrily, barely waiting before pressing it even more irritably a second time.

Taylor was upstairs when she heard the front doorbell ring. She had been standing staring out of the window of Bram's bedroom, the same room she had shared with him yesterday afternoon and last night.

Beneath her clothes her body started to burn hotly at the memory of the way she had responded to Bram's lovemaking.

They had made love in the truest and deepest sense of the word, and not just once but . . .

She bit down hard on her bottom lip, forcing back her tears as she tried to banish the image of Bram's expression this morning when she had withdrawn from him, physically, mentally and emotionally; the confusion and hurt in his eyes as he released her from his arms, his pain when she had refused to talk to him or to explain.

But how could she . . . ? How could she tell him that she had no right to accept the gift of his love, no right to give him hers; that to allow him to love her and to love him in return would be to expose him to danger.

Yesterday, she had been overwhelmed by a reckless tide of selfish need. This morning . . .

He had had to go out to an urgent, unexpected business meeting, but he wouldn't be gone long and when he came back . . .

When he came back she would not be here. She had already made that decision.

Her fingers curled so tightly around the photograph frame she was holding that the silver almost cut into her skin.

Bram had brought it back from her flat. The frame was slightly damaged and the glass gone, but the photograph inside was unharmed.

Taylor had almost refused to take it . . . to acknowledge it as her property, but she had seen the thoughtful curiosity in his eyes.

'It's . . . she's . . . she's my goddaughter,' she had explained jerkily. 'My. . .her parents live abroad now. I. . .I don't see them any more.'

'She's a very pretty girl,' Bram had responded gravely.

How quickly had the thief found the photograph? Taylor wondered sickly now. . . . Immediately, or had he merely come across it by accident when he was rummaging through her drawers?

Downstairs, the doorbell pealed imperiously. As the sharp noise pierced the heavy silence of her own despair, Taylor realised it had rung several times already.

Unsteadily she went downstairs, hesitating in the hallway as she saw the forbidding outline of the man standing outside.

'The police know you're staying here. They will probably want to interview you again,' Bram had warned her.

Shakily, Taylor went to open the door, her fingers trembling as she secured the safety chain first.

She could hear the man on the other side cursing her as he tried to push the door open. 'Where's my father?' he demanded furiously. 'And who the hell are you?'

So this was Bram's son. She would have recognised him anywhere, Taylor acknowledged. She released the safety chain and stood back as he strode into the hallway. He exuded an air of pent-up rage and tension. She could almost see and feel it shimmering around him like an angry, crimson aura.

She saw his eyes narrow, his gaze sharpening as he studied her. 'My God,' he breathed softly. 'You're her, aren't you? Where's my father?' he repeated, his tone suddenly very harsh as he passed her heading for the study door.

'He's not here. He had to go out.'

She had heard so much about this son of his from Bram, had recognised the love in Bram's voice when he spoke of him and had sensed how much pain was tangled up with that love. But nothing had prepared her for the reality of Jay's reaction to discovering her here in his father's house . . . in his father's life.

Had she been in a position to commit herself to Bram, to acknowledge her love for him and to have him return that love, she would have been afraid of this man. As it was, once her initial shock had faded, she felt unexpectedly calm.

There was, after all, something about him that was familiar, very familiar.

'You must be Jay,' she said quietly, placing the photograph she had been holding down on the table between them. She saw the way he glanced at it, frowned and then looked at it again before looking at her.

'Your daughter?' he demanded acidly. 'So it's not just you my father is going to be expected to keep in luxury, is it? It's her as well, is that it?'

Taylor's face flushed with angry indignation. 'No, she's not . . . my daughter,' she denied. 'She's—' to her dismay she could hear her voice trembling openly '—she's my . . . my goddaughter. And as for your father being expected to keep either of us—'

'What?' he challenged her. 'No such thought ever crossed your mind . . .? Do me a favour. Why the hell else would you have inveigled and crawled your way into his bed? And don't try telling me that you haven't . . . I can still smell the sex on you,' he told her insultingly.

Taylor gasped, her face white as she stepped back, her hand going instinctively to her throat as though to protect the fragile life-force beating there.

'Oh yes, I've heard all about you,' Jay continued savagely. 'And about how besotted my father is with you. But you're not married to him yet, and I intend to make sure that you never are, no matter what it takes. You—'

'Jay!'

Neither of them had heard Bram walk in through the still-open door. Taylor's face was as pale with shock as Jay's was dark with fury as they both turned at the stern commanding sound of his voice.

'Taylor, are you all right?'

Ignoring his son, Bram walked past him and gently placed his hands on Taylor's shoulders, drawing her towards him in a gesture at once protective and unexpectedly possessive.

'I . . .' Taylor tried to speak, to tell him, to tell them both that Jay had nothing to fear from her. . . . But to her shame, all she could do was stand mutely within the protective circle of Bram's arms, while hot tears ran down her face.

'Can't you see what she's really after?' she heard Jay begin fiercely. But Bram didn't let him finish.

'Please leave, Jay. You've already upset Taylor enough.'

'Dad—'

'Leave. Now!'

'If I leave here, there's no way I'm coming back. Not while she's still here, still in your life,' Jay warned him bitterly. 'Take your choice—it's either her or me.'

Taylor shivered, closing her eyes. The decision was made now . . . out of her hands.

'Taylor *is* my life, Jay.'

Taylor felt her stomach lurch as she saw the expression in Jay's eyes, the open disbelief, the brief flash of unbearable pain, the tremor that ripped through him before his face hardened into granite.

As he turned and walked slowly towards the door, closing it after him, Taylor held her breath, waiting for Bram to stop him to retract his words of dismissal and denial. When he didn't, she tugged on his sleeve. 'Bram, he's your son. You mustn't . . .'

'And you are the woman I love,' Bram told her sombrely.

'He's your son,' Taylor repeated, her throat tight with tears. 'You love him.'

Jay would never forgive her for this, never forget, never stop blaming her.

'I can't let you do it,' Taylor whispered. 'You and I don't . . .'

'You and I don't what?' Bram challenged her. 'You and I don't have any right to be together . . . to be happy . . . to love each other?'

'He's afraid of losing you.' Despite the softness of her voice, her expression was haunted almost, her eyes dark with fear.

'It's all right,' he told her huskily. 'There's no need for you to be afraid. I heard what he said to you, and I promise you that there is no way Jay or anyone else could ever come between us, or change the way I feel about you.'

Taylor stared at him. 'How can you say that? How can you be so sure?' she demanded fiercely. 'We hardly know each other. I—'

'I know that I love you,' Bram said with quiet conviction. 'I know that so much of my life has already gone by without you in it, that I'm not prepared to risk losing another second of loving you. I knew when I held you in my arms, when you held me in your body, that what we shared was something special and rare, a gift that few people are blessed to experience. To turn our backs on it, to spurn it—' he shook his head '—I can't.

'I know what Jay said must have frightened and upset you, and the last thing I would want is for you to feel obliged to stay with me because I chose you above Jay. That was my decision, and I had the right to make it. Just as it is your right to make your decisions, to choose your life.

'And the only way I want to be part of that life is if you choose freely to have me there.'

'You mean if I said that I wanted to leave . . . that I didn't want to stay, you'd just let me go?' Taylor's mouth had gone dry and she was shaking convulsively inside.

'If that was what you wanted, then, yes,' Bram agreed gravely.

Taylor closed her eyes remembering how, this morning, she had told herself that she couldn't stay . . . that she had to leave.

Now she had even more reasons for leaving.

Her eyes were swimming with tears when she opened them and looked at Bram.

For the rest of her life and beyond it she would carry with her the memory of how it had felt to have his hands caressing her body, his mouth . . . to hear his whispered words of love and to receive the ultimate physical gift of his body's aching release within her own.

She opened her mouth to tell him she couldn't stay, that she had to go for his sake as well as for her own. But instead of those words of denial, all she could manage, as she walked into his arms, was a shakily sobbed, 'Bram . . .'

13

It couldn't be allowed to go on . . . it had to end. . . . She would have to find a way of making it end, but not now . . . not today . . . not yet.

Taylor was like a dieter, a drinker, a druggie, continually promising herself that tomorrow she would make a fresh start. Tomorrow she would break free of her addiction. She was in denial, refusing to acknowledge her own weakness and inability to do what she knew had to be done, she thought, deriding herself as she bent to remove the spent heads from Bram's roses.

How long had she been living here in Bram's house? A month, slightly more. And how many times during that month had she warned herself that it was impossible for her to stay?

Love was such a very fragile bloom. Like these roses, seen in full flower, it seemed impossible to believe that it could ever wither and die.

She would miss this garden when she left, just as she would miss the space and comfort of Bram's house. . . . And Bram himself, she taunted herself. Was she allowed to acknowledge that she would miss him too? Could she let the words, the thought, creep stealthily into her mind, or would it be safer for her to deny its existence altogether until the time actually came when she had to confront it, alone on her own, somewhere far, far away from the warm, loving protection of Bram's arms.

Bram had left this morning for a conference in Strasbourg, where he was the principal speaker. He had wanted her to go with him, but she had refused.

'I don't like leaving you on your own,' he had told her this morning as he held her in his arms and kissed her gently. 'But you'll be safe here, and I'll be back tomorrow evening.'

She was missing him already.

Now would be an ideal time to leave. In a city like London it was easy enough for someone to disappear. Thanks to Bram the insurance company had been very prompt about settling her claim, so she had a fairly substantial amount of cash at her disposal.

She could rent a room somewhere until she found another flat. Her own would have to be sold. She could never live there again.

If she left now, Bram was bound to come after her. He could trace her through her job, and besides . . .

Besides what, she taunted herself. You will want to sleep with him one more time and then one more again. To hold him, and be held by him, how often, once . . . twice . . . a thousand times.

Every extra day she spent with him increased the risk she was already taking. What would happen once he found out the truth? Would he still love her then—how could he?

Hadn't she already caused him enough pain? He might pretend to her that he had no regrets over his quarrel with Jay, but she had seen his face when he thought she wasn't watching him, had seen the sadness in his eyes.

Jay, after all, was his son and Bram loved him.

Once she was out of the way, they would make up their differences and . . .

'Why have you never married?' she had asked him one night as she lay in his arms in the dark. It was easier for her to talk to him when she knew he couldn't see her expression, guess what she was thinking.

'Because I never met you,' he had responded, kissing her. But later he had admitted that it was because of Jay and his behaviour as a child that he had decided he could not commit himself to a relationship.

There was also the problem of what to do about her flat. Sooner or later she was going to have to visit her flat. She had already told Bram she wanted to sell it.

'Would you like me to arrange for an agent to go round and view it?' Bram had asked. He was like that, offering her his help with open-handed generosity but never behaving towards her as though he considered her incapable of making her own decisions.

He was the first man she had known who possessed that kind of intuitive delicacy about other people's feelings; she liked it in him. Dominant, controlling men made her feel wary and ill at ease.

Illogically, she found the almost exaggerated care taken by 'new men,' with their aggravating determination to behave in a way that was totally politically correct, equally unappealing.

With Bram though, she knew instinctively that his sensitivity was an intrinsic part of his personality. Unlike Jay, who she suspected had never exhibited sensitivity for another person's feelings in his entire life. It was obvious to her that Jay needed to feel in control. She found him both emotionally aggressive and manipulative, but she was careful not to criticise him to Bram; not because she thought Bram would dislike it but because she worried that it might hurt him.

Bram had told her that the rift between him and Jay had been unavoidable, something which had been destined to happen, and that there was simply no way he would ever allow Jay to come between them. But she knew that what had happened must have hurt him. And she knew that, far from having accepted his father's love for Taylor, Jay was still determined to bring their relationship to an end.

She had no doubt at all about Jay's reaction if he ever discovered the truth about her past—not that he was likely to do so. Had she been a different kind of woman, the kind of woman Jay obviously wanted her to be, she might have derived a good deal of cynical amusement watching Jay trying to undermine her relationship with his father, knowing the secrets of her own past were potentially far more destructive than Jay could ever be.

But she wasn't that kind of woman. God knew, she had tried in these last few weeks to pretend that the past had never existed, that she had every right to accept Bram's love and to return it, but she knew she was lying to herself.

To leave Bram, having known the joy of being loved by him, would be to commit herself to an emotional wasteland, a landscape of pain and agony, joyless and empty, stretching into eternity. But she could not stay with him, deceiving him, lying to him, all the time afraid that . . .

She looked up as she heard the front door open. Bram had told her he wouldn't be back until tomorrow evening, but . . .

She went into the house and came to an abrupt halt, the smile dying on her lips as she saw not Bram but Jay standing in the hall.

'Bram isn't here,' she informed him coldly, frowning as she saw the keys he was pocketing. Bram had told her that he had asked Jay to return his spare house keys to him and that he had done so.

'I know,' Jay responded. 'In fact, I'm just on my way to the airport to catch a flight to join him. He rang me this afternoon and said he'd been offered a couple of days' fishing.'

The words were said casually, carelessly almost, but Taylor didn't miss the gleam of triumph in Jay's eyes.

She knew, of course, that the two were still in contact at work—how could they not be? But she had gained the impression from Bram that the atmosphere between them was still very tense and that Jay had been displaying a marked tendency to sulk.

'He's behaving more like a child than an adult,' Bram had told her one evening in exasperation. 'Anyone would think that we were the ones at fault.'

'In his eyes, we probably are,' Taylor had replied wryly. 'He's obviously still very angry about our relationship, Bram. Outwardly he may be an adult, but inwardly he still feels as he did as a child—resentful, and threatened by anyone new coming into your life.'

'Well, I'm afraid it's a situation he's just going to have to get used to. I don't know whether it's a sign that I'm getting older or what, but I'm becoming increasingly less tolerant these days where Jay's concerned. To be honest with you, Tay, I'm tired of being made a scapegoat, of having to make amends for the past. Yes, I do regret what happened, and of course I'll always blame myself for it. But I can't go on for ever paying for that mistake. Will *our* children blame me for their conception, I wonder...?'

'Our children,' Taylor had whispered huskily. 'But...'

'But what? Do you think I'm too old, is that it...?'

'No, no, of course not,' Taylor had assured him immediately and honestly. But she hadn't been able to say any more. Her throat had been too thick with tears.

Children... Dear God, if only that were possible. Only she knew how much, over all these long, barren years, she had ached and yearned for that fulfilment. And to have Bram's children . . .

'Jay won't like it,' she had warned Bram lightly to cover her emotion.

Bram's response had been lost beneath the pressure of the increasingly passionate kiss he was giving her.

No, there had been no indication in anything Bram had said that he and Jay were now back on terms that would lead to them going on a fishing trip together. So far as she knew, he still intended to return from Strasbourg as he had originally planned.

'What's wrong?' Jay asked her with mock solicitude. 'Didn't Dad tell you we're going fishing? But then he wouldn't, would he? He's never been one for confrontations . . . feminine hysterics and scenes, and God knows he's had to endure enough of them. He seems to have this ability to attract a specific type of woman. You know the type I mean, Taylor? Strong-willed— forthright, some people would call them—domineering and strident is probably a better description.

'Dad is so easygoing he tends to let them manipulate him, lets them believe . . . Inevitably, of course, he finds himself in a situation he's desperate to get out of. With that kind of woman, though, it can sometimes be difficult to get them to accept the end of a relationship. You know what I mean, don't you?'

Oh, yes, she knew, Taylor acknowledged silently.

He was enjoying this, she realised.

'Why have you come here, Jay?' she asked quietly, refusing to be drawn.

She saw her response had angered him. What had he expected her to do—argue with him, get upset, threaten to tell his father?

'Dad asked me to collect his fishing gear. I'll go and get it. I take it he's still sleeping in the same room.'

'Yes, he is, but I think you'll find what you're looking for in the spare bedroom. Bram moved some of his clothes into there to give me more room for mine.'

Two could play the game that Jay was playing, Taylor reflected as she watched the way his mouth clamped shut in fury, the angle of his jaw hardening and lengthening.

'I shouldn't get too comfortable there if I were you,' he remarked as he headed for the stairs. 'I'm afraid you won't be staying very long. You might think you hold all the winning cards now, but the whole pack hasn't been dealt yet. My father's almost fifty, and there's never been a woman yet who's managed to get him to the altar. Believe me, plenty of 'em have tried.'

'He's forty-two, not fifty,' Taylor corrected sharply, 'and while he may have made allowances for you when you were a child, Jay, and put your needs before his own, somehow the thought of him continuing to do so for an adult of your age is about as ridiculous as imagining you're still in nappies, sucking a dummy. But then, of course, if that is how you choose to see yourself . . .' She gave a small, dismissive shrug.

If things had been different, if, for instance, she had been able to stay with Bram and share his life, she would probably have been more reticent. As it was, it was high time that someone gave Jay a taste of his own medicine.

She made sure she was out of the way when Jay left the house. Why hadn't Bram said anything to her about asking Jay to join him? Surely not, as Jay had implied, because he felt that she would object or complain that he was going back on his ultimatum to his son.

It was ridiculous to suggest that Bram felt that he needed to keep time spent with his son a secret from her, like a man betraying his partner with a secret lover.

But Bram was a very sensitive man. He wouldn't want to hurt her and . . . And Jay was his son and he loved him very deeply. No, no matter what he might say to her, Jay had to be important to him. More important than she was?

What did it matter now. Soon she wouldn't be here.

Less than half an hour after Jay left, the telephone rang. Taylor knew instinctively that it was Bram. Love did that to you, she acknowledged wryly. It brought out emotions, needs, heights and depths in a person that they had never even dreamed existed; caused them to dream impossible dreams and believe, even if only fleetingly, that they could come true. It ignored reality, chafed at obstacles, recognised no authority other than its own.

'It's good to hear your voice,' Bram said, adding more fiercely,' 'God, I'm missing you, Tay. It's been less than twenty-four hours and I'm walking around like a zombie. I feel like part of me is missing. It's like being taken off a life-support machine.'

'Very romantic,' Taylor teased, all the stern talks she had given herself, all the vows she had made to end it were forgotten as she listened to his voice.

'Romance is for operettas,' Bram told her wryly, 'insubstantial or light-hearted. That isn't how I feel about you. Are *you* missing *me?*'

'Yes,' Taylor admitted. 'But you'll be home soon, tomorrow.'

She hadn't been trying to test him, to trip him or trap him, she told herself later, which only made the pain so much harder to bear. She had simply been trying to offer him the reassurance she had believed he wanted. But in the silence that followed, she was suddenly aware of a feeling of unease and discomfort.

'I'm afraid it's going to be a little longer than that. Something's come up . . . a meeting . . . and I'm going to be stuck here for another couple of days.'

'Didn't Dad tell you we're going fishing?' Jay had said. 'But then he wouldn't, would he?'

'A meeting,' she repeated. Her body had gone icy cold and she could feel her teeth starting to chatter. What kind of meeting? she wanted to demand. And who with? But her pride stopped her.

'I'm really sorry, Tay,' she could hear Bram telling her. 'You'll be all right on your own, won't you . . . you won't—'

'Yes, yes. I'll be fine,' Taylor told him quietly.

Fine . . . Just as long as she didn't allow herself to think about the way he had lied to her. Just as long as she didn't let herself picture the gloating look in Jay's eyes. Just as long as . . .

Was it her fault? Had *she* forced him into a position where he felt he had to deceive her in order to see his son. She might not *like* Jay, but she had never never asked Bram to choose between them.

But Jay had!

'Taylor, are you still there?' Bram asked urgently.

'Yes. Yes, I'm still here.'

'I can't wait to get back . . . to see you . . . hold you. Tell me what you are wearing. No. No, don't . . . I'm aching for you already. I should have brought you with me, but it didn't seem fair, not when I was going to be tied up in meetings for most of the time. I miss you like hell at night, though. It's just not the same, sleeping alone.'

For a moment Taylor was tempted to point out that if she had been with him it would have been rather difficult for him to arrange to go fishing with Jay, but she managed to resist the impulse. That kind of reaction was exactly what Jay would like. She could all too easily imagine him questioning Bram, asking him in mock innocence how she had reacted to the news that they were going fishing—when he knew that Bram had not told her.

Ten minutes later, as she replaced the receiver, she admitted that she could not blame Bram for wanting to make his peace with his son. But to do so in a way which undermined her and allowed Jay to hurt and torment her, that was different.

It seemed so out of character for a man who, for so long as she had known him, had displayed extreme sensitivity towards her emotions.

Bram frowned as he replaced his receiver. Something was wrong. Taylor had sounded so reserved, so remote almost. He never should have left her, not when their relationship was so new and vulnerable.

Right now, all he wanted to do was to get home and take her in his arms and reassure himself that everything was all right... that she was all right. But he couldn't cancel the arrangements he had made with Jay, and he hadn't had time to explain the full situation to Taylor. Bram had arrived at his hotel to find an unexpected message from Jay advising him that an additional important meeting had been set up for the day after tomorrow. Not good timing as far as Bram was concerned, but there didn't appear to be a way out of it.

He closed his eyes and mentally pictured Taylor, forming her out of the dark space, clothing her face in his favourite smile, her eyes in teasing warmth, the tilt of her head that meant that she was feeling happy, secure. But the image refused to stay static, it fragmented and then reformed.

Why was it so much easier for him to picture her anxious and on edge, than happy, her skin still warm from lovemaking, her body relaxed?

Why, when she had said nothing, done nothing to make him feel like this, did he have this gut feeling that something was wrong? That she was . . .

That she was what? Going to walk out on him?

God, he was far too old to feel this kind of emotional anguish. It was a reaction that belonged to youth and youth's intensity.

Hadn't he warned himself, told himself all along that if she wanted to leave, if she wanted to walk away from him, then he had no right to try to stop her?

Hadn't he said over and over again in the deepest privacy of his own thoughts that the last thing he wanted was to put any kind of pressure on her? That the only reason, the only way he wanted her with him was because that was what *she* wanted?

What was the matter with him? She had admitted that she loved him.

Admitted. That said it all, didn't it?

He loved her! He welcomed his love for her, found joy and pleasure in it, wanted to shout it from the roof tops.

She loved him, but *her* love made her fearful and angry, defensive and deprived of her freedom. The last thing he wanted to do right now was to spend time away from her, but if he returned home now, Jay would . . .

Perhaps Taylor was right. Perhaps the habits of a lifetime, of protecting and loving his son *were* too strong for him to throw off. Habits he was doomed to carry with him to his deathbed and perhaps even beyond.

The girl at the booking desk thought Jay was quite definitely the most smoulderingly sexy man she had ever set eyes on. As he paid for his ticket to Strasbourg she wondered impulsively if it was worth getting someone to cover for her and booking herself onto the same flight.

'Have a good trip,' she told him as she handed him his ticket with a smile.

Jay smiled in response and was still smiling five minutes later as he crossed the airport concourse and made his way to the first-class departure lounge. He had enjoyed seeing the expression in Taylor's eyes when he had given her the news about his fishing trip with his father. She had tried to hide her reaction, of course, but he had seen the tell-tale flicker of doubt, the uncertainty and the pain.

For the first time since his father had refused to agree to the Japanese venture, Jay was aware of the return of a sense of power.

Standing in the hallway of his father's home watching Taylor as she absorbed the news he had given her, he had felt it almost like an electric current, a fierce, triumphant sensation, heating his blood and driving it through his veins.

There was no feeling quite like it, not even that last explosive heartbeat before orgasm. It was unique, erotic, life-enhancing—it was the wheels which drove the machinery of his person, his reason for being.

He flicked open his paper, skimming the headlines. The local news was dominated by the death of a man whose body had been found slumped over his desk in a prestigious London office. He had not, as had first been assumed, committed suicide because of some threatening business failure or disgrace, but apparently because his marriage had broken up.

Jay's mouth curled in a sneer as he read the comments of the dead man's friends and acquaintances about the depth and intensity of his love for his wife.

As far as Jay was concerned, love was, at best, a mawkish, sentimental concept, publicly lauded by those who made their living by commercialising it, and privately derided. For those who suffered from it, it was a disease—a mental disorder which made them vulnerable and weak objects of pity or contempt. It was a cloak which people, society, used to cover the raw, primitive essence of sexuality and its demands, a trap, a means of control by which the powerful controlled the weak.

In Jay's eyes, people claiming to experience love were as suspect as those claiming to have met beings from outer space.

The knowledge that his father believed he was in love filled him with a mixture of emotions so intense they were like a volatile cocktail of raw energy inside him.

His father could not be in love. It was impossible. She was impossible. And the idea of their relationship continuing... enduring... But it wasn't going to continue. He was going to see to that.

His father didn't need this woman in his life. He didn't need other children... other sons who might... Angrily, Jay flung down the newspaper and got up, striding over to the lounge's viewing area.

There was nothing for him to worry about. He had already done the groundwork. He had no qualms about what he was doing, no doubts that he would succeed. Why should he have?

'Plum, of course, is being dreadfully difficult about her dress. But then I suppose it's only to be expected—when has she ever been anything else? And then this morning the florist rang to say that she'd heard that the Duchess of Kent had agreed to be the guest of honour at a charity ball and that they were planning on using white lilies for the floral decorations and since it was the same night as Plum's party, it was going to be hard to get as many lilies as we need and did I have an alternative in mind, just in case.

'I knew I should never have used that girl,' Helena continued in exasperation, as her husband walked into their bedroom from his dressing room, 'but Daphne insisted that she was good, and not outrageously expensive. Now I know why. No one, but no one, decorates their ballroom with coloured lilies. I just don't know what I'm going to do....'

'You could try getting in touch with an importer direct,' James suggested, as he inspected the navy-and-maroon striped tie he was wearing.

He had a board meeting in the city this morning, and then he was having lunch with his uncle at his club. The old boy was slightly eccentric and rather frowned upon by the more conventional members of their family. James himself had expressed disapproval on more than one occasion over his uncle's behaviour; there had been that plan to sell off his family seat and allow the house to be converted into luxury apartments. James had assumed that, as his uncle's closest male relative, he would in the natural order of things inherit the place himself, and the very last role he saw for himself was that of landlord, no matter how wealthy his potential tenants.

'Really,' Helena went on, 'organising something like this birthday ball is so exhausting. And, of course, Plum has taken no interest whatsoever in it, nor offered me the slightest little bit of help.

'I really don't know why I'm bothering. She's just so un-grateful—after everything we've done for her! I was going to suggest she come with us to Florence, but—'

'Not a good idea,' James interrupted grimly. 'You know the problems we had the last time we holidayed *en famille*. I did not particularly enjoy having Signor Cavelleri complaining to me that my stepdaughter had seduced his son.'

Helena compressed her mouth. 'That's typical of her, of course.' Her expression registered acute distaste as she added tersely, 'It's her father's fault. He's the one she's inherited her . . . unfortunate tendencies from.'

He would have to change his tie, James decided. Over half the members of the board were ex-Guards and bound to think he was trying to imitate them. He knew how they looked down on a striped tie that did not have exclusive regimental status.

It still amazed him that a woman like his wife, who was fas-tidious in every single attitude she had, especially when it came to sex—prudish some might call her—could ever have been married to a man like Flyte MacDonald, whose appetite for the pleasures of the flesh was uninhibitedly gargantuan. Even now, on the rare occasion when James and Helena did have sex, she insisted on wearing her nightdress and having the lights out. Not that he minded. There was, in his opinion, something rather suspect about a woman who enjoyed sex. One certainly did not wish to marry such a woman, or to have her closely related to one.

He had scrupulously distanced himself from the problems Plum had caused her mother as she grew up. She was not, after all, his daughter, and it was not up to him to attempt to correct or discipline her.

He and Helena had both been in complete agreement that the best environment for her was a strict, all-girl boarding school. Her turbulent, troublesome presence under their roof had strained his temper to its limits, and he had been determined that his own daughters be protected from her influence. Which was why, instead of following her to boarding school, they attended small, private day schools. That way he could monitor their friendships and forestall any tendencies they might develop to follow in their halfsister's footsteps.

Like Helena, he was inclined to believe that the genes responsible for Plum's outrageous behaviour had been inherited from her unpredictable and outrageous father.

'I still haven't got the final numbers in.' Helena continued to fret as James changed his tie and walked back into their bedroom. 'And, of course, Flyte hasn't bothered to reply.'

'Flyte?' he queried, frowning.

'Yes, Plum insisted on inviting him. I know he's her father, but honestly, you'd think that since you and I are paying for everything and he hasn't even offered to contribute a single penny and it isn't that he can't afford it . . . I read in the *Times* only the other day that he'd been offered a fortune by some American collector for one of his pieces.

The thought of his immaculate, cool-blooded wife in the arms of that hirsute, unabashedly and unashamedly oversexed bear of a man made him feel acutely uncomfortable. As a result, the subject of her previous marriage was not one that they often discussed. He shared and applauded Helena's belief that it was an aberration best ignored.

'Typical of him not to reply. Now I'll have to go round and see him. Otherwise Plum will try to make a big issue out of the whole thing and complain publicly that he wasn't invited. I can't understand why he continues to live in that ridiculously small house when he could afford something far better.

'It's quite absurd how famous and sought after he's become. Plum was saying that there's ever talk of a royal commission.'

James was still frowning. Flyte MacDonald was the last person he wanted to see at Plum's coming-of-age party, even if he was her father. He opened his mouth to tell Helena that he refused to have her ex-husband as a guest at a ball he was paying for when Helena, guessing what was coming, neatly forestalled him, adding with apparent casualness, 'Of course, I suppose it could look as though we were being petty, or even worse as though we were afraid of him in some way, if we *didn't* invite him. It's quite the done thing these days for ex's to be included in family celebrations.'

Helena was a woman who had learned the hard way that to oversell something was often counter-productive. She had not been married to James for close on fifteen years without knowing the way his mind worked. If Plum had displayed the tell-tale signs of having inherited her father's notorious sexuality before she and James had married, Helena doubted that the marriage would ever have taken place.

James was a man who took his responsibilities seriously. Through their marriage, Plum was now one of those responsibilities. She knew how much Plum's behaviour offended and angered him. As a child, Plum had stubbornly refused all his efforts to make friends with her.

The trouble with Plum was that she enjoyed causing trouble and ill-feeling, Helena acknowledged now. She had no sense of control or self-restraint, no respect for convention. If Plum hurt, she didn't endure the pain in stoical, stiff-upper-lipped silence; instead she screamed it to the world delighting in the noise and the pandemonium that followed.

She was so totally removed from the kind of daughter Helena had expected to have, so unlike her other two daughters, that sometimes in the dark early-morning hours of the night when her normal tight grip on her thoughts and her reactions was slightly suspended, she wondered if somehow she had left hospital with the wrong child, if by some miracle it could be proved that Plum was not hers, and that therefore she was not in any way responsible for her, not in any way to blame for the problems she caused them all.

However, with daylight came reality. Plum might not have anything of Helena in her but she was quite definitely Flyte's child.

In a boy such excesses might—just—have been acceptable; deplored, of course, and controlled as best one could, but boys were a different species from girls and permitted a certain licence and indulgence.

But Plum was not a boy. Plum was—Plum was unfortunately Plum.

'Yes, you're right,' she heard James saying. 'I suppose we have no alternative other than to invite him.'

'Don't worry,' Helena reassured him. 'I intend to call round this morning and see him just to make sure that he just doesn't turn up . . . with someone unsuitable. . . .'

She paused as she looked across at James.

'One of his women, you mean,' he guessed. 'If he's likely to do something like that, then . . .'

'I'm sure he won't,' Helena soothed. 'After all, he would look just as bad if he did something to embarrass Plum as we would.'

'Embarrass Plum?' James gave her an astonished look. 'Impossible. She's more likely to revel in the fuss it would cause.'

'I mean from a public point of view, not a private one,' Helena told him.

'Well, you know best, but I can't say I'm altogether happy at the thought of him being here.'

Helena wasn't either, but she was even less happy at the thought of Plum throwing a temper tantrum.

'He is my father, after all, and not James,' Plum had pointed out when she had first demanded he be invited. 'Even if you and James would both prefer to pretend that your marriage to my father never existed. I bet you wish you could forget me just as easily, don't you?'

Helena had refused to respond. After all, she had heard many, many variations on this particular argument all through her second marriage.

'It is James who is paying for your ball and not your father,' she had pointed out coldly, ignoring Plum's petulant expression.

'*My* ball . . . that's a joke,' Plum had retaliated. 'It's not me you're doing it for. I don't even want the damn thing. You're just doing it so that you can show off to your friends and James's.

'Well, it's true, isn't it? How many of *my* friends have been invited, the people *I* know and want? It's all your friends, James's friends . . . people you want to impress.'

'I wasn't aware that *you* had any friends,' had been Helena's freezing response. 'At least none that possess both a dinner suit and some modicum of social adeptness.'

'If you don't invite Daddy, then I'm not coming,' Plum informed her. 'Anyway, he's much richer than any of your friends, and more fun too.'

Once in stride there was no stopping Plum. Old arguments, old grievances were dragged out and trailed deliberately in front of her, Helena recognised. And as always the more heated and emotional Plum became the more Helena found herself withdrawing from her.

'I don't know why you ever insisted on having custody of me,' Plum yelled furiously at her, her face flushed, her impossible tangle of curls almost standing up on end.

'You've never loved me or wanted me. You and James couldn't wait to get rid of me, send me to boarding school.'

'You're being ridiculous,' Helena had told Plum icily, but it was true, of course. She *had* never loved her, not wanted her; Plum's conception had been a mistake, the unwelcome and unpalatable visible confirmation of Helena's own lack of self-control, of the extraordinary physical effect Flyte had had on her—an effect which she had resented and which ultimately had led to the breakdown of their marriage.

The sexuality which Flyte had brought to life within her had been an aspect of herself which had filled her with loathing and disgust, and the knowledge that Plum was the direct result of her inability to control the sexual frenzy Flyte generated within her had prejudiced her against the child even before her birth.

Had Plum turned out to be a different kind of child...*her* child rather than Flyte's, things might have been different; she might eventually have been able to forget how she had been conceived.

It had taken a good deal of self-control and patience to persuade Plum to agree to this ball, which was not, as Plum had so succinctly guessed, really for her benefit at all.

To throw a ball for one's offspring's coming of age was the done thing in the circles in which Helena and James moved. They could not completely turn their backs on Plum and dissociate themselves from her without causing a good deal of speculation and gossip.

It didn't matter that almost everyone in their circle knew, or had heard, about Plum's outrageous behaviour. Nor that Helena had, on countless occasions, had to grit her teeth and appear to be grateful for the sympathy of other women whose daughters were models of perfection and saintliness. While she continued to give Plum her long-suffering support, she was recognised and acknowledged as a wonderful mother; if she turned her back on her . . .

Alongside her deepest wish concerning Plum's future ran her darkest fear. The former was that impossibly Plum would meet some suitable young man who would fall so desperately in love with her that he would insist on marrying her before he realised the truth about her. The latter was that Plum would triumphantly announce that she was pregnant and that she had no idea what was the name—or the colour—of the child's father. She knew the fear was more likely to be fulfilled than the wish.

Plum had known exactly why it was so important that they hold this ball, and predictably, she had used that knowledge. Not because she particularly wanted her father there, but because she knew how much Helena did not. And it was for precisely that reason that Flyte was likely to accept.

And if he did accept there was the problem of where to seat him. It would have to be at the top table, unfortunately. And since she did not want any hitch in her carefully arranged table plan, she was going to have to call round and find out what his intentions were.

There was no point in telephoning. Flyte loathed the instrument. Once when they had been making love and the phone had started to ring, she had insisted on going to answer it. It was, after all, the middle of the afternoon. Flyte had been so furious that he had taken the instrument from her, ripped its wires from the socket and thrown it down the lavatory.

She had been the one, though, who had had to explain to both the plumber and the telephone engineer what had happened.

Helena was not given to introspection or self-analysis or to thoughts of retribution and persecution. Such indulgence would have run counter to the ethics of her class, for one thing, and to her nature for another. But there were times when she felt as though everything that Plum was, everything she did, was designed to cause her mother the maximum amount of embarrassment and irritation.

Take this ridiculous crush Plum claimed to have on Bram, for instance. Bram of all men. Bram, who she herself . . .

She frowned briefly at her reflection in the mirror as she clipped on her gold-rimmed pearl earrings. Real, of course, and on clips, since in her youth pierced ear lobes were something one associated with a certain class of women and foreigners.

'You won't forget that we've got the Hacketts coming for dinner, will you?' she reminded James as she firmly pushed away the thought which had been about to form at the back of her mind.

In many ways, like Flyte, Bram too belonged to the past, but whereas Flyte was someone Helena preferred to forget she had ever known, never mind married, Bram was a friend she was proud to acknowledge.

'No,' James assured her, 'I intend to keep lunch with Uncle Bertie as short as possible.'

As he came towards her, Helena dutifully inclined her cheek for his kiss.

She had made up her mind she would marry James when, after their sixth date, he had still not made a move to get her into bed, and it was a decision she had never regretted.

They were physically, emotionally and intellectually similar, both possessing the long, narrow bone structure of the British upper classes, the pale, fine hair and the equally pale blue eyes. They were often referred to as a good-looking couple. Helena was not a woman who followed fashion—she considered herself above all that sort of thing—but appearance *was* important to her, as was creating the right impression, projecting the right kind of image.

She smiled as she saw the approval in James's eyes as he looked at her reflection in the mirror.

The pearls she was wearing had been his wedding present to her. She wore them virtually every day, apart from the month-long holiday they took in Tuscany every summer. Her wedding ring was a plain gold band, old and worn since it had originally been James's grandmother's. Her engagement ring was a triple twist of stones which had come from the same source, and fell just satisfactorily short of being vulgarly large.

Helena's hair, skilfully lightened from mouse to a more flattering beige, was kept just long enough for her to twist into an elegant knot in the nape of her neck. With the number of formal occasions she and James were called upon to attend, a shorter style would have been impossible. Long hair worn up was a must for women in her social circle, and already her two younger daughters wore theirs past shoulder length, confined by the ubiquitous Sloane hair band.

Her shirt was silk and several years old, and like her hair and the skirt she was wearing, it was a neutral beige. Her, make-up was as discreet and controlled as everything else about her.

Helena had everything in life that she had ever wanted—her family, her husband, her home, her charity work, her friends. A lifestyle that many would envy. And yet sometimes, when she caught sight of herself unexpectedly in the mirror, she was confused by the haunted expression she saw in her eyes.

Plum's fault, of course, the one remaining wild, out-of-control element in her otherwise safe, controlled world.

14

—▶ ◀—

'Jay, what are you doing here?' Bram asked as his son walked towards him across the busy hotel foyer.

'Everything go all right with the minister?' Jay asked, ignoring his question. 'You did get my message about the extra appointment, didn't you? It could open up a whole new market for us if we get involved in designing programs for Eurocrats.'

'Perhaps,' Bram conceded. 'Although I'm afraid your optimism is a little premature. As yet, the minister doesn't seem to have too clear an idea of what role, if any, we could ultimately play.' Bram paused, studying his son thoughtfully. He had gained the impression during his earlier appointment that the meeting could quite easily have been put off until a future date, the discussion being more exploratory than anything else. Knowing his son, Bram had the distinct feeling that Jay was up to something, operating by a hidden agenda which would be designed to benefit Jay and no one else—certainly not Bram.

'I don't suppose you fancy a couple of days' fishing with me?' Jay asked casually. 'There's that place in the Gironde where you used to take me.'

'Which you said you hated,' Bram reminded him dryly. 'And Strasboug is hardly en route to the Gironde.'

'No,' Jay agreed, smiling, shrugging his shoulders as he added with apparent sincerity, 'It's okay, I do understand. It was just a thought, but obviously you're keen to get back to Taylor. She sends her love, by the way.'

'You've seen Taylor?' Bram demanded, frowning.

'Yes. I called round on the off chance last night, cap in hand, dressed in sackcloth and ashes and bearing an olive branch, so to speak, but she was just on her way out.'

'Taylor was going out?' Bram's frown deepened as he ignored the first part of Jay's speech, even though it was oddly out of character for his son to behave in such a generous and warm-spirited way to someone whom he considered to be his opponent.

'Yes. A friend was taking her to Quaglino's, she said. She didn't introduce us. I expect she was worried that they might lose their table if they were late,' he added carelessly.

'Now, about that fishing trip, you don't have to make up your mind right now. Why don't we have lunch and you can update me with what the minister had to say. New business is, after all, my area of responsibility.'

'*You* were the one who arranged the meeting,' Bram reminded him.

Taylor going out to dinner with a man? It seemed so out of character. He wasn't even aware that she knew any men other than Anthony and himself. He caught himself as he recognised how idiotic such thoughts were. Of course, she was bound to know other men; he, after all, knew other women. But Taylor was not like him. She was, in fact, not like anyone else that he knew; she guarded her privacy and was openly reluctant to let anyone of either sex into her life. Alongside the sharp flare of jealousy was an equally strong, if not stronger, sense that the image that Jay had portrayed not only jarred but just did not ring true.

He gave his son an assessing look. Jay was in a remarkably good humour. Too good perhaps.

As a child, Jay had deliberately and openly tried to sabotage every relationship Bram had. In more recent years, there had been no close relationships in Bram's life for Jay to feel a need to destroy, until now . . . until Taylor.

Surely Jay had understood when he banned him from the house until he apologised to Taylor that this time, things were different. That this time and for the first time he intended to put his own needs and those of the woman he loved before those of his son.

'He won't give you up easily,' Taylor had warned him sombrely one evening when they had been talking about the situation. 'That kind never do.'

And her eyes had been haunted, full of dark shadows and tightly controlled fear.

He had hated knowing that he was responsible for that fear and had instantly reassured her that there was no way he would ever let Jay come between them.

'He'll always be your son,' Taylor had said, her voice and her eyes remote. 'Nothing can change that.'

'Yes,' he had agreed quietly, 'and you will always be the woman I love.

'As my son, Jay will always have a place in my life and in my heart, but he's an adult now, not a child. One day he will fall in love, marry. . .have a child or children of his own. Then, hopefully, he'll feel differently. . . understand.'

Taylor had given a small, fierce shiver. 'I pity the woman he does love,' she had told Bram. 'He's too possessive. . . too obsessive. . . .'

Her voice had stumbled slightly over the last word.

Now as he watched his son, the tiny cold grain of suspicion grew and hardened into an icy lump of conviction. Jay was up to something, he was sure of it.

Jay had only one aim in life and that was to control absolutely everything and everyone around him. Because he believed it gave him power, when in fact—

Jay had turned away from Bram and was studying a girl walking across the hotel foyer. It wasn't anger he should be feeling towards his son, Bram recognised tiredly. It was pity.

'So, shall we have lunch?' Jay turned back towards him.

Bram shook his head. 'I'm sorry, Jay, I've got to go.' He glanced at his watch. 'I've got some calls to make.'

'What about our fishing trip.' Jay was frowning now, his mouth starting to harden.

'*Your* fishing trip,' Bram corrected him gently. '*I* can't make it, I'm afraid. I have other commitments . . . other priorities in my life.'

He didn't trust himself to say more. Suddenly, he badly wanted to hear Taylor's voice to reassure himself that she was all right.

He turned his back on Jay and walked away. He hated feeling this way about his son, suspicious of the motives behind what he said or did.

* * *

Helena parked her car outside her ex-husband's Chelsea home, and hesitated for a few seconds, then got out.

As she walked past a statue of writhing figures in Flyte's garden, she automatically averted her eyes. A thin mousy-haired girl, whom Helena guessed to be Flyte's latest housekeeper cum secretary, eventually answered the door. She chewed nervously at the ends of her untidy hair as Helena explained that she wanted to see Flyte.

'He's working at the moment,' the girl told her.

Working? Helena doubted it. Flyte was a night owl, his mornings spent either in bed or slumped over a mug a bitter black coffee, liberally laced with whisky. That was just one of the unsociable habits she had not been able to cure him of.

The hallway smelled of dust and stale air. Flyte's studio was built on the back of the house, but the dust from his work filtered everywhere, leaving a fine grey film over everything.

Helena shook her head fastidiously as the girl suggested that she could wait in the sitting room. The sitting room was a small dark room at the front of the house that no one ever used, furnished with a haphazard collection more suited to a junk yard than someone's home. Helena certainly wasn't going to risk either her pristine person or equally pristine clothes in it.

'I'll wait here,' she told the girl with icy authority. 'And you can...'

The sound of female giggles and protesting shrieks accompanied by the familiar booming bass of her ex-husband's voice interrupted. Two sets of female giggles, she observed with distaste, as the door in the passage to the studio opened and Flyte strode through. He was followed by two extraordinarily beautiful, wraithlike young women with Pre-Raphaelite haloes of dark brown curls and startlingly sapphire eyes set in matchlessly perfect and matching faces. Twins, and from the looks of them, not much older than Plum. Helena doubted that Flyte's interest was the least bit paternal. But it was the girl who had let Helena in who blushed when Flyte fondled the breast of the twin he was embracing with his left arm, while turning to kiss the one on his right.

'Same time tonight, girls,' he told them as he finally released them. 'Don't forget.'

'You can stop looking at me so disapprovingly, Helena,' he added as the mousy girl ushered the twins to the front door. 'My interest in them is entirely professional. They're models.'

'I've come to talk to you about Plum's coming-of-age ball,' Helena told him coldly, ignoring his comment.

She knew very well that Flyte considered it a perk of his work to have sex with his female models, a fact which had caused her horrified disbelief when she had first discovered it, six months into their marriage. She had walked into his studio one afternoon and discovered him very energetically and noisily engaged in oral sex with the wife of his then current patron.

What had made matters worse was that neither of them had appeared to be the least bit embarrassed at being caught in such a vulgar act of unfaithfulness.

As Flyte had reluctantly removed himself from between her thighs, his partner, as shameless as he, had simply lain there watching Helena triumphantly, her thick bush starting to dry and curl in the studio's heat as she mocked Helena.

'You should try it some time, Helena. Your husband is really the best pussy licker I've ever known.'

She had been pregnant with Plum then, otherwise she would have left him straight away. That night, when he had tried to repeat on her the intimate caress she had witnessed him giving the other woman, she had clamped her legs together, hissing at him that he was never to touch her like that again.

He had laughed at her, ignoring her anger and her refusal, touching her, teasing her until . . .

A hot surge of shock jolted through Helena's body, her face burning now with the embarrassment she had not betrayed earlier. Fortunately, Flyte had his back to her as he led the way to his studio, where he told her they could discuss things more comfortably.

As he opened the door and stepped back to allow her to precede him into the studio, Helena was immediately swept back in time by the unforgettable smell of stone and dust intensified by the heat in which Flyte always insisted on working; mingled with the fruity smell of the red wine which he drank as though it was water, and the unmistakable scent of Flyte's sweat and his sex.

Helena faltered on the threshold as she fought not to breathe in the heady atmosphere.

She remembered the first time she had visited Flyte's studio, which in those days was in a run-down terraced house in London's East End. Then, too, she had been immediately and fastidiously aware of the strong, raw smell of the studio. Fatally, in direct counterpoint, had run a strong dangerous chord of sexual excitement.

They had met at a party. He had been, if not drunk, then certainly intoxicated, and the friend giving the party had asked her if she would give him a lift home. Reluctantly, she had done so. She shuddered now, not wanting to remember what had followed.

She had not been a virgin when she met Flyte. She was in her twenties, after all, a university graduate with a high-powered city job in a firm of commodity brokers owned by a friend of her father.

Fresh from a humiliating defeat at the hands of Jay, then a repulsively over-mature eight-year-old, she had attended the party in an attempt to make Bram jealous.

'You want my father to have sex with you and make you pregnant so that he'll marry you,' Jay had accused her in the flat hard childish voice she had come to loathe.

'But he doesn't want to go to bed with you. Anyway, he's already going to bed with someone else. I've heard them. She makes a lot of noise. She screams and . . .'

Never in her whole life had Helena felt such an urge to take hold of a child and physically hurt it. She had had to walk out of the room to prevent herself from doing so. She loathed and detested Jay almost as much as she craved and wanted his father.

She didn't need Jay to tell her that much as Bram liked her as a friend, he did not desire her. And she certainly didn't need him to lay bare her fragile dreams that one day Bram would turn to her, not in lust and desire . . . perhaps not even in love. But maybe, just maybe, in need, and from that need . . .

It was a dream she had cherished ever since their days at university together; a secret . . . which Jay had now made her see in the cruel light of reality.

And so she had met Flyte and taken him home, and he had seduced her with rough red wine and even rougher lovemaking, which had ripped away all her preconceptions about her sexual self and which had made her scream quite certainly every bit as loudly and pleasurably as Bram's envied lover.

She had never meant it to be anything other than an affair, and neither, she suspected, had Flyte. But then one night, totally out of the blue, he had told her that he wanted to marry her, and if necessary force her to agree by impregnating her with his child.

Drunk on wine and sex, and the drugging pleasure of being so intensely physically wanted, so physically in need of the strong powerful thrust of his body within her own, she had accepted. Her family, of course, had been horrified, but stubbornly she had refused to change her mind.

The memories were like a raw, ulcerated spot that refused to heal and which, fatalistically, she could not resist touching.

A fierce shudder of disgust ran through her as she caught sight of the half-finished sculpture in one corner of the studio.

Two naked girls, long-limbed with full rounded breasts and swollen pubic mounds, as sensually flushed and pouting as their open mouths, were draped with sexual abandon around the figure of a solitary male. The threesome, despite the solidity of the stone, managed to convey a writhing, excited mass of rampant sexuality. One of the girl's hands was reaching for the man's erect penis while the man suckled the breast of the other girl; his hand positioned as though just about to slip between her open legs. Despite the slenderness of the girls' bodies and the fact that Flyte had sculpted them without any body hair, it was obvious that they were fully adult and sexually aware—and equally obvious who had modelled for them—and for the man.

She had known immediately that Flyte and his twin models had been lovers—it was the kind of situation Flyte delighted in.

'Like it?' he taunted her now, knowing full well what her reaction would be. 'It's a private commission—a man who's made millions from renting out soft porn videos. He said that this was every man's most basic soft porn fantasy, to be serviced by two women at the same time. I did try to find a set of triplets. I thought it would give the whole thing a certain extra licentious appeal, and besides . . .'

Helena knew from experience what was coming next.

Angrily she averted her gaze from the sculpture, her mouth compressed as she heard Flyte's soft mocking laughter.

'You might fool everyone else with that tight-lipped look of disgust, Helena, but not me. I know the real you—remember? The Helena who moans and screams and begs for more, who claws a man's back until she draws blood, who makes him—'

'Stop it! Stop it!' Helena could feel the tension building up inside her. She knew he was manipulating her, tormenting her, forcing her to concede control of the situation to him. She had never liked losing control . . . which was why . . .

'Remember how it was between us?' Flyte was saying softly now, as he nodded towards a dusty shabby-looking sofa pushed into the far corner of the room. 'Remember how we—'

'No, I don't remember,' Helena lied frantically. 'I don't *want* to remember.' It was anger that was making her heart beat so fast, that was all. . . . She knew perfectly well that Flyte had no more desire for her than she had for him; that he was simply trying to torment her because he was that kind of man.

'I could always refresh your memory for you,' she heard him saying silkily. 'In fact—'

'I haven't come here to discuss the past, Flyte,' Helena managed to interrupt, at the same time strategically placing herself closer to the door and further away from him. She thought her subtle movement had gone unnoticed until she saw the look in his eye.

'Do you ever think of me when you're in bed with that dull worthy husband of yours, Helena?' he asked softly.

'No, I don't,' she returned furiously, finally losing her temper with him. 'In fact—'

'What? You don't do anything as physically intimate as having sex? No, I don't expect you do.'

'Will you stop this?' Helena demanded. If he was being like this now, what on earth would he be like at Plum's ball?

Having him there would be like having an unexploded bomb in the room. Flyte could be the most charming man anyone could hope to meet when he chose, out-sophisticating everyone else in sight, making even the starchiest society matriarchs melt when he wished. But he could also be so destructively cruel that he could inflict razor-sharp wounds that could never heal.

'All I want to know is, do you intend to come to Plum's coming-of-age ball?'

'Ah yes, of course. Who else is going?' he asked her carelessly. 'Or can I guess...? Certainly not any of Plum's friends from what she's told me.'

'Plum doesn't *have* any friends,' Helena responded bitterly. 'All Plum has in her life is a succession of men who—'

'All...? What about her family? Her stepfather...her mother?' Flyte asked her smoothly.

Unable to hold his gaze Helena looked away from it. 'Naturally we've invited the family,' she told him stiffly. 'Both James's and mine. And our friends, and then, of course, there are certain social obligations one has to fulfil, and certain business associations...'

'My God, no wonder Plum says she doesn't want to go. You'd be better off giving her the money and—'

'And what?' Helena asked him bitterly. 'You might not care that our daughter has the habits and reputation of a...of a whore...but I do. She isn't going to be this age for ever. She needs—'

'She needs what, Helena? A husband who'll imprison her in the kind of life you think is best for her? Pity it isn't still possible to immure rebellious problematic daughters conveniently in convents, eh? What Plum needs is love. That's L-O-V-E, just in case you aren't familiar with the word, but then of course I know that you aren't,' Flyte accused acidly.

'Poor little sod, she hasn't had much of a life, has she? Our fault of course. We—'

'How dare you say that!' Helena interrupted angrily. 'She's had everything...*everything* any girl could possibly want.'

'Liar. She's had nothing. Oh, materially, you might have showered her with guilt gifts, but emotionally, physically, you've given fuck all, and it shows.'

'Are you saying that it's my fault that her behaviour is so outrageous? Because if you are...'

'It's *both* our faults,' Flyte silenced her by saying quietly. 'We're *both* responsible for her conception, Helena, *both* of us. And we're both responsible for what she is . . . or is not, though I've no doubt that *you* don't see it that way. In *your* eyes all her faults . . . her flaws are down to me.

'I'll tell you something, though. I'd say she's got a hell of a lot more going for her than those whey-faced passionless, personality-less girls James gave you.'

'You would think that,' Helena replied coldly. Inside she was shaking with anger.

She wished she had never come here, that she had flatly refused to even entertain the idea of allowing Plum to invite her father to the ball.

'You really don't want me at this affair at all, do you?' Flyte asked her mockingly, reading her mind with amused accuracy.

'You're Plum's father,' Helena said tightly.

'Oh yes, I'm her father and she wants me there, she's already told me that. Will Bram Soames be going?'

'Bram *has* been invited,' Helena agreed carefully. 'He is, after all, one of our oldest friends.'

'One of *your* oldest friends,' Flyte corrected.

It had always been a sore point between them, her friendship with Bram, not because Flyte did not like Bram—he did—but because . . .

'There, at least, Plum is very much your daughter. Odd, isn't it, how we do burden our offspring with the curse of our own weaknesses.'

'I haven't the faintest idea what you're talking about, Flyte,' Helena said crushingly. 'And since I'm already running late . . .'

'Oh, yes, you do,' Flyte corrected her fiercely. 'I'm referring to the fact that our daughter, *your* daughter, believes herself to have a god-almighty crush on Bram Soames. . . . And she's not the only one, is she? *Is* she, Helena?'

'Bram is a friend,' Helena told him woodenly, 'and if—'

'And if what? If on our honeymoon you cried out his name while you lay in my arms . . . that means nothing. Is that what you're going to tell me?'

Helena had had enough.

'All right,' she admitted, white-faced, her eyes blazing with a mixture of exhaustion and pain. 'Yes, I loved Bram . . . but that was all a long time ago.'

'And he never reciprocated your feelings. Poor Helena... You certainly tried hard enough to make him. But then, of course, you did have some pretty powerful opposition. Never underestimate the power of a determined self-obsessed child who believes he has sole claim on his parent's emotions and life. A child like Jay.'

'Jay was never a child,' Helena snapped. 'He was a . . .'

'A what? An incubus,' Flyte replied mockingly. 'Poor Helena—and poor Bram, although I understand from Plum that Jay has relaxed his grip on Bram's life enough for Bram to find himself someone—and a very special someone, too, if Plum is to believed.'

Helena looked away from him.

'Plum always was inclined to exaggerate things and overdramatise. I don't imagine that this woman is anything more than a business acquaintance of Bram's.'

'Don't you? Why not? Because to do so would be too painful? Would it arouse too many uncomfortable memories of a Helena you don't want to admit ever existed, a Helena who knew what it was to feel real emotion, real need. You can't suppress her for ever, Helena. One day the real you is going to prove too strong for the control you exercise over her, and when she does . . .'

'I'm not listening to any more of this. I *am* the real Helena,' Helena told him angrily. 'The other Helena . . . the other . . .' She stopped, folding her mouth into a forbidding line. What was she doing, allowing him to goad her like this to . . . to . . . ?

'The other Helena what?' Flyte taunted. 'Never existed? Oh yes, she did . . . and I could take you to bed right now and prove her existence to you. Would you like that, Helena? Is that—'

'No, I would not like it,' Helena denied furiously. 'And—'

'But if it was Bram standing here making you the same offer, you wouldn't be saying no, would you?' Flyte asked softly.

He had tricked her, trapped her, and he knew it, Helena acknowledged as she stood staring at him, unable to force herself to make the denial she knew she ought to make.

It was all Plum's fault that she was here being subjected to Flyte's taunting and goading. There was nothing he enjoyed more than provoking people.

'I've got to go,' she said stiffly. 'I need to have final numbers for the ball by the weekend so that the table plans can be drawn up, and . . .'

'Oh, I shall definitely be coming,' Flyte assured her carelessly. 'I wouldn't miss it for the world. Where will you seat me, I wonder, Helena? What do the etiquette books suggest in such circumstances?

'The top table? Or am I to be banished to the Siberian wastes of some dark, shadowed corner. It will be interesting to see where Bram is to sit.'

'Bram is Plum's godfather. Naturally, he will be seated at the top table,' Helena informed him coldly. 'And now, if you'll excuse me, I really must go. . . .'

Her voice might sound cold, but she knew that her face was hot, like her body, like her churning, chaotic emotions.

Bram . . . Even now, after all these years . . .

She could still remember the first time she had seen him across the university quadrangle, the sunlight burning his hair so that he seemed to be standing in a halo of golden warmth, like some young warrior god newly come down to earth. She had been reading Classics, a serious-minded, serious-looking young woman who had thought she knew exactly what would happen in her life.

A degree, a career, marriage to some suitable young man, two children, a house in the country as well as a base in London, holidays in Tuscany, winter dinner parties; in short, a solid, safe, upper-middle-class lifestyle.

And then she had seen Bram and fallen in love.

But Bram had not loved her in return. Oh, he had liked her well enough, had liked her and been kind to her. He might even have taken pity on her enough to take her to bed, from where she would have worked hard to ensure that she remained there. Bram, being the man he was, would have been far too soft-hearted to have ever ejected her from it. Eventually, they would have married; she would have had his children. . . .

But she had not taken account of Jay.

She had done everything she could to persuade Bram that it was in the boy's own interest for him to be brought up by someone else. By anyone else, just so long as it was not Bram himself.

She had cited numerous examples of Jay's appalling behaviour to support her claim that he needed a different kind of environment and upbringing than the one Bram could provide. But to no avail. Jay had retained his ironclad, suffocating grip on Bram's life.

Throughout the years, Bram had maintained the bonds of friendship she had initially forged as a ramp from which to fight for a more intimate relationship. After her disastrous marriage to Flyte and the far more successful one to James which had succeeded it, she had told herself that she no longer desired Bram; that their friendship was enough, because she had finally had to accept that was all there could ever be; that the moment when she might have turned the balance of their burgeoning relationship in her own favour had gone.

She was, she assured herself as she drove away from Chelsea, perfectly content in her marriage and in her life. Or at least she would have been if it were not for the problems that Plum constantly caused her.

If Bram had at last found someone to share his life, then she was glad for him . . . as a friend should be . . . if Jay was prepared to allow that someone to remain in his father's life—which she doubted.

It was none of her business, she reminded herself starkly, except that she and Bram were old friends, and *as* an old friend she was naturally concerned for him . . . and curious about this new woman in his life. It would be only good manners for her to get in touch with Bram and to extend the invitation to Plum's birthday ball to include his . . . friend.

But not today. She already had the beginning of a tension headache and her hair desperately needed trimming and retouching with colour. Bram had always been the kind of man who noticed how a woman looked, who paid genuine compliments and made genuinely concerned enquiries if he thought something might be wrong.

Bram . . . Bram. . . . Bram. . . . She braked just in time to avoid driving a through a red light, her face flushing in mortification as she realised what she was doing.

15

Taylor had asked the taxi driver to wait. The telephone in the apartment was still connected, but she needed the security of knowing that if she chose she could just turn round and walk away. Walk away... or run?

Her throat was tight with tension as she inserted the key in the lock, the new lock that Bram had had fitted for her.

The air inside the apartment tasted stale and unlived in. It held a faint chemical smell, which she realised must come from the professionally cleaned carpets and curtains. Something else Bram had organised.

As she hesitated in the doorway to the sitting room the first thing Taylor noticed was the empty space where her sofa had originally been. The insurance company had agreed to cover the cost of everything that had been damaged or destroyed. But Taylor had not given any thought to replacing anything. Living with Bram, cocooned from reality by the protective warmth of his love, there had been no need to do so. No need and certainly no desire.

The very thought of coming back to live here now, after what had happened, made her feel queasily cold, her eyes lifting instinctively to the locked windows, her heart starting to flutter in panic.

After the comforting lived-in clutter and warmth of Bram's home, the apartment felt barren and inhospitable. The moment she stepped into the room a feeling of claustrophobic fear engulfed her, paralysing her so that she could neither advance nor flee.

Oddly, Taylor found the atmosphere even more menacing now than she had done on the night of the break-in. Then she had had shock to protect her from some of the terrors of her own imagination; now she did not. It was all too easy to picture the intruder stalking her, watching her, waiting.

The door to her bedroom was open. She could see inside it. The bed was almost corpse-like with its plain white single covering; her bedding had been destroyed, but even if it hadn't . . .

Her skin started to crawl. Already she could sense the terror waiting for her, a yawning black chasm, its mouth reaching greedily towards her, wanting to suck her down into its dark, destructive vortex. A living hell from which she might never escape.

Before the break-in, the moment she was inside the flat she would lock the doors and windows, close the curtains, to hide herself away from the outside, prying eyes of the world; now, she was even more terrified of the opposite, of being locked away in here with it . . . with him. . . . She could almost smell him, feel him, see him. . . .

The front door, which she had left open, suddenly swung closed.

She tried to scream, but she couldn't. She was suffocating . . . drowning, dying in the thick, black fog of terror that engulfed her.

And then she heard Bram's voice.

She was laughing and crying as he held her in his arms, apologising for frightening her, telling her that he had cut his stay in Strasbourg short because he hadn't been able to be away from her any longer.

'But how did you know I was here?'

'I just knew,' Bram told her huskily, holding her even more tightly in his arms.

He wasn't sure himself why he had had such a sudden and sharp conviction that he had to get home, breaking several appointments to do so. What he did know was that entering his house, empty of her presence, had been like walking into a graveyard, cold, empty, shadowed by a miasma of lost dreams and hopes.

'I had to come here. I wanted . . .' Taylor shivered, unable to tell him of her decision to end their relationship. Tears filled her eyes. She loved him so much. Needed him so much.

She murmured a soft protest against his mouth as his palm cupped her jaw, turning her face to meet his.

The feel of his mouth on hers was already so belovedly familiar; for her there could never be boredom or lack of excitement
in such familiarity. For her it could only enhance and enrich love,
giving it a depth and intensity that inwardly she had always
craved and needed.

Her mouth opened beneath his, welcoming the gentle stroke
of his tongue, her own returning the caress.

'Thank God, I found you.'

Bram looked as shocked by his words as she felt. Her heart
missed a beat. Had he known that she meant to leave, to disappear...?

Had she somehow conveyed her thoughts to him, subconsciously willed him to stop her?

'Let's go home,' Bram suggested softly, releasing her from his
arms but still holding on to her hand, his actions mirroring the
anxiety she could still see in his eyes.

Instinctively, she raised her free hand to his face, touching him
gently. To leave him now was an impossibility, she acknowledged achingly, as he turned his mouth into her palm and kissed
it passionately.

'Let's go home, Taylor,' he repeated urgently. 'I can't make love
to you here and . . .'

'No,' she agreed, suddenly shivering.

As Bram shepherded her towards the door, she said, 'I thought
you were supposed to be going fishing with Jay. He called to see
me on his way to the airport.'

She was proud of the way she managed not to let him see how
hurt she had been by his failure to tell her about his fishing trip.
Bram's grim 'Yes, I know' made her search his face curiously.

'I'll tell you all about it once we get home,' he added, as he
opened his car door for her, bending his head towards hers and
whispering in her ear, 'after we've made love. . . .'

They were lying in bed together, her body aching deliciously
from the fierce urgency of his lovemaking, when she suddenly
remembered the waiting taxi driver.

Bram laughed when she told him. 'He'll have gone by now,'
he assured her. 'Although I expect we'll get a pretty hefty bill. But

who cares...I've got far more important things on my mind right now than taxi fares.'

'I thought you were going to tell me about Jay and your fishing trip,' Taylor reminded him provocatively as he leaned over her and started kissing his way along her jaw and then down her neck.

'Later...' he promised, his glance resting lingeringly on the still flushed, temptingly erect nipple that was his goal.

The warmth of her breast against his palm was an erotically soft weight; he could feel her slight quiver as she felt the warmth of his breath against her skin.

It amazed and bemused him, this unexpected, unfamiliar, intense sexuality she aroused in him, not by doing anything, simply by being.

He felt the now familiar coiling arousal of his body as his mouth opened over Taylor's breast and he heard her swift indrawn gasp of pleasure followed by the tiny keening moan she made whenever he touched her like this.

By all the laws that governed such things, he should have already expended everything he had to expend. Emptied himself completely and totally inside her in that initial, mutually urgent bout of lovemaking which had left them both slick with sweat and breathing heavily. But this time, if anything, the emotion between them was even more intense. Her openness to him, his penetration of her, by some almost mystical combination were such that his body defied logic and reality not just to carry her through the hot, tight spasms of her orgasm, but to share it with her and to leave within her a single, unexpected powerful spurt of semen.

He felt her shudder as he ejaculated, her fingers digging into his flesh. At first he thought her reaction was caused by the fading pulse of her orgasm, until she told him, her eyes wet with tears, 'I felt that...I felt you come...it was...it felt like...'

When she stopped, he asked softly, 'It felt like what...?'

'It felt like you were right inside my womb,' she continued huskily, 'as though you were reaching out to the very deepest, most elemental part of me...as though...as though the two of us...'

As though the emotion of the moment was too much for her, she suddenly started to tremble. Wrapping her tightly in his arms, Bram tried to ease her away from what he could see was a painful intensity by teasing her. 'You're doing wonders for my ego.'

Bram held on to her. No need to ask her if she loved him, nor to tell her that he loved her—such words were superfluous, unnecessary.

Taylor's womb still ached from the intensity of her orgasms. Her emotions, like her skin, felt acutely sensitive and so responsive to him, so in need of him, that she felt she couldn't bear him out of her sight, never mind out of her life. She couldn't bear the thought of him being even a heartbeat away from her . . . of anything or anyone coming between them.

She tensed, remembering. 'You were going to tell me about Jay.'

'Yes,' he agreed. 'What exactly did he say to you when he came here?'

'He told me you'd telephoned him and that you'd asked him to fly out and join you for a fishing trip. He said . . .' She hesitated, not wanting to reveal the rest of Jay's conversation.

'He told *me* that he caught *you* just as you were on your way out to dinner with a friend,' Bram informed her dryly.

'He what? But that's not true.'

'Neither was what he told you about the fishing trip,' Bram explained. 'I should have guessed that he might do something like this . . . warned you, but I thought . . .'

'Divide and conquer,' Taylor suggested.

'It was one of his favourite tactics as a child. I don't understand him, Taylor,' he admitted. 'He's my son and I love him, but if he wasn't my child . . .' He shook his head.

Taylor reached out and touched him lovingly. It frightened her sometimes, this need she had to touch him and be close to him. She of all people, who had never, not even in the days before . . . not even as a child, been in any way a tactile person. Somehow Bram brought out a sensory hunger in her.

'I'm afraid he's still as determined as ever to try to come between us . . .' Taylor heard Bram saying.

'Yes,' she agreed. It would be so easy... so sensible to use the excuse Bram was unwittingly giving her. Bram would be hurt if she left. He would try to persuade her not to allow Jay to influence her, but in the end, he would accept her decision. Yes... it would be so easy—and so cowardly.

Which was her more damaging option—being a coward, or risking Bram discovering the truth?

'His behaviour is quite unforgivable,' Bram added. 'But for the moment at least, I think it would give us a little bit of breathing space if we simply said nothing rather than tax him with his deceit. What do you think? Am I being a coward? I know I should—'

'No, let's leave things as they are,' Taylor interrupted, placing her fingers against his chest. After all, who was she to preach morals to Bram when her own... And besides... She gave a tiny responsive shiver of pleasure as Bram started to kiss and then gently suck her fingertips, her heartbeat picking up and matching the quickened rhythm of his.

'Jay can't help the way he is,' she began unsteadily, 'and he's desperate, so . . .'

'I disagree. He *could* change, but he refuses to,' Bram replied tersely, the gentleness returning to his voice as he smiled into her eyes. He said, 'You're a very understanding and compassionate woman, Taylor.'

'Understanding, yes,' she allowed. Her voice was suddenly harshly stark as she added, 'But compassionate, no. Compassion is the last thing I feel for Jay, Bram.'

'Forget about Jay,' Bram ordered thickly as his hand cupped her breast and his eyes started to darken with desire. 'Tell me what you feel for me instead.'

'So, today's the day, is it?'

Fate raised her eyebrows with lofty disdain and asked in a puzzled voice, 'What day?' But there was a dimple of laughter beside her pursed mouth and her eyes gleamed with excitement and amusement as she shook her head at her father.

'It's only one interview out of dozens that I need to make. I doubt I'll even get to see Bram Soames himself. My appointment is with his PR representative.'

'Oh, I see, so the reason you were up half the night pacing up and down in your bedroom, talking to yourself, had nothing to do with preparing questions for this interview then? Ah, I've got it. You're rehearsing for a play, the young amateur dramatics....'

Caroline scolded them both as her husband expertly fielded the piece of toast Fate threw at him, determinedly repressing the comment that sprang to her lips as she surveyed her daughter. In her day a young woman hoping to make a good professional impression did not do so attired in a pair of jeans (albeit clean ones), one of her father's white cotton shirts and a well-worn soft tweed jacket, acquired from the same source. Nor would she have worn her hair in Fate's shiny mop of urchin curls, or her face, apparently free of any trace of make-up. In her day, a young woman in Fate's position would have aimed to look 'smart' and that would have meant wearing a neat, well-cut suit—with a modest knee-length skirt, tights and polished shoes, a silk shirt and, perhaps, if one was frightfully self-confident, a pair of plain gold or pearl earrings. An immaculate hairstyle and some attempt at make-up would also have been *de rigueur*.

Caroline sighed regretfully. Fate looked anything but a would-be professional woman. Fate looked...

As she surveyed her daughter Caroline felt her heart melt with love and pride. Fate might, at first glance, look little more than an unruly, untidy teenager, but Caroline had seen the second and third glances that men gave her daughter. The pursed, thoughtful look of other women reinforced the knowledge that there was no way that Fate was the kind of girl who could ever be constrained or compelled into a specific mould or image.

'What time do you have to be there?' Oliver was asking.

'My appointment is at twelve,' Fate said, wrinkling her nose slightly. 'I suppose that means that I'll have no chance of meeting the great man himself. He'll probably be out at some executive lunch somewhere.'

'Maybe if he was an executive,' Oliver agreed wryly, 'but he isn't. He's the self-made head of a successful business. They don't have time to waste on long, leisurely lunches.'

'What train are you planning to come back on?' Caroline asked.

'I'm not sure,' said Fate between bites of a fresh piece of toast.

'No doubt it all depends on whether or not Bram Soames invites her to join him for an executive lunch,' her father teased.

Pulling a face at him, Fate picked up her mug of coffee. 'It's no big deal, really,' she told her parents firmly. 'It's only a preliminary interview and once they realise what angle I want to take...'

'You don't know for sure yet that your interviews will confirm your view that success and wealth do not enhance the quality of their lives.'

'It isn't so much *their* quality of life—no doubt *they* will claim that they do. It's the effect they have on those people close to them, their wives, families.'

'You've set yourself a pretty formidable task,' her father pointed out dryly.

'It's a very worthwhile area of research,' Fate defended fiercely.

'There's nothing wrong in being idealistic,' Oliver told her gruffly. 'Not at your age at least.'

As Fate lowered her head to study a headline in the *Daily Telegraph*, he looked across the table towards Caroline. They were proud of her, this daughter of theirs, Caroline especially so. They had to fight hard not to be over-protective with her.

'I'll give you a lift to the station, if you like,' Oliver told Fate after he and Caroline shared their silent secret moment of love and pride over her bent head.

'Mmm... Thanks.'

She was their beautiful, shining link with the future, their hostage to fate.

Caroline gave a small shiver. Fate was so vibrant, so quiveringly joyously full of life and energy that she seemed totally invulnerable. Every bit of her glowed and it seemed impossible to imagine that anyone or anything could ever possibly want to hurt her.

Caroline blinked away threatened tears as Fate leaned across the table to hug her.

'Good luck,' Caroline whispered as she kissed her.

Jay was smiling as he pushed open the outer doors and walked into the Soames Computac foyer. He had returned from Strasbourg three days ago, and, so far, he was rather pleased with the result of his carefully sown seeds of potential destruction.

It was too early to tell how well the plants would flourish, and digging up the seeds before they had had a chance to germinate would negate all the hard work he had put in. At this stage, it was enough to know that Taylor looked tense and on edge, that she seemed to have lost weight.... His smile became unkind. A woman of her age could not afford to be too thin; it would make her look scraggy and old.

He had seen Taylor and his father walking down the corridor to Bram's office this morning and had silently rejoiced over the distance between them, the way Taylor had moved away from his father as Bram tried to close the distance between them.

She was, no doubt, still punishing him in that way that women had, for saying nothing to her about his supposed 'fishing trip'— giving him the silent treatment. In bed as well as out of it, Jay hoped. She was that type. Not for her an outburst of temper followed by furious accusations. No, she would keep her resentment, her anger to herself, and brood over them.

Once the affair was over, his father would soon come to realise what a lucky escape he had had. For now, Taylor might still be accompanying his father to work, sharing his office with him, encouraging him to waste his time on this charitable venture he was so keen on—his crusade, as Jay mockingly called it. But it wouldn't last.

It wasn't just for his own sake, or even his father's, that he had sown seeds of doubt, Jay told himself virtuously. There was the business to consider as well. Once Taylor had removed herself from his life, Jay had no doubts that his father would return his attention to where it rightly belonged.

And then, psychologically, it might also be a good time for him to press for a greater degree of power and control in the company, Jay decided, his eyes narrowing thoughtfully. A bit of judicious manipulation of their accountants, a few words dropped in the right ears about the possible consequences of his father's dalliance with his 'charitable venture,' the risks of leaving complete control of the business with one man. The need for a more youthful input, a hint that profits were falling, could only serve to add weight to his case. His mouth started to curl upwards, while the receptionist, who had watched his progress through the foyer with a wooden expression, allowed herself to breathe more easily.

Fate, early for her appointment and seated in the waiting area, had seen Jay come in and observed the receptionist's body language with interest. The young woman had greeted Fate warmly, but reacted quite differently to the man.

This man, whoever he was, was seriously mega-sexy. Not even the staidness of his city suit could disguise that body. And as for his face . . . those eyes . . . that incredibly sexy mouth—This guy was pure, hunky male sexuality and, on full charge, was likely to be responsible for serious knicker meltdown in every female within visible radius. Or at least he should have been. The receptionist was careful to avoid looking at him, as though he were the Hunchback of Notre-Dame—and carrying the plague as well.

Which, Fate observed, presented a rather interesting puzzle.

He quite plainly was familiar with the building; he had walked in as if he owned the place. And the receptionist was obviously not new to her job. It could be that the sheer fact of having seen him before had diminished in her the eye-popping hormone-racing effect of his presence. But not to the extent that the wooden po-faced look into the middle distance merited; Fate doubted that even a lifetime of looking at him could do that. No, it was more as though the girl was actually reluctant to look directly at him or make eye contact with him. Afraid almost. Why? In case he turned her to stone? He was more likely to burn the flesh right off her bones with those sexy eyes of his, Fate decided. God, imagine having him look at you with them all hot and hungry while he . . .

Forget it, she advised her libido with kind, motherly firmness. He's out of your league, babe, and just you be glad about it. . . .

Fate could think of only one explanation of the receptionist's attitude to the man—that no matter how gorgeously the goods were wrapped, whatever was inside the wrapping was nothing quite so mouth-watering.

Shame, Fate reflected and turned her attention back to her newspaper.

Jay gave the receptionist a mocking smile as he walked past her. She had come on to him pretty strongly when she first started with the company, until he had told her coolly and un-equivocally that he didn't have the time to take her to bed, but if she was that desperate, they could make use of the executive lift, adding that of course afterwards she would lose her job.

'I never have sex with the staff,' he had informed her.

She hadn't spoken to him or looked directly at him since.

As he drew level with the waiting area, he saw Fate out of the corner of his eye, noted the tousled mop of curls, the shining bright beauty, the clothes and the look of laughing, intelligent curiosity she gave him. He saw something else as well. . . .

Something that made him stop several paces past her and frown slightly as he closed his eyes and mentally conjured up the image he was searching for.

Her hair might be different, short instead of long, and she was certainly older, but he had no difficulty recognising her.

Taylor's goddaughter.

His heart started to beat in heavy, fast thuds, caused by an emotion which his brain called anger and his heart refused to re-cognise as jealousy.

Taylor must be feeling far more confident of herself and her position than he had believed. Certainly confident enough to go public on her relationship with his father, as she had arranged to meet her goddaughter here.

No doubt she intended to strengthen her grasp on his father's life over an intimate 'family' lunch. His father was one of those men who should have had daughters. He could remember hear-ing Helena say so in the early months after Plum's birth, when she had compared the genuine pleasure with which Bram had held her baby and given her her bottle, to Plum's own father's outright refusal to involve himself in anything to do with the practical side of 'parenting' his child.

And Jay had only to think of the way his father had spoiled and indulged Plum all through her life to know that what He-lena had said had been true.

As his anger fed on itself he turned on his heel and retraced his steps.

Fate could feel herself starting to blush as he walked purposefully towards her. He looked absolutely furious. Surely he couldn't have guessed what she had been thinking. . . .

'You must be waiting for Taylor,' Jay began curtly.

'Er, yes . . . well, at least, I suppose . . .' She must be even more nervous than she had thought, Fate decided as she took a deep breath. She said more calmly, 'I do have an appointment with someone from the PR department, but I'm afraid I haven't been given a name. Taylor . . . that's very unusual. I've never heard it before. Does it belong to a woman or a man . . . ?'

She stopped as she saw the sharp narrowing of Jay's eyes.

'So you don't actually know Taylor then,' he asked smoothly.

'No. I'm afraid I don't,' Fate confirmed, acknowledging ruefully that her mother had probably been right to point out to her that her clothes did not exactly project a businesslike image. She forced herself to meet and hold Jay's piercing, sharp gaze.

As he studied her face, Jay was convinced that he was right and that she was the same girl whose photograph Taylor had claimed was that of her goddaughter. But this girl, quite plainly, did not have the slightest idea who Taylor was, had not even heard her name before.

Two thoughts struck him simultaneously; the first was that the situation obviously required closer investigation, and the second was that he ought to remove her from the foyer before either Taylor or his father saw her.

He glanced at his watch.

'Well, I'm afraid there's been a small crisis in the PR department,' he lied, 'a minor emergency. . . perhaps I can help you instead. I'm Jay Soames, by the way, and you . . .'

'Fate. . .' Fate responded dizzily, wondering frantically whether he was as aware as she was of the tingling sensation of excitement scudding through her body as he shook her hand.

'So what exactly was the purpose of this appointment you had with our company?' Jay asked her.

Determinedly pulling herself together, Fate told him.

'Well, of course, a man's wealth and success have an effect on the lives of his close family,' Jay said, after he had listened to her brief explanation.

His mouth was already curling with dismissive contempt. In another moment he would be walking away from her, Fate recognised. But he had not listened to her properly; he had not really heard what she said, but had instead placed his own interpretation on her words.

'I agree,' she told him, adding challengingly, 'but what I want to discover is whether those effects are genuinely beneficial.'

'Ah, I see. You're hoping to prove that they aren't, is that it? Of course, you would be,' Jay murmured dryly as his glance subjected her to a slow and thorough scrutiny. 'Try telling it to someone who has lived in poverty all their lives. I doubt they'll be convinced.'

'Lack of money isn't the only poverty,' Fate retaliated sharply. 'A child can be brought up with every financial benefit there is and still suffer emotional and mental poverty.'

'The poor-little-rich-kid syndrome?' Jay taunted.

'Women married to workaholic men complain that they would far rather their husbands earned less and spent more time with them and with their families. That is a known fact.'

'Mmm...until the man goes bust or is made redundant. Then they sing a different song. However, it's a very interesting and provocative theory,' Jay acknowledged. 'We can't discuss it here, though. Look, I've got an hour or so free, why don't we go and get some lunch and you can interview me at the same time, and we can discuss the whole concept in more detail.'

Why, when he sounded so sincere, did she have the feeling that he was hiding something? Fate wondered.

Everything about him suggested that he would not have the least sympathy or empathy with her views. Logically she would have expected him to dismiss her and them, and refuse to discuss the matter any further, not offer to take her out to lunch.

There had to be another motive for his invitation, and the only one she herself could think of, the most obvious one was . . .

Was that he wanted to take her to bed. But he didn't come across to her as the type of man who would need to manoeuvre or manipulate a woman into a position where he could proposition her.

No, he looked far more like the kind of man who was used to women coming on to *him*. Who, if he wanted a woman, would simply and no doubt arrogantly tell her so.

Curiouser and curiouser, Fate decided. 'Thank you,' she said. Mischievously she thought that while he was pursuing his own agenda she could hopefully disarm him enough to get at least some of her questions answered—even if, as she suspected, the answers would run counter to her theories.

The next hour or so promised to be extremely. . . interesting, Fate told herself as she waited for Jay to rejoin her after going to inform the receptionist that he was taking her out to lunch and to cancel her appointment with PR.

16

'So now that I've answered your questions, how about you answering some of mine?' Jay suggested.

They were seated opposite each other in the semi-privacy of a small alcove, tucked discreetly out of sight of most of the other diners. It was, Fate recognised, the kind of table a man might book for dinner with a lover—or someone he hoped would become one.

It was certainly not a table for someone who wanted to see and be seen, and she was pretty sure Jay had specifically requested it, because initially the *maître d'* had been about to show them to one far more prominently placed.

It could be, of course, that Jay had simply wanted some degree of privacy for her interview. But he had expressed neither unease nor, if she was honest, very much interest in the questions she had asked, answering smoothly and easily, without giving her very much information.

He seemed amused and even slightly contemptuous and had skilfully tried to trail a small red herring in front of her at one stage by asking her how many wealthy and successful female executives she was interviewing.

'As many as I can,' she had responded evenly. There was no sexual bias in her report.

They had now ordered their coffee, and Jay was watching her intently as he waited for her response to his request that she tell him more about herself.

'I don't know if I should,' she said carefully, acknowledging now that it was the woman in her that urged caution. The same woman whose hormones had jumped in that dizzying, whirling dance of sexual awareness when she had seen him in the foyer.

'It's quite simple,' Jay told her softly. 'You just open your mouth and let the words come out....'

As he spoke he was looking at her mouth, focusing on it, concentrating on it as though...

Fate swallowed nervously, praying that he couldn't tell that a tiny, betraying rash of goose bumps had spread right up over her arms and that her heart was thumping frantically, while her nipples . . .

She knew what he was doing, of course; she wasn't *that* green and naïve. She had, after all, emerged unscathed from the incident with her tutor.

Jay wasn't attempting any subtlety at all, and any woman—any female over the age of sixteen—idiotic enough to fall for that long, lecherous, deliberate look at her mouth didn't deserve to call herself adult.

Fate had lost count of the number of times she had been subjected to similar tactics. She found it either annoying or enjoyable, depending on how lenient she felt towards the bloke who attempted it. This time . . .

This time, her whole nervous system was going into total overload, her legs were trembling, her pulses racing, while her mouth and her lips . . .

How *could* they possibly be softening like that, swelling subtly, parting without her being able to do a damn thing to stop them.

'There is . . . there isn't much to tell,' she managed to respond as she indignantly fought her body's reaction. It was behaving like a wayward child, totally oblivious to any danger, headstrongly determined to have its own way, or rather to let Jay. . . .

Hastily, she suppressed her thoughts and gave Jay a brief history of her life.

'So, like me, you're an only child,' he commented as he waved away the waiter, after ordering them both a liqueur.

Fate frowned. She had already had two glasses of wine and she wasn't sure any more alcohol would be a good idea. She certainly did not care to have it ordered for her without being consulted.

But before she could say so, Jay continued. 'No large extended family? Aunts, uncles, cousins . . . godparents?'

Fate, who had been trying without success to catch the waiter's eye and cancel her own drink, responded absently. 'No, I'm afraid not. My father is an only child, and my mother did have a sister but she died before I was born, in a car accident along with their parents. My mother doesn't like to talk about it. It happened when she was working abroad—that's where she met my father. My godparents live in Australia. They were close friends of my parents before they married. Aunt Ann is older than my mother, and I rather think they became close when my mother lost her family. We keep in contact but it's been years since I last saw them.'

'So, no doting godmother close at hand to spoil you...'

'Unfortunately, no.' Fate laughed. 'What about you?' she questioned. So far, her queries had all been directed at discovering what impact his father's success had had on his life, and she had steered clear of personal questions about his family background. Now though, with his having steered the conversation to her, the temptation to discover more about him was too strong to resist.

Careful, she warned herself as the waiter brought their drinks, he's not for you. 'Mad, bad, and dangerous to know,' as Lady Caroline Lamb had reputedly said about Byron.

'Much the same,' he told her. 'It's really just my father and myself. Both he and my mother were only children when I was born. None of my grandparents are alive, and as for godparents...' His face hardened. 'Due to the circumstances of my birth, my mother's parents decided that it would be morally wrong to have me christened.'

When he saw that she didn't understand, he explained tersely, 'I was illegitimate.'

Fate knew that her expression had betrayed her shock. Not because of what he had said but the way he had said it. The word was rather old-fashioned and seldom used. Never in her experience had she heard it filled with such anger and bitterness.

'You haven't tried the chocolates,' she heard him saying to her as easily as though his previous statement had never been made.

Fate started to shake her head in rejection but he had already picked up a strawberry, thickly coated in rich chocolate, and was leaning across the table.

'Bite,' he ordered her.

Easier and perhaps safer to give in than to refuse, Fate decided, firmly avoiding making make eye contact with him as she opened her mouth to bite into the chocolate-covered fruit.

In not making eye contact with him she had made a dangerous mistake, she discovered seconds after as, instead of the fruit,
her lips closed round the hard flesh of his fingertips, fingertips
which were openly and seductively brushing against the soft inner flesh of her lips, caressing it.

Furiously Fate drew back from him.

'What's wrong,' he asked softly, 'didn't you like the taste?'

Oh, she had liked it well enough, and he knew it, damn him.
But that wasn't the point. The point was . . . the point was . . .

'What are you doing this evening?'

'I . . . er, nothing,' Fate responded truthfully, grinding her teeth
in irritation as she saw the look he was giving her.

'You are now,' Jay told her softly. 'Meet me in the foyer at six.
I've got a couple of appointments this afternoon . . . unless, of
course, you want me to cancel them and come back with me now
to my apartment. We could spend the rest of the day in bed and
the night as well.'

'No.'

Jay laughed, a genuinely amused laugh, Fate noted crossly.

'Very proper and conventional,' he approved mockingly. 'But
both of us know that you—'

'I can't see you tonight,' Fate interrupted him quickly.

'Why? Because you're afraid that I'll persuade you to go to bed
with me, or because you're afraid that you'll want me to?'

'Neither,' Fate denied firmly. 'I . . . I just don't think that it's a
good idea to mix business with pleasure.'

To her chagrin he laughed again. 'Ah, so you do admit that
there would be . . . pleasure,' he taunted her.

She intrigued him, Jay acknowledged, this clean, fresh, serious woman-child, who was all the things that he was not. He had
no idea yet exactly what the connection was between her and
Taylor, but there *was* one. He was sure of it. He had a gut feeling
about it . . . an instinct. *She* might not know the connection existed, but it was there, nevertheless. The photograph in Taylor's
possession proved it.

It would have been interesting to witness Taylor's reaction had
she discovered Fate sitting in the foyer. Very interesting . . . There
was a lot more Jay wanted to know about Fate and her background . . . her family.

And there was a lot more he wanted to know about Taylor as well. Right from the start it had struck him as odd that she was so alone, so isolated, but when he had said as much to his father, Bram had sprung to her defence so immediately that Jay had dropped the subject.

Dropped it but not forgotten it.

Jay hadn't forgotten, either, the way she had reacted over Fate's photograph. And he was now convinced that it *was* Fate's photograph. Her looks were too striking to mistake. All right, so the long hairstyle had been replaced by a gamine's mop of curls, which on any other woman he would have immediately dismissed as unattractive and butch, but which on her... It added an extra piquancy to the situation that he should find her such a sexual turn-on, he admitted.

'I have no doubt that you like to think you're a good lover— most men do,' Fate was saying as she started to stand. 'But sexual athletics don't have much appeal for me these days. I grew out of that phase a long time ago,' she added loftily.

'So, what is it you are looking for?' Jay drawled as he, too, rose. 'Or can I guess? Commitment... permanency... love?'

'I'm not looking for anything—or anyone,' Fate contradicted him calmly.

'Thank you for having lunch with me,' Jay murmured as he forestalled her attempt to walk away from him by taking hold of her upper arm.

His fingers were strong enough and long enough to completely span her arm, Fate noticed as she shivered slightly from the heat of the physical contact.

'I've enjoyed it immensely.'

'Sure you don't want to change your mind? It's not too late for me to cancel those appointments.'

Jay knew perfectly well, of course, that there was no way she was going to say yes. He also knew that despite her valiant attempts to both deny it to herself and conceal it from him, she was intensely, physically aware of him.

What would she be like in bed? he wondered, once they were outside on the pavement and she was walking away from him, having thanked him curtly for her lunch and refused his offer of a taxi. Not passive and clinging, not from the way she moved, the way her body, her whole person vibrated with life.

He suspected, though, that she wouldn't be as physically aggressive or perhaps as experienced as she would want him to think.

A secret smile curled his mouth.

She would be both angered and chagrined, he knew, if she realised how much he was enjoying the contrast between the angry stiffness of her back and the soft roundness of her bottom.

Despite her airy attempts to convince him that her experience and self-awareness were such that sex held no mysteries or surprises for her, he didn't think it would take him very long to show her otherwise.

She had long legs and the muscles, he knew, would be supple, her skin smooth and silky, faintly tanned.

He continued to watch as she crossed the road, smiling in triumph when she couldn't resist the temptation to turn round and look to see if he was still there. Arrogantly, he raised his hand in acknowledgement, laughing as he pictured the flush that was staining her skin, and the way she was fighting to control it.

Back in his office, his secretary would, no doubt, have placated the man whose appointment he had so ruthlessly ignored in order to take Fate to lunch. He had two other appointments booked for the afternoon; they would have to be cancelled. He had other more urgent matters to attend to.

Later that afternoon Jay got up from the desk in the main lounge area of his apartment and paced over to the window, his body taut with suppressed triumph. No matter which way he looked at the facts, they always added up the same way. There could be no doubt. He was convinced he was right.

Fate had laughed when she mentioned over lunch that both because she had been born prematurely abroad, just before her parents planned to return to Britain for her birth, and because of some additional complications, she had been several months old before her birth had been properly registered.

Jay had laughed too, but mentally filed the information. Had the delay really been caused by the explanation she had obviously been given by her parents? Or was it possible that while she might legally be their child, they might not be her actual birth parents?

If only he could provide incontrovertible evidence that he was right . . .

Jay frowned. In order to do that he might have to employ the services of a private investigator, something he didn't want to do. To share something so intensely personal and important with anyone else ran totally counter to Jay's deepest beliefs. He walked back to his desk, and stared hard at the notes on his pad. His frown suddenly lifted as he remembered the way Taylor had reacted to his enquiries about the photograph. She had been quite definitely on edge and ill at ease. If she betrayed herself so easily, merely at the sight of Fate's photograph, what would she do if she was confronted with Fate herself? And if Taylor *was* Fate's mother, then somewhere Fate must also have a birth father, a man who had been Taylor's lover and whose existence Jay was pretty sure Taylor had neglected to mention to his father.

Deceit in any form was abhorrent to Bram. His father could be surprisingly intransigent and unforgiving when it came to someone's being deliberately deceitful. As Jay had good cause to know.

And how much more deceitful could a woman be than to conceal from a man she was supposed to love, the birth of a child?

What other secrets—lies—lay hidden in Taylor's past?

Who was Fate's father? A married man, perhaps, with whom Taylor had conducted a secret affair. No doubt she would plead with Bram that she had had no option but to give up her child for adoption.

But Taylor had obviously remained in touch with Fate's adoptive parents. Otherwise, how had she come by that photograph?

From what Fate had told him, Jay had gained the impression that her parents were comfortably off. Could Taylor perhaps have been blackmailing them? The apartment Taylor had lived in before moving in with his father—in *on* his father was how Jay thought of it—had certainly cost more than Taylor would have been able to afford on her modest salary. The photograph frame itself had been solid silver and expensive.

How would his father feel when he discovered that the woman he believed he loved had sold her own flesh and blood . . . her child?

She would fall apart, Jay decided cruelly, and not even his father would be able to defend her then.

As he pondered on how best to bring about such a confrontation, he glanced towards the fireplace and a long, slow smile curled his mouth.

Still smiling, he walked over and picked up the stiff white invitation from the mantel. Jay laughed out loud, his eyes blazing with triumph.

Of course . . . It would be perfect. Plum's coming-of-age ball. There was no way his father would not go, and no way he would not take Taylor with him.

He had already insisted that Jay must accept the invitation. As for Fate . . .

She was aptly named, Jay decided as he replaced the invitation, and glanced at his watch, then picked up the phone.

His secretary was just on the point of leaving, but she knew better than to protest or object. She gritted her teeth silently as she listened to Jay's instructions.

It would take her at least half an hour, maybe even longer — *if* the people he wanted her to speak to were actually still in their offices.

'You're back earlier than I expected. How did you get on?' her mother demanded excitedly as Fate walked into the kitchen. 'Did you see Brampton Soames himself, or —'

'No, I saw . . .' Fate stopped. 'The interview went reasonably well,' she said in a composed voice. 'I got the impression that Bram Soames is not quite your typical, successful entrepreneur type. I would have liked to interview him personally,' she added, 'but somehow I don't think I'm going to get the chance.'

Jay had completely stonewalled her when she had hinted that she would like to interview his father, and had not just looked irritated when she pressed the matter, but almost angry.

He had a temper, she guessed shrewdly, but she also suspected that he kept it pretty firmly under control. She still wasn't sure she had done the right thing in refusing his offer of dinner. She might have been able to persuade him to arrange for her to meet his father.

Not a chance of a snowball in hell, her brain derided her. The only arrangements he would have been interested in making were those which would have ended up with her in his bed.

'So who did you interview?' her mother asked. 'Come on, tell me. The head of their PR department?'

'No, actually it was Soames's son . . .' Fate admitted reluctantly.

She had no idea why she was so reluctant to discuss Jay with her mother. Well, all right then, so she was lying, she knew exactly why she didn't want to discuss her meeting with Jay Soames with anyone else. Her brain might be convinced that the best thing there could ever be between them was a good, healthy distance, but her body . . .

'His son? What was he like, what did he . . . ?'

What was he like? How about body-achingly, lust-longingly, downright sexy? Fate's mind wandered back over her shocked delight at her first sight of him.

'He was very helpful,' Fate said, 'but I should still have preferred to interview Brampton Soames himself.'

'And did his son confirm any of your theories?'

'No,' Fate admitted ruefully.

'Oh, darling,' Caroline sympathised. 'Will you be in for supper this evening? Your father telephoned to say he'd be late. He's got to go and see someone.'

'I'm not really hungry,' Fate told her. 'I think I'll go up and have a shower and wash my hair. London always leaves me feeling so dirty somehow. And then I've got some notes to write up.'

'It's the traffic,' her mother agreed. 'All those fumes. I always end up with a dreadful headache.'

She was not going to think about Jay Soames, Fate told herself firmly as she went upstairs. More specifically, she was not going to think about the dinner date she could have been having with him this evening.

Bed and breakfast was probably a closer description of what he had had in mind.

An hour later, dressed in an old pair of leggings and an old sweater, her hair smothered in a hot-oil treatment and wrapped in a towel, she was writing up her notes when she heard the front doorbell ring.

A couple of minutes later her mother called, 'Fate . . .'

Groaning to herself, she put down her pen and went downstairs. The sitting room door was open and she could hear her mother's voice, slightly breathless and unfamiliarly girlish.

Puzzled, Fate entered the sitting room, her hands going instinctively and protectively to the towel-wrapped hair as she saw Jay smiling tauntingly up at her from the sofa.

'Don't tell me you've forgotten our date,' he complained.

Like her, he had changed from the clothes he had been wearing earlier. The blue jeans looked as though they fitted him like a glove, the soft shirt had tempting wide spaces between the buttons, wide enough, she was sure, for a determined and slender-fingered female to reach between them and stroke the satin softness of the flesh beneath. The leather blouson jacket had to have been made in Italy and, like the jeans, it had a well-worn, almost shabby softness about it.

Very sexy, Fate acknowledged once she recovered from her shock. Very, very sexy.

Ignoring her mother's slightly flustered flapping—his effect was quite obviously not restricted to one age group, Fate noticed wryly—she gave him a narrow-eyed look as she replied sweetly, 'I didn't forget. I told you that I couldn't see you tonight.' Despite the way her heart was racing, her voice was strong and firm.

'Pity. . .' His voice was soft, but the look he was giving her certainly wasn't.

'I was very interested in what you had to say over lunch,' he went on. 'I was hoping we could take things a bit further. I've been in touch with one or two people I know to see if they would agree to be interviewed by you. I don't know if you've heard of them. . . .'

He mentioned several names, and Fate struggled not to look impressed. Heard of them? Of course she had. Who hadn't?

They were internationally known—men in very much the same mould as his father, who had built up successful businesses from virtually nothing. And at least three of the people he named had already responded to her tentative enquiries by stating that they couldn't spare the time to give her an interview.

Why had Jay Soames gone to so much trouble on her behalf? Not just to get her into bed, surely.

As she saw the way he was watching her, the knowledge and confidence he wore as easily as his clothes, she badly wanted to tell him that she wasn't interested, that he was wasting his time because she didn't need his help and she certainly didn't want his company. But if she refused him now, her mother would want to know why. . . .

Why was he pursuing her like this? Fate wondered as she dried her hair.

To have gone to the trouble of getting her address and coming out here, never mind securing those interviews for her, must mean . . .

Must mean what? That he didn't like being thwarted . . . that he wanted to teach her a lesson? Not very pleasant traits in any man and certainly not in a potential lover.

Be careful, she warned herself as she slipped into some clean clothes and checked her reflection in the mirror. The Joseph separates had been a treat from her father, and she knew they looked good on her, fashionable, with just a discreet hint of sexiness.

When Fate went back downstairs, her mother's face was prettily flushed and Jay was studying a photograph of her which had been taken just before she started at university. Her hair had been long then, her face still immature and soft with youth.

Jay was smiling as he studied it, and for some reason her heart started to race in a fast, erratic beat.

'So what made you change your mind about our date?'

'I didn't know I had changed it. I never actually agreed to it,' Fate said dryly.

'You could always have refused. You wanted to come with me,' Jay challenged.

'I'd have been a fool not to,' Fate told him. 'You're obviously a very useful person to know. Those interviews alone . . . ' She paused, but she knew that Jay wasn't really deceived.

'Ah, I see,' he mocked her. 'Your desire for my company is simply cerebral—fuelled by ambition. I don't think so. I think that if you and I were on our own right now, it wouldn't be the thought of free access to my computer files that would be on your mind.'

'Don't be too sure,' Fate checked him. He was taking far too much for granted, she decided, far too much.

They were seated in a small, local bistro Fate had recommended when Jay had asked her to suggest somewhere they could eat.

That had surprised her. She had automatically assumed that he intended to drive her back to London for dinner, followed by the suggestion of a nightcap at his apartment. She had already rehearsed her refusal.

'Oh, before I forget, since this is what you claim you want, here's a list of the people I've contacted. I'd better give it to you, hadn't I?' Jay handed her a sealed envelope. 'You can speak directly to their secretaries. Their names and the telephone numbers are included.'

As she took the envelope from him, carefully avoiding allowing her fingertips to touch his, Fate just managed to stop herself from asking him why he was going to so much trouble on her behalf.

She could just imagine his amused and no doubt extremely sexually explicit response to her naïveté, but it wasn't just wariness that made her face start to flush slightly.

All right, so sexually she did find him a turn-on. So what? she demanded irritably. Acknowledging the fact didn't mean that she was going to end up in bed with him. She wasn't.

Whatever pleasure she would have with him would be more than cancelled out by the pain that would follow. And there would be pain. Fate knew.

He wasn't just the kind of man that women wanted to go to bed with, he was the kind they fell in love with as well—if they were foolish enough or crazy enough to ignore all the warning signs which said that falling in love with him would be just about the worst possible thing they could do. And she wasn't foolish, was she?

Jay smiled to himself as he watched her. He knew exactly what she was thinking, but she was wrong. Getting her into his bed wasn't the only thing he wanted—no way. She was too valuable a pawn for him to risk alienating her or, even worse, losing her.

Bed would only complicate things, and he needed to maintain his contact with her, to keep her in his life. As well, at this stage at least, he needed to keep her away from Bram and Taylor.

'You've arranged for me to be able to interview everyone in here,' Fate commented, tapping the envelope, 'but you haven't said anything about my interviewing your father.'

'I shouldn't have thought that would be necessary. I've already told you everything you need to know.'

'From your point of view.' For some reason her comment angered him, she noted, but she wasn't going to back down. 'Your father might see things differently. Parents and children often do.'

'I see. Is that observation spoken from a personal point of view or a general one?'

'I get on very well with my parents.'

She gave Jay a challenging look as he started to laugh.

'You're their only child and it's obvious that you're the focus of their whole lives. They, no doubt, loved and cherished you from the moment of your birth.'

'You're an only child, too,' Fate replied pointedly. 'You must—'

'No.'

The harshness of his denial shocked her. She looked uncertainly across the table at him.

'You,' he told her fiercely, 'are very obviously a child who has been surrounded by love always. It shows in the way you look, the way you move, the way you talk. It's like a patina that people like you wear as carelessly and casually as the wealthy wear expensive clothes—without any thought for, or awareness of, those who have not had your advantages.' He stopped abruptly.

Because he felt he had said too much? Fate wondered. She wanted to ask more, but she sensed he wouldn't allow her to pursue the subject.

'You look like a little girl at times, do you know that,' Jay asked.

'But I'm not,' Fate warned him hardily.

'No,' he grated, 'but you are very dangerous.... Very, very dangerous,' he added softly.

'I am not a child,' Fate repeated.

'No? Then why were you so afraid of seeing me this evening?' he probed.

Fate took a gulp of wine and almost choked on it as she tried to avoid looking into his eyes and found, instead, that her glance was lingering quite openly—and dangerously—on his mouth.

Men with that kind of full bottom lip were supposed to be sensual and demanding lovers. Would he...?

'I...I wasn't,' she lied, adding, 'I just didn't think you were serious, that's all.'

'About what, taking you out to dinner or taking you to bed?'

'It was very kind of you to go to the trouble of arranging those interviews for me,' Fate said, refusing to rise to the bait and trying to ignore the heavy excited hammering of her heart at the same time.

'Yes, wasn't it,' Jay agreed.

He was watching her far too closely.

'Of course I was serious,' Jay continued softly, 'on both counts, but then you already knew that. It's all part of the game...you run, I chase....'

'I don't play that kind of game.' She was beginning to feel angry now, to feel that not just the situation but, more important, her own reactions as well were somehow slipping out of her control.

'It's all right,' Jay told her in that same soft voice which was sending dizzying, sweet little shivers racing up and down her spine, and doing far more dangerous—and anything but sweet—things to other parts of her anatomy.

'I'm not going to coerce you to do something you don't want to do. Oh, no. When the time comes, it will be what you want. You'll be the one coming to me and telling me how much you want me.'

Jay could tell from the way she was fighting so hard to suppress it, just what kind of effect he was having on her. He could see it in her eyes, in the way she was breathing, the way she was moving... Oh, she would protest, prevaricate, say it was too soon, but once in his bed...

It was a very necessary part of his plan that she remained in thrall to him for long enough for him to do what he planned to do. That was why he could feel the surge of excitement seizing his body, releasing itself in a physical sexual response, which had him tensing and moving uncomfortably in his chair, glad that the physical sign was not visible to others.

His arousal, he assured himself, had nothing to do with Fate herself. It was simply a reaction to the knowledge that he had found a way of removing Taylor from his father's life. That was what was important to him, not this too young, too naïve... too idealistic girl, who looked nothing like the kind of woman who normally appealed to him.

She was too tall, her hair was too short, she was too forthright, too opinionated, and she would probably go and complicate everything by falling in love with him. But that was her problem, not his, he told himself guardedly.

God, but he was arrogant, Fate decided. Did he really think he knew women so well that he could predict that she would beg him to take her to bed? If so, perhaps it was time he realised that not all women were so predictable, or so foolish.

It was late when they left the bistro, and Fate knew that her parents would already be in bed. As soon as Jay stopped his Jaguar in the drive, she thanked him for the evening and reached for the door handle.

He made no attempt to stop her, nor to get out of the car and open the door for her, Fate noticed ruefully. The Jaguar's engine was still running—not that she had any intention of asking him in.

Jay let her get as far as the front door before he got out of the car. He caught up with her just as she was inserting her key into the lock.

When he touched her lightly on the arm she swung round in shock, dipping her head so that he wouldn't see her expression.

'You forgot this,' he said softly, handing her the envelope he had given her earlier.

Fate was furious with herself. How could she have done such a stupid thing? She could have sworn she had put the envelope in her pocket.

Now, of course, he was going to think that she had left it behind on purpose so that he would come after her like this and...

'And this,' Jay added in an even softer voice, as he stepped towards her, gathered her in his arms and moved them both into the shadows of the house wall in one swift, smooth movement that caught Fate off guard and unwillingly impressed.

He didn't kiss her, as she had expected him to do, aggressively and demandingly. Instead he looked down into her eyes, and she could hear the smile in his voice, even if the shadows prevented her from seeing it on his lips as he teased her. 'I shouldn't really be doing this. You don't deserve it, you know. Not after forcing me to come running up here to find you.'

Well, don't then, Fate wanted to reply, but his mouth was already moving very gently over hers, so gently and briefly that it reminded her of a very first taste of ice cream, no more than a small lick of someone else's spoon that left you longing for more...much more...much, much more.

'Not enough,' she heard Jay saying as unnervingly as though he had read her thoughts. And then his arms tightened round her, and his mouth came down again, but this time...

She was still trembling when he released her, her eyes blind with the shock, her body so close to the brink of orgasm that she couldn't understand how he had possibly aroused her so intensely, simply by kissing her. Or how she had let him.

She knew that he was aroused, too, but she doubted that she could possibly have had the same effect on him that he had on her. She didn't look at him as he unlocked and opened the door for her, but she still knew that he had turned round and started back to his car even before she had closed the door.

Her reaction to him had shocked her. As she went upstairs she reminded herself of everything she already knew. He was dangerous...he was devastating...he was out of her league, lethally so, and he didn't give a damn about her or how he might hurt her. If she had any sense, any sense at all, she simply wouldn't see him again.

Jay didn't look back as he walked to his car. It was only a kiss, he told himself grimly, just another step on the road to ridding his father of Taylor.

All right, so for a second... a heartbeat of time, he had felt... had wanted...

Angrily, he put the car in gear. She was a means to an end, that was all. A means to an end. If for a second, when he had looked down into her shocked eyes and seen in them the knowledge of what was happening to her, he had wanted to reach out and hold her, comfort her... so what? He hadn't done it, had he? And he never would.

He had seen the resistance and the anger in her eyes when he told her that she would be the one to come to him, to ask him to take her to bed. In different circumstances it would have been a tempting challenge to prove to her that he was right, to slowly and methodically, inch by inch, piece by piece, destroy her self-esteem and pride, and to do it so subtly that she would never know what was happening to her until it was too late and when she did eventually lie beneath him, her body quivering with need for him, he would...

A passer-by turned to stare at the Jaguar as its driver missed a gear. What a waste. Some people had no idea how to treat a decent piece of machinery.

17

'Plum, please try to concentrate. Have you ticked off Lord and Lady Ferrars?'

Helena sighed as Plum pouted sullenly and then sent the neatly stacked pile of invitation acceptances off the table and onto the floor.

'I don't know why there has to be all this fuss,' Plum grumbled, pushing back her chair so that she could help Helena to pick them up.

'No, leave them, you'll only get them all out of order,' Helena snapped at her. She had been right, it had been an idiotic idea to persuade Plum to come home for the weekend. She had already upset the girls by telling them that her old pony, now too small for her to ride, would probably end up as dog food. Then she had annoyed and embarrassed everyone by walking around the house wearing nothing more than a G-string and a thin cotton lawn shirt—quite obviously a man's, and still, Helena had noticed in distaste, smelling faintly of his sweat.

She had gone out on Saturday evening without telling them where she was going and had only returned midway through Sunday morning. It was now almost noon on Monday, and Plum had been up for less than half an hour.

'And the fuss, as you call it,' Helena added, tight-lipped as she retrieved the last of the scattered pieces of paper, 'happens to be for your benefit. Something you might try to remember occasionally, Plum. Couldn't you at least have a shower and brush your hair before you come down?' she complained, changing tack.

Plum wasn't listening; she was studying one of the acceptances she had just picked up.

'Who invited him?' she demanded angrily.

'Who?' Helena asked, frowning, looking to see whose card she was holding.

'G. McKenzie? Oh, he's related to your friend Justin Gardner. Justin's mother telephoned and asked if it would be all right to bring him with them. Do you know him?'

'I've met him. He's boring,' Plum responded disparagingly. At least she would have Bram there to turn to for comfort. If it weren't for him, she would have been tempted not to turn up at all.

And why on earth did The McKenzie have to be there?

It irked her that she hadn't been able to completely dismiss the way he had rejected her. A man who looked as though he didn't even have a clue what sex was really all about. He was lucky she had even offered. Well, she wouldn't offer again.

'I suppose Bram's bringing *her* with him?' she challenged her mother, dismissing Justin's cousin from her thoughts and concentrating instead on someone far more important to her.

'Bram has asked if he can bring Taylor with him,' Helena agreed sedately.

Both Bram and Jay had in fact asked if it would be all right for them to bring someone with them, and while Jay had described his partner as a 'friend,' Bram had told her that the person he wanted to bring with him was someone who was 'very special to him' and whom he very much wanted her to meet.

She was delighted for Bram, of course she was!

Fate chewed the top of her pen as she read through the paragraph she had just written. At five o'clock on a Sunday morning, she ought to have been in bed fast asleep. She had been unhappy with the way she had recorded her interview with the wife and daughters of one of the contacts Jay had arranged, and that dissatisfaction had nagged at her even in her sleep. She had woken up an hour ago and known she wouldn't be able to do anything else until she got it right. A goal she had not yet reached, she acknowledged irritably.

During the interview, she had felt certain that despite their loyal attempts to pretend otherwise, the family did not share the man's belief that they were blissfully happy and content with a husband and father who, while providing them with every material luxury, spent so little time at home that the cleaning lady had assumed the couple were divorced.

The wife had laughed when she related this story, but Fate had seen the pain behind the smile. However, trying to convey this impression was not proving easy. Emotions were such ephemeral things. So difficult to put into words, but so powerful to feel, as she had good cause to know.

She touched her newly shorn hair. The style suited her with its elfin wisps and soft curls, but there was no doubt that it was short . . . very short.

'You should grow your hair,' Jay had told her. He had just driven her home and they'd been sitting in his car. She had seen him several times since the evening he had turned up at her home, and as he had bent his head to kiss her he had complained mockingly that when he slid his hand into the back of her hair he could almost be touching a boy.

'That's your problem, not mine,' Fate had replied flippantly. But his comment had hurt—as she was quite sure he had intended.

She liked her hair short, and Jay had to realise that he couldn't manipulate her or dominate her by trying to undermine her self-confidence. And so she had had her hair cut.

She started as her telephone rang. So early in the morning, a ringing telephone could signify some kind of emergency, and it sent the adrenalin racing through the veins. Uneasy, she reached for the receiver.

'Did I wake you?'

'Jay. . .' The adrenalin was still pumping, even faster than before now, but for a very different reason.

'No, as a matter of fact you didn't. I was working. What on earth are you doing ringing this time of the morning?'

'I've got half an hour to spare and the lines are fairly quiet at this time so I thought I'd give you a call. I've got a small favour to ask, by the way, something I forgot to mention before I left.'

Fate waited. Jay had been in Japan for the past week and she had missed him, but she certainly wasn't going to let him know it. As for the timing of his call . . .

'What kind of favour?' she said instead.

He laughed and the sound made her body ache and her heart melt.

'Not what you obviously think from the suspicion in your voice. If I wanted telephone sex I'd get a professional. Or was I mistaking suspicion for something else quite different? No response?' he taunted softly. 'Well, never mind. Although if the shoe were on the other foot, how long do you think it would take me to arouse you? Not long, I suspect. In fact I'd like to bet that right now if you're honest, all it *would* take—'

'Jay.' Fate interrupted him warily, but she knew there was a slightly breathless and wholly betraying note in her voice.

'All right.' She could tell that he was smiling. 'Look, I'm due to attend a rather dull coming-of-age party next Saturday and I need a partner. I was wondering if you would come with me.'

'You're ringing me from Japan at five o'clock in the morning to ask me that?' Fate demanded in disbelief.

Jay laughed again, and this time the sound was somehow nearer, warmer . . . as though . . . as though he was holding the receiver very close to his mouth.

His mouth . . . Fate closed her eyes unwillingly, remembering just what it felt like to be in close contact with Jay's mouth, to feel it feathering against her own, to feel it . . .

'No,' Jay told her softly. 'I rang because I'm getting tired of sleeping on my own, of waiting for you to stop being a little girl and grow up. You want me, Fate, and we both know it. When you dropped me off at Heathrow you were practically having an orgasm in my arms. What is it holding you back? All you have to do is say the word. I can come home if you like. There's a flight later today.'

Fate closed her eyes. Her fingers were trembling so much she could hardly hold the receiver. It would be easy to say yes, to give in, because that was what she would be doing.

'You'll be the one to ask me for sex,' he had told her. She had known then there could be nothing of any real value between them.

Once you took the sexual excitement and challenge out of their relationship, what was actually left? What would be left once they had actually been to bed together? Oh, he might listen to her when she talked about her plans . . . her hopes for the future. He might even encourage her to talk about her childhood and her family but he rarely responded with any real information about himself, and she was always aware that he was somehow distancing himself from her.

One evening she had persuaded him to see a film with her. In it, the male hero had undergone a transformation which had allowed him to show his emotions and his vulnerabilities. Afterwards Jay had been sarcastically critical of the film and the male character.

It was a myth that society valued the so-called 'new man,' he had told her contemptuously. Men were by their very nature competitive with one another, respecting only those who were stronger and more powerful.

'Show me a woman who is sexually involved with one of your so-called 'new men,' and I'll show you a woman who secretly fantasises about being bedded by a lover who's everything that her wimp of a partner isn't.'

Fate had stood her ground and argued the issue, but Jay had refused to give way.

'Well?' she heard him saying softly now, on the other end of the line.

'No, Jay,' she said huskily. 'I don't play games with my body or my emotions. I value myself too much.' She replaced the receiver before he could say anything.

She wasn't sure she was strong enough to resist him if he continued to undermine her by taunting her about what she was missing.

Yes, the sex between them would be wonderful, probably the best she had ever experienced or would ever experience. But the experience would be purely physical, she acknowledged miserably, without any kind of real emotion, because Jay would never allow himself to feel or express any emotion.

She wondered sometimes why she continued to see him when she knew there was no future, and when she half suspected that a good part of the reason Jay continued to see her lay in her resistance.

Once she had slept with him, once he had 'won,' there would be no reason for him to go on seeing her. Perhaps for both their sakes she ought to stop fighting and give in, get the whole thing over and done with. That way she might stop lying awake at night aching for him, and he would stop pursuing her.

Oh, the temptation of it. If he rang back and she conceded defeat, by this time tomorrow . . . But he wouldn't ring back, she acknowledged wryly. That wasn't Jay's way. Right now he would be enjoying knowing what his telephone call had done to her and how much she wanted him. She knew him well enough to know that.

She stared unseeingly through her bedroom window. Whose coming-of-age party did he want her to accompany him to? She knew so little about the rest of his life . . . his family . . . his friends.

Perhaps it was just as well that he had made that derogatory comment about her begging for sex, she reflected. She had never as yet been involved in a relationship where she had felt that her emotions might not be reciprocated or where they might get out of control and if she was honest with herself, she had always felt slightly superior to girls who had done so, pitying them for what she had perceived as their lack of self-esteem and their neediness.

Now unexpectedly she could see how easy it might be to fall into that kind of trap, to persuade herself that all it would take to transform Jay into the perfect man was love . . . her love. It was as fallacious as telling a child that all it took to transform a frog into a prince was a kiss . . . and as tempting.

Nothing and no one could change another human being unless they wanted to change. And Jay most certainly did not. He *liked* being the way he was. He liked *himself* as he was . . .

But did she . . . ? Fate pursed her lips. She rather thought not, but that did not stop her wanting him, aching for him, lying awake at night trying to stifle a hunger for him, which was a physical pain.

18

Plum sulkily read the horoscope predictions of her favourite astrologer, and threw the paper aside in disgust. Today was her eighteenth birthday, and tonight the evening of her celebration ball, and according to Patric Walker, the planets in their courses had decided to mark the event with a planetary sequence so extraordinary that not a single star sign would remain unaffected by their confrontational and transforming influences.

Her own horoscope warned of setbacks and unexpected problems followed by the dawning of a new age. Well, it wouldn't do, Plum decided crossly, since it was her birthday. She had already had one argument with her mother over the seating plan. Helena had refused to seat Bram next to her, despite all Plum's pleas and protests.

Virtually the only reason she had agreed to go along with this dreary ball was that she knew Bram would be there. And now, not only was he bringing another woman with him, but *she* wasn't even going to be sitting next to him. Added to that, she hated and loathed her dress, which made her look grotesquely fat and about twelve years old. And that horrible cousin of Justin's would be there. *And* after three weeks of fine weather, it was raining. . . .

Bram's brow furrowed as he studied Taylor. She hadn't been well recently, having picked up a summer bug, which on top of the tension she had already been suffering had completely wiped out her appetite. She looked too pale and too finely drawn, he thought as she started to brush her hair. The emotional closeness they had shared following his return from Strasbourg had been replaced by her withdrawal from him. Something was wrong, even though Taylor denied it when he tried to talk to her, claiming that he was simply imagining it.

He had tried again last night in the quiet time after they had made love.

'I just don't like the thought that I'm coming between you and Jay,' Taylor told him. 'He hates me, Bram, and if he could, he'd destroy us.'

'Jay can't do anything to hurt you,' he told her, holding her close. 'I won't let him.'

It hurt to know she doubted the strength of his love for her and its endurance. To him it was all so simple. He loved her and he knew himself well enough to know that the quality and intensity of that love meant that nothing anyone could ever say or do would change his feelings.

She hadn't really wanted to go to Plum's birthday ball this evening. She had pointed out that it wasn't fair to Helena to expect her to include her at the last minute and that she would be an encumbrance to him since she wouldn't know anyone.

'That kind of thing isn't my scene,' she had protested. 'I'm not a party person. I'm not sociable or fun.'

'I need you there with me,' Bram had told her simply, and in the end she had given in. He had gone with her to buy the dress she was now wearing, a slim silky cream crêpe tube, round-necked and long-sleeved. On the hanger it had looked plain and dull, but on Taylor... The fabric had a sensuous fluidity to it that mirrored every movement she made. It was a dress that hinted at its wearer's sexuality rather than emphasising it. It had a matching hip-length jacket with a swing back and an open vent embroidered with a scattering of freshwater pearls.

Initially, when he had given Taylor pearl and diamond earrings to wear with it, she had refused to accept them.

'They're too expensive,' she had told him. 'I can't wear them. Everyone will know...'

'What?' Bram had asked her gently. 'That I love you? Are you really ashamed of me, Taylor...of our love?'

In the end she had given way. This evening, as he stood at the doorway of his bedroom—now their bedroom—he had watched, unseen by her, as she put them in her ears and then touched them, love and pleasure shining in her eyes, her mouth suddenly trembling slightly as her eyes filled with tears.

He had gone to her then, taking hold of her and wrapping her in his arms despite her protests that she would get make-up on his dinner jacket and he would disturb her hair. She had returned his embrace though, and the kiss which followed. Now as she rebrushed her hair he could almost read the thoughts going through her mind.

It had taken him days and days of careful coaxing to get her to let her hair down and loose, and now he could sense that a part of her still wanted to coil it up tightly out of sight.

'Leave it,' he whispered softly from behind her. 'It looks wonderful. *You* look wonderful.' He gave a small groan and would have taken her back in his arms if she hadn't shaken her head and stepped back from him.

Bram might think that she looked wonderful, but if he could read her mind . . . Every morning when she woke up, the first thought that came into her head was that it couldn't go on and that somehow she must find the strength to leave him.

Every morning!

There were many, many times when she wanted to be able to tell him the truth, all of it, to share the horror of her past with him. But how could she?

'Ready?' Bram asked her.

Taylor nodded her head. Tonight would be such a bittersweet occasion—the first time she would meet his friends, be seen publicly as his partner. The first time and the last time. The only time.

Fate pulled a wry face at her reflection in the mirror. The last time she had worn this outfit had been more than twelve months ago for a May ball. Her hair had been long then and she had worn it up. The graduate she was accompanying hadn't been able to keep his eyes off her all evening. He had insisted on punting her down the river in the early hours of the morning, just as dawn had broken, proposing to her on bended knee and almost causing the punt to capsize. She had been seized by a wild desire to giggle, but fortunately had managed to control herself. She had made the lilac shot-silk full-length skirt herself, gathering up the yards of fabric into a tiny waistband and grimacing over the layers of net needed for the underskirt.

She had found the cream silk bustier with its hand-stitched seed pearls on a market stall, and the cream satin stole she had worn with it had been borrowed from her mother. The most expensive part of the outfit had been the satin shoes she had dyed to match her skirt.

Was a long skirt the right thing to wear with her short urchin crop? she wondered. If not, it was too bad; it was the only outfit she possessed which was remotely suitable for this kind of occasion.

Her parents would gladly have bought her something new, but she had robustly refused, announcing that it was a complete waste of money to buy something new and expensive that she was likely never to wear again. Anyway, she liked her lilac skirt. The colour suited her, and she liked the swishing sound the silk made when she moved. The top did reveal rather a lot of cleavage, and under the light of her bedroom her skin gleamed silkily, her bare shoulders a soft honey colour.

The outfit made her waist look impossibly tiny, and her breasts unfamiliarly voluptuous. She looked, she decided, rather temptingly sexy.

Tempting enough for Jay to forget, ignore his edict and ask *her* to stay the night with *him*. Her heart started to beat a little bit faster.

Jay was mentally calculating the order of events of the evening as he drew up outside Fate's home. He intended to make sure that when he confronted Taylor with Fate, there was no way she could escape or that his father could fail to notice her reaction. And there would be a reaction. Jay was sure of that.

He had no doubts at all now that his assumptions about Fate's true parentage were correct. All the facts were there and everything slotted far too easily into place for there to be any mistake. He smiled to himself, imagining Taylor's reaction when he asked her,

'Haven't you introduced your daughter to my father yet?'

Earlier in the week he had overheard his father praising Taylor for the help she had given him with his charity project, claiming that it was all because of her that he had made so much progress. Unaware of Jay's presence, Bram had taken Taylor in his arms, kissing her with slow thorough passion.

Enjoy it, Jay had thought furiously and silently, *because you aren't going to have him for very much longer.*

* * *

Plum stared at her mother in disbelief.

'You've done what?' she cried. 'Well, that's it. I am definitely not going. Not if I have to have that Scots idiot sitting next to me all evening, lecturing me on how I should be living my life. He's worse than you are,' she accused her mother shakily, 'and I—'

'Stop being so hysterical, Plum,' Helena interrupted angrily. 'I've put Gil McKenzie next to you simply to even out the numbers. Neither of you had a partner and—'

'Oh yes, that's right, rub it in. It's my party, supposedly, but *I* haven't got a partner.'

'And whose fault is that?' Helena demanded icily. 'Certainly not mine. We've done our best to bring you up properly, respectably....'

'I wanted *Bram* to sit next to me,' Plum told her bitterly. 'And even Dad would have been better than that ... than ... him.'

'There is no way I could possibly put your father near you on the top table,' Helena told her coldly. 'Apart from anything else, it simply wouldn't be fair to James. He is the one who is paying for all this, you know.'

'Well, he need not have bothered on my account,' Plum muttered under her breath. 'None of this was my idea....'

This was all she needed ... to be forced to spend the evening under the grimly watchful eye of Gil McKenzie.

She hated him, loathed him. He would ruin *everything*. How could she throw herself into flirting hard enough with Bram to entice him away from Taylor with Mr Self-Righteous sitting next to her like a jailer?

The whole evening was going to be a complete disaster, just as Patric had predicted.

'Not hungry?' Bram had asked Taylor quietly as he watched her push her food around her plate.

Taylor shook her head. She had been feeling queasy all evening, a recurrent problem and an unpleasant feature of the bug she had picked up.

Bram had tried to persuade her to go and see a doctor, but she had refused. What was the point? She was suffering from the combined effects of the trauma from the break-in and a virus; she already knew that.

She also knew that she was under a considerable amount of tension from this whole evening. She suspected that Helena probably wondered what on earth Bram saw in her. And who could blame her? She knew the history of their past relationship from Bram and had guessed that Helena must have loved him.

However, if her love now lay in the past, her daughter, Plum's, was very much in the present. She had been aware of Plum's hostility throughout the meal. Plum had made no attempt to conceal it, flirting openly and desperately with Bram all evening—or at least attempting to.

Bram had gently but very firmly made it plain to her that he simply wasn't interested. How many other men would have been able to resist such open adoration? Not many, Taylor recognised.

Jay timed his moment carefully, waiting for the brief hiatus between the ending of the more formal part of the evening and the beginning of the dancing. Standing up and pulling Fate to her feet, he ordered, 'Come with me.'

'Where are we going?' Fate protested. 'No one else is dancing yet.'

'We aren't going to dance,' Jay told her. 'I'm going to introduce you to my father. You *do* still want to meet him, don't you?'

Fate stared at him. Every time she had brought up the fact that she would still like to interview his father, Jay had stonewalled her, evidencing not just resistance to the idea, but some degree of antagonism as well.

'This way... they're at the top table,' he added carelessly.

As they walked past the other tables Fate was well aware of the attention they were receiving, or rather the attention Jay was receiving. She rather suspected she was not the cause of the oblique, and in some cases not quite so oblique, glances they were attracting, the speculation and curiosity, especially from female guests.

Through the law of the universe through which such events seem to be governed, as though by some alchemic process, a pathway cleared in front of Jay and Fate as they approached the top table. Taylor saw them first, the shock bringing her to her feet without her quite knowing how she got there. Her small agonised sound alerted Bram, causing him to look first at her in anxiety and concern and then towards his son.

It was working, Jay exulted. Taylor couldn't have betrayed herself more clearly. She was holding on to the edge of the table for support, her face white with shock, her eyes wide and blank as she focused compulsively on Fate. They were close enough now for Jay to be able to see the way she was trembling, visible violent shudders racking her body, which she made no attempt to control as she moaned a husky denial.

'Jay,' Fate protested anxiously at his side. But he ignored her, shaking off the constraining hand she had placed on his arm as he closed the distance between himself and his father.

Plum, too, was curious to know what was happening, frowning irritably as Gil said pedantically, 'I rather suspect that Taylor is not feeling very well . . . and no wonder. It's far too warm in here. She obviously needs some fresh air.'

Fresh air? Plum raised her eyes heavenwards. *Why* had her mother insisted on lumbering her with this . . . this dullard?

Only the width of the table separated them now. Taylor couldn't take her eyes off Fate, who was looking back at her in puzzled concern. Jay. . . Jay had done this, Taylor thought, and it was a hundred thousand times worse than she had ever imagined it could be. How had he found out?

There was a buzzing sound in her ears, a sense of a huge inescapable pressure bearing down on her. She could see Jay turning to say something to his father, but no matter how hard she strained to hear the words he was using to denounce her, she couldn't—the buzzing was too loud.

Jay was trying to speak to him, to introduce him to the extraordinarily pretty girl at his side, Bram guessed, but all his attention was concentrated on Taylor. He didn't need the Scots burr of Plum's young man warning, 'Watch out, she's going to faint,' to alert him to what was going to happen. He was already prepared for it. He caught Taylor deftly as she slid into a dead faint, gently lowering her to the floor.

Jay was still trying to say something to him. Without even turning his head, Bram said grimly 'Not now, Jay.'

The young Scotsman was offering to see if he could find a doctor. Helena suggested that it might be a good idea if they moved Taylor somewhere cooler and quieter.

Bram declined both offers. 'If you could just help me get her to the car. I'll take her home and get my own doctor out to see her. She hasn't been well for some time...a virus...' Fate watched, a tiny frown pleating her forehead as Jay's father and the young Scotsman gathered up Taylor's limp body and carried her towards the exit.

Why hadn't Jay helped his father? Why was he standing there staring at the woman who had fainted with his eyes full of such venomous hatred?

'Jay, what is wrong?' she asked.

'Nothing,' he told her abruptly. Grabbing hold of her arm, he added, 'Come on, we're leaving.'

She wasn't given the opportunity to protest or resist, as the other guests who had gathered round discreetly to see what had happened made way for them.

She could feel the tension in Jay's body as the crowd forced her against him. From the pieces of information he had reluctantly given her about his childhood, she had begun to draw her own conclusions about his relationship with his father. Did his anger now stem from the fact that Bram had turned to someone else to help him with Taylor?

But Jay could hardly blame his father for doing that. Fate admitted to herself that the hostility she had seen in Jay's face as he looked at the woman at his father's side had shocked her.

Jay had not discussed with her his father's relationship with Taylor, but it had been obvious to Fate that the older couple were very much in love. In fact, if she was honest with herself, it had given her an unfamiliar jolt of pain to recognise in Bram Soames just where Jay's spectacular and very male sexual appeal came from, and at the same time to recognise also that in Bram it was softened and gentled by a nature just about as different from his son's as it was possible to be.

Bram might not have Jay's sexuality to quite as intense a degree, but he had something of far more value, far more appeal to her own sex. But even so, Fate did not envy Taylor for being the recipient of Bram's love.

She might have Bram's love, but she also had Jay's hatred, and Fate suspected she knew which of them would prove the stronger.

Plum was furious. How dare that horrid stupid woman ruin her evening by fainting like that and taking Bram away!

Plum could feel the angry tears trickling down her face, ruining her carefully applied make-up, but she didn't care. What did it matter *what* she looked like now? What was the point in anything? All these years, for as long as she could remember, the only man she had really wanted was Bram, and she had gone on hoping, believing, promising herself that one day he would look at her and—

Plum tensed as she heard the door to the ladies' cloakroom open, anticipating her mother's entrance. But it wasn't her mother who had opened the door and was now advancing very purposefully and determinedly towards her, it was Gil.

'You can't come in here,' she squeaked in protest. 'Get out at once before someone sees you.'

Was that actually a smile curling Gil's normally rigid and disapproving mouth? Heavens, it was! Plum blinked and stopped crying as she recognised something else. It wasn't just a smile, it was a rather astonishingly sexy and teasing smile as well.

'I'm not going back there,' she told Gil. Her mother had obviously sent him to find her, and he would, of course, have to be the one to witness her complete humiliation and to know that he wasn't the only man to reject her.

Fresh tears filled her eyes, as self-pity overwhelmed her. What was wrong with her...? *Why* didn't Bram want her... *why* didn't he love her? Why didn't *anyone* love her?

'I'm not going back,' Plum repeated, her voice wobbling between defiance and misery. 'I won't, I...'

'So where are you going to go?' Gil asked, cocking an eyebrow enquiringly and, she was quite sure, insufferably mockingly at her. 'Or are you planning to set up home permanently in here?' he added interestedly.

'Don't be stupid, of course I'm not. I don't care where I go, or what I do. What does it matter any more?' Plum demanded mournfully.

'Your mother will be wondering where you are . . . if you are all right . . .'

Plum gave him a scathing look. 'No, she won't. She doesn't care *what* happens to me just as long as I don't embarrass her. She's never cared . . . never . . . She wishes she'd never had me.' Her voice wobbled again. 'Go away. Leave me alone.'

How could she face people now when they knew . . . when they could see? Only now could she admit to herself how much faith she had pinned on tonight, how much she had hoped that it would change things. They would all have to pay attention to her, to admit how much they had misjudged her. Even her mother respected Bram's judgement and was slightly in awe of him. With Bram's love to support her . . . to prove to everyone that she was worthwhile, no one would be able to tell her any more that she wasn't. Everyone would have to admit how wrong they had been about her.

Only it wasn't going to happen. Bram *didn't* love her and he never would; no one loved her . . . no one ever would.

'I might as well be dead,' she wept. 'I can't go back out there, I can't . . . .'

'So what are you going to do?' Gil asked again, and then before she could answer him, he added unexpectedly, 'I'm going home tonight, back to Scotland. Why don't you come with me?'

Plum stared at him. 'What?'

'You heard me,' Gil told her.

'You want me to go home with you? But why? You don't even like me.' Then, 'What's it like . . . your home?' she added suddenly and frowned as though her curiosity had come as a surprise to her.

'It's beautiful,' Gil told her quietly, his eyes darkening slightly with emotion. 'Special, the best place on earth as far as I'm concerned. The Scottish Borders are the most beautiful countryside there is. The land has been in our family for centuries, and the house was built at the beginning of the eighteenth century. It costs a fortune to run and God knows how much longer we'll be able to hang on to it.'

'The Scottish borders . . .' Plum gave a disdainful shudder. 'I'd rather . . .'

'What?' Gil challenged, 'Stay here?'

He had no idea why he was doing this. In their short, very short acquaintanceship she had said and done things that set his teeth on edge and filled him with dislike and despair. But then, listening to his cousin's revelations about her family and the way she had been brought up, he had been filled with compassion for the lonely, unloved child she must have been. He wanted to take hold of her and protect her, give her everything that she had never had, take her and gently teach her how to value herself . . . how to love herself.

She would hate his home and she would hate the life he lived there; she would cause friction and mayhem in his household and total disorder to his carefully ordered life. She would also most certainly ruin his family's name.

'Are you serious?' he heard her asking him tentatively.

He paused for a second, saw the uncertainty and longing behind the protective insouciance and said firmly, 'Yes.'

'And we could go now. . .without telling anyone. . .just leave?'

She was still, in so many ways, a child, he recognised as he nodded his head. He would have to find a way of leaving a message for her mother, of course. His aunt already knew that it was his intention to drive north from the ball.

Who would have believed that a man like Gil was capable of behaving so impetuously, so romantically? Plum marvelled as she picked up her trailing skirts and walked towards him.

It was all rather like something out of a Regency romance . . . with the heroine being swept off by the hero. Well, maybe not quite so romantic as that—after all, she and Gil didn't even like each other, Plum remembered—but then if she *didn't* go with him, what was the alternative?

Go back to the ballroom, where everyone knew what had happened? Where everyone had seen the awful way in which Bram had made it so obvious how much he loved Taylor, the way he had totally ignored her?

And she needn't stay in Scotland long, need she? Just long enough for people to forget what had happened.

19

'Jay, what are you doing?' Fate demanded as he dragged her out of the ballroom and into the hotel lobby.

'Your father—'

'My father's a fool,' Jay interrupted harshly. 'My God, she's got him exactly where she wants him, or she thinks she has, but she's not—'

He broke off, cursing under his breath as he almost collided with another man who was obviously also on the point of departure from the hotel, the collar of his heavy coat turned up, shadowing his face. Fate gave the man a brief, sympathetic smile in mitigation of Jay's irritation and bad manners.

'Jay, where are you going? You can't just walk out like this,' Fate protested, as she realised he was heading for the hotel exit.

'No? Watch me,' Jay ground out. 'My God, did you see what that clever bitch did? But all she's done is buy herself some time . . . so that she can come up with some more lies to deceive my father. . . .'

He was talking about Taylor, Fate realised in dismay. His enmity towards the other woman had shocked her. It had revealed a side of him she had suspected existed, but it had been a suspicion she had buried deeply and tried to ignore.

'Where are you going?' she asked worriedly.

'Home,' he told her curtly. 'Are you coming?'

Fate stared at him. This was the first time he had invited her to his apartment, if 'invite' was the right word. When she had visualised the first time she went to his home, it had certainly not been under these circumstances.

As she hesitated, torn between concern and wariness, he turned towards her, watching her.

Fate hesitated. 'I . . . I'll think about it while you're getting the car. . . .'

'I'm leaving the car here,' Jay said. 'We can walk from here.'

'Walk?' Fate stared at him, and then looked down at her thin shoes and long skirt.

'Jay, it's raining,' she protested. 'And . . .'

He was starting to turn away from her, shrugging his shoulders, his mouth set and hard. And yet, as she looked at him, it was not an angry adult Fate saw, but a small, insecure, frightened child.

She caught up with him just as he strode through the door. He didn't look at her or speak to her until she told him breathlessly that he was walking too fast for her.

He stopped abruptly, turning around so sharply, sliding his hands into her hair and holding her head so tightly, that she made a small protest of pain.

'What's wrong? This is what you wanted, isn't it?' he demanded roughly as he covered her mouth with his, expertly silencing any response she could have made; kissing her with an intensity and demand that made her head spin and the blood pound through her veins.

She could feel her body reacting to him, responding to him . . . wanting him.

When he released her, her mouth was swollen, throbbing from his kiss. Her hair and her face felt damp from the rain and tears of emotion filled her eyes as she looked up at him.

'Oh, Jay . . .'

'Oh, Fate,' he mimicked mockingly. 'You're amazingly easy to arouse, do you know that? I rather envy you. Hasn't your mother ever warned you that sometimes it's wise to hold back a little . . . that the male likes a challenge?'

Fate eyed him warily. 'Jay, what is it . . . what's wrong?' she asked him quietly.

He had been in an odd mood all evening and the way he was behaving now frightened her. If she was not careful he could hurt her very badly.

'Nothing's wrong,' he told her tersely. 'I thought this was what you wanted.'

He had started walking again but this time tempering his stride to allow Fate to keep pace with him.

'To go to bed with me. Or are you going to lie to me and pretend that it isn't? That's something your sex is very good at,' he told her savagely. 'Lying . . . you've made it into an art form . . . a way of life and—'

'I have *never* lied to you,' Fate interrupted him, and added steadily, 'and yes, I do want to go to bed with you.'

'So why the coy hesitation?'

'I'm not being coy,' Fate denied. 'I was just surprised, that's all. After all, you're the one who's always said that *I'd* have to do the asking. . . .'

The smile he gave her was hugely unkind and made her heart miss an anxious beat.

'But you *have* asked,' he told her softly. 'You never *stop* asking . . . and now I've decided to say yes. What's wrong?' he taunted. 'And please don't tell me that you've changed your mind and you want to go home to Mother. Children change their minds, adult women do not, and as you're very fond of telling me, you are an adult woman, way past the age of consent. Which reminds me, I trust you carry some form of protection with you. If not . . . I seem to remember there's an all-night chemist just round the corner here, although I can't remember the last time I had call to use it. See how honoured you are,' he mocked her. 'All those fevered still-adolescent fantasies you've no doubt been creating about my varied sex life are way, way off the mark.'

Fate gave him a troubled look. He was deliberately goading her, but why? As she mentally reviewed the evening, trying to pinpoint what she might have said or done to have caused his present mood, she suddenly frowned.

She was falling into a trap already far too familiar to many women, she recognised sombrely, that of taking on the responsibility for another person's moods and happiness.

She shivered as they turned the corner, and she saw the lights of the small shopping precinct.

'I don't have anything with me,' she said truthfully.

For a moment she half expected he was going to send her into the shop, but then he gave a small shrug and told her curtly, 'Wait here.'

He wasn't gone long. Fate had deliberately turned her back on the shop as she waited for him.

Why was it that even as she applauded Jay's common sense in broaching such a subject, she also mourned the lack of romance and spontaneity that went with it?

'It's this way...' Jay touched her arm lightly, guiding her round the corner.

They were in one of the most expensive and exclusive parts of the city. The large houses which lined the streets and the square up ahead of them were the property of the Duke of Westminster.

They walked through the square and turned down a street which led off it. As they did so, Fate was surprised to see an empty, boarded-up building site.

'It was demolished without proper planning permission,' Jay told her dryly when she commented on it. 'The company that owns the site has gone into liquidation apparently, and in the present climate no one seems to want to buy the site. London is full of empty office blocks.

'It's here,' he said, indicating the modern block on the corner and gesturing towards the flight of steps which led up to the main door.

The building looked cold and bleak, which was exactly the way she felt. The passion and arousal she had felt when Jay kissed her had faded, and she shivered.

'Now, what is it?' Jay demanded heavily.

'I...I don't think this is a good idea,' Fate said truthfully. 'I...you...this isn't the way I wanted it to be....I don't think—'

'You don't think what?' Jay was angry now. 'Don't start playing games with me, Fate,' he warned furiously. 'I'm not in the mood for it. You've left it a bit late to play the coy virgin role,' he added unkindly. 'And don't bother trying to lie to me—'

'I have no intention of lying to you,' Fate interrupted him crisply. She was becoming angry herself now.

'All women lie,' Jay corrected her. 'Look at the way that bitch Taylor has deceived my father—'

Silently Fate looked into Jay's face. The control she had so deplored had gone now, and she felt, rather like poor Pandora must have when she finally unlocked and opened the forbidden box. A small quiver of prescient fear shivered down her spine.

This, she suspected, was the *real* cause of Jay's volatile mood tonight. Not her, and certainly not any desire for her, but the relationship between his father and another woman.

She had seen the hatred in his eyes in the ballroom and had pushed it aside. Now she couldn't ignore it any longer.

'Your father's relationship with Taylor is *his* concern, not yours, Jay,' she pointed out quietly.

'It's obvious how much he loves her and how much she loves him. Just because *you* find their closeness...hurtful...' She was trying to choose her words carefully, trying desperately not to provoke the fury she could see glittering in Jay's eyes. 'That doesn't mean that Taylor is deceiving your father. Why should she... what could she hope to gain...? No woman who loves a man wants to deceive him, and she *does* love him.'

Fate was genuinely puzzled by Jay's insistence that Taylor was deceiving his father.

'*Why?*'

Jay's control broke and he reached for her, taking hold of her upper arms and shaking her as he howled the question into the night.

'Do you *really* want to know...? Then I'll tell you. She's lying to him because she doesn't want him to know the truth about her. She doesn't want him to *know* what she really is, because she knows that *if* he does, *when* he does, there'll be no place in his life for her. A woman who abandoned her own child... denied her... sold her. My God, where do women get the reputation for "mothering" from. You don't care about the emotions... the needs, the lives of your children. You just use them as pawns, pretending to love them when it suits you, and then ignoring them... denying them when it doesn't....'

Fate stared at him. Even if he had allowed her to speak, she had no idea what to say. This torrent of abuse and hatred that was pouring from him left her torn between shock and pity, too numbed by what he was saying to be aware of his painful grip on her arms or the curious scrutiny of a couple watching them from the other side of the road.

'Whatever Taylor has done in the past... she loves your father now, Jay,' Fate said gently. 'We all make mistakes and—'

'So rational and forgiving... I wonder if you'd be quite so forgiving if you knew the whole truth?' Jay taunted. 'Shall I tell you what she is ... what she's done?'

Fate discovered that her mouth had gone dry and she was starting to tremble. What on earth had *she* to fear from hearing Jay's 'truth' about a woman she didn't even know.

Besides, it was obvious that Jay intended to tell her whether she gave him permission or not.

'She's your mother, Fate . . . the woman who gave birth to you and then rejected you, gave you away to another couple, abandoned you. She's your *mother!* God knows who your father was—some student she met at university perhaps, an already married man, or maybe she doesn't even know. Haven't you ever thought it strange that your birth wasn't registered until you were several months old, that your parents haven't had any other children.'

'I . . . I was born abroad. My parents didn't register my birth until they came back to this country. Don't you remember? I told you at lunch the day we met.'

Fate could hear the panic in her voice, feel it in her body. It couldn't be true . . . it was impossible. She would have *known*. She would have been told. Jay was just making it up, trying to frighten her, to punish her for supporting and defending Taylor.

Out of the corner of her eye she saw the couple on the other side of the road, embracing in the shadows. The woman was giggling . . . protesting, the clear night air carrying the sound to Fate as easily as it must be carrying the sound of their quarrel to them.

'Taylor isn't my mother,' Fate denied painfully. 'She can't be . . . I . . . I would have known. . . .'

Jay laughed mockingly.

'*How?* If she isn't your mother, how do you explain the fact that she has a photograph of you, the exact same one that takes pride of place in your parents' sitting room.'

He ignored Fate's agonised 'no,' continuing brutally. 'She told me you were her goddaughter, but *that* was a lie, wasn't it, Fate. *You* didn't even recognise her name, never mind know who she was . . .'

Fate stared at him, her face pinched and haunted. 'You're lying, Jay. I don't believe you.'

'Oh, yes, you do,' Jay contradicted her. 'You don't want to . . . but you do. Be honest. What other explanation can there be? Why would she lie if she didn't have something to conceal.

'Oh, no, my dear, Taylor *is* your mother—if indeed that is her name. And even if you do not know her, she certainly knows you. Did you see the look on her face tonight when she saw you?'

'That was very quick of her to stage that faint, but all she's done is buy herself some time. I knew right from the start that she was hiding something . . . concealing something.'

'You've done all this deliberately, haven't you,' Fate whispered.

'It was a lie,' she accused, her voice starting to rise with the pain exploding inside her, 'all a pretence. You *never* wanted me. All you wanted was to *use* me!'

'You had it all planned, right from the start, didn't you!'

Fate knew she was shrieking and that the couple on the other side of the street were openly listening, but she didn't care. She was too furious to care.

How could she have been such a fool? How *could* she have let Jay manipulate her, use her like this!

She felt sick with humiliation and shock. Jay was still holding her. She tried to wrench herself away from him but he refused to let her go.

'How far were you prepared to go, Jay?' she asked hoarsely. 'How could you possibly have wanted to take me to bed when you feel the way you do about the woman you claim is my mother? Or are you so . . . so emotionally perverted that that kind of thing turns you on?' she asked in disgust.

'She *is* your mother. The way she reacted when she saw you tonight proves that,' Jay told her savagely. 'And as for what turns me on and how far I was prepared to go . . .'

Fate was unprepared for the way he pulled her against his body and its arousal. As she struggled to break free she could feel his hands moving down her back, pressing her even more closely against him.

His heart was hammering heavily against his ribs and she could feel her own body reacting to his physical excitement even as her mind froze in revulsion.

'You're sick,' she said shakily, trying to break free.

'I'm sick? Because I tell you a truth you don't want to hear? Don't blame me, Fate. I'm just the messenger. If you're looking for someone to blame, then the person who's really responsible is Taylor. Blame your mother.'

Did he know what he was doing to her, Fate wondered, or was he so self-obsessed, so caught up in his own needs that he had no conception of what he was doing, the pain he was inflicting on her?

Her parents would have told her if she'd been adopted. Honesty was very important to them—and to her.

She shuddered as she felt his hands sliding forward to cup her breasts, her teeth chattering with a mixture of shock and revulsion.

She could feel the heat of his breath against her skin, tiny shivers of sexual recognition shimmying down her spine. Tears clogged her throat and burned her eyes.

She couldn't remember ever feeling such anger or such helplessness. He had deceived her, betrayed her, deliberately and cold-bloodedly taken her hand and brought her to this place of pain. Her feelings, her pain, her life—they weren't important to him. She was simply a tool he had used in his obsessive desire to control his father's life.

'You don't love your father,' she told him quietly as she tensed her body against him. 'You don't know *how* to love, Jay, either anyone else or yourself. You only know how to hate, how to inflict pain. You say you want to protect your father from Taylor, but that's a lie. You don't want to protect him—you want to *destroy* him, to make him suffer because you blame him for . . .'

She saw anger ignite the darkness of his eyes and just had time to give a small, protesting gasp of denial as his mouth came down on hers, the weight of his body crushing the breath from her lungs as his teeth bit savagely at the inner softness of her lips and her frantic cries of protest were smothered beneath the cruel pressure of his kiss.

She had thought she knew all there was to know about herself and her sexuality and she had worn that self-assurance like a banner. Now suddenly he was ripping that banner from her showing her its frailty and inability to protect her. Showing her that against her will, her pride and her mind, her body could be made to respond to a male desire that was fuelled not by desire, but by anger.

The grief and pain of her self-knowledge froze her body into stiff rejection. Jay raised his head and looked into her eyes. 'Don't tell me you don't want me, because we both know it's a lie.'

'Yes, I want you,' Fate admitted steadily, 'but I want my self-respect more.'

Quietly she stepped back from him.

'Right now I'm not sure which one of us I pity and despise the most, Jay,' she told him shakily. 'You or myself . . . On balance I rather think it's myself. I, at least, should have known better. You . . . !'

'Very dramatic,' Jay sneered, 'but the truth is that no matter what the hell you'd like to imagine you feel, right now I could take you to bed and make you forget that any of this conversation ever took place. In fact I'd guarantee it.'

'Oh, yes,' Fate agreed calmly. 'I've no doubt that you've got the skill—and the cruelty to use my own body against me. But it isn't you who arouses me. It's the image I've created of you in my own mind that I'd be responding to, and that man simply doesn't exist.

'You think you've got all the answers, Jay, all the power, but life isn't like that. You think that the moment you reveal the secrets of Taylor's past your father will reject her. But he loves her, and love, real, genuine love, can be a very forgiving and compassionate emotion.

'After all, he still loves *you*, doesn't he?' she added with cutting emphasis before turning on her heel and walking away, her head held high, her vision blurred by the tears that filled her eyes.

She heard him calling her name, but she didn't turn round and she knew that he wouldn't come after her.

Fate might have thought she had had the last word, but she would soon come crawling back, Jay told himself sardonically, as he crossed the foyer and took the stairs to his first-floor apartment two at a time.

It wasn't his fault if she hadn't liked hearing the truth. He wasn't the one who had lied to her. She ought to be thanking him for showing her how she had been duped and deceived, not treating him as though . . .

Silly little fool.

Angrily Jay tugged off his damp jacket and flung it down on the sofa, cursing savagely beneath his breath.

She was the one who had goaded him into telling her the truth. If she hadn't . . .

If she hadn't, right now she'd be in his bed, her long supple body spread out beneath him, her legs wrapped round him, her eyes dark with longing and arousal as she looked with bemused awe and delight into his and felt the inexorable thrust of his body within her.

She would have been a generous lover, giving everything, holding back nothing, uninhibited in her response to him, glorying in her womanhood. The kind of woman who . . .

The kind of woman he neither needed nor wanted in his life, Jay told himself harshly as he walked into his small kitchen, banging open drawers until he had found what he was searching for.

He seldom drank either at home or alone, and the raw spirit burned his throat as he emptied the full glass in one gulp.

Tonight was Fate's loss, not his, he assured himself as he poured himself a second glass. She would ache for him a hell of a lot more than he was aching for her, and for a hell of a lot longer.

The taxi driver gave Fate an anxious look as he dropped her off at her front door. She was a tall girl, not the vulnerable-looking type at all, he would have thought, but there was a look about her, an air of sadness, of forlornness and pain that brought out all his male protective instincts.

Perhaps it was just as well that her parents were away, Fate reflected as she unlocked the door. They would know the moment they saw her face that something was wrong, and being them, they would want to know what.

She went into the sitting room and switched on the light, walking across to the photograph of herself which had been taken when she had learned that she had got into university. Did Taylor really have a copy of this photograph, or was Jay simply lying to her?

She didn't for one moment believe his claim that she was Taylor's daughter. She couldn't possibly have been as close to her parents as she was if she was not their child. There would have been something, some clue, some sense within herself of not being a part of them.

But that look of shock and fear on Taylor's face this evening. *Had* she caused that? And if so, why? So many questions and so few answers. Her head ached with the combined weight of them and the pain the evening had brought her.

Logically, she knew she had done the right thing in walking away from Jay. He had shown her what he really thought of her . . . how unimportant she was to him.

No matter how badly she might be hurting right now, she would have hurt a hell of a lot more if she hadn't discovered the truth until after they had become lovers.

Lovers . . . She closed her eyes. Dear God, what a word to use in connection with what there would actually have been between Jay and her.

What would happen if his father chose Taylor over Jay? What would he do? How would he react? Fate shivered.

There was no way that he would simply accept defeat and walk away, leaving his father and Taylor to get on with their lives. No . . . he would rather destroy them both and himself as well, than allow them their happiness. . . .

She closed her eyes and then opened them again.

'My mother never wanted me,' Jay had once told her brutally in response to her innocent question about his family. 'Nor did my father, although he made a better job of concealing it, or at least attempting to. Making atonement, he's very good at that . . . but not good enough.'

'Oh, Jay,' Fate whispered now. Tears burned her eyes but she refused to let them fall. What was the point? They wouldn't help Jay and they certainly wouldn't help her. . . .

—▶ ◀—

20

T aylor heard the bedroom door open and immediately tensed. She could see from the look on Bram's face that he was aware of her withdrawal and was trying to control his reaction.

Tears blurred her vision as he sat down on the edge of the bed, carefully giving her enough room so that he was not invading her space.

'How are you feeling?' he asked gently.

'Fine,' Taylor said unconvincingly, avoiding meeting his eyes.

The doctor had been at first amused and then concerned by her reaction to the news he had given her after he examined her.

He had wanted to send for Bram then, but she had stopped him, explaining shakily that she needed to have some time on her own to absorb what he had said. She knew that he would have spoken to Bram before he left.

'I think I sensed right from the first moment I saw you that you could have a very powerful and transforming effect on my life,' Bram told her softly, as he reached for her hand.

Taylor let him take it, her cold flesh warming in the tender hold of his.

'But I must admit I never dreamed . . . never dared dream per- haps, just how powerful and transforming that effect was going to be.

'Perhaps it's old-fashioned of me,' he continued when Taylor gave no response, 'or even worse, a sign of my own increasing maturity that what, as a boy, was a prospect that filled me with stomach-churning fear and disbelief should now fill me with an equal sense of disbelief. But this time a disbelief born of awe and joy. Perhaps we do have to reach a certain degree of maturity to recognise that our ability to create new life is in its own way a very special miracle.'

'Try telling that to a girl—a woman—who discovers she's pregnant with a child she most emphatically never planned and doesn't want,' Taylor said grimly. But her eyes still filled with tears at the sincerity in his voice and the love in his eyes.

'Are you very angry with me?' Bram asked quietly.

Taylor shook her head, 'I'm more angry with myself,' she told him truthfully.

'You don't want our child.' It was a statement rather than a question.

'Do you?' she challenged Bram forcefully.

'Yes,' he said firmly. 'Oh, I know what you're going to say, and I agree that this baby wasn't planned or even anticipated by either of us, but when the doctor told me, I felt what I can only describe as a sense of rightness, of . . . of great pleasure and happiness . . . a sense of . . . of fate almost.'

'You mean that being a man it makes you feel good to know that you've impregnated me,' Taylor said pointedly.

'No, I don't mean that at all,' Bram denied. 'How could I, of all men, feel like that? I've learned the folly of that kind of male chauvinism the hard way, Taylor, and what it costs—to everyone involved.

'No, what I meant, but obviously didn't put across very well, was that it seemed right and good...meant to be, in some sense, that you and I through our love should have created a new life. All the more so, in some ways, because we didn't plan to do so . . . because it wasn't a conscious decision. An . . . an affirmation of our love, if you like. . . .'

Taylor swallowed hard on the hot tears scalding the backs of her eyes.

She had known instinctively and immediately that he would feel like this, that he would want their child, that he would want them both.

She knew that the doctor thought her angry denial was because she didn't want her child, but he had been wrong. Of course she wanted him or her. Of course she did. Her reaction had been caused by her feelings of anger and guilt, and fear of the burdens, the danger she was imposing on her child even before it was born.

'I want us to get married,' Bram told her, adding quickly before she could interrupt him, 'and no, not just because of the baby.

'Or, at least, not in the way that you might mean. I want us to be married because I want to show the world the commitment we're making to each other. A commitment I wanted to make before the doctor told me about the baby, but I was afraid to push you in case it was something you didn't want as much. But now...?' He paused and looked at her.

'The doctor was concerned about you. You do want this baby, don't you, Taylor?' he asked her huskily. 'You aren't thinking of—'

'No...no. Never,' Taylor denied fiercely and truthfully. Abort her child...no... She couldn't even think of it, but that didn't stop her from dwelling on the guilt she would always feel about his or her conception. 'I want us to get married,' Bram had said. If she refused, if she left him...disappeared...how would her child—Bram's son or daughter—feel when he or she was old enough to understand that she was responsible for Bram's absence from the child's life? Had she any right to deprive her child of its father...and such a father...? Taylor knew she didn't. But the alternative meant exposing Bram, as well as her child, to so much danger. Had she the right?

'I don't want this child to suffer as Jay has done. I don't want to inflict on it the wounds I've inflicted on him. I want this child to know right from the start how much he or she is loved and wanted. I want to be always and for ever a part of its life. But even without this baby I would still have wanted to marry you, Taylor.'

'I know that,' Taylor acknowledged chokingly. And she did. She had known right from the start. She had known *everything*, but she had not known this. She had not known, had never thought, dreamed, imagined that she might have already conceived Bram's child. It had simply not occurred to her; there had been so many other things to worry about, and at her age...

It was only just beginning to dawn on her what she had done, and the nausea that churned in her stomach had nothing to do with her pregnancy.

Bram saw her face turn pale and frowned anxiously. 'What is it? Aren't you feeling well? Shall I...'

Taylor shook her head. 'I shouldn't have done this,' she wept. 'I should never have let this happen. Oh God, Bram...'

She was crying in earnest now, her body shaking, as the days, months, years of suppressed emotion and fear finally broke through the barriers she had buried them behind.

'I can't marry you. I can't put you in so much danger....'

'What danger?' Bram demanded gently. 'You're the one who'll be at risk. You're the one who's carrying our child?'

'No, it's not that...it's not the baby...you don't understand.'

She was sobbing uncontrollably, her body shuddering. Instinctively Bram realised that if he was ever to learn what in her past had caused her so much distress and pain, it was now.

'Tell me, Taylor,' he coaxed gently, taking her in his arms. 'Tell me what's wrong, darling. Whatever it is it can't hurt you now. Nothing can hurt you now.'

Taylor started to laugh hysterically. 'Oh God, if only that was true,' she told him. 'But I can never be safe, Bram . . . not while he's still alive. And neither can you and our baby. . . He'll try to hurt you too. Oh God, what have I done, what have I done?'

'Jay knows . . .' she added wildly. 'Somehow he's found out. That's why he was there last night with her....'

Bram frowned. He had already suspected that the appearance of his son with that incredibly pretty girl, who was somehow vaguely familiar, had been responsible for at least part of the stress which had led to Taylor's fainting. But the discovery that Taylor was pregnant had pushed his son's part in the events to the back of his mind.

'Jay can't hurt you,' he told her firmly now. 'I don't care *what* he knows . . . what he's found out. *Nothing* can change the fact that I love you, Taylor. Nothing!'

'Not even if...not even if I decided that I...that I couldn't have this baby?' Taylor tested.

She could see the pain in his eyes and her own heart ached in response. The mere thought of losing this child she had only known she was carrying for a handful of hours, was almost as bad as the thought of losing Bram himself.

'Not even that,' he assured her huskily. 'I couldn't force you to have my child, Taylor. No man has a right to force a woman to do that. If you don't want our baby—'

'I do ... I do ...' Taylor interrupted him fiercely. She paused, then said slowly and clearly, 'I believe that Jay thinks that Fate is my daughter, but she isn't....'

Bram waited, hardly daring to breathe in case she changed her mind and retreated behind that wall of reserve of hers.

'She's my niece,' she told him hesitantly, so obviously waiting for and wary of his reaction that Bram's heart ached for her. Steadily, his eyes met hers, willing her to feel his acceptance of her, whatever her past might hold. It must have worked because when she started to speak again, her voice was firmer and more confident. 'My sister's daughter ... But she doesn't even know I exist.'

Bram fought to hide his compassion. He could hear the pain in her voice, see it in her eyes, feel it in the air around her. It was, he recognised now, such a constant part of her life that it was always there with her—even if it was only now that he was being allowed to see the full extent of it for the first time.

What had happened? Had they quarrelled, these two sisters, and so badly that one of them had never allowed her child to know of the other's existence? But if that was the case, how did Taylor know Fate's name, how did she come to have her photograph? Because Bram realised now where and why he had found Fate's face so familiar. He waited.

'Caroline is my older sister,' she explained. 'She met Oliver, her husband, when she was working in Australia. My parents, our parents, didn't want them to marry. They...' She swallowed painfully. 'They never knew about Fate.... They were killed before ... before Caroline could tell them she was pregnant.'

'They were killed in a car accident, you once told me,' Bram said gently.

'Yes, that's right,' Taylor agreed dully. 'Only it wasn't an accident ... it wasn't an accident at all, and it was all my fault. Because of me ...'

She was crying again, her whole body shaking uncontrollably as Bram comforted her and rocked her.

What did she mean? Had she been driving the car? He could think of no other way in which she could blame herself for her parents' deaths. He could well understand how a sensitive young woman could and would blame herself.

As gently as he could, he tried to reassure her. 'Even if you were driving, that doesn't mean that—'

'No,' Taylor interrupted, shaking her head violently. 'You don't understand. It wasn't me...I didn't kill them. It was him....'

'Him?' Bram repeated. He was completely mystified now, but of much more concern to him than his own confusion was Taylor's deathly pallor, the tremors that shook her body, the blank, shut-in look in her eyes when she turned her head to focus on him.

'*Him,*' she repeated insistently, angry almost that Bram should question whom she meant. 'Dennis Phillips,' she whispered, her lips trembling as they formed the two words. 'He's in prison now. He was sentenced to serve two consecutive life sentences... and an extra term, for... for... rape as well. But they won't be able to keep him there for ever.'

She was trembling so violently her teeth were chattering, a hectic flush burning the previously pale skin of her face, her eyes dark and brilliant as though she was in the grip of some fever. Her words tumbled over themselves so quickly that Bram had to concentrate to make sense of them.

'And when he gets out, he's going to come looking for me. I know he will and when he does—' She turned to Bram and his heart ached with pity and shock as he saw the terror in her eyes.

'He's already killed my parents. He swore he'd never let anyone else have me, that he'd never let anyone come between us. I thought then...' She closed her eyes and then opened them again.

'He'll find me...us...and then he'll try to kill you, Bram, like he did them. And our baby...he'll.... I should never have let this happen.... I never meant it to happen.... Don't you see? I *can't* stay with you.... I *can't* marry you.... I can't put you in that kind of danger. It's bad enough that *I* have to live like this, dreading each day, never knowing...always being afraid...knowing that one day he'll get out of prison and that then he'll try to find me.

'I know the police told him that I was dead, that I'd been in the car with my parents, but I *know* he won't believe them. I know! He's like that, you see—obsessed—and even though they've changed my name, given me a new identity, Jay found out. He must have to have brought Fate to show me. And if Jay can find out . . . Jay reminds me of him in a lot of ways . . . in the way he is . . . with his obsession about you. I can't go on living like this, Bram. I can't take any more. It was bad enough before, but now that I've met you. . . I had no right to let you get involved with me . . . to let you love me. No right to put you in this position.'

'You couldn't have stopped me from loving you,' Bram told her huskily. 'As for exposing me to danger . . . he's only a man, Taylor, and you've said yourself, he's in prison now. . . .'

'He's *not* only a man . . . he's . . . he's possessed,' Taylor told him frantically. 'You don't understand . . . you don't know . . .'

'Then tell me,' Bram invited.

Taylor stared at him. 'I don't know if I can.'

'Try,' Bram encouraged her, stroking her hair and holding her close. 'I promise you it doesn't matter what you say, it won't change anything. It won't stop me loving you. Nothing and no one could ever do that.

'Did you once love him, Taylor . . . is that it? Did you love him and because of that . . . because he was somehow responsible for your parents' deaths you feel that you share his guilt?'

'I do share it. He killed them . . . murdered them because of me . . . because he wanted me and because he knew that they . . . He thought it was just because of them that I didn't want to see him any more, but it wasn't.'

'He was my first boyfriend. We met when I was sixteen. I was very naïve . . . very young for my age. My parents . . .' Taylor gave a small shrug. 'They loved us in their way, but they had such high standards, such ambitions for us both, and I was so afraid that I might disappoint them. They were also so cold, so critical, so distant somehow. When I met Dennis and he was so kind to me . . . so loving . . . so warm, so possessive, I thought. . . .' Bram's heart ached for her as she had to stop to swallow. He wanted to tell her that there was no need for her to go on, that it didn't matter, that she had no need to bare her soul to him. But instinctively, he knew that she needed to talk, to bring out into the open all the pain and fear she had kept hidden.

'My parents didn't approve. They thought he wasn't good enough for me. He was eighteen and he had already left school. They wanted me to go to university as my sister had done. I used to meet him secretly after school and in the evening when my parents were out. We . . . we became lovers. I . . . I . . . enjoyed it. It made me feel . . . it made me feel valued, loved. It both shocked me and excited me to discover that I was . . . that I liked sex.

'I knew my parents would be horrified . . . disgusted. My sister and I . . . my parents considered academic achievement much more important than emotional happiness.

'I suppose, if I'd been more experienced, more aware, I'd have realised sooner that he was too intense . . . too possessive, but then . . . Well, it just seemed to me that it was wonderful to have someone to love me so much. He used to make jokes about killing any other boy who looked at me, about killing me if I left him, and that used to make me feel so protected and wanted . . . knowing that he loved me so much. Oh God, if I'd only known that he wasn't joking, but I didn't . . . I didn't know that . . .' Anxiously Taylor turned to look up at Bram. 'I didn't know. . . .'

'No, of course you didn't,' Bram comforted her. 'How could you . . . ?'

Inwardly, he was wondering how on earth her parents could have been so uncaring, so unseeing, not to have known what was happening to her. He could picture her so clearly, feel her need . . . her innocence and her hunger to be loved and his heart ached for her.

'At first, all I wanted was to be with him. He made me feel so good . . . so happy. But then . . . he started to get angry, to pick on me, demanding to know where I was and who I was with whenever I wasn't with him. Once he saw me talking to a boy in the street—his parents were friends of my parents—I just stopped to say hello, that was all, only Dennis thought . . . he . . . there was a fight and Paul, this other boy . . . he was very quiet, very shy. He was quite badly hurt. Dennis said afterwards that he was sorry, that he had been jealous and that he'd lost his temper. I was upset at first, shocked. But then . . .' Taylor bit her lip and looked nervously at Bram.

'It was flattering to think that I meant so much to him,' she admitted, with painful honesty. 'I was so selfish, so . . . so self-obsessed.'

'You were young,' Bram contradicted her gently. 'Young and very vulnerable.'

'By the time I began at Oxford, I was beginning to realise just what he was. But he was so persistent, and although I tried to end it, he just kept on turning up, insisting that I loved him really, threatening to kill himself if I left him.

'He got a job right in the city of Oxford. Everywhere I went he seemed to be there. I knew he loved me, but . . . I was afraid of him. He would get so angry. Once, when I tried to end it, he punched a hole through the door to my rooms. He was so jealous that I daren't make . . .

'He didn't like me spending any time with other people, not even with other girls. One day, when I was out at a lecture, I got back to find out he'd moved into my rooms. He refused to leave. He said I couldn't be trusted, that he had to do it to make sure that I didn't leave him. He gave up his job. He told me he was afraid I'd try to leave when he wasn't there. He wanted me to leave university. He wanted us to go away together, but by then . . .'

'Wasn't there anyone you could ask for help?' Bram queried gently. Inwardly, he was more shocked than he wanted her to see. He had guessed that there was someone in her past who had hurt her, but he had imagined an unhappy love affair, perhaps with a married man. It had never occurred to him that she had endured anything like this.

'It didn't matter what I did, how much I tried to appease him, to reassure him . . .' Taylor continued in a low voice. 'He just became worse. The more I gave in the more he demanded. I . . . afterwards I had some counselling and I was told then that such obsessiveness like that feeds on itself. . . .

'I had started to fall behind with my studies . . . I was terrified that I would be sent down. I knew how my parents would react to that. They didn't even know that I was still seeing Dennis. I hadn't dared to tell them.'

'But surely, when they visited you they saw him . . . realised . . .'

'They didn't visit me,' Taylor told him, shaking her head. 'My father was very involved in his own career, and in fact they had moved temporarily from our home near Oxford to a flat in London, just before I began university. They were concerned then about my sister, as well.'

Bram looked away from her, not wanting her to see the anger in his eyes. What kind of people had they been not to have known, not to have guessed, not, apparently, to have cared . . .?

'Things got worse. Dennis . . . he started accusing me of seeing other men.' She gave a bitter laugh. 'He must have known it wasn't true. By then he was insisting on accompanying me to my lectures and waiting outside for me. I never went anywhere without him.

'He bought some handcuffs. . . . I don't know where . . .' She gave a deep shudder, shame and anguish darkening her eyes as she gave Bram a look of anguished appeal.

'He said he wanted . . . he fixed them to the wall by the bed . . . just out of sight so that no one else . . .' She stopped, shaking her head, unable to go on.

'He did that to you?' Bram couldn't conceal the revulsion he was feeling.

'He—he threatened to,' Taylor told him, 'but he never . . . well, only once and that was . . .'

She bowed her head. 'I hated him by then, but I was terrified of him as well.

'My counsellor told me later that . . . that it was tantamount to kidnap and rape. But how could it be when we were already living together . . . and he was already my lover, even though by then I didn't want—

'Rape isn't something that only happens with a stranger,' she told Bram painfully. 'I felt so guilty, so dirty. . . . I wanted it to end so desperately, but I was so afraid of him . . . of what he said he'd do. Sometimes, when he said he'd kill himself if I left him, I almost wished he would,' she admitted in a whisper.

'My tutor wasn't happy with my work. He kept me behind one afternoon after my lecture to talk to me about it. Dennis was outside. He . . . he . . . he was always very suspicious and when I didn't come out at the usual time . . .

'He came looking for me. I was crying...my lecturer... Dennis thought...he attacked him, and it was worse this time, much worse than before. The police became involved. My parents...

'My father told Dennis that he was never to see me again, that he would never be allowed to see me again. I moved out of my rooms and went to live with four other girls. My parents applied for a court order banning Dennis from coming near me.

'I never saw him, but I knew that he was there. I could feel him watching me. He joined the army after he left school but...but he'd had to leave....'

'He'd...there'd always been a violent, possessive streak there apparently. He'd never known his father. And his mother, she couldn't cope with him, and when she remarried, it was decided that he should be fostered. It wasn't all his fault. I—'

'He...he broke into the house one night. He locked the other girls in one room. He told me that he was taking me away, that we were going where no one would ever be able to find us. He said that he'd kill anyone who tried to come between us. He said it was all my parents' fault, that they had never liked him...that they had turned me against him.

'I didn't want to do what he said, to go with him, but he was making all kinds of threats, not just against my parents, but the other girls as well.... He...he said he was taking me somewhere where no one else would ever find us....'

Taylor's face had gone white again, but her eyes were burning with emotion, haunted with remembered anguish.

'He...he took me into my room...' Taylor started again. 'He had destroyed it—everything—my things, my work, the furniture. It was...it was horrible. He told me that if I didn't go with him, if I didn't do what he wanted, if I tried to escape, he would hunt me down, find me wherever I went. I asked him why he was doing it...what he hoped to gain...' She looked at Bram.

'He said it was because he loved me.' Her mouth trembled. 'It was obscene. How could he love me? *That* wasn't love....'

She closed her eyes and took a deep breath, trying to steady herself. 'I went with him. He had a car. It was very old, very rusty. He...he said there were handcuffs in it.... He...I...I begged him not to touch me, but he wouldn't listen to me. I was so afraid, so sickened by what he was doing, by what he was. He said he wanted me to have his child. He kept going on and on about it, telling me over and over again that all he wanted was for us to be together with our child.

'It had gone dark by this time. I had no idea where we were. God knows what would have happened if the brother of one of the girls I was living with hadn't turned up unexpectedly and discovered what had happened. The police were alerted, and they set up roadblocks. I found out later that he'd virtually been driving around in circles.

'I . . . the police and my parents wanted to bring a case against him for abducting me. He was taken into custody but allowed out on bail. It was then that he killed my parents. . . . They had moved back to Oxford by then. He did something to their car. The police found the evidence afterwards. There was an accident . . . the brakes . . . They were both killed outright. Fortunately no one else was involved.

'I . . . It was suggested that I should be given a new identity . . . a new start, to . . . to protect me for the future when he eventually came out of prison. I . . . there was another girl who died in Oxford the same day as my parents. She . . . there were drugs involved. And so the police decided that I should "die" in the accident with my parents and assume this other girl's identity. She had no family . . . and . . .' Taylor shuddered.

'In some ways that was the worst of all. I felt almost as though I had taken the clothes off her body and put them on, still warm from her flesh. It was so, so . . . I felt like a thief . . . almost as though I had, in some way, been responsible for her death, just as I had for my parents'.

'The police told my sister what had happened. She was still in Australia then, and pregnant with Fate. She wanted to fly home to be with me, but I told her that we must never see each other, that I couldn't take the risk that through me she, too, might one day be hurt.

'I knew, you see, no matter what the police said, that one day he would be free and that when he was . . .'

As she spoke, Taylor wrapped her arms protectively around her body. 'He would kill me . . . both of us . . . all of us, if he knew I had conceived your child,' she whispered.

Listening to her, watching her, Bram knew that no matter how far-fetched what she was saying might seem to him, to her it was very real. Now he could understand why she had reacted the way she had when her flat had been broken into.

No doubt she had feared then that somehow he had, against all logic, found her.

'Taylor. Taylor. I can understand why you feel so afraid . . .' Bram told her as he held her. 'But, my love, there really is nothing to fear. He's in prison. You said so yourself, and unlikely to get out for a very long time, I should imagine, and even when he does, even if he does go looking for you, what can he find? Officially you are dead. Isn't that true?'

'Yes . . .' Taylor agreed. 'But he could still find me. I know he could. He could still discover the truth. Jay did.'

'No,' Bram corrected her, shaking his head. 'Jay may have thought he had discovered something to your discredit, but he can't possibly have learned the truth.'

His son, Bram suspected, probably believed as he himself had initially been inclined to do, that Fate was Taylor's child.

His eyes hardened.

Listening to Taylor's story he had recognised all too easily the echoes of Jay's obsessive possessiveness over him. No wonder she feared Jay's influence so much.

And now there wasn't just Taylor to consider; there was their child as well. He doubted that Jay would seek to harm the baby physically, but emotionally. . .

The sheer lack of concern for anyone else's feelings, the intensity of emotion, the single-mindedness and cruelty Jay had displayed in confronting Taylor with Fate had shocked Bram.

It was hard, if not impossible, to go on loving someone, even one's own child, when they had displayed that kind of behaviour.

Jay was an adult with his own life and, quite patently, his own code of behaviour. Bram now owed it to Taylor and to their child to put them first, to protect them from Jay's malice. He owed it to them and he owed it to himself.

As he held Taylor in his arms and recognised all these things, he came to a decision.

'What is it? What are you thinking?' Taylor demanded, look-ing up and seeing his expression.

'I'm thinking that it's considerably less than flattering to hear how little faith you have in my ability to protect you and our child,' Bram told her ruefully. 'And I will keep you both safe, Taylor. I promise you that.'

'It's *your* safety I'm worried about,' Taylor stressed.

'You have every right to love me,' Bram said, 'and I have every right to love you back. Don't deny my love and protection, Tay-lor.'

Taylor looked at him. What could she do...? If there was just herself to consider, but there wasn't....

'You can't marry me,' she reiterated, but Bram could sense that she was weakening. 'Jay will hate it. He'll—'

'Jay has his own life to lead,' Bram told her, 'and I intend to make sure that he knows from now on, his life is to be lived completely separately from ours.'

Taylor stared at him, surprised by the unfamiliar hardness in his voice.

'I've come to a decision,' Bram told her. 'One of Jay's greatest fears is that somehow he'll lose the company. I intend to stand down and give him full control.'

He saw Taylor's expression and kissed her mouth gently. 'Don't look like that. It isn't any sacrifice. I've already made more money than I'm ever likely to be able to spend. I'm not in-terested in expanding the company, in making more profits. My other work... *our* work is what interests me now, giving some-thing back to the community, not taking from it. That's what I want to do.

'I've never particularly liked living in London. I prefer the country. My ideal would be a rambling country house with a fair bit of land, a stream for fishing, a couple of ponies, you by my side, our children....' He laughed at Taylor's expression. 'This program we're working on now is only the start of what I'd like to do. And it's something we can do together, Taylor, some-thing we can share as I believe two people should share their lives.

'Jay will have what he's always wanted, full and complete control of the company, and I'll have you and our children.'

Taylor looked uncertainly at him. He sounded so confident, so happy. She ached to believe him. He made it all sound so easy, so simple....

'Jay doesn't just want the business, he wants you as well,' she told him.

'No, Jay doesn't want me,' Bram corrected her gently. 'What Jay wants is to control everyone and everything around him. Once I'm no longer a part of his life—'

'He'll blame me,' Taylor whispered. 'He'll—'

'Have faith in me, Taylor,' Bram urged. 'Trust me. I promise you, you have nothing and no one to fear. Not Jay, and not this other man. No one,' he repeated firmly.

He knew he was right, but he was also thinking that it wouldn't do any harm to get in touch with a high-ranking police official he knew. Just so that he could truly set Taylor's mind at rest...

'There's only one thing you need to worry about now,' he told her as he cupped her face so that he could kiss her.

'What's that?' Taylor mumbled, admitting to herself that it was useless trying to fight him... trying to fight herself, when she knew that what she wanted, what she ached for was to spend the rest of her life with him.

'How quickly can you find something to be married in? Because I want you and I'm not prepared to wait....'

'Well, at least we shan't have to worry about drawing up a guest list.' Taylor laughed, but Bram could see the pain in her eyes.

'No, it will just be the two of us and our witnesses,' Bram agreed. But he was already planning to get in contact with her sister. She and Taylor had obviously kept in touch over the years and he knew that Taylor would want her there at her wedding, even if she refused to admit it.

'Stop worrying,' Bram told her. 'Everything's going to be fine. There's absolutely nothing for you to worry about, apart from looking after yourself. If there's any worrying to be done, let me do it.'

21

'Remember the doctor said you had to eat,' Bram told Taylor as he leaned across the table to kiss her.

'I've made an appointment to see the vicar and I've been in touch with a couple of estate agents as well. I've told them what we're looking for. We shouldn't have too much trouble finding something suitable.'

'Oh, Bram . . . are you sure you're doing the right thing? I . . .'

'I'm sure,' Bram said firmly.

Now, as he studied Taylor's wan face across the table, he acknowledged he was glad he had made that call to an old acquaintance very high up in the Metropolitan Police.

He had listened to what Bram had said to him in silence and then announced, 'Two consecutive life sentences—well, even with the maximum amount of time off, he's going to be in prison for a minimum of twenty years. Then when you add the sentence for the attempted kidnap and rape... Plus, as you say, with the victim being given a completely new identity... No, I shouldn't imagine for one moment that there's the remotest chance of him causing you any trouble. Such people *are* extremely dangerous, of course, all the more so because of the intensity of their obsession. If you give me his name I'll make some enquiries for you, just to set your mind completely at rest.'

Their conversation had confirmed what Bram had already known, but it might go some way to putting Taylor's mind at rest.

'Since neither of us have been married before, there's no bar to us being married in church,' Bram told Taylor.

'A church wedding.' Taylor looked at him uncertainly. 'Oh, Bram, I don't—'

'Isn't that what you want?' he asked her firmly.

Taylor nodded her head. 'Yes, but . . .'

'No buts.'

'Jay won't like it,' Taylor protested. 'He—'

'Leave Jay to me,' Bram instructed. 'What we choose to do with our lives is our concern, not his.'

When he saw her expression he shook his head and touched her mouth gently with his fingertips.

'No, don't waste your compassion on him, Taylor. He'd have destroyed our relationship and you if he could have, and that's something I can never forgive him for.'

'You still love him?'

Bram shook his head sombrely. 'No, I don't think I do. God forgive me for saying it, but I don't think I do.'

'Don't reject him completely, Bram. He's going to find it very hard and...'

He reached across the table and took both Taylor's hands in his own.

'He doesn't deserve your compassion,' Bram told her quietly. 'He's pushed me too far this time. I'm going to ring the company's solicitors later and ask them to draw up all the necessary papers to hand full control of the business over to Jay. It's for the best,' he told her gently. 'He won't let matters rest where they are. We both know that.'

'No,' Taylor agreed unhappily, 'I wonder what he's told Fate. She can't possibly know the truth. I'm afraid that he might try to hurt her because of me, Bram. She's so young and he's...' She bit her lip again. 'If he thinks she's my daughter...'

'I'll speak to him,' Bram promised her.

Jay had quite plainly intended to use the girl to get at Taylor, picking up on the connection between them from Fate's photograph. But how had he tracked her down?

There was only one way he was going to find out.

'Jay, have you got a moment?'

Dismissing his secretary, Jay followed his father into his own office, lounging easily against the wall, his hands in his pockets as he watched Bram close the door and then turn to face him.

To judge from his father's appearance, he hadn't had a particularly refreshing night's sleep—which made two of them, Jay acknowledged grimly. The difference was, his body being younger, he was slightly better at concealing it.

What irked him even more than his inability to sleep was the fact that once he had dropped off, he had been disturbed by a succession of confusing dreams about Fate.

He was glad that he couldn't remember the full content of those dreams, just as he was glad that he had resisted the temptation to reach for the phone and punch in Fate's number.

What was there to say, after all? That his body, his loins ached intensely for her...so what? That would pass, and right now he had far more important things to deal with than an inconvenient itch.

Bram had gone to stand behind his desk. He looked surprisingly formidable and remote. Jay hid a small smile. He remembered his father looking similarly impressive on one or two occasions during his childhood, when he had felt it necessary to discuss the inappropriateness of certain aspects of his son's behaviour.

His father had a certain way with words, but although Jay had always acknowledged Bram's appeal to his better nature, he had never acted on it, neither had he ever felt the remorse which Bram seemed to expect him to exhibit for his wrongdoing.

And he didn't feel any now.

Bram must have probed the cause of Taylor's dramatic faint and, with any luck, she would have saved him the trouble of unmasking her by panicking into doing the job herself.

Bram, no doubt, now wanted to talk to him to seek corroboration of what she had told him. And if not . . . Jay gave a brief, mental shrug. It wasn't his fault that Taylor had lied to his father, concealed the conception and birth of her child.

'I have two things to say to you, Jay,' he heard Bram telling him quietly, 'and neither of them is open for discussion. The first is that Taylor and I are getting married and that we are expecting a child. The second is that I am standing down from the chairmanship of the company and handing over full control to you. Taylor and I intend to move out of London just as soon as we can, and I think it best that, for the future, you and I agree that our lives will follow different paths, which should seldom, if ever, cross.'

Jay stared at his father in disbelief. He wasn't lounging in a relaxed, easy confidence against the office wall any more; neither was he smiling.

'If this is supposed to be some kind of joke...' he began ominously.

Bram looked at him steadily. 'I'm not laughing, Jay, and I certainly wasn't laughing last night either, when, through your behaviour, you caused Taylor to faint.'

'*I* caused her to faint?' Jay defended himself harshly. 'I'm not the one who concealed the existence of my illegitimate child, who—'

'Neither is Taylor,' Bram interrupted him coldly. 'You're barking up the wrong tree, Jay. Fate is not Taylor's child, and in assuming that she is, you—'

'*She* told you that,' Jay sneered, 'and *you* believed her. You always were a soft touch.'

'Perhaps. But I scarcely think you can legitimately find fault with that aspect of my personality. After all, it has certainly benefited you in the past. However in this instance—'

'So come on then, tell me. How did she explain away Fate's existence and her lies about being her godmother?'

'Taylor's past is no concern of yours,' Bram said firmly, 'and I have no intention of discussing with you either it or your gross misconceptions about it.' Bram's eyes narrowed assessingly. 'You haven't told Fate you believe she is Taylor's child, I hope.'

Jay stared at him angrily. 'She insisted on knowing,' he told Bram irritably. 'For God's sake,' he exploded when he saw Bram's expression, 'she isn't a child.'

'Maybe not,' Bram agreed quietly, 'but to be told that a complete stranger is her real mother must have shocked and upset her. Where is she now, Jay?'

Any hopes Bram had been cultivating that when it came to Fate, his son might have at least shown a little compassion and concern were trampled as Jay shrugged his shoulders and said coldly, 'I neither know nor care.'

'You used her deliberately to try to hurt Taylor, didn't you?' Bram accused him quietly.

'She's an adult. If she thought—'

'How did you find her, Jay?' Bram interrupted, sickened by his callous response.

'I didn't,' Jay replied. '*She* was the one doing the looking.'

Jay smiled at his father's frown. He had no intention of explaining how he had come to meet Fate. Let him think that Fate was as suspicious of Taylor's past as he was himself.

He could feel the cold, hard ball of fury filling his chest cavity, swelling and throbbing. The thought that Taylor might already be carrying his father's child and that she might use that fact to pressure his father into marrying had simply never occurred to him. For some reason, Taylor hadn't struck him as the kind of woman who would take such a risk. She was too cautious . . . too careful.

He had underestimated her, he recognised savagely, and now he was paying for that mistake. But the game wasn't over yet. He still had some cards to play.

'So, Taylor's pregnant,' he commented, smiling coldly. 'I hate to pour cold water on your obvious enthusiasm, but are you sure it is *your* child? You're an extremely wealthy man and . . .'

For a moment he thought that Bram was actually going to hit him. The thought sent the adrenalin racing challengingly through his veins.

But even as Bram raised his fist, he dropped it again. His flesh was drawn back tightly against his facial bones, suddenly making him look much older, and there was, Jay gloated with secret triumph, the sheen of barely suppressed tears in his eyes. But as Bram looked at him, that sheen disappeared to be replaced by icy coldness.

'I shouldn't dignify that question with an answer, Jay. But I shall. Let me tell you this. It would be easier by far for me to doubt *your* paternity than it would that of the child Taylor is carrying.'

Jay stared at him. An odd feeling of dizzy vagueness had come from out of nowhere to invade his body like mist coming out of sunshine on a mountainside, obliterating everything that was familiar, changing the known landscape out of all recognition and rendering it dangerous and alien.

He opened his mouth to speak, but no words would come. He was aware of Bram walking past him and opening his office door.

He was even aware of lifting his own hand to stop him, but Bram ignored him, quietly walking through the door without looking at him and then closing it after him.

* * *

Fate's hands were trembling as she turned the wheel of her mother's car and reversed out of the drive. She still wasn't sure if she was doing the right thing, or why she was doing it, when she knew . . .

A council workman on the other side of the road, clearing up the verge, paused in his work to watch her, smiling at her. Automatically Fate smiled back, but her heart wasn't in it.

It might have been different if her parents had been at home. Then she could . . .

She glanced sideways at the passenger seat, checking the address she had written on the piece of paper, even though she now knew it off by heart.

Her face still burned as she remembered the lie she had told Jay's secretary in order to get it. The woman had never even questioned her. Fate was normally a confident driver, but by the time she had reached her destination, her knuckles were white as she gripped the steering wheel, and two dark spots of tension-betraying colour burned in her otherwise pale face.

The house rather surprised her. It wasn't what she had expected. Pretty, cottagey, almost in some indefinable way, it looked . . . it looked like a home. She parked the car and then simply sat where she was, waiting for the spasms of nausea and apprehension to subside before she could get out.

She had dressed carefully, scattering nearly everything in her wardrobe as she searched frantically for something that would convey the right impression. In the end she had settled for a simple button-front dress in copper-coloured linen, which her mother had bought her in Italy the previous year. The colour suited her and the styling was irreproachably Italian. It was the kind of dress which instantly bestowed on its wearer a sophisticated femininity.

The previous night's rain had given way to clear skies and sunshine. Fate could feel its heat on her bare legs as she crossed the pavement to the house's front door.

She rang the bell and waited, fighting down the impulse to turn and run away. She felt alternately hot and cold, her body perspiring and then shivering.

The door opened.

Wordlessly Fate studied the woman watching her.

'Fate.' Taylor welcomed her gently. 'Good, I was hoping you would come. I did try to ring, but there was no answer. Come in. Are you on your own or . . . ?'

'My parents are away. They . . . they don't know I'm here.'

Was that really her own voice uttering those disjointed, stumbled, staccato words? Was this really her following this woman who was a stranger to her but who spoke of her parents as though . . .

'Sit down,' Taylor invited her. 'Would you like something to drink? Tea, coffee, something cold . . . '

Fate shook her head, refusing both the offer of a seat and refreshment. To her horror she could feel tears flooding her eyes. She bent her head to hide them, but it was too late.

Quickly Taylor crossed the floor and took her in her arms.

'It's all right . . . it's all right,' she soothed her, holding her tightly and rocking her trembling body gently. 'It's all right, Fate. I promise you, everything's all right . . . ' As she released her and stepped back from her, Taylor smiled into her eyes and told her softly. 'I think I know what's happened, what Jay has told you. But he's completely wrong. I'm not your mother, Fate . . . I'm your aunt . . . '

'My aunt!' Fate stared at her. 'But that's impossible. I . . . I don't understand.'

'Let me explain,' Taylor told her. 'But first, what about that drink?'

'Yes, yes, coffee, please.'

Taylor wasn't her mother. Fate felt almost giddy with relief. Her parents hadn't lied to her, deceived her. They were really her parents. She was truly their child . . . and Taylor's niece. . . .

'I'm sorry,' Taylor apologised as she came back into the room with two mugs of coffee. 'I know how much of a shock all this must have been for you. Sit down and I'll explain.'

While Taylor talked, Fate listened, silent apart from the occasional shocked protest of sympathy.

'Your mother never wanted to keep my existence hidden from you,' Taylor said, 'but I insisted. I was so afraid. It's hard to explain the kind of fear. . . . It's probably something one has to experience to totally understand. I'm sorry that you've been hurt and distressed by...by what's happened. That was the last thing I wanted to happen. I . . . it never occurred to me that Jay would track you down and—'

'He didn't. He saw me in the office, in the foyer. I had an interview. He recognised me from a photograph you had,' Fate explained quietly.

'Yes.' A look of pain crossed Taylor's face. 'Your mother and I have kept in touch. Letters to a post box address, and occasional telephone calls. She sent me the photograph as a birthday present several years ago. I think she was trying to get me to change my mind. She was trying to show me what I was missing out on. And I was tempted. Perhaps I ought to have given in to that temptation....'

She looked into Fate's eyes. 'Don't let Jay hurt you, Fate. He—'

'He was just using me,' Fate supplied dryly. 'Yes, I know. He . . . he can't bear the thought of your relationship with Bram and . . .'

'I know,' Taylor agreed. Her eyes clouded as she added, 'Bram thinks it best if the two of them lead separate lives from now on. He . . . he wants us to get married. I . . . I'm expecting his child. He intends to hand full control of the business over to Jay, which he hopes will satisfy Jay's hunger for power and control and, at the same time, it will allow him to concentrate on the charity work he's involved in.'

'It...it sounds the ideal solution,' Fate commented, but as the two women's eyes met, each knew what the other was thinking.

'Has . . . has Bram told Jay yet?' Fate asked eventually.

'I'm not sure. He was going to tell him this morning. I keep telling myself that Jay isn't a child, he's an adult. And I keep reminding myself of all the ways he's hurt Bram over the years. And yet...I can't help thinking about how I would feel if Jay were my child . . . how much it would hurt me to know that . . .'

'Bram had turned his back on him,' Fate supplied quietly for her.

'Bram's concerned that Jay might . . . It isn't just ourselves we have to consider. There's the baby as well....'

Taylor heard Fate's shocked gasp and smiled painfully. 'Oh, no . . . I don't mean that Jay would do anything to *physically* harm us, but there are other ways, which are far more painful and effective, as Jay himself knows. His grandparents, especially his grandfather, were unspeakably cruel to him when he was a child, telling him that he wasn't wanted or loved, that he had blighted his mother's life, making him feel . . .

'Bram has done his best to reassure Jay, to not just tell him but to show him as well that he is loved and that his grandfather lied to him, but—'

'Oh, poor little boy,' Fate blurted out compassionately.

'Yes,' Taylor agreed sadly, 'poor little boy. But,' she reminded Fate, 'he isn't a boy any longer.'

'No,' Fate agreed.

They talked for another hour, laughing sometimes, and sometimes allowing themselves to be overwhelmed by their emotions and giving way to their tears.

'I might wish that things had happened differently, but I'm still glad that they did happen,' Fate announced defiantly, when she finally stood up to go. 'I just wish we hadn't had to wait so long to meet each other.'

'That's my fault,' Taylor told her sadly, reaching up to touch her face.

'Don't let Jay hurt you,' she warned Fate, seeing the unhappiness in her niece's eyes. But sne suspected that her warning was already too late.

Taylor walked out to the street with Fate and watched as she unlocked the door of her car.

'Am I going to have a surprise for Mum when she comes home,' Fate told Taylor as she turned round to hug her. 'Not only have I found an aunt I never knew I had, but I'm going to have a cousin. I'm so pleased for you and Bram,' she added warmly. 'After everything that you've gone through, to have found each other and to know that you're carrying Bram's child . . . I'm so happy for you and I know that Mum will be too.'

'Tell her to ring me,' Taylor whispered chokily to her as they exchanged a final hug.

There was a car in the parking space behind Fate's. She saw the driver in her rearview mirror as she glanced in it before driving off. He was leaning on the open window reading a newspaper. He had blond hair, which looked as though it was a toupee. Poor man, Fate reflected. Why on earth, with all the marvels of modern science at their disposal, had no one yet been able to produce a hair piece that looked real?

Bram found the message waiting for him on his return from a meeting with his accountants.

He had spent the best part of two hours withstanding their appalled protests at his decision to step down from overall control of the business.

'By all means hand over the chairmanship to Jay if that is what you want,' they had advised him, 'but not total financial control. There *are* ways we can limit—'

'No,' Bram had interrupted them harshly. 'I've made my decision and I don't intend to change it. I agree that we can set up a trust fund to finance the charity work I want to get involved in, but as far as the company itself is concerned . . .'

They had backed down in the end, but very reluctantly. Jay wouldn't have been flattered had he witnessed their obvious unwillingness to accept him in Bram's place, Bram acknowledged. But that was his son's problem—not his.

Life and time were too precious to waste any more on things that were no longer important to him. Including Jay?

He pushed the thought of his son to the back of his mind as he punched in the telephone number on the message slip.

The Deputy Assistant Commissioner was just on his way to a meeting when Bram's call came through, but he still took the call.

'It seems that your man is not in prison any more,' he informed Bram. 'He appealed the sentence and won, and he was released approximately six months ago.'

Released. Dennis Phillips was free? Bram frowned into the receiver.

'However, you really have nothing to fear,' the DAC assured him, 'given the victim's change of identity. There is absolutely no way he could ever track her down, always supposing that he wanted to.'

Bram was still frowning as he thanked the man for his help and replaced the receiver.

How was Taylor going to feel when he told her that Phillips was free? He had seen for himself what it had done to her when her flat was broken into . . . the way she had reacted, the sheer terror that had gripped her.

He had always believed complete honesty was essential in any worthwhile, close relationship. If he withheld the truth from Taylor, he would in essence be lying by omission. But if he told her, he would completely destroy her fragile peace of mind.

He had no option, he recognised, but to keep to himself what he had learned. After all, as the DAC had assured him, there was no way that Phillips could possibly find Taylor.

He was glad, though, that he had managed to convince her to marry sooner rather than later.

Another change of name would distance her even further from Dennis Phillips and could only add to her safety.

22

Having spent the first half of the long drive north alternately demanding that Gil turn the car round and take her straight home and crying noisy tears; protesting her undying love for Bram, coupled with her equally undying hatred of him for not loving her back; and the second half of it fast asleep, Plum finally woke up to discover that the journey was over and that she and the car had come to rest in the inner courtyard of the ancient Scottish keep which was Gil McKenzie's ancestral home.

Just as she was about to open her mouth and demand again that she be immediately taken back to London, Gil forestalled her by saying firmly, 'Wait here, and don't attempt to get out until I come back. The dogs don't know you yet.'

'The dogs . . . ?'

While Plum peered uneasily out into the dimly lit darkness of the courtyard, Gil opened the driver's door.

As he did so, a heavy wooden door on the opposite side of the courtyard creaked open, allowing not just a very welcome beam of light to escape but, to Plum, something far less welcome and ominously large—lurcher dogs.

'Gil,' Plum protested tearfully, but he was already closing the car door. He paused briefly to say something to the dogs, which, instead of following him, were now standing watchfully on either side of the car—her protection or her prison? Plum wondered woefully as she asked herself what on earth had possessed her to come north with Gil in the first place. He was a man she didn't even like, a man she had come close to acutely loathing, in fact, on more than one occasion.

All right, so she had needed to escape from the sight of Bram with Taylor. But there were other and far more hospitable places she could have escaped to, and other and far more hospitable people.

She tensed as the elderly woman revealed in the beam of warm light from the open doorway was warmly embraced by Gil. His mother? Didn't she remember Gil saying that both his parents were dead? Lucky him, she thought with a petulant sniff. She could well imagine the barrage of questions and recriminations *she* would eventually have to face from her mother.

She guessed that Gil was saying something to the woman about her, because they had both turned to face the car and Gil was gesturing towards it.

Inwardly fuming at her enforced imprisonment, she promised herself she was going to make Gil extremely sorry that he had bullied her . . . *forced* her into coming to this God-forsaken part of the world with him.

Just look at this place, for instance. All that stark granite, those walls that seemed to go on forever, those tiny narrow windows—the place was more like a fortress than a home.

Gil and his companion had started to walk towards the car, the dogs bounding so enthusiastically and playfully around them that Plum couldn't help wondering suspiciously just how dangerous they actually were.

The woman, who she could now see was well into her sixties, seemed completely unfazed by their presence, shooing them away as she and Gil rounded the car and Gil opened the passenger door.

'Plum, I want you to meet Nanny Fairburn,' Gil announced, forestalling the angry comment Plum had been about to hurl at him.

'Here you are, Nanny,' he told his companion, turning away from Plum. 'You're always complaining that this place needs a woman and a handful of bairns to keep you occupied. I think you'll find that Plum fits both of those descriptions,' he added dryly, while Plum glowered at him.

How dare he talk about her like that, laugh at her like that! She opened her mouth a second time to demand that he turn the car round and drive her back to London, but got no further than an angry, 'I am not . . .' before she was interrupted.

A soft Highland voice crooned, 'Oh, but she's a bonnie lassie. But half-starved by the look of her. What on earth have you been doing to her, and leaving her out here in the car as well . . . ?'

Still scolding Gil she reached out and took one of Plum's hands between her own soft plump ones, smiling warmly at her as Plum gaped back in astonishment.

Those of her London friends brave enough to venture north had often spoken of the dour, inhospitable Scots, suspicious of anyone born south of the border. She had shuddered in sympathy and disbelief at hair-raising tales she had heard about unfriendly treatment by ancient family retainers; about the freezing, draughty, ancient piles with their equally freezing and ancient staff, cold baths, clammy sheets, horrendous heaps of stodgy food; about the appalling ordeal of day-long shoots ... and the even more arduous rigours of the Highland ball.

She shot a wary glance at the woman now urging her to come inside and get warm. Like her hands, Nanny's face and body looked soft and warm, the bright blue eyes filled with the kind of motherly concern that made Plum's own eyes widen.

'Come away in and just ignore those great fools of dogs. Why on earth you keep them I don't know,' she castigated Gil. 'Daft as brushes and even less use.'

'They're excellent guard dogs, Nanny,' Gil protested.

To Plum's delight the older woman wasn't going to let him off so easily. 'Guard dogs, my foot. Lolling about in front of the fire is their idea of guarding anything—either that or jumping all over the furniture. You'd be better off with a nice modern alarm system like the Lindseys at Coldporter have just had fitted. A wonderful thing it is, and it doesn't come jumping on your bed at night and half frightening you to death.'

Plum laughed; she couldn't help it. The mingled look of protest and sheepishness on Gil's face was enough to set her off giggling mirthfully.

'Nanny, that isn't fair,' he began.

'Oh, stop your havering and blethering,' Nanny told him firmly, 'and let's get this poor child inside. My ... what on earth has he done to you?' she demanded as Plum stepped out of the car, still wearing her ball gown.

'He abducted me from my own party, Nanny,' Plum told her mischievously, darting Gil a challenging look as she did so. 'Snatched me up without so much as a by-your-leave.'

'Did he so?' Nanny retorted. 'Well, of course, it's in the blood. I well remember how I was told about the way his great-grandfather abducted his bride, and right from under the nose of her rightful bridegroom. Caused quite a stir that did, and it wasn't the first time that a McKenzie has taken his chosen bride by force.'

Plum gaped at her. It was impossible for her to imagine that anyone as stoical and staid and downright respectable as Gil could ever be even remotely related to someone who sounded so dashing and romantic.

'Tell me more,' she breathed enthusiastically, allowing the older woman to urge her towards the house, 'about the man who abducted his bride, I mean. He must have been so romantic.'

Behind her Plum could hear Gil give a derisive snort but she ignored him, tossing her head dismissively. Suddenly the warm glow through the open doorway beckoned invitingly. Nanny Fairburn was making soothing, comforting noises about running her a hot bath and tucking her up in bed with a hot water bottle and some of her special tisane.

Plum gave a small, blissful sigh of acceptance and recognition. This was what she had wanted all her life, someone who would take care of her, somewhere where she would feel safe....

Perhaps coming to Scotland had not been such a bad idea after all, she decided as she followed Nanny Fairburn towards the open door. It was a pity that Gil had to be here, of course. But then every Eden had its serpent, and Plum was smugly aware that with Nanny's firm eye on him he seemed to be holding in check his normal acerbic and critical treatment of her.

One of the dogs pressed its cold nose against Plum's hand, its whole body wriggling with pleasure when she paused to stroke it.

London...her mother...Bram...all of them offered only pain, whereas here . . .

'Come on now, it's time to wake up. I've drawn you a bath and brought you some tea. You'll have a proper breakfast downstairs, although you'll have to eat alone this morning, I'm afraid. The master is already away over the hill.'

Plum blinked sleepily as Nanny Fairburn pulled back the curtains and let the sharp, bright daylight into the bedroom. It sounded odd to hear Gil referred to as 'the master.' It was somehow such an ancient, almost feudal term of address, and it sounded so much more spine-tinglingly masterful and, yes, sexy even, than the far more prosaic and staid 'my lord' she was accustomed to hearing.

'What do you mean, he's away over the hill?' she asked, obediently swinging her legs out of the bed as Nanny Fairburn pulled back the covers. The starched lawn nightdress she had worn last night had originally belonged to Gil's grandmother, she had been told. The lawn was delicately fine, pin-tucked and hand-sewn, Plum guessed. A world away from her normal choice of bed wear—when she did wear anything. But as she caught sight of her reflection in the dressing-table mirror, she was aware of how much the old-fashioned nightdress suited her, of how chastely feminine it was.

'It isn't even seven o'clock,' she added, appalled as she realised how early it was. In London she wouldn't have been *thinking* of getting up at such an early hour, but as she paused to turn back towards the bed, Nanny Fairburn was already opening the door to the private bathroom. It wasn't, Plum decided judiciously, worth protesting. After all, she was up now.

Nanny laughed. 'The master's been out since six with his hawk.'

'His what?' Plum stared at her.

'His hawk,' Nanny repeated, adding dolefully, 'Although what he wants with such a creature, I'll never know. Raised it from a fledgling, he has. One of the keepers brought it in. Some boys had been caught robbing the nest.'

'A hawk,' Plum breathed, impressed in spite of herself. There was something so romantic and male about the image the word conjured up, with its echoes of medieval knights and acts of valour and daring.

Were all the furniture and fittings in the castle giant-sized? she wondered idly half an hour later as she lay, full length, in the huge, deep Victorian bath and gazed dreamily at the vaulted ceiling above her. The four-poster bed she had slept in last night had been equally huge, like the room's heavy, polished oak furniture.

It must be wonderfully romantic living in a castle, she decided, far more so than living in the neat, dull perfection of the Regency style so beloved by her mother.

Nanny had gone downstairs, promising to bring back the underclothes she had apparently laundered for Plum overnight, plus something more suitable to wear than her ball gown.

She hadn't thought about clothes when she made her impetuous decision to leave with Gil, which just showed how upset she must have been. Thinking about clothes was, after all, one of the major concerns of her daily life.

The huge plain white towels Nanny had left warming for her might look dull, but they felt wonderfully warm and soft, Plum acknowledged as she stepped out of the bath and wrapped herself in one. She sniffed the towelling appreciatively, breathing in the clean scent of fresh air and sunshine.

In the bedroom she found her clean underwear plus a pair of equally immaculately laundered jeans, a T-shirt and a pair of shoes, all of them the right size.

She was just slipping her feet into the shoes when Nanny Fairburn came back, retrieving the damp towel Plum had discarded and starting to strip back the bed.

'Where did these come from?' Plum asked her curiously. 'They can't possibly have belonged to Gil's grandmother.'

'Certainly not,' the older woman agreed, shocked. 'The mistress would never have worn such things. The master sent down to the village for them.'

When she saw that Plum was looking puzzled, she explained, 'They belong to the daughter of one of his tenants. She's away at St Andrews at the moment, learning to be a doctor.

'Come away, now, and have your breakfast. I've made you some porridge and then there's toast with our own moorland honey.'

Porridge and toast! Plum stared at her.

'I don't eat breakfast, Nanny,' she told her plaintively.

'Of course you do,' Nanny corrected her firmly.

And, of course she did.

It was the trauma of the previous evening that had made her so hungry, Plum decided as she discovered that she had not only finished her enormous bowl of porridge, but eaten three pieces of toast as well, all washed down by a large breakfast cup of deliciously fragrant French coffee.

The family had French blood in its veins, Nanny had told her, owing to the marriage of the master of the time to a French countess in an age when the Scots had had closer connections with the French than with the English.

'What time will Gil be back?' Plum wanted to know.

'Oh, he'll be gone for the best part of the day now,' Nanny told her. 'And then there's a tenants' meeting this evening. And then tomorrow he's to see the keepers about the moor. There's a Japanese gentleman who wants to rent it next year for the shooting.'

'It sounds as though he's going to be very busy,' Plum responded. She was glad, of course, because that meant that she wouldn't have to spend any time with him, which was exactly what she wanted. He bored her to tears, and she knew *he* disapproved of her. They had absolutely nothing whatsoever in common, and if she hadn't been so desperate she would never have dreamed of running away with him as she had . . .

Running away . . . A small, mischievous smile touched her mouth. How dramatic and romantic it sounded and how irritated Gil would be if she told him so. That was, of course, if she ever got the opportunity to tell him. It sounded as though he was going to be far too busy to find time for her.

Her smile died away to be replaced by a small frown. Why should she care? The last thing she wanted was to have to spend any time with him, wasn't it?

Of course it was, she assured herself. It was just . . . it was just that it wasn't very nice . . . it wasn't very flattering, knowing how little people wanted her company. Her mother didn't want her — she never had . . . Her father had his own life to lead . . . her friends . . . Bram . . . Bram didn't want her. . . . Tears of self-pity started to fill her eyes. And now it seemed that Gil didn't want her either.

'I don't know why Gil bothered bringing me here if all he's going to do is ignore me,' Plum announced petulantly.

'No?' Nanny responded dryly, giving her an old-fashioned look. 'Well, I dare say he has his reasons.'

Plum looked puzzled.

'He always did have a weakness for rescuing hurt young things,' she added, further confusing her.

* * *

'But why did you have to tell my mother that I was here in the first place?' Plum demanded angrily.

'Someone had to,' Gil responded grimly.

It was almost a week since Plum had arrived in Scotland, and she had almost forgotten the events which had led to her precipitate flight from London, until yesterday, when her mother had telephoned. She had icily demanded to know when Plum intended to return home, and pointed out to her that once she did, there were apologies to be made for her behaviour in leaving her own party without any warning or explanation.

'Have you any idea how much you've embarrassed me?' her mother had demanded to know. 'If it wasn't for Gil we wouldn't have had the faintest idea where on earth you were . . . What exactly are you doing with Gil anyway?' she had added.

'He kidnapped me,' Plum had told her flippantly, telling herself that it served Gil right. After all, he was the one who had gone behind her back and told her mother where she was. That was typical of him too . . . interfering, bossy. 'Apparently it runs in the blood.'

There, let him explain his way out of that one. She darted a glance at him on the opposite side of the room.

'Stop being difficult, Plum,' her mother had warned her. 'No doubt you find it very amusing to have persuaded poor Gil to take you home with him, but I certainly don't and I'm sure Gil is regretting his act of kindness now. I want you to make arrangements to return home immediately. You'll have to travel by train, I imagine.'

Home. Plum stared angrily into the receiver. She had felt more at home in the few short days she had spent here in Scotland with Nanny Fairburn to fuss protectively over her and spoil her, than she had ever done living under her mother's chilly roof.

'People are beginning to ask where you are. You've got thank-you letters to write. I want—'

'I'm not coming home,' Plum had told her mother. 'I'm staying here.'

Plum had watched Gil's expression as he overheard what she was saying. Well, if he didn't want her that was his problem. He was the one who had brought her here, and what, after all, was there for her to go home for . . . or to . . . ?

Her mother had been furious, of course, but in the end she had been forced to acknowledge that there was nothing she could do. Not that she could have any objections to the fact that she was with Gil, Plum reflected gleefully.

She had never met anyone who took life and his responsibilities so seriously. It had startled Plum to discover how very wealthy Gil was. In her experience, young men of Gil's age who were wealthy were more interested in enjoying themselves than involving themselves in the kind of boring duties that seemed to fill Gil's life.

If he wasn't attending some tenants' meeting or other, he was doing equally dull and worthy things with numerous groups of people who seemed to need his help and advice.

'Well, you were the one who brought me here,' Plum reminded Gil challengingly now.

She thought she heard him mutter under his breath, 'I must have been mad.' But since her pony had fallen slightly behind the large chestnut he was riding, she couldn't be quite sure.

It had been the boredom of her own company, coupled with a strong desire to provoke some kind of reaction from him, which had first prompted her to insist that Gil take her out with him on his morning ride, and she had seen the surprise—and the irritation— in his eyes when she had actually presented herself at the stables at six o'clock.

The mare she had been given to ride was pretty and docile, but she was no match for Gil's far more high-spirited Arabian, just as Plum's schoolgirl riding was no match for the enviably easy way Gil sat in the saddle, the reins looped round one hand, leaving the gauntleted arm of the other free to carry the hooded falcon perched on it. Behind them the dogs gambolled happily, sniffing at the dew-damp grass. The sky above was perfectly clear and empty.

If she hadn't known Gil so well, it would have been easy to persuade herself how very romantic he looked, how very sexily male, Plum acknowledged as she watched the small breeze flatten the thick darkness of his hair against his skull.

In London she had found him boring and slightly ridiculous and stuffy beyond belief. But up here he seemed different somehow, more . . . more aloof . . . more . . . more dangerous.

Dangerous? Gil? She hadn't forgotten the lack of interest he had displayed in her . . . his near rejection of her. *That* showed what kind of man he really was, how boring and sexless—even if right now he looked as though he could have ridden straight out of a novel by Sir Walter Scott.

He had already reached the top of the hill and had now stopped to wait for her.

Her borrowed T-shirt and jeans had been replaced with some clothes she had bought in the nearby market town. Not her normal style at all, but Gil seemed to approve of them. It had been an unfamiliar experience to have a man want to see her dressed in something that concealed more of her body than it revealed.

As she reached the top of the hill, Gil dismounted, tethering his own mount and then doing the same with hers.

'I know how to do it,' Plum objected crossly, giving him an angry look as his mouth tightened in disbelief. Did he really think she was so totally incapable?

The dogs were investigating a patch of bracken several yards away. As Gil unfastened the hood around the falcon's eyes, he was speaking softly to it . . . lovingly almost, Plum realised . . . as another man might to his lover. He removed one of the pieces of raw meat from the pouch he was carrying and fed it to the predator. Plum shivered as she watched. There was no doubt that the bird was magnificent, and no doubt either that it was extremely dangerous.

As Gil finished untying the bird and threw up his arm, it soared upwards into the blue arc of the sky, its powerful wings beating the air.

'How long will it be gone?' Plum asked Gil.

'*She* will be gone for as long as *she* needs,' he told her.

'She . . .' Plum gave him a taunting look from beneath provocatively half-lowered lashes. 'Anyone would think she was your lover from the way you talk about her and to her. Why haven't you got a lover, Gil? Don't you like women? Are you afraid of them? Don't you like sex?' she taunted him deliberately.

'Yes, I do like sex,' he told her finally, when she had just decided that he wasn't going to reply. 'I like it very much.' He turned towards her and added softly, 'Unlike you. You don't really like it at all, do you, Plum?'

'Yes. I do,' she contradicted him quickly, but she could feel her face start to burn and her stomach muscles to tighten. 'I like it very much. Everyone knows that. And I'm very good at it,' she added purringly. 'Very, very good. Do you want me to show you?'

She knew, of course, what he was going to say. He would tell her curtly and rejectingly that he most certainly did not.

She tensed slightly as he removed the sleeveless leather jerkin he was wearing, carefully placing it on a large boulder.

Once he had done so, he turned to look at her and told her evenly, 'Very well, then, Plum. Come and show me.'

Plum gaped at him. Her mouth had gone uncomfortably dry and her heart was beating frantically fast.

'Come on, then,' Gil repeated, challenging her softly. 'Come over here and show me.'

For a heartbeat of time Plum was tempted to refuse, to turn on her heel and ignominiously accept defeat. But how could she . . . ? And besides . . . besides. He was just trying to outface her, that was all. She hadn't forgotten what had happened the last time she made sexual overtures to him and she was pretty sure that he hadn't, either, and it wouldn't be any different this time. Gil was the kind of man who took his sex seriously, who liked his partners pure . . . who believed in love.

She started to walk towards him, reminding herself as she did so that it was just a game. A game she had played over and over again, countless times before. A game she *always* won, just as she was going to win this time.

Gil didn't move. His gaze was locked on her face. Plum wanted to look away from him, to break the powerfully magnetic force of his unblinking stare, but somehow she could not do so.

Once she was close enough to him, she reached towards his belt, a small half-smile playing round her lips. This was the bit she liked the best, the bit that always took them by surprise, the bit that gave *her* full control.

Her fingers trembled slightly as she tried to unfasten it. It was leather and slightly stiff and, disconcertingly beneath it, she could feel the taut hardness of Gil's stomach. Most of the men she did this to had soft stomachs . . . most of them . . .

She let out her breath in a leaky sigh of relief as Gil's fingers snapped round her wrists.

She had known, of course, that he would stop her. There had never really been any doubt in her mind about that. In her triumph she was tempted to taunt him verbally to underscore her victory, but as she raised limpid eyes to meet his hard stare, the words she had been about to speak died unspoken. Gil looked anything but defeated. He looked . . . he looked . . .

'That isn't how I like my sex, Plum. At least not to start with. I like it like this,' she heard him saying to her with unnerving gentleness.

The fingers curling round her wrists weren't just there to hold her away from his body, she realised in a sudden shock of surprise, they were there to trick her, to trap her, to imprison her as he pulled her firmly against him and kept her there, ignoring her angry attempts to break free.

'I like my sex to be a slow, leisurely, mutual exploration of each other's needs and desires,' he told her softly, 'starting like this.'

He had captured her mouth before she had even guessed what he intended to do, kissing her with such sensual expertise that she was left floundering helplessly, torn between alarmed shock at the way he had tricked her and confused sensual excitement at the way her body was responding to the slow, caressing movement of his mouth.

She tried to protest when his tongue breached the closed defences of her lips, parting them so skilfully and determinedly that the sensual impact of what he was doing to her made her cling dizzily to his shoulders.

She couldn't believe that it was actually *Gil* who was doing this to her, who was making her feel like this, and she had to open her eyes to look at him to make sure that he hadn't somehow been replaced by one of his passionate and romantic ancestors.

Gil's eyes were open too, blazing hotly with passion, which made her shiver in awed recognition of just how wrong she had been about him.

His hands were already unfastening her shirt, unclipping her bra, cupping the full warmth of her breasts and caressing them in a way that made her breath catch in her throat and a feeling she had never experienced with anyone else before, run through her like a rush of little hot, fiery darts making every part of her body ache and throb but most of all making her want . . .

She gave a small, choked gasp as Gil's mouth trailed down her throat, nuzzling the smooth soft flesh of her breast, caressing it with a careful delicacy that made her tremble frantically.

As though that shudder had been a signal he had been waiting for, his mouth opened over her nipple with hot passion, sucking on it so potently that Plum, who had never experienced a sensation like it in her entire life, took immediate fright and started pounding his chest and shoulders with her fists, terrified by her own response to him and her inability to control it.

She, who was always the one in control, who had never, ever really, really wanted a man, who had always been secretly amused and slightly contemptuous of the ardour she invoked in her would-be lovers; she who had never, not even once in her whole life, actually physically felt any compulsion to open her body to a man, never mind ache to have him bury himself completely and deeply inside it, to fill her so totally that she could feel him within the deepest, most feminine and female recesses of herself—but she wanted that now.

She wanted it so badly that she was openly terrified of that wanting, her panicky flailing in his arms reminding Gil of the terrified attempts of his falcon—as a fledgling—to break free of him. But, as he had tamed the falcon, he would tame Plum. He would love her, reassure her and make her feel so safe with him that she would never want to break free of him. But first, as he had done with the falcon, he had to master her. With the falcon he had gone three nights and three days without sleep to do it; with Plum . . .

He suspected he knew already what it was she feared, that loss of self . . . that fear of being vulnerable, of being rejected. And when finally he laid her down on the soft grass and removed her clothes, laying bare the secrets of her sexuality, first to his tender careful exploratory touch and then to the far more intimate, and to Plum almost shockingly, unbearably arousing, thorough loving of his tongue and lips, he knew that he had been right.

Half-wild with fear and panic, Plum tried to stop him, to halt her own inevitable humiliation as she tried frantically to hold back and control the response she could feel overwhelming her, her lips clamped tight against the betraying sounds she was making in her throat, the betraying words which would tell him how unused she was to this much pleasure, how afraid of it and of him . . . how afraid that once he had seen her vulnerability and recognised her need of him, he would turn his back on her and walk away from her.

But Gil would not stop. When she tried to wrest away from him he used his superior weight to pin her down, when she tried to claw at him and tug his hair with her hands, he pinned her wrists down. When she screamed and sobbed and told him that she hated him and that she loathed what he was doing, that no man who was really a man—who wanted her respect—would ever perform such an intimate act on, or for, a woman, he simply continued to caress her tenderly with his mouth, so that in the end her angry screams of denial and abuse turned to anguished tears, which shook her body almost as much as the great climactic surges of pleasure that contracted within her and made her cry out to him, and afterwards, huddle weakly in his arms, drained and defeated, her head bowed as she waited to hear him reject her.

'Now,' he told her softly, and she shivered in mute awareness of the scent of herself on his mouth when he kissed her gently. '*Now*, you are mine, Plum, and no other man is ever going to touch you again. No one will ever arouse you the way I have done. No man will ever love you as I love you. You're mine, do you understand?'

Numbly Plum nodded her head.

'Good,' Gil told her firmly. 'Now you're going to get dressed and I'm going to take you home. We'll ring your mother and tell her that we're engaged, and that we're going to be married. Here . . . just as soon as it can be arranged. And then, when we've done that—'

'Married . . .' Plum blurted out. 'But . . .'

'But what?' Gil asked her gently.

'But you can't want to marry me...not me.... You don't...you haven't even ... we haven't ...'

'*You* were the one who needed to know how much I desire and love you, not me,' Gil told her dryly. 'I already knew. I don't need to take you to bed to know how I feel about you, Plum.'

She could barely take in what he was saying.

'But how can you love me? You've always ... You've never ... When ... when ...?'

'The moment I set eyes on you in that accursed wine bar. I wanted to grab hold of you then and bring you back here with me.'

'You wanted me then? You wanted to kidnap me and run away with me,' Plum breathed, 'just like your ancestor ...?'

'Just like him,' Gil agreed solemnly. But his eyes were full of laughter and something else as well, Plum recognised, suddenly filled with heart-stopping, dizzying, dazzling joy.

Gil loved her. He really loved her. He loved her and she would marry him and stay here being loved and looked after for all the rest of her life.

She felt ... she felt ... she felt wonderful, she realised. Wonderful, ecstatic ... she felt as though ... as though ...

'Oh, Gil, I love you. I really, really love you,' she told him happily, flinging her arms around him and kissing him enthusiastically.

'I still can't believe that Gil actually wants to marry Plum,' Helena told James. 'It seems ...'

'Like a miracle?' James suggested wryly. 'I just hope he knows what he's letting himself in for. I wouldn't ...' He paused and shook his head.

'Oh, just think what this means,' Helena marvelled. 'No more dramas ... no more ... It's such a relief. Gil says they want the wedding to take place as quickly as possible. Just a quiet ceremony, close family only.'

'It sounds almost too good to be true,' James responded. 'I know she's your daughter, Helena, but sometimes ...'

'I've never really felt that she was my child,' Helena confessed. 'There's always seemed to be so much more of Flyte in her than of me. Just like him, she seemed to delight in causing trouble, in being difficult....'

Maybe in the past, secretly, there had been times, brief, occasional moments of betrayal when she had compared James unfavourably to Bram and even to Flyte; but there was no doubt about which of the three men had the best genes, Helena now reflected complacently.

You only had to look at Plum and Jay to recognise the difference between them and James's daughters. It made her shiver now to think what she could have been letting herself in for if she hadn't conquered those foolish desires she had once had for Bram, if he had returned those feelings. Plum had been bad enough. If she had had a child like Jay...

No, she was lucky to be married to a man like James, to have children like her two daughters by him. This was where her future lay, here with James and their children. Those silly yearning regrets she had been having about the past, about... things ... were best forgotten.

She smiled, picturing her friends' disbelief and envy when they learned that Plum was to marry Gil. Perhaps, after all, her daughter did have something of *her*. Perhaps they could begin again...form a new relationship now that Plum had finally come to her senses....

She, certainly, had no idea why on earth Gil wanted to marry her daughter. A man like that, titled, wealthy—she was just thankful that he did, that Plum would soon be off her hands, her responsibility no longer.

Gil had said they wanted a very quiet, small wedding, but there were certain people who would have to be invited, of course, if only to correct the very unfortunate impression Plum's unscheduled disappearance from her birthday ball had caused.

Plum could wear cream satin; it would suit her colouring perfectly. She could wear her hair dressed with flowers and just have her two half sisters in attendance, Helena decided, her mind suddenly busy. Did Plum realise how much organisation even a small wedding—especially a small wedding—could take?

There were guest lists to be drawn up, the wedding breakfast to be planned, the church, the music, accommodation for the guests who would have to travel north.

Helena came to a decision.

'James, I'm going to have to go north to see Plum. There's so much I'm going to need to do...to organise, and you know how useless Plum is at anything like that.'

Helena smiled happily at James.

In Scotland Plum gazed lovingly into Gil's eyes. He had told her that there was no way he was going to take her to bed 'properly' until after they were married.

'Nanny would never let me,' he had insisted teasingly, when Plum had protested. But although he had stuck to his decision not to take her to bed 'properly,' it had certainly not stopped him from being extremely inventive about finding ways of stretching that promise to its utmost limits and, in doing so, giving her so much pleasure that Plum curled her toes in blissful anticipation of what their wedding night was actually going to be like, if this was how he could make her feel without penetrating her.

'You know what's going to happen now, don't you?' she warned him, nibbling his ear playfully. 'My mother is going to come rushing up here, madly organising everything and everybody....'

'Good. That's what mothers of brides should do,' Gil responded promptly, equally teasingly and far more productively caressing the nipple of her bare breast.

They were in the stable block, lying half-naked in the big airy loft above the stables, because Plum had pouted that there was something deliciously erotic about the sight of a man dressed for riding and that she had always had a secret fantasy about being made passionate love to in such lusty surroundings.

Gil had promptly pushed her up against the wooden stall of an empty stable, holding her there while he kissed her and pulled open her blouse, baring her breasts.

'Stop. Someone might see us,' Plum had squeaked, remembering that there were men working outside in the yard.

'Let them,' Gil had challenged, well aware that his employees were far too well trained to risk interrupting them.

Torn between shock and excitement, Plum had continued to protest verbally, while her body responded physically to his touch, until he had suggested that they continue their love play in the relative privacy of the loft.

Now the afternoon sunlight shone softly on Plum's bared breasts, and as she saw the way Gil was looking at her, a flood of aching sweetness filled her. Leaning forward, she placed her lips against the base of his throat and whispered, almost shyly, 'I love you so much.'

Instead of teasing her as she had expected him to do, Gil took hold of her hand. Pushing himself back from her slightly so that he could look down into her eyes, he raised her hand to his mouth, slowly kissing each finger.

The look in his eyes made Plum's face burn and her heart pound.

'Oh, Gil, I don't think I can wait much longer,' she protested plaintively, her mouth trembling.

'*You* can't wait?' Gil growled, placing her hand over his body. 'How the hell do you think I feel?'

'You were the one who said that we had to wait,' Plum reminded him.

'And so we shall,' he confirmed, adding in a whisper as his breath feathered warmly against her mouth, 'Just think, in twenty years' time you'll be the one planning our daughter's wedding.'

They had already agreed that they wanted children. 'Lots and lots of them,' Plum had suggested eagerly.

'Well, we've certainly got the space for them,' Gil had agreed.

Gil's children . . . Plum gave a small wriggle of pure, blissful pleasure. She couldn't wait . . . in fact . . . Her hand stroked provocatively over the hard ridge of flesh beneath his clothes. . . .

23

'Happy, Mrs Soames?' Bram asked Taylor gently as he brushed some of the lingering confetti from her hair and bent his head to kiss her.

'Yes,' Taylor whispered back, her eyes bright with shining tears.

Bram and Fate had organised the wedding between them, refusing to listen to her protests that she didn't want any fuss.

Her sister and Fate has whisked her off on a shopping spree, during which Taylor had almost magically found herself transported back in time, transformed into someone whose excitement and enthusiasm were more appropriate for a girl of nineteen or twenty than a mature woman of almost twice that age . . . or so she had complained to her sister.

The three days in Paris were ostensibly to buy Taylor a wedding outfit and a trousseau. When was she ever going to wear so many ridiculously flimsy, delicate pieces of silk and satin lacy underwear? she wondered, since instead of a honeymoon trip, she and Bram had agreed they would rather spend their time viewing country properties they had selected as possibilities for their new home.

'Of course, you'll wear them,' Caroline had assured her with wonderful elder-sister bossiness. 'Think of the fun Bram is going to have taking them off. . . .'

'And think what's going to happen to these silk stockings when I have to pull a pair of wellingtons over them,' Taylor had mourned.

Being with her sister again was somehow like finding a missing piece of herself. Their years apart might never have been. They meshed so well together, had so much to talk about, so much to share and relearn about each other, and she knew quite well that Bram's insistence that she go to Paris with them on a shopping spree had, in reality, been his way of ensuring that she had time alone with Caroline and Fate, so that the three of them could begin to form the relationship they should have had but which they had been denied.

His sensitivity had touched Taylor, even more because she was aware of how he must be contrasting the renewal of her relationship with her family, with the final destruction of his with Jay.

She had tried gently to suggest to him that he might have been too harsh with Jay, to let him know that no matter what *her* feelings were towards his son, she had no wish to be the cause of Bram's severing the bond between them.

Where had it come from, this new generosity, this new tenderness? Automatically her hand rested for a second against her womb.

'Are you okay?' Bram asked her instantly.

'I'm fine, we're both fine,' she reassured him immediately. But her smile was replaced by a small frown as she touched his arm and asked tentatively, 'Bram, Jay—'

'No,' Bram interrupted firmly, 'it's over, Taylor. He's had his chance.'

Despite his words, Taylor suspected that he must be wishing that things were different, that Jay could have been there with them this morning in the small and homely little church a handful of streets away, where they had been married, and now too, here in the sunny garden of Bram's house, where caterers had provided a deliciously satisfying and stunningly appealing buffet luncheon for the five of them.

If they had been surprised to be asked to cater for a wedding reception for so few people, they had hidden it well, Taylor acknowledged. She acknowledged as well that despite her own protests and initial objections, she had been glad to have Caroline and her family with her, both in church and here now. And if *she* had felt that need for the support and approval of her family, then how must Bram, who had always been so close to Jay, really feel about his son's absence . . . ?

And Bram wasn't the only one who might secretly be wishing Jay was with them, Taylor decided as she glanced across the garden at her niece.

Fate had been talking animatedly to Bram, but now that he had come over to rejoin her, she was on her own, her mouth drooping slightly, anxiety and unhappiness shadowing her eyes.

Taylor and Caroline had had several lengthy discussions about Jay's relationship with Fate in Fate's absence.

It was plain to Taylor that her sister had a decidedly weak spot for Bram's son, who she suspected had shown a far different face of his personality to Fate's parents than he had ever done to her.

For her part she didn't, for one moment, doubt Jay's ability to charm and flatter, but she had seen the unhappiness in Fate's eyes. Although by an unspoken but mutual agreement, both she and Fate had played down the cruelty of Jay's role in bringing Fate into contact with Taylor, Taylor knew how much Jay must have hurt her niece, even if Fate herself refused to acknowledge or discuss it.

Fate loved him, Taylor suspected, even if she was trying very hard to both ignore and destroy that emotion.

'You haven't opened your wedding presents yet,' Caroline reminded Taylor, coming over to join them.

Taylor grinned at her. Even as a child Caroline had never been able to resist the lure of a wrapped parcel, much to their parents' disdain.

'I'm saving them for later.'

She brushed a few more pieces of confetti off the cream silk of her dress. Simple in style, it was the kind of dress that immediately imbued its wearer with a glamorous elegance, which had shocked Taylor the first time she had seen herself wearing it. Standing in the mirrored salon of the exclusive couture house where she had bought it, she had protested that such an expensive outfit was a complete waste of money, and that it was ridiculous of Bram to want her to buy it.

A futile protest, for Bram had given Caroline explicit and strict instructions that his bride wear something that wouldn't cause his son or daughter to accuse him of jealousy when they saw their wedding photographs.

'Jealousy?' Taylor had asked him, mystified.

'Yes, jealousy,' Bram repeated, 'because that's what they would think if they saw a photograph of their very beautiful mother wearing something, anything on her wedding day that did not do her justice, and which was not almost as beautiful as she is herself....'

'Oh, Bram,' Taylor had protested, shaking her head, but he had had his way. The cream silk would no doubt be carefully packed away in tissue paper for her daughter or granddaughter to ooh and aah over in the future, Taylor admitted ruefully.

Inwardly she marvelled at the extent to which Bram had changed her life. If anyone had told her a year ago that she would be standing here today, celebrating her marriage to a man whom she loved so intensely that sometimes merely to glance across the room at him was enough to make the ground rock beneath her feet in a flood of intense emotions, supported by her sister and her family; carrying her new husband's child, she would not just have flatly denied the possibility but, would have also assumed bitterly that they could only, by the impossibility and implausibility of their predictions, have been making fun of her in the cruellest and most unbearable of ways.

But there were still clouds on the horizon, shadows threatening the brilliance of her personal shining blue sky, she acknowledged.

Not so much because of the past. Bram, bless him, had made her see that her fear that Dennis could somehow track her down and find her ... find them ... had become almost as much of an obsession as had Dennis's supposed 'love' for her. No, her pain was on Bram's behalf and not hers.

Already, with their child little more than the merest tell-tale bulge, she was keenly and very fiercely aware of just how strongly protective she felt towards it. Of just how antagonistic she would feel towards anyone who dared to cause him or her a single second's unhappiness or pain. And that was after just four months. How would she feel were she in Bram's shoes, a parent of some twenty-seven years' standing?

Quite irrationally, given what Jay had done and what he might still do, she longed for there to be some way in which Bram and Jay could be brought together, and for the lives of them all to somehow be harmonised.

And Bram's unhappiness wasn't her only dark cloud. There was Fate as well.

Fate...

Taylor looked round in vain for her niece.

'She's gone,' Caroline told her when Taylor asked where she was. 'She said to tell you that she had some unfinished business to attend to. She said you'd understand.'

The sisters exchanged a look. 'Do you think she's gone to see Jay?' Caroline asked Taylor.

'Yes,' Taylor confirmed.

'I hope he doesn't do anything to hurt her.' Caroline sighed unhappily.

Silently Taylor echoed her hope, but without much conviction.

'You still haven't opened your presents,' Caroline reminded her again.

'No. I think I'll save them for this evening,' Taylor told her. She was beginning to feel tired—something she felt increasingly lately—the baby, of course. She spoke to it silently now, reminding it that it was at least in part responsible for today's events.

There had been a moment in church, listening to the reading of the lesson, when she had looked at Bram and seen the tears in his eyes, felt the intensity of his emotion and matched it with her own. She knew then, beyond anything that ever had or ever could happen, that nothing in her life had ever been more right or meant to be than for her and Bram to celebrate their love with this kind of solemnity, bringing a spiritual blend of tranquillity and joy.

As she knelt there in church, exchanging her vows with Bram, even Jay had ceased to threaten her. He would miss out on so much in life because of his obsessive needs. He would live for ever in the shadow cast by those feelings, as she had once lived in the shadow of her fear.

Yes, she felt compassion for him, but she also felt concern for her niece.

Fate loved him, and because of that he would hurt her. Doubly so, because she was Taylor's niece. And Fate knew it.

'Are you okay?'

Taylor smiled up at Bram as he put one arm around her and rested the palm of his hand against her belly.

Two mornings ago she had woken early to find him already awake beside her, his hand resting gently on her stomach while he talked to their child, telling it how much he already loved it . . . how much he loved them both.

'I love you, Bram,' she said emotionally now, remembering that moment.

As she lifted her hand to touch his face, the diamonds in the ring he had given her flashed white fire.

Caroline had gaped in open awe at them, but Taylor had shaken her head reprovingly at her.

Her rings were beautiful and had, no doubt, been very expensive, but the gift Bram had given to her which she valued the most was the gift of his love.

'I hope Fate's all right . . .' she told him quietly now, mentally contrasting her own happiness with the unhappiness she knew Fate had been trying valiantly to conceal beneath a façade of determined brightness.

24

It was totally illogical to have come here like this, Fate admonished herself fiercely, as she paused halfway up the flight of stone steps leading to Jay's apartment building. She had been impulsive and emotional in deciding to do so. Even if Jay was at home, he would hardly be pleased to see her, not today of all days and certainly not her of all people.

So why had she come?

Because, for one crazy heartbeat of time, as her eye had been caught by that photograph in Bram's house of him standing with Jay—Bram looking slightly anxious, Jay all of somewhere around eight years old looking fierce and independent—she had suddenly felt for that eight-year-old boy, had felt the anxiety and dread that lay behind his outward show of hostility, had known how mortally afraid he had been, and known, too, that the grown-up, adult Jay was just as afraid, even if he would never allow himself to admit it.

How on earth was he feeling today, knowing that he was excluded from such an important celebration and from the rest of Bram's life? Was he regretting what he had done, wishing he could turn back the clock, wishing he could find the words to repair the damage he had done to his relationship with his father, but too proud still to admit it?

Fate's heart had ached for him, overruling her more pragmatic head.

She wasn't aware of having made any conscious decision to come and see him, she only knew that somehow she had found herself on the pavement outside Jay's house and that she was now here in the hallway of his apartment building, looking uncertainly towards the stairs.

What if he wasn't in? What if he was in but refused to speak to her? What if . . .

Taking a deep breath, she squared her shoulders and headed for the stairs.

Jay stared morosely at the empty glass in his hand and reached
for the bottle on the table beside him, frowning when he realised that it, too, was empty.

He had started drinking late last night after walking out on the
astounded and furious woman friend he had taken to dinner. He
had flirted with her heavily enough throughout the meal to make
her feel comfortably confident that the two of them would be
spending the night together.

Dropped unceremoniously outside her own flat after what she
had thought was a promising ten minutes or so of heavy-duty
snogging in the shadowy darkness of Jay's car before they left the
restaurant car park, she had been not only disappointed but
infuriated.

She had told Jay, with biting accuracy, just what she thought
of him, adding as her parting shot, 'You never were much of a
fuck anyway, as I remember it. You were always all muscle and
no heart, and now it looks as though you can't even manage the
muscle.'

Jay didn't bother to argue with her. He could manage it all
right, but the problem was he could only manage it in a certain
set of circumstances, or rather in connection with a certain specific person, and it was *her* image which had sparked off the intense and promising session of foreplay. It was also her image
which had brought it to an end.

He picked up the empty bottle and walked into the kitchen
with it. It made an ominous sound as he dropped it into the gar-
bage, the empty chink of bottle against bottle.

He could hear his front doorbell buzzing as he walked back
into the living room. His secretary had strict orders that he was
not to be disturbed under any circumstances, and no one else
knew he was here—or cared?

He cursed as he opened the drinks cabinet door and realised
that the empty bottle of Scotch he had just thrown out had been
his last.

The doorbell was still buzzing. He had already switched off
his telephone and fax machine, just in case his father should try
to get in touch with him, to plead with him to change his
mind . . . to wish him well.

Yesterday he and his father had signed the first of the papers which would eventually give him control of the business. They had signed them separately, in their separate offices, attended by their separate legal representatives.

He had never thought it would come to this, had never dreamed . . . imagined that his father would reject him in favour of *her*, never mind that he would marry her . . . or impregnate her with his child.

A sudden desire to be violently sick gripped his belly. He fought against it, subduing it, controlling it as he had done everything in his life, turning, not towards the bathroom but towards the front door.

As the door opened, Fate's eyes widened in shock. Jay's normally healthy, slightly olive-toned skin looked distinctly sallow. His eyes, slightly bloodshot, the skin around them swollen and puffy, focused unsteadily on her and as he leaned forward she could smell the spirits on his breath.

'Well, well, if it isn't the daughter of the bride,' Jay taunted her. 'Just as well we never made it to bed together, eh, stepsister? Or have I got it wrong? Have you come to tell me some good news— like the wedding's off, or better still, the bride's dead?'

If he hadn't closed the door behind her and wasn't right now leaning against it, surveying her with all the malicious pleasure of a bored and feral cat given a mouse to play with, Fate knew she would have turned round and walked away—run away. Even without the fact that he had obviously been drinking, the mood he was in was too dangerous for her to stay.

He might very well be suffering, but it certainly wasn't from remorse or regret. The little boy she had come here to comfort existed only in her own foolish imagination.

'*You* were there, of course, to watch the happy event,' she heard him say with quiet savagery, enunciating every word clearly and carefully, as well as spacing them out with single-minded control that belied his drunken state.

'Yes, I was there,' she agreed gently. 'You should have been there too, Jay. It was a beautiful service.' She spread her hands, recognising the impossibility of trying to convey to him the way the simple service had touched her, moved her, uplifted her.

'*I* should have been there? My God . . .' Jay started to laugh. 'What for? To complete the happy family circle, my father, your mother, both of *us*? Have you thought yet that *their child* will be half-brother or -sister to *both* of us?'

'No. No, it won't, Jay,' Fate corrected him quietly. 'Taylor isn't my mother. She's my aunt.'

'She told you that . . . ? And you believed her? You're a fool,' he told her contemptuously.

'Better a fool than a knave,' Fate quoted lightly before repeating more firmly, 'Taylor *is* my aunt.'

'Your aunt. . . I see.' Jay laughed contemptuously. 'So why did she lie and tell me she was your godmother. . . if she's really your aunt?'

He was sneering openly at her now, and smiling at her as well—always a dangerous sign where Jay was concerned.

It wasn't Jay himself who made her feel so uneasy and wary, she recognised, it was his total refusal to accept any view other than his own.

'She lied because she felt she had to . . . to protect us,' Fate told him, with quiet emphasis on the 'us.'

'To protect you?' Jay's eyes narrowed. 'What the hell from?' he demanded sarcastically. 'Yes, I admit, she isn't someone I want added to my own family tree, but—'

'Stop it, Jay,' Fate interrupted angrily. 'You don't understand. This isn't a game where you win by scoring off points on someone else. This is reality. . . life. Taylor cut herself off from us. . . her family because . . . because she was afraid for us. Because of something, of someone.

'There was a man,' she told Jay in a low voice, 'and he . . .'

Tersely, she outlined what had happened to Taylor, not looking at Jay until she had related the full story.

She lifted her head and looked at him, searching his eyes for any sign of disbelief, gathering herself up to defend Taylor if he showed any signs of refusing to accept what she had told him. But his expression was unreadable.

'She told you this, did she?' he eventually asked her, almost tenderly.

'Yes. Yes, she did,' she confirmed.

'And you believed her.'

This time she didn't wait to check his expression, replying immediately and confidently. 'You were wrong about her, Jay,' she told him gently, 'but even if you hadn't been . . .'

While outwardly Jay was listening to Fate, within, his brain had gone into overdrive. Did she honestly expect him to believe what she had just told him? Taylor was a quick thinker, he admitted, he had to give her that. He doubted that even he would have been able to come up with something so clever and at such short notice. Clever, but outrageously implausible. He doubted that anyone less gullible than Fate would have believed it. Someone such as his father, for instance. But then his father had his own reasons for publicly, at least, accepting Taylor's fiction.

Now that his father had cast in his lot with Taylor, he could hardly turn round and admit that she had deceived him. In the same circumstances, Jay admitted that he would certainly not have done so. His pride alone would have stopped him. He smiled bitterly to himself. His father was going to pay a hell of a price for Taylor, and not just in financial terms. That knowledge alone ought to be all the revenge Jay needed.

And as for Fate, she, too, had a vested interest in believing Taylor's story. If she didn't, she would no longer be able to wear that bright shining raiment of her parents' love.

As he glanced at her, he remembered how often he had wanted to take hold of that invisible protection and wrench it from her, to make her see the world . . . people, as they really were, to show her what it felt like to hurt . . . to suffer.

'You should have been at the wedding, Jay,' Fate was saying softly to him. 'I . . . I can understand how . . . how you must feel. How hurt and alone you must feel. But just because Bram loves Taylor, that doesn't mean that he doesn't . . .'

As she talked, Jay was suddenly aware of a sharp twisting sensation inside him, a desire to make her stop so that he wouldn't have to listen to what she was trying to say. Strong emotions were gripping him. He could feel them tightening his chest, pressing outwards against his ribs, squeezing the muscles of his heart, until all he could feel was a red-hot, searing pain.

Once, years ago, another woman had spoken to him in that same, soft voice, sugar-coated with a pseudo-warmth that covered an icy cold.

"Your father doesn't love you. How could he? How could anyone love a horrid child like you, Jay...?'

Helena ...

He closed his eyes as he heard her words coming back from the past to taunt him, instinctively reaching for Fate, his fingers digging into the vulnerable flesh of her shoulders as he dragged her against his body, driven by the need to silence her, to reject the compassion and pity he could hear in her voice.

With just a few words, Fate had splintered the armoury of his defences with the same impact that a home-made bomb of sharp, rusty spikes and broken glass would have on the unprotected human body. Not lethal perhaps, but cruelly destructive and painful.

It was an attack designed to maim rather than kill, and Jay reacted to it in the same way as a pain-crazed victim of a physical attack would do, desperate to annihilate the pain that was threatening him. His method was to hold Fate imprisoned against his body, use his mouth to silence the soft compassionate words he couldn't allow himself to hear, words which crazed him with an agony he couldn't bear to endure.

Fate's body stiffened, her breath drawn in in an involuntary, muffled protest.

Her eyes flashed their message of angry denial and rejection into his as she fought to release herself from his grasp. Her body might be unwarrantedly and inconveniently aroused by the proximity of his; irritatingly excited by the intensity Jay was exhibiting, the breakdown of his fierce control. But mentally, she was fully aware that it was desire for her that was motivating him ... not love....

Neither was she alone in her arousal, she discovered. Her body refused to respond to her mind's admonishments, to ignore the hardening of Jay's body against hers, but reacted instead rather like a giddy, untrained young puppy on a leash, responding in joyous abandonment to its pleasure in recognising a special friend.... A very special friend, Fate decided grimly, as totally without any permission from her, her lower body pressed closer to Jay's, her hips rotating tellingly.

The rhythmic penetration of his kiss was making her whole body ache. Somehow he had managed to back her up against the door, and as he used his weight to keep her pinned there while he lifted her arms above her head, Fate knew that whatever had originally caused him to kiss her, if she didn't stop him soon there could be only one outcome.

Illogically, she panicked. This wasn't what she wanted. Jay wasn't what she wanted, not now...not anymore...not like this, no matter how much her body might tell her differently.

As her efforts to twist her body free failed, her panic increased and, without thinking about the possible consequences, she bit sharply into Jay's bottom lip, drawing blood. She could taste its salt on her lips and in her mouth. The shock of what she had done widened her eyes and tensed her whole body into stunned stillness.

When Jay released one of her hands to touch his fingers to his bleeding mouth, she followed the action, her gaze lifting involuntarily from his mouth to his eyes.

The anger she had expected was there, but so was something else. Something else which made excitement kick dangerously through her body and her heart start to race.

'You're going to be sorry you did that,' Jay told her thickly, 'very sorry.'

The heavy-lidded, sensually aroused look he gave her left her in no doubt about what he meant. She could possibly, just possibly, have escaped, ended it there and then, pulled herself free of his restraining arm and left. But she hesitated just that second or so too long, long enough for him to read the message contained in the betraying flood of heat that flushed her skin, the way she couldn't quite look him in the eyes, the way her breath caught slightly in her throat as he trailed the hard pads of his fingertips down along the exposed line of her neck. She shivered and closed her eyes without making any attempt to pull away, simply standing there allowing him to take control, to dominate the situation, to dominate her.

'Nothing to say...no objections to make,' Jay murmured as his mouth teased and then possessed the racing pulse point in her throat, welcoming the reaction he drew from her until he had her trembling openly and violently in his arms.

'But then this, after all, is what you want, isn't it?' he added cynically. 'What you've always wanted.'

Fate tried to deny it, but as she met the look that blazed from his eyes, her gaze dropped helplessly to his mouth and the denial was silenced.

'Kiss me,' she heard Jay demand roughly. 'Kiss me and feel what you've done to me, taste it . . . taste my blood and then remember what kind of man I am, Fate. No crime against me ever goes unpunished . . . no crime.'

She drew in a sharp, protesting breath as Jay's hand cupped her breast, protesting because of what she was feeling rather than what he was doing. To her chagrin, she could see quite clearly beneath the silk, the pouting outline of her swollen nipples.

Jay, of course, could see it as well and she had to turn away from the look of angry unkindness in his eyes as he deliberately licked the tip of his forefinger then drew a slow, stomach-churningly sensual circle of fire around one aching point and then equally deliberately, and even more destructively, bent his head and ran his tongue over and over the taut point.

She had always known with that inner knowledge that women possess about the hidden secrets of their sexuality that it would be like this between them; that he would touch her and that she would ache, melt, yield, *burn* for him every bit as fiercely as any martyr at the stake, welcoming, embracing, wanting a total sublimation of self that he, in his arrogant maleness, would silently demand. It had been this recognition, this knowledge of the impossibility of reconciling the two so completely divided parts of her own nature which had held her back from making an earlier sexual commitment to him.

Her whole body shuddered as Jay continued to caress it. She reached blindly for him, trembling, shivering, oblivious to the sharp, muted cries she was making, oblivious to everything but her need and his desire.

She wasn't aware of them making their way from his sitting room to his bedroom, nor of the trail of abandoned clothes they left behind them. The cool, pale cream linen of his bedding felt slightly rough against her skin, but not unpleasantly so, the sensation even slightly erotic as Jay laid her on the bed and then simply looked at her, his gaze absorbing every detail of her nakedness.

Fate lay still, watching him watching her. Pleasurable though it was to see the faint, betraying reaction to the sight of her that Jay was not quite able to control, she found far, far more pleasure in looking at him.

His body was every bit as athletic as she had imagined, his muscles firm and hard without being unpleasantly overdeveloped, his body hair dark and tantalisingly soft, his nipples unlike hers, small and dark but just as erect. She touched one with her fingertip, circling it as he had done hers, her lips parting in anticipation of the way his flesh would feel and taste inside her mouth, her eyes widening slightly as she felt the way Jay's muscles clenched and saw the dark spread of colour burning his skin.

He wasn't used to being held victim to his own desire, she guessed shrewdly, as his fingers bit into her wrists, lifting her hand from his body, his mouth curling tautly before he placed his lips against the flesh of her inner wrist and watched the way she responded to him, her breath catching softly in her throat.

She had been made love to before, by men who were far more anxious to please her than she suspected Jay would ever be, but her body had never been anything like as responsive to them as it was to him.

The sensation of Jay's mouth caressing the soft flesh of her stomach made her quiver in pleasure. His head bent over her body; she could feel the warmth of his breath against her skin, her sex. If he touched her now with his mouth, caressed her with his tongue as she knew he was going to do, there was no way she would be able to hold back her orgasm, and when it came for the first time, she wanted it to be while he was inside her, while they were both sharing the same pleasure, the same intensity.

Fate saw the darkness in his eyes as she reached out her hand to stop him, the arrogance, the hint of triumph, the pleasure in knowing how much she wanted him, but they were only of secondary importance, things to be noted and then dismissed as she told him huskily what she wanted.

When he hesitated, she reached out to him urgently, imploring him to hurry.

He felt smooth and hard, filling her, and she felt as though her body were a moist, clinging, oh, so-sensitive supple sheath, which he fitted into with perfect harmony. Every movement, however small, even each breath he took was registered by her body—*every* movement—so that well before he began the long, slow thrusts that were the build-up to the climactic urgency of his own release, her orgasm had already overwhelmed her, flooding her with convulsive waves of pleasure, drowning her, submerging her in the shock of its intensity.

When his body finally surged orgasmically within hers, she willed him to focus on her, to meet her own gaze and to share with her the awesomeness of what they were experiencing. But he refused to respond to her silent plea for communication and oneness, his glance sliding away from hers, his eyes closing as he arched the tension from his spine and the tiny droplets of sweat fell from the damp tangle of his body hair onto her own flesh.

Fate reached out towards him, caressing his breastbone, raising her head so that she could place her lips to his throat. But he moved back from her and she had to content herself instead with sucking the moistness of his skin from her fingertips, shivering finely in mute pleasure as she clung to the intimacy they had shared.

At the same time as her mouth trembled in a smile, her eyes wanted to fill with tears. She wanted desperately to reach out to Jay, to hold him and to be held by him, but he was already retreating from her, turning his back on her.

'Jay . . .'

Tentatively she said his name, her voice low and slightly uncertain. Her stomach muscles clenched as he turned to look at her. His eyes were cold and hard, his voice flat and merciless as he taunted her.

'It's a funny thing the way you can want a woman almost to the point of distraction until you've had her, and then you realise that you've been duped, that she just doesn't have what it takes, that there's no way she comes anywhere near living up to your expectations and that the sex you thought was going to be so good is barely even average, pedestrian and totally uninspiring, the kind of thing that proves the old adage that it is better to travel hopefully than to arrive.'

As he moved his hand he glanced at his watch and told her emotionlessly, 'I've got to leave in half an hour. It won't take you long to get dressed and leave, will it? Oh, and by the way,' he added before turning away from her, 'I still don't believe a word of what you've said about Taylor. She *is* your mother, whether you choose to accept that fact or not. Did you really think I'd allow myself to go on wanting you, Fate, once I knew you were *hers?*' he added cruelly. 'There's only one reason I took you to bed, and it had nothing to do with desire, or even lust....'

Fate looked back at him. Her heart was beating heavily and very slowly, too slowly. She felt like someone standing on the edge of a precipice, knowing that for her own safety she must step back, and knowing that she must not allow Jay to torment her into asking the question he so obviously wanted her to ask, and knowing just as well that she would.

'Then what...*why*...why *did* you make love to me?' she asked him tonelessly.

'Make love to you...' His mouth twisted maliciously. 'My God, no wonder you're able to convince yourself that Taylor isn't lying to you. I didn't "make love" to you, Fate, I "fucked" you.

'My wedding present to my father and your mother, if you like. You didn't really think I wanted *you*, did you? How could I? *Why* should I?'

He turned round and looked mercilessly at her, studying the tears slipping silently from her eyes before reaching out and gripping her chin as he told her quietly, 'You're nothing to me, Fate...less than nothing. You didn't even rate as a particularly good fuck. Now get dressed and get out.

'Oh, and Fate,' he added over his shoulder to her as he headed for the bathroom. 'Don't bother coming back, will you, because next time you won't get past the front door.'

He looked at his watch again.

'You've now got twenty minutes left.'

'Haven't you opened them all yet?' Bram groaned in protest as he watched Taylor slowly and carefully unwrap the small, gold-bowed box he had slipped in among the other presents. He adored giving her presents. It made his heart ache with love for her to watch the way she tried so desperately to control her anticipation and excitement. How many times as a child had she received presents that must have disappointed her to have learned that guarded carefulness, he wondered.

'I'll bet you were the kind of child who drove everyone else mad by taking forever to unwrap your birthday and Christmas presents,' he teased her lovingly now.

'Our parents stopped buying us surprise presents when we were seven,' Taylor told him wryly. 'My father believed it encouraged immaturity. We were given a list of approved items from which we had to choose one and then justify that choice by writing an essay, detailing the reasoning behind our choice and the benefit we believed we would derive from the gift. One year Caroline rebelled and refused to choose something from the list. She said, instead, that she wanted a bike. She didn't get one, needless to say.

'Oh, Bram, you shouldn't have . . .' Taylor exclaimed, pleasure and excitement in her voice, as finally she had the box open.

Bram heard Caroline gasp in admiration as she saw the earrings he had bought for his wife.

Sapphires in an antique setting. He had seen them by chance in a jeweller's window and had immediately known that they were exactly right for Taylor.

'They're beautiful,' she told him as she reached up to kiss him. 'But they're far, far too valuable for me to risk wearing them. I'd be petrified of losing them. And besides, once we've moved out to the country, I'm hardly going to have much opportunity to flaunt this kind of serious jewellery,' she laughed softly.

'We'll *make* the opportunity,' Bram told her firmly. 'Even if we have to wait until he or she comes of age to do so,' he told her as he touched her stomach gently.

All of them laughed, and Bram knew that despite Taylor's protest, she was thrilled with his gift. He could see it in the happy sparkle in her eyes, the tender warmth of her smile.

'Open this one next,' he urged her, picking up a large, carefully wrapped box. 'Come on, let me help you with it,' he teased her as she reached to take it from him, making a playful grab for the bow adorning the top of the box.

'It's addressed to me,' Taylor pointed out to him, retaining her hold on it and batting his hands away.

Still laughing, Bram stood back to watch her open the gift, Caroline and Oliver standing next to him. None of them had made any reference to Jay's absence nor to the fact that Fate had disappeared. Bram knew that Taylor felt that he had not mentioned Jay because it hurt him too much to do so, but she was wrong. It frightened him a little at times to recognise that where there should have been a gaping, hurting wound in his life, there was simply nothing...no regret...no guilt...no pain...nothing.

Taylor had opened the box and was removing the packing of scrunched tissue paper, smiling teasingly into his eyes as she did so, so that he saw them change, the laughter shift to blankness and, with devastating speed, to horror, seconds before she started to scream.

As he wrenched the box away from her it was the smell that struck him first. The box gave off a stench of unbelievable putridity. The sort of smell that, in a different time, one would have instinctively associated with hell and eternal damnation.

As he stared into the box, gritting his teeth against the stench, Bram felt his gorge rise.

Beside him he could hear Oliver enquiring urgently, 'What the hell is it . . . ?'

'It's a dead foetus...I think,' Bram told him quietly as he closed the box and placed it on the table with care. Taylor was leaning against her sister's shoulder. She stared unseeingly into space as he tried to comfort her.

'I'm going to ring the doctor,' Bram told Taylor, as Caroline tried to urge her out of the room.

Who would do something like that? Bram asked himself, sickened, as he picked up the telephone and punched in the doctor's number.

Who would send a pregnant woman a dead foetus on her wedding day...? Who . . . what kind of person would do something like that?

Obviously someone who hated her, who wanted to hurt her and to kill their unborn child.

The deliberately cruel and malevolent significance of what the box had contained couldn't be ignored. Who had the most reason to resent Taylor and the child she carried . . . ? *His* child . . . Jay?

He closed his eyes, praying that he was wrong. That Jay would not, could not, act with such bitter vindictiveness.

But if not Jay, then who?

Taylor, it seemed, believed she knew. Half an hour later, when he escorted the doctor up to their bedroom, she was pacing the room, her arms wrapped tightly around her body, her face bleached and exhausted.

'It's him. I know it's him. Somehow he's found me . . . found us. Somehow . . . Oh God, Bram, what have I done . . . ? This is all my fault. . . . If anything happens . . .'

'Nothing is going to happen,' Bram soothed her. But even as he said the words he was aware, for the first time in his adult life, of a feeling of helpless impotence . . . of knowing that all he was doing was mouthing platitudes. Quite obviously he could not protect her and their child. He couldn't even protect her from her *fear* of Dennis Phillips, never mind the man himself, he recognised bitterly.

Dennis Phillips. His body stiffened as he remembered what he had not told Taylor—that Dennis Phillips was now a free man.

But it was impossible for him to have found Taylor. Totally impossible.

Bram could hear Taylor arguing with the doctor, protesting that she did not want to be sedated. 'What good will it do . . . ? Now that he knows . . . now that he's found us . . .'

Bram tried to soothe her. 'Taylor, we don't *know* yet that Dennis Phillips *is* responsible for—'

'I know,' Taylor interrupted him. 'I know! But there's no way I'm going to let him do anything to hurt my baby. . . our baby,' she cried fiercely, her eyes suddenly burning with passionate intensity. 'No way. I'll kill him first. . . .'

She spoke so softly, but with such emphasis that Bram's eyes widened slightly.

She meant it, he recognised, marvelling at nature's determination to protect the vulnerable life that Taylor carried.

'I'll be all right now,' she told the doctor firmly and then turned to Bram.

'Show him, Bram, show him what was in the box. I want to know...' She stopped and swallowed, before continuing huskily, 'I need to know what... what it is....'

'Well, I can tell you what it isn't,' the doctor announced after he had seen the gruesome contents of the still partially wrapped box. 'It is not a human foetus. Some animal's, I suspect, but I'm not sure which. Even so... hardly the kind of thing one would want to inflict on a pregnant woman...' He frowned as he wrapped the foetus in the newspaper he had asked for and started to return it to the box.

'There appears to be a letter here,' he told Bram, removing it and handing it to him.

The sealed envelope was tainted with the same sickening smell which now permeated the whole room. Grimacing, Bram ripped it open, removed the typewritten letter it contained and read it.

It was addressed to Taylor:

Remember me. You thought that you'd deceived me, fooled me, lying about your death, just as you lied about loving me. But liars have to be punished. You punished me for loving you and now I am going to punish you for lying to me and for lying to our child, *my* child. The child you were unworthy of having, just as you were unworthy of my love.

The child you denied and abandoned, gave away... my child. You don't deserve her, so now I'm going to take her away from you. You never deserved her. You would have killed her in your womb if you could, you and your accursed parents. They're dead now and you should have died with them. You won't come between us any more. She's mine now and nothing, no one, will keep us apart any longer. She's mine....

Bram's hand was shaking when he put the letter down.

Taylor's eyes filled with panic. 'It's from him... from Dennis Phillips, isn't it? But how?' She looked at Bram, her eyes stark with shock and knowledge.

'He's out, isn't he?' she demanded, her voice rising accusingly. 'They've let him out...after everything they said.... He's free and now...'

'He took his case to the appeal court,' Bram confirmed gruffly. 'I suppose, with the prisons being so overcrowded, the judge...'

'You knew.' Taylor stared at him. 'You knew and you didn't tell me. You...'

Bram closed his eyes, unable to find the words to defend himself.

'Oh, Bram. What have I done...what have I done?' She wept. 'He thinks Fate is his child,' Taylor whispered. 'How *can* he think that? No one...' She looked at him with pain-filled eyes and breathed, 'Jay. Jay knew.

'Tell me that Jay hasn't done this, Bram. That he wouldn't hurt Fate like this. You're his father, you know him best. Tell me....'

Bram shook his head, shamed to the depths of his soul that he couldn't give either Taylor or Fate's parents the assurance they needed and deserved.

'Fate's with Jay now,' Taylor told him anxiously, clutching at his shoulders. 'That's where she was going when she left here. Ring him, Bram. Ring him and tell him to keep her there. Tell him that she mustn't leave. Oh God, if anything happens to her...'

'Nothing *will* happen to her,' Bram promised her forcefully. 'If necessary we can arrange for her to have twenty-four-hours-a-day protection. We'll keep her safe, Taylor, I promise you that. Whatever it takes. Everyone will be safe.'

'They told me that he would never be able to find me,' Taylor mumbled, her eyes blank and her mouth trembling. 'They told me that it was impossible. They told me that I'd be safe.'

'And where exactly is the young lady you believe is in danger now?' the policeman asked Bram in concern.

Bram looked at Taylor before answering him.

'We believe she's gone to see my...my son, but since there was no answer when I tried to telephone him...'

'I see. So as of now you have no real idea of the young lady's whereabouts.'

'No,' Bram agreed heavily. 'No, I'm afraid we don't.'

The only sound that broke the heavy silence that followed was the sob of fear that Caroline tried unsuccessfully to stifle.

25

Jay stared at the tight wad of fabric he was balling in his hand and then realised it was his discarded shirt. He remembered the way Fate had looked at him when he had walked out of the bathroom to find her dressed and standing quietly in the middle of the bedroom.

'It's all right,' she had told him with composure. 'I know you want me to leave and I'm not going to make a scene. One day there'll be a man in my life who values me and all that I am.' Her voice gave a betraying tremble. 'I had hoped that man might have been you. Now I just hope we never have to meet again.' And with those words she was gone.

The ringing of the doorbell brought Jay out of his thoughts, and he headed for the door.

His surprise at seeing his father there, and not as he had expected—hoped?—Fate, was clearly discernible in his expression, and Bram took advantage of it to step into the apartment and close the door. 'Is Fate here?'

Shock...anger...disappointment...pain... Jay wasn't sure which emotion was the strongest. All he did know was that his father—*his* father, who had told him point-blank that he wanted nothing further to do with him—should have come here, not to see him, not, quite obviously, seeking a reconciliation, but in search of Fate. The realisation unleashed inside him the most intense surge of pure rage he had ever experienced.

Typically, he reacted immediately to it.

'Why, do you fancy bedding her as well? Tired of the mother already, are you, and want to try the daughter...? Well,-I shouldn't bother. She isn't worth it. And besides, right now I should imagine she's pretty well shagged out.'

Bram was and always had been the kind of man who didn't welcome male crudity and Jay enjoyed seeing the look in his eyes as his jaw clenched. But he wasn't prepared for the way Bram took hold of him, his fingers digging painfully into the hard muscles on Jay's upper arms, as he demanded thickly, 'Stop it, Jay. For God's sake, don't say any more. *Is* Fate still here? Just answer me, yes or no.'

'No.' Angrily he pulled himself out of his father's grip.

'Look, I don't know what the hell's going on or why your new wife—I presume she *is* your wife now—should send you round here looking for her precious daughter—so precious, in fact, that for damn near twenty years she's denied her existence and still continues to do so, if Fate's to be believed—'

Bram interrupted him, cutting across his sardonic comments. 'When did Fate leave? Did she say where she was going?'

'About an hour ago and no, she didn't say. . .'

The tone of Jay's voice and the expression in his eyes made Bram demand curtly, 'What have you done to her, Jay? What have you said?'

'Done to her?' He gave a small shrug. 'Well, what does one say to a woman who's proved to be a bit of a sexual disappointment and who you've got an unhappy suspicion is going to prove difficult to eject from your life.'

He gave another shrug and informed Bram, in a mocking tone of voice, 'I told her that sexually, the experience wasn't worth repeating, and since that was the *only* reason I had taken her to bed in the first place, there was really no point in her staying.'

'You rejected her,' Bram said flatly. 'You took her to bed and then you rejected her. My God, Jay. . .'

Bram closed his eyes, only too well able to imagine the state Fate must have been in when she left Jay's apartment. She could be anywhere now. . .*anywhere*. But please God, nowhere where Dennis Phillips could find her.

'So, I rejected her,' Jay drawled. 'So what? So what's the big deal?'

'The big deal is that Fate's life is being threatened and we need to find her to warn her and to make sure she is safe. Not that that will be of any interest or concern to you, but naturally it is to me and to her father and her mother and to Taylor. . . .'

'Oh, come on, don't try to tell me that you've fallen for that story Taylor's made up about being Fate's aunt—Taylor *is* her mother. She's lying to you if she says anything else!'

'Fate, like her parents, was someone who Taylor wanted to protect. You, by your meddling, your interference, your downright vindictive cruelty, have now been instrumental in exposing Fate to danger and, I suspect, in intensifying it. I have no idea how the hell Dennis Phillips got the idea that Fate is his daughter, but there's only one other person I know who shares his delusion about Taylor and that's you. Do you know him . . . ?'

'Dennis Phillips . . . no, I don't know him,' Jay denied angrily. Bram could tell that he was speaking the truth. 'I had never heard of the man until Fate told me about him. And I still think—'

'What,' Bram demanded harshly, 'That I'm lying? No, Jay, you're the one who's doing that. You're lying to yourself, deceiving yourself because your ego won't allow you to accept the truth.

'But, if anything has happened to Fate, your ego isn't going to protect you from your conscience and it certainly won't protect you from me.'

As Bram turned away from him, Jay half moved towards him and then stopped.

It wasn't his fault that this Dennis Phillips believed that Fate was his daughter. He didn't even know the man. How could he possibly be to blame?

Just before he reached the door Bram turned round and began, 'If Fate should get in touch with you . . .' He stopped and looked at Jay, his eyes flat and hard with contempt.

'But she won't do that, will she, Jay? You've made sure of that.

'For years I blamed myself for what you are, cursed myself for being responsible for the circumstances that moulded your nature, but now—' He shook his head. 'There's no excuse for your kind of cruelty, Jay. If anything, your own experiences should have taught you. You do know, don't you, that Fate loves you?'

'I know she believed she did,' Jay told him harshly, ignoring the guilt he could feel threatening him. He couldn't meet his father's eyes. His heart started to beat too heavily and too fast; an emotion he didn't want to identify seeped painfully through him.

He tried to defend himself. 'But then Fate doesn't really know me, and if she did—'

'Save it for someone else, Jay,' Bram advised him, opening the door. 'I've heard it all before, remember, the trauma of your past . . . I am, after all, that past, and right now I've got far more important things to worry about than your imagined—'

Both of them froze as the telephone suddenly shrilled.

Jay reached it first, picking up the receiver and then, after a few seconds, passing it to Bram. 'It's Taylor . . .'

'Bram, we've had another letter,' Taylor said tearfully. 'He says that he's got Fate and that he's never going to let her go. He says that I've had her for twenty years and that now it's his turn—that she's his child . . . his daughter, that I rejected her in the same way that I rejected him, that he's going to make sure that I never see her again. Oh God, Bram, I'm so afraid for her . . .' She started to cry, unable to go on.

Bram tightened his grip on the telephone receiver. Out of the corner of his eye he could see Jay, standing a few feet away, a nerve beating visibly in his jaw.

'I'm on my way back,' Bram told her. 'Have you informed the police of what's happened?'

'Yes. Oliver and Caroline are with them now.'

As he replaced the receiver and turned back towards the door, Bram heard Jay say tersely, 'Dad . . .'

Bram shook his head. 'Not now, Jay. Whatever it is you want to say, it will have to wait. I've got to get back to Taylor.'

Bleakly Jay stared after him as Bram opened the door and walked out.

There was an unfamiliar, cold feeling in the pit of Jay's stomach and his heart was still beating very fast. Old emotions, emotions he had denied and suppressed for years, were trying to crowd in and threaten him, to break through the barriers he had built around himself. He felt . . .

He felt, in some odd and terrifying way, rather as he had done when he learned that his mother and grandparents were dead, when he realised . . .

Only Fate wasn't dead. She couldn't be. It was less than an hour since she had been here with him . . . less than a handful of hours since she had lain in bed beside him, beneath him, opening her body to him with the same extravagant warmth and generosity that hallmarked everything she did . . . everything she was.

Fate . . . Fate . . . He closed his eyes and clenched his fists.

Fate . . . It couldn't be his fault that this man . . . this Dennis Phillips, had kidnapped her. It couldn't be his fault that Phillips believed Fate was his daughter.

'No . . .'

It wasn't until he heard the sound of his own anguish echoing back from the silent walls around him that he realised he had screamed his denial aloud.

She had to be somewhere. She could not have just disappeared.

Without even realising what he was doing, Jay opened the door and went out into the street, looking left and then right and then breaking into a jogging run as the silent Fate-less pavements taunted him with her absence.

Which way had she gone when she left him? Where had she been going?

Logically, she should either have returned to his father's house or gone home to her parents' place, but Fate had been far from being in a logical frame of mind.

So where would she have gone, and how had Dennis Phillips found her . . . ?

Bram had said that only Jay and Phillips believed Fate was Taylor's child; he had implied that Phillips got the idea from Jay.

But Jay had not confided that belief to Fate's abductor. How could he have done?

The supermarket was fifteen minutes away from closing and almost empty. The girl on the till gave Dennis Phillips a teasing smile as she rang up the bowl of lilies and the expensive chocolates, commenting archly as he handed over his money, 'Someone's going to be lucky.'

'They're for my daughter,' he told her proudly. 'We've been apart but we're together now.'

He was a very ordinary-looking, nondescript man of medium height with medium-brown hair whom she wouldn't normally have given a second look if it hadn't been for the intensity in his eyes and voice.

His daughter, whoever she was, obviously meant the world to him, she reflected. Lucky girl. She wished that her dad thought as much about her.

Dennis Phillips frowned as he checked the car park. His own car was parked well away from any of the others, but even so, he still took a slightly circuitous route to get to it, making sure that no one was watching him or following him.

He had always been interested in survival and surveillance tactics, and before they had sent him away, he had built up quite a good collection of books and articles on the subject.

Nowadays, of course, it was different. There were videos you could buy and study. The prison library hadn't stocked any-thing in that line that would have been of any use to him, but he had still made good use of its facilities. The staff had praised him for the dedication and determination he had shown in his study of genealogy and drama. Little had they realised that his at-tempts to plot his own family tree had served as a screen for his real purpose, which had been to track down and then punish that bitch who was responsible for what had happened to him. . . . He had left prison determined to find her and make her pay for what she had done. Only it hadn't been quite as easy as he had hoped. He had found her sister easily enough. A scornful look dark-ened his eyes. Oh yes, finding her had been easy. He had watched the house, waiting . . . not realising then . . .

If he hated the bitch before for what she had done to him, the way she had betrayed him, then that was nothing to the hatred he felt for her now that he knew the truth—now that he knew about the way she had stolen his child from him, giving her away to someone else to bring up.

He could kill her just for that alone. She was just like his mother—first of all driving his father away, forcing his father to leave them—to leave *him*. And then, when he had tried to pun-ish her for separating him from his father, she had told the coun-cil that she didn't want him any more, that she couldn't cope with him, and they had taken him away, put him in a home.

He had hated it there, and he had vowed that he would get even with his mother for what she had done.

She had been on her own the day he went to see her. The man she had put in his father's place had been at work. She had pretended to be pleased to see him, but Dennis had known that underneath she wasn't. It had pleased him to see that he made her feel afraid. He had enjoyed that. It made him feel very powerful. He had let her think that he had forgotten what she had done, how she had sent his father away, how she had sent him away, and then just as she had started to relax and the fear had started to leave her eyes, he had hit her. He had only been doing what his father would have wanted him to do, he had told her sternly. It was his right to punish her, his duty. She had cried at first and then she had screamed, but not for very long. He hadn't killed her, but he had heard that later her man friend left her, unable to put up with the nightmares she suffered and the scars on her face and body.

All women were the same—bitches who needed to be punished. He hated all of them, all except one. . . . His daughter. She was so beautiful, so perfect. . . . He hadn't known then, when he had been watching her house and following her, that she was his. He had simply been looking for Anne—Taylor as she called herself now.

His eyes darkened with fury as he unlocked his car door. That bitch had known how much he wanted a child. . .she had known and yet had still lied to him. All these years he had been a father and had not known it, would never have known it if he hadn't overheard that man in the street.

He didn't like him, Jay Soames, the rich, arrogant bastard who had hurt his precious girl and made her cry. But she wasn't going to cry any more . . . not now . . . not now she had him to protect and love her.

The love he had felt for Taylor might once have been the focal point of his life, but he understood now that it had simply been a training ground, a nursery school, a learning process preparing him for what was to come. The love he felt for Fate, his child, his daughter, far eclipsed anything he had ever felt or thought he had felt for the women he had believed he loved before her— his mother, her mother. They had betrayed him, scorned his love, destroyed it. They had not deserved his love, but he had learned from their treachery.

He parked the car within a reasonable walking distance of his actual destination, concealing it by the simple expedient of not

concealing it, parking it among a row of others on an anonymous street. Tomorrow he would choose a different street. Who,
in this busy indifferent city, would notice another car, grey and
dull, not worthy of their curiosity or concern?

Having checked that no one was following him, he got out of
the car, removed his purchases and then meticulously locked it.
Not that anyone would attempt to steal it, it wasn't that type of
car. He had learned many things while in prison besides how to
trace a person's forebears—and present family.

The acting classes had been particularly useful. Fate hadn't
realised he had been following her for days, weeks, knowing that
ultimately she would lead him to Anne. That was how he had
overheard Jay Soames telling her who she really was, who her
mother really was, and he had known then that Fate was his
child.

It was Fate who had led him to Taylor, as she now called herself. He had known from the first that if he was patient and careful he would eventually find her, just as he had known they had
lied to him when they told him she was dead, that she had been
with her parents in the car when it crashed.

He hadn't told Fate yet that he would still have to punish her
mother, for keeping them apart, and her 'parents,' as she called
them, for trying to take his place in her life. He wanted to win
her trust first, to make her see the great wrong that had been
done to both of them. He wanted her to share his own sense of
fury and hatred . . . to feel as he did, which she would. She must.
She was, after all, his child, flesh of his flesh, body of his body,
soul of his soul. . . .

His footsteps quickened impatiently, he couldn't wait to be
with her again. His thoughts seethed and boiled inside his head
in a frenzy of excited energy. Fate was his, his . . . Gloating, he
savoured what Taylor must be experiencing now. The pain, the
anxiety, the knowledge of how powerful he was and how weak
she was herself. But then she deserved to suffer. He had given her
his love and she had rejected it. He had given her his child and
she had rejected her.

Poor Fate. But he would make it up to her, show her how much
he loved her and how much she must love him in return.

26

Fate tensed as she heard something rustle in the darkness outside her line of vision...a mouse...a rat. She shuddered. Or was it him returning? She shuddered more deeply.

She was sitting on a low camp-bed with her back against a wall covered in something which felt slick like plastic or polythene and very cold, the kind of cold that came from being damp, although the wall itself felt dry enough. Her hands and feet were tied and she was also handcuffed and fastened to a thick metal post. She knew because she had seen it in those few seconds before he had snuffed out the light and left her here in the darkness.

Even now that she had been here God alone knew how long and her eyes were just about able to make out vague shadows in the darkness, she could still barely see anything—only her silk dress, a thick coat he had wrapped round her and, if she twisted her wrist, the dial of her watch.

It was almost as though she had been buried alive, entombed . . . as though he intended to leave her here to die. Panic clawed at her throat, sending her heartbeat into frantic overdrive. She felt more afraid now than she had done in the street when he had come up to her and she had known, even before he touched her, that she was in danger.

She had tried to escape, to turn and run, to cry for help, but the street had been empty and he had been too quick for her. He had grabbed hold of her with a steely strength that had made her wince, pulling her against him, and then holding that pad of noxious-smelling cloth over her nose and mouth until she passed out.

When she came round she had been here in this place, which felt and smelled like all her very worst nightmares. Only then, at least, there had been light and she had not been alone.

She had thought at first that he meant to hurt her, rape and then murder her, and had not believed him when he told her she had nothing to fear from him. But then he had stunned her, telling her that he was her father, that she was his and Taylor's child, that Taylor had betrayed him, betrayed his love, betrayed them both.

She had known instantly then who he was, whispering his name through half-numb lips.

He had pounced. 'So, she has told you about me. What did she say? Did she say that I gave her everything, that I loved her... worshipped her, that I swore that I would never let anything or anyone come between us and she swore the same? But she was lying. She was just using me. She cheated us both. She cheated me out of my child and you out of your father, but we're together now....

'What were you doing with Jay Soames?' he had asked her, frightening her with the look she could see in his eyes. 'Why did you go to see him? He wants you, doesn't he, but he can never have you. You're mine, and no one will ever take you away from me.... You know that, don't you, Fate? You know that you must always stay with me now. You know that you must never let anyone come between us. Not like your mother... She did that.... She tried to hurt me, to leave me, and I had to punish her for it.... I had to do it, Fate... I had to show her how much I loved her... how much she meant to me. But she didn't understand. She caused me a lot of trouble.... Why did you go to see Jay Soames?'

Fate had licked her dry lips, more frightened than she had ever been in her whole life. Nothing she had ever experienced had prepared her for this. It was the kind of thing that happened to other people, not to her, and even now, she felt somehow as though what was happening was unreal, so unthinkable and terrifying that she dared not allow it to be real.

Already she knew that Dennis must not be allowed to guess that she and Jay were lovers.

'I... I went to see him to... to try to persuade him to... He had quarrelled with his father and—'

'His father... you mean Bram Soames. He and Anne were married today, weren't they? I sent them a present,' he added conversationally. 'He'll soon regret it. She's nothing but a whore....'

Fate froze as his voice started to rise. 'She's a whore and she always has been, even if she did try to persuade me that she wasn't, that she was a virgin. How could she have been a virgin? She didn't bleed, and all virgins bleed, don't they, Fate? I hope that you are still a virgin, that you've kept yourself pure. But then, you're my daughter, you wouldn't do anything else, would you, Fate? My daughter. I wanted a child so much, but she wouldn't let me . . . she told me she didn't want . . . but she lied to me. She was carrying you all the time, but she didn't want me to know it. She lied about that just as she lied about being in that car with her parents. But I knew all the time she wasn't. I knew she wasn't dead and I promised myself that I'd find her. . . . I knew I would. The governor thought I was being such a model prisoner, studying genealogy, tracing my family tree. . . . That's how I found you, Fate. . . . I knew she had a sister, living in Australia, she told me. She'd fallen in love with someone out there but her parents didn't approve. They wanted her to come home, but she wouldn't. She, Anne . . . she said she missed her.

'I suppose she forgot all about that when she changed her identity, but I didn't forget. She thought she'd been so clever, hiding from me by stealing a dead girl's name. But she'd forgotten she'd told me about her sister.

'Bitch . . . giving away her child . . . my child . . .'

Fate shivered again as she relived their conversation.

She wondered what it must be like, what it must do to someone, to be so caught up in one person, one compulsion, one obsession, that it dominated the whole of one's life, possessed one's thoughts for year after year so that there was no room for anything else.

Dennis frightened her, terrified her, but at the same time she also felt a deep pity for him, for the narrow emptiness of not just his life, but his whole person. She was also uncomfortably aware of the tiny threads of similarity between his behaviour and beliefs and Jay's.

Of course, Jay was not a murderer, a kidnapper, a man so obsessed that he would kill to get what he wanted, *who* he wanted, and then justify his behaviour by blaming it on others. But he would warp and twist the truth, he would lie and scheme, he would use other people to protect his own interests, his relationship with Bram.

Jay... Did *he* know what had happened to her? Did he care...? She could feel the hot weakening burn of tears stinging her eyes. Fiercely she blinked them away.

She knew, from what Dennis had told her, that her parents and Taylor must know by now what had happened to her. The knowledge that they would be instigating a search for her, thinking about her, worrying about her, made her feel both comfort and pain; pain because she knew how much anguish they must be suffering and comfort because she was able to draw the warmth of their love and care for her around her like a protective blanket, to protect her from the icy grip of her own terror.

But what if they never found her? What if, despite all his assurances to the contrary, Dennis Phillips did intend to hurt her...to kill her? He had said that he would never let her go, that they would always be together, that she was his....

She must not panic. She must not give way to her fear and horror, Fate warned herself frantically. She needed to concentrate instead on remembering everything she had ever read about kidnap victims who survived their ordeal....

Talk to your captors, wasn't that what you were supposed to do . . . form some sort of bond with them? Well, she already had that, in Dennis's mind at least.

She had been too afraid, too shocked so far to deny his claims that she was his child, and perhaps she would be wiser not to try to do so.

But how could anyone hope to find her? She herself didn't even have any idea where she was.

She tensed as she heard a noise in the darkness.

'Fate. I'm back. I'm sorry I had to leave you, but there were things I had to do.'

Fate shivered convulsively, blinking in the harsh light from the powerful torch which Dennis had turned on.

'Look what I've brought for you,' he told her, thrusting the lilies and the chocolates towards her with the enthusiasm of a young boy.

Fate had to swallow back a sob of hysteria. The lilies would die in here without light, without warmth.... Like her? And as for the chocolates ...

She shrank back, away from him, as he reached towards her, trembling as she saw the angry look in his eyes.

'Silly girl,' he warned her. 'I'm not going to hurt you. I'm your father. I love you. Let me untie this and then we can talk.... I've got such plans for us, Fate,' he told her as he untied the gag he had wrapped around her mouth, 'such plans. Just be patient.'

'What...what plans?' Fate croaked. The words felt as though they were sticking in her throat. If she could only get him to tell her something, give her a small piece of information, it might help her to feel stronger, braver. But she could see that he hadn't liked her question. Even though he hadn't said anything, his body language, the restless, shifty way he was moving his weight from one foot to the other, warned her not to push him too hard.

'You'll know soon enough. Look. Look what I've brought you,' he commanded, excitedly ripping the cellophane wrapping off the chocolates. 'Which are your favourites?'

Sick with fear and exhaustion, the last thing Fate wanted was chocolate, but she automatically reached out towards the box, wanting to placate him, and then whimpered in shock and pain as he smacked her hand away roughly.

'No ... naughty ... you mustn't snatch,' he told her wrathfully. 'I'll choose one for you. You can't have them all. Open your mouth.'

He had already removed one of the chocolates from the box and was lifting it towards her mouth. Fate could feel the gagging mixture of nausea and pain rising in her throat, but she dared not refuse the sweet.

The chocolate felt smooth and cold against her tongue, melting quickly away from the soft, sticky, over-sweet centre.

'It's a strawberry cream,' he told her gloatingly. 'I knew you'd like it. They're my favourite, too. She...your mother, never liked them. She preferred plain chocolate, hard centres—like her. I should have known then....' His voice had dropped as though he was speaking more to himself than to her, and Fate wondered in silent horror how many hours over the years he had spent in such conversations, with himself as the only audience.

'I'm going to take these cuffs off in a minute,' he told her as he gave her another unwanted chocolate. 'And then I'm going to take you to where you can perform your bodily functions. But I'm going to have to blindfold you first, and don't try to struggle or escape, because if you do . . .'

'Perform her bodily functions.' How prim and Victorian the phrase sounded, and yet, she supposed, she ought to be grateful to him for his humanity.

Fate shivered as she felt him refastening the blindfold around her eyes and the gag around her mouth. It took all her strength to stop herself from lashing out in a panicky attack against him— instead of quietly submitting to it.

The place he took her was some distance from her prison. She could feel cool, fresh air on her skin as he walked her across some rough ground and then made her wait while he unlocked another door. The enclosure he guided her into was small and very basic.

'I'll be waiting outside,' he told her as he closed the door and left her. He had removed her blindfold, but despite her pleading, had refused to allow her any more light.

By the light of the lantern he had left her she examined her crude surroundings. She was in what looked like a wooden hut, furnished with a chemical toilet of the type one might use on a camping holiday, and a portable shower.

There was also an old wooden chair in the hut with some rough, but clean, towels on it, some soap and a sponge and, she noted, her eyes widening, a change of clothes—her own clothes.

Well, the jeans and the T-shirt and the warm sweater he had obviously stolen from her bedroom at home would certainly be far warmer than the outfit she had on—and far less distinctive?

What chance of escape would she have if she pushed open the door and tried to make a run for it now? Fate wondered. And then she remembered the steely strength he had exhibited when he manhandled her into his car, and she knew that it was a risk she simply dared not take. Not until she knew a bit more about her surroundings.

She would have to talk to him, question him, try to gain his confidence and find out as much as she could from him.

She flushed the toilet and carefully started to remove her soiled clothes.

At least she need not have any fears of him in a sexual sense—that was one burden she did not have to bear.

What were her parents doing right now...? What was Jay doing...? Did they...did he...?

As her hot tears mingled with the cold water of her makeshift shower she allowed herself the luxury of giving way to her emotions.

27

'Hey, watch it, mate!'

Jay tensed his body antagonistically towards the staggering lurch of the man who had addressed him.

What was the point in telling him that he had been the one in danger of walking into him and not the other way round? Jay asked himself wearily. What was the point in anything, any more? It was close on two o'clock in the morning, and he had spent the past six hours searching the streets around his apartment block, looking for some sign of Fate, even though he had known all the time that he was not going to find her.

It was, he thought as he forced back the emotions threatening to overwhelm him, the realisation of all his worst nightmares, the nightmares he had kept so deeply hidden, had so denied that he himself had not even known they existed, until now.

As he turned to retrace his steps to his apartment, he hesitated for a moment. Then, before he could question his decision too deeply or reject it, he changed direction, heading not for his apartment but for his father's house.

Lights blazed from every window. A police car was parked on the roadway outside. Jay crossed the road and walked up to the front door.

Bram had obviously seen him coming, because he opened the door before Jay reached it. His father's face looked lined and tired, pain etched deep into the narrow grooves around his mouth, and shadowing his eyes. As he caught sight of his reflection in the hall mirror, Jay realised that they had never looked more alike.

Jay didn't need to ask his father if there was any news; it was obvious from his expression, from the way he moved, that there wasn't.

'I had to come,' Jay told him. It was all he could find to say, but it seemed to be enough. Bram touched him briefly on the shoulder, as though in silent acknowledgement of all that couldn't be said.

'Fate's parents have gone home. The doctor felt that it was best. Fate's mother...the shock...and as the police said, there's really nothing they can do at this stage, other than wait.'

'The police?' Jay asked. 'I saw the car outside....'

'Yes, they're with Taylor. One of their expert consultants is with them, trying to build up a psychological profile of Dennis Phillips in the hope that it will help them assess what he is likely to do. And, of course, Taylor probably knows him better than anyone else. She's had firsthand experience of what he's like. She blames herself for what's happened, for—'

'*She* blames *herself?*' Jay cut in harshly. 'I'm the one who virtually threw Fate out on the street and... What the hell kind of man is this Dennis Phillips anyway, to do something like this?'

'He's a psychopath,' Bram told him starkly. 'From what Taylor has told me about him, he's so obsessional that once he gets an idea in his head, once he becomes fixed on some purpose, nothing else matters.'

'And now, because of me, he believes that Fate is his child and that is why he's kidnapped her.'

'We're not sure *why* he believes Fate is his child,' Bram told him quietly, but he couldn't quite bring himself to meet his eyes, Jay noticed. However, whatever his father thought of him, it couldn't be any worse than what he thought of himself.

Jay tensed as he saw Taylor walk into the room, flanked by two uniformed policemen and accompanied by another older woman.

She was still wearing what was obviously her wedding outfit, and the incongruity of it alongside a face streaked with tears and pale with exhaustion was almost surreal.

'I'm sorry I can't do more to help you,' she was saying to the woman, who Jay guessed must be the psychologist Bram had told him about.

'You have helped us,' she assured Taylor. 'The details you've given us of your relationship with him, and especially what happened when he kidnapped you, will help us, if not to find your niece, then at least to establish where not to waste our time looking.

'It sounds, from what you've said, as though he's the kind of man who prides himself on his survival skills, on his ability not so much to live off the land but to camouflage himself against it.

'You said that he often talked to you about his childhood fantasies, of living in the woods and making himself a den....'

'A lair, was what he used to call it. He used to say that animals went to earth and so it was only natural that human beings should have the same instincts. He told me that when he was in bed at night, he used to imagine that he was lying in a burrow he had made for himself, hidden away from everyone else, so that, no matter how hard they searched, they couldn't find him. It was a . . . a fixation with him....' Jay saw Taylor shudder, her face blanching.

'Look, we'll go now and let you get some rest,' the psychologist said. 'But I'll come back in the morning if I may—there are still some points I'd like to go over again with you.'

'We can do it now, if you like,' Taylor offered, shaking her head when the woman suggested that she might be too tired.

'No,' she told her tightly, adding quietly, 'after all, I can sleep as much as I like once we've found her.'

She sounded calm and in control, but Jay saw the way her mouth trembled and sensed the enormous effort she was having to make to not give way to her emotions.

As he was studying her she looked up at him, their glances meeting. Jay saw in her eyes the knowledge and the pain that he knew were in his own . . . and he knew that no matter what anyone else might say to her, she, like him, blamed herself for what had happened. They shared the awful inescapable burden of their belief in their own guilt.

For the first time in his life, Jay wondered how different things might have been had he had someone to share the traumas of his childhood with...a brother...a sister... For the first time in his life he realised that to have had that brother or sister would have meant that he had an ally rather than a competitor, a friend rather than a foe, vying with him for his father's love.

An hour later, hearing both the exhaustion and the grim determination in Taylor's voice as she still refused to go to bed and insisted on finishing the interview with the psychologist, Jay felt an odd and unfamiliar emotion. It was, he realised, respect. Respect for Taylor for what she was doing, for her control, her gritty determination, her ability to deny her own needs and to put Fate's first. She was, he recognised, a woman it would be good to have on your side, in whatever capacity she might enter your life.

Had things been different, had she been older and he younger, could *she* have been the stepmother who might have changed things for him, who might have changed *him?*

It was too late now to ask himself that question, too late to regret the enmity which existed between them. They had both made their choices and taken up their opposed positions.

'I'd better go,' he told his father. 'If there's anything new you'll—'

'Why don't you stay here? There's plenty of room, and the police are going to want to interview you sometime. . . .'

Bram and Jay both turned to look at Taylor. She pushed her hand into her hair, lifting the heavy weight of it off her neck. She wasn't sure why she had suggested that he stay the night. He was, after all, the last person she wanted staying under the same roof. He was her enemy, dedicated to destroying her relationship with his father, as obsessive about his desire to control every aspect of Bram's life as Dennis had been about his professed love for her. . . .

But Jay wasn't Dennis, she reminded herself firmly. Jay was not a murderer, not an abductor.

Jay turned towards his father, his face carefully blank of all expression while he waited for his reaction to Taylor's suggestion. But beneath his outward calm, his heart was thumping heavily as he looked for some sign that his father knew, that he understood, that he . . .

That he what? Jay derided himself bitterly. That he still loved him?

Why *should* Bram love him? Once, he would have manipulated his father into inviting him to stay, and then used that as a power base from which to launch an attack on his and Taylor's relationship.

Nothing could destroy the love that existed between his father and Taylor. He could see that as clearly as he could see the shared pain and anxiety in their eyes. He had no right to try, no right to . . . to what? To Bram's love. Love, to be truly worth-while, had to be freely given, not demanded as a right.

Fate had tried to show him that with her own love for him, but he had scorned her, mocked her, rejected and taunted her.

'Yes, you can stay if you like, although . . .' Bram shrugged tiredly. He didn't need to finish his sentence, Jay reflected grimly. All three of them knew what Bram had been thinking. What was the point in Jay's staying? What help could he be?

'How . . . why does this man . . . this Dennis Phillips believe that Fate is his child?' he heard himself asking Taylor. Did she, like his father, believe that he had somehow *told* the man that Fate was his child? He knew that he could put his hand on his heart and swear that he had not. He had not after all, discussed the subject of Fate's birth or his conviction that she was Taylor's il-legitimate child with anyone other than Fate and his father.

'He . . . he desperately wanted me to conceive his child,' Tay-lor told him quietly. 'I think then he felt that it would give him additional power over me. . . . But now it seems somehow as though he may have transferred his obsession to Fate. . . .'

Jay turned to his father. '*I* didn't tell him that Fate was his child. I don't even know him. I haven't told anyone. . . .'

Bram only said, 'It's almost four o'clock. We're all exhausted. Let's try and get some sleep.'

'The police will be coming back in the morning,' Taylor re-minded him. 'The psychologist wants to go over everything with me again, just in case I think of something I might have missed.'

Bram frowned. 'Surely you've told them all you can. You—'

'I want to do it, Bram,' Taylor said with gentle firmness, her hand resting betrayingly against her stomach for a second. She continued, 'Fate isn't my child but . . .' She gave a small shudder and closed her eyes. 'Even if we get her back safely, none of us is ever going to be the same. We all will carry the scars of this with us for the rest of our lives.'

Jay could feel his heart hammering frantically against his ribs. At one and the same time, he felt like a small child again, fright-ened by the evidence of adults' vulnerability, and like the adult male he was, wanting to grab this man who had abducted Fate and was subjecting her to all kinds of terror, and to physi-cally . . . He swallowed hard. Fate . . . Why . . . why hadn't he kept her with him where she was safe? Why hadn't he told her he loved her?

He froze, shocked by how easily the emotion he had fought so hard to deny and destroy had pushed past the barriers he had thought he had erected against it. She means nothing to me, he had told himself over and over again. But he had been lying. His subconscious mind had known that all along, and now his conscious need, his heart, his body, his soul, knew it too—knew it and was filled with the pain of it, the anguish, the remorse, the knowledge of his own unworthiness.

Jay looked away as Bram went over to Taylor and took her in his arms. His envy of their love for each other, their closeness... their togetherness, swept over him with all the cold bleakness and intensity of a Siberian snowstorm.

He closed his eyes against the weight of his own pain.

'Scars heal, given time and care,' Bram told Taylor gently, 'and what remains of them reminds us of the pain we suffered and our strength in overcoming it. Don't forget that there are still cultures where they wear their scars with pride as badges of growth and personal achievement. To know pain is part of the human experience, to overcome it, to live with its residue and to have learned not to fear it is one of the hallmarks of maturity and wisdom. But who am I to tell you that? You've already suffered enough and...'

'That was different,' Taylor told him swiftly. 'That doesn't matter any more. I was young. It's not the same. Fate—'

'Fate is also young and strong and, according to the police psychologist, while Dennis Phillips continues to believe that she is his daughter she will be safe.'

Ten minutes later as Jay made his way upstairs to the guest bedroom, he glanced out of the landing window and saw the policeman on duty outside, guarding them, protecting them. It was Fate—who was God alone knew where, suffering God alone knew what trauma of terror and pain—who needed that protection, not him... least of all him, Jay acknowledged savagely as he continued on his way upstairs.

If only he had not done what he did, said what he had said. If only he had told Fate what he felt about her, shown her... If only.

It was too late now by a lifetime for him to wish that things were different, that he was different.

It took Jay a long time to fall asleep, and when he did he started to dream, the old frightening childhood dream he had not had in years. He tried to wake up, to fight free of its grip on his sub-conscious . . . but he couldn't.

Jay had felt excited and important when they first arrived at the hospital in the police car. He had stared at the ambulances, his eyes widening as he watched everything going on in the busy area around the Accident and Emergency Department. The teacher who had come with him in the police car and the police-man were talking in low voices, both occasionally glancing at him and then looking away without meeting his eyes.

Something had happened, something important. But the sense of excitement which had filled him when the teacher and the po-liceman had come into his class and taken him away with them faded, to be replaced by a sharp, funny pain that filled his stom-ach and his head as he walked with them down a long shiny cor-ridor that smelled horrid and felt cold.

He felt cold and, when they stopped outside one of the cor-ridor doors, he started to panic, backing away from them, shaking his head and crying that he didn't want to go inside.

The teacher was getting cross with him. Her face was all red and angry-looking, like his grandfather's when he told him he had done something wrong. She had tight, wiry-looking hair, and her body was bony and angular, not like his mother's, which was all soft and warm. He used to like climbing up on his moth-er's knee and cuddling against her warmth, but his grandfather had said that he was too old to be such a baby and his mother wasn't allowed to give him cuddles and spoil him any more.

Sometimes, at night when he was sure that he couldn't be overheard, he cried into his pillow, wishing that his mother would come in and sit with him, that she would take him away somewhere where it could be just the two of them. He had tried to tell her how much he wanted it just to be the two of them, but she had looked frightened and unhappy and he had known, without knowing how he knew, that he must never say what he had said to her, in front of his grandfather.

His mother had a new boyfriend. He knew because he had overheard his grandparents talking about him. His grandfather liked him. He said he was the 'right sort.' But Jay didn't like him. He had sharp, bright, hard eyes, which looked through Jay rather than at him, and Jay knew, without its being said, that he shared his grandfather's dislike of him.

He had tried to tell his mother how he felt, but she had shushed him and told him he was being silly. But he had heard his grandparents discussing what would happen to him if his mother married her boyfriend.

'You couldn't expect him to take on the responsibility of another man's child,' his grandmother and grandfather had said. They would have to start looking round for a suitable boarding school for Jay.

When he had told his mother that he didn't want to go to boarding school, she had looked upset and told him that his grandfather knew what was best for him, and he must try to be a good boy and not make him angry.

In his dream, Jay relived the fear and desolation he had experienced at the hospital when the nurse had come to talk to the policeman and the teacher, inadvertently leaving open the door she had come through, so that Jay could see inside it. His mother was there inside, lying on a bed, only somehow she didn't look like his mother. She lay still and white, her hair scraped back off her face and covered with a cloth that was even whiter than her face. There was a swollen, ugly discoloured patch of flesh on her cheek and her eyes were closed.

Something about her stillness, something about the silence of the room around her, hurt deep inside his chest. He felt very frightened and badly wanted to cry, but his grandfather had told him that boys didn't cry. The nurse was still talking in a low voice to the policeman and the teacher; none of them paid any attention to him. He moved closer to the door and looked deeper into the room. His heart started to pound as he saw that there were two other beds in the room and that his grandmother and his grandfather were lying on them in the same still silence as his mother—at least he thought it was his grandfather, although his face . . .

He took a step into the room, although he badly, desperately wanted to turn and run away, to forget what he had seen, to pretend he hadn't seen it at all. Only there was a man blocking the way, a big, very angry-looking man who was shouting at the others as he reached towards Jay and grabbed hold of his arm. He pulled Jay towards him, demanding, 'Who the hell let this child go in there? Who is he, anyway, and what's he doing here?'

'He's the... the deceased's son,' the nurse said very quickly and tightly. She bustled towards Jay and said fiercely, 'You're a very naughty boy. You shouldn't have gone in there....'

As she spoke, she was pulling the door closed. Jay panicked. His mother was in there and something was wrong with her. He wanted to be with her... but the nurse wouldn't let him go to her. He started to cry and then scream, kicking out wildly as the policeman picked him up.

'Poor little sod,' he heard the policeman telling the teacher. 'Still, I suppose he's lucky he wasn't in the car with them.'

'Were there any survivors?' the teacher asked.

'No, a head-on crash. The younger woman, his mother, was still alive, just barely breathing. The others were dead when we got them out.'

Dead... his mother was dead. His grandparents were dead. Jay went very still. How often in his most secret and hidden thoughts had he wished that his grandfather would die, that he and his grandmother would just disappear and leave him on his own with his mother. But now God had punished him for his wicked thoughts, just as his grandmother had always told him he would, by taking his mother away. Jay started to cry....

Taylor heard the sound in her sleep, recognised it and responded to it automatically, her feet on the floor, her hand on her dressing gown even before her eyes were properly open. It was only when she was outside their bedroom door that she recognised that the crying was not, as it had been so many times in the past, the sound of her own pain bringing her sharply from her sleep, not just to escape the torment of her bad dream, but to succour the hurt child within herself whose grief and pain could only be expressed in the protective silence of the night.

No, she wasn't the one who was crying in her sleep. It was . . .

She turned her head in the direction of the room where Jay was sleeping and walked tentatively towards it, pushing open the door.

Jay was lying on his side, facing the door, his eyes tightly closed, his hands balled into the defensive, anxious fists of a small frightened child.

He was talking in his sleep, protesting between his sobs that he hadn't really meant it, that he had never meant his grandfather to die, that he wanted to see his mother . . . that she mustn't be dead, that he needed her and wanted her.

Just as her senses automatically recognised that it was Jay the child who was held fast in the grip of his nightmare, reliving some incident from his childhood, so her emotions responded to that child and his needs. It was the child who cried out for his mother and the child to whom Taylor responded, seating herself on the bed beside him, taking one of his clenched fists in her own hands, speaking soothingly to him as she smoothed the tumbled hair back off his hot forehead, her actions maternal and caring, like the steady soothing tone of her voice as she responded to Jay's cries for his mother.

'It's all right, Jay, I'm here,' she told him softly. 'I'm here now. Everything's all right.' Beneath the bedclothes his body trembled slightly, reminding her that he was, after all, human and vulnerable, his bones, his flesh, his emotions just as capable of being damaged and knowing pain as her own.

He was responding to the gentleness of her touch, the calming reassurance of her voice, relaxing into a quieter, deeper sleep.

As his breathing eased and slowed, without knowing why she did so, Taylor leaned over him and kissed his forehead—the gesture any mother might make to her child, an expression of understanding and love . . . a benediction.

They had, after all, a great deal in common, she suspected, this son of Bram's who had been so antagonistic towards her; much more in common than just their undoubted love for Bram.

She knew that Jay expected her to blame him for what had happened to Fate, in the same way that he obviously blamed himself. But he was simply one of several links in the chain of tragedy which imprisoned her niece.

He was sleeping naturally and quietly now, the man once more and not the child.

Poor little boy, how he must have suffered when he lost his mother, believing himself unwanted and unloved. No wonder he had fought so desperately to keep Bram for himself.

Taylor touched his face gently with her fingertips before getting up. In his sleep, Jay smiled.

It was four o'clock in the morning but Dennis couldn't sleep. He paced the small floor of his hiding place in excited elation, stopping every now and then to assure himself that she was still there . . . his daughter . . .

She lay on her side, huddled up inside the sleeping bag he had prepared for her. She had wanted him to untie her ankles and the handcuff that was still attached to her wrist, pleading with him, fighting hard not to cry when he had refused. He had wanted to free her, but he had reminded himself sternly that she was still at the same stage as a young, wild animal being tamed; if he untied her now, she might try to escape, to leave him, and injure herself in the process. Later, when she was more quiescent, things would be different.

He glanced at her short, shorn hair and frowned. She would have to grow it long. Girls should have long hair. He would buy her such pretty clothes and everywhere they went people would comment on her beauty. He would be so proud of her . . . and everyone . . . every man would envy him for having such a daughter.

Once all this was over and it was safe for them to leave, he would take her such places, show her such things, just as he had once promised her mother. They would go away together, travel all over the world . . . he had saved money while in prison and he could work, earn enough to support them both. They would go to Canada or America. No one would ever find them there.

He had given her some pills to make her sleep. He had stolen them from the prison hospital, not intending to use them on her, then. . . . After all, he hadn't known then that she even existed.

Would she realise that he was the man Jay had knocked into in that hotel lobby, or the man who had watched her quarrel with Jay in the street outside his apartment block? She had been disgustingly drunk, that woman he had persuaded to walk along the street with him. She had wanted him to go home with her. His face crinkled in disgust. She had become angry and abusive when he had thrust her away from him and refused to go with her. It hadn't been his fault that he had had to hit her. He had done it for Fate's sake....

Fate... He crooned her name over and over again. She was his now. His...

28

The first thing Jay noticed when he woke up was the scent, light, delicate, floral and wholly feminine. It surrounded him.

It had danced in and out of his dreams, a will-o'-the-wisp that disappeared every time he tried to catch hold of it. Dreams of his mother. Of being held by her, comforted by her, told by her how much she loved him, told that he was safe, that everything would be all right, that there was nothing to fear, that her love surrounded and protected him. Dreams such as he had never before experienced. Dreams which had nourished and empowered him rather than the debilitating, humiliating nightmares he was so used to.

It wasn't with the image of his grandfather—stern, implacable, denouncing Jay and his illegitimacy—that he had awoken this morning, but instead with a deep sense of having been loved and nurtured.

But the perfume he could smell now wasn't imaginary, nor was it his mother's. He sniffed the air curiously and then his pillow. The scent was tantalisingly familiar and yet, at the same time, unrecognisable.

It wasn't Fate's. She smelled of herself, warm, feminine, feisty and, sometimes, although he knew she would have fiercely denied it, she still had a hint of that delicious baby vanilla scent of the very, very young.

He looked at his watch. It was just gone seven o'clock in the morning, but he knew he wasn't going to be able to get back to sleep.

Was Fate sleeping, or was she too lying awake somewhere, afraid and not knowing what was going to happen to her?

What *was* going to happen to her? What was he planning to do, this man who had taken her...claimed her as his child? What would Jay be thinking of doing, in his shoes? Jay closed his eyes, trying to concentrate on how he would feel if he had a child, and someone had taken it from him. You read about this all the time, fathers who had seized their children, breaking the law rather than be parted from them. But they were fathers who had known their sons and daughters, who had lived with them, seen them born, watched them grow. Try as he might, Jay could not put himself in their shoes. And besides, this was different. Dennis Phillips had not known that Fate even existed until . . .

Until Jay had, somehow or other, given him that knowledge.

Jay sat up, pushing away the bedclothes and swinging his feet to the floor.

The house was quiet, his father and Taylor obviously still asleep, as Jay let himself out to walk along the sun-streaked, early-morning street.

At this hour there was hardly any traffic—a milk float, its battery starting to run down as it chugged its way along the street; the odd car of someone going out exceptionally early or coming home very late; a couple emerging from one of the houses opposite, their arms wrapped around each other as they shared a passionate embrace.

Jay looked away from them. Something about the way the woman had turned up her face towards the man's had reminded him of Fate.

Where was she now? Oh God, why couldn't he be with her?

For the first time in his life he recognised that there was something worse than being hurt yourself, and that was the knowledge that someone you loved was suffering and that you couldn't do anything to help them.

The sound of a church bell broke the silence that surrounded him. He stopped, frowning as he looked around him. The sound was coming from the small church tucked into a corner of the square he had just walked into.

Almost without being aware of what he was doing, he changed direction and walked towards the church. The door stood open, and as he looked through it he could see the flicker of candles illuminating the church's dark interior.

A priest smiled vaguely at him as he walked past him.

No religion had ever meant anything to Jay, and yet he discovered that he had somehow walked inside and taken up a candle, his hand shaking as he lit it.

He could see a woman deep in prayer several yards away. When she stood a few minutes later, he recognised her. Taylor obviously recognised him as well, although she gave no indication of it as she walked past him other than a brief, exhausted glance in his direction and the vague hint of a perfume he recognised instantly.

How long had she been here...? Hours by the look of her. Had she come here after leaving him...comforting him, to seek comfort herself?

Tears blurred his eyes as he tried to focus on the altar and form his thoughts into some kind of order. What was the point in his coming in here to pray for Fate when he couldn't even call to mind something as familiar as the Lord's Prayer, which he had repeated hundreds of times as a child.

Where was the peace, the reassurance, the comfort such a place should bring?

Angrily, he turned away from the altar and walked back towards the exit. As he stepped out into the sunshine and saw Taylor waiting for him, he came to an abrupt halt.

His memories of his bad dream and the way she had comforted him were still too fresh and raw for him to simply walk past her as he wanted to do. When he hesitated, she started to walk towards him.

'You must hate me,' Jay blurted out.

'No, I don't hate you,' Taylor said quietly. 'But I *do* fear you.' She gave a small shiver. 'You remind me too much of him. Your possessiveness towards your father, your obsession with him, almost.'

Jay stared at her as he realised what she was saying. 'You think I'm like him, like Phillips? You think I'd do what he's done...?'

The silent answer in her eyes shocked him. Dennis Phillips had broken the law. He had been in prison. He was a murderer and a kidnapper; he was, so Jay believed, mentally deranged. Whereas he...

'You believe that, and yet last night you still...' Jay stopped, unable to go on.

'Last night was different. Last night you were a child, alone and in need.' Her hand touched her stomach.

'I . . . I didn't mean to hurt Fate. . . . I . . . I love her.'

Jay couldn't believe what he was saying, what he was doing. He, who never confided in anyone, who trusted no one, who had never once in his whole adult life felt any need for another person's understanding and support. But then he had never loved anyone before. 'You can't love me,' Fate had told him, 'you can't love anyone, because you don't love yourself.' But she had been wrong. And so had he in thinking he was immune to love.

'Yes, I know,' Taylor told him gently.

'Oh, God, what has he done with her? Where has he taken her?'

Taylor watched him in silence. What response, after all, could she make to him, Jay acknowledged bitterly, other than to remind him that everything he was suffering, Fate must be enduring a hundred-, a thousand-fold and more?

Taylor was starting to walk away from him. Jay glanced back towards the church as he fell into step beside her, then said sardonically, 'A bit of a pointless exercise my going in there to ask for help from a deity I don't believe in. A bit like a man who's kept his money stashed in a suitcase under the bed all his life, going to ask the bank for a loan when it's been stolen. Why should God, any God listen to me, help me . . . ?'

'For Fate's sake?' Taylor suggested. 'Isn't that, after all, why *both* of us went there? For Fate's sake, and because there's nowhere else left for either of us to turn?'

'I promise you that we're doing absolutely everything we can to find her,' Jay heard the police inspector gently reassuring Fate's mother, as he walked into Bram's house.

Fate's parents had just arrived having made an early start from home. Fate's mother went straight up to Taylor and hugged her fiercely. 'I did some thinking last night and it dawned on me that perhaps Dennis Phillips was able to trace our family because we've moved back into the Oxford area—not too far from where our parents lived.' Caroline's pale face revealed how this worrying thought must have preyed on her mind through the long night. 'Oliver and I were concerned about that at the time.'

Taylor hugged her sister even tighter and said that Dennis would have tracked them down wherever they had moved to. 'You can't blame yourselves for this.'

'We're making a house-to-house search in the area around where she was last seen,' the inspector told them. 'We're pretty sure he will be holding her somewhere close to where he snatched her. He doesn't have a current passport and Fate's passport is at home....'

'Yes, we've brought it with us this morning,' Oliver confirmed.

Jay knew that the police believed, from the information Taylor had already been able to give them, that Dennis Phillips would behave in much the same way as he had done when he had kidnapped her, taking Fate to a secure den or lair he had prepared earlier, which would be very close to where he had kidnapped her, to lessen the risk.

The inspector frowned as his radio crackled into life, excusing himself to go outside to his car parked in the street.

He was gone about ten minutes and when he came back he announced, 'We think we may have discovered where he's holding her.'

'Where?' Everyone spoke in unison, while Taylor and Caroline clung to each other and started to cry softly.

'One of my men saw someone he thought might be Phillips leaving a supposedly derelict building site a short distance from your apartment,' the inspector told Jay. 'We've placed the whole area under observation and—'

'Under observation!' Oliver interrupted him angrily. 'If you think Fate's there, why the hell can't you just go in and get her out?'

'Initially, we need to ensure that the man we're watching is Phillips. And then—' he paused, adding carefully '—he may have booby-trapped the area around wherever he is hiding Fate.'

'Booby-trapped...? What do you mean?' Caroline's face went pale as she asked the question. Jay could feel his own heart pounding with a mixture of fury and fear.

'When will we know...when will we know if it is Phillips, and if he is holding Fate there?' Bram asked quietly.

'I can't answer that question, not yet,' the inspector told them. 'But I can promise you that we are doing everything we can. I must ask you all to remain here for the time being.' He looked deliberately from Oliver to Bram and then to Jay. 'Any attempted heroics are out of the question. They could endanger not only the lives of my men, but Fate's life as well.'

Jay knew that he was speaking the truth, but at the same time . . . At the same time he was thinking exactly what Oliver and his own father were thinking. Like him, they felt the same need to be there, to physically release Fate from her imprisonment and to make sure that never, never again did Dennis Phillips ever go anywhere near her.

Jay looked at his watch. It was after two o'clock in the morning and well over eighteen hours since the inspector had told them they might have found where Phillips was keeping Fate.

The inspector wasn't here now. A young police constable had arrived to keep them informed of what was happening—and, Jay suspected, to prevent them from leaving the house. Although the constable was polite, he looked disgruntled, occasionally forgetting himself and betraying his disgust with the passive role he was being forced to take.

Just before the inspector left, he had told the worried group that the police were sure that the man seen leaving the building site was Dennis Phillips and that the area was now surrounded and sealed.

'What are they waiting for?' Oliver ground out irritably, as he got up for the umpteenth time to stride over to the window and look out into the street. 'How long are they going to let him keep her there?' he demanded, turning round to confront the young constable.

How long? The same question was echoing through the heads of them all, Jay suspected, as the long night hours dragged slowly through every minute, every second. They were all exhausted, none of them willing to sleep.

Dawn came, the sky pale and clear. The young constable disappeared, to be replaced by another.

At eight o'clock, the constable's radio crackled into life. Another meaningless message, another false alarm. In the same tense, edgy silence they all heard some anonymous radio controller ask for cars to attend a shop break-in.

Jay looked across at his father. The two of them had barely spoken since Jay returned to the house with Taylor. But then what was there for his father to say? Jay wondered bleakly. What would he say in Bram's shoes? How would he feel?

The radio crackled again.

'They're going in,' the police constable told them excitedly. 'Phillips has left the site and they're going in.'

It was Bram who saw Jay look towards the door and Bram who stepped in front of him, his hand on his arm, staying him.

'I need to be there,' Jay told his father fiercely.

'For Fate's sake, or for your own?'

Jay closed his eyes. His father was right, of course, as always . . . As always . . .

The next half hour was the longest Jay had ever known, longer even than those awful minutes he had endured as a child when he had feared his father would refuse to take him in.

No one spoke or moved. Bram and Taylor sat together, Bram's arm wrapped tightly around Taylor's waist. Fate's parents stood clutching each other by the window, their gazes locked on the constable and his radio.

Only he was alone, Jay recognised, just as he always had been, just as he always would be.

Jay saw the car first. It had no distinctive marking to single it out as a police car, but something about the way it was being driven, some sense of urgency and excitement kept his attention fixed on it as it came up the street and stopped behind the patrol car already there. He was the first to see the inspector, with a night's growth of beard on his jaw, gently helping Fate out of the car.

As she looked towards the window she saw him, her lips parting slightly, her face starting to flush.

'Fate.'

Jay wasn't even aware of saying her name until the others suddenly crowded around him.

Fate blinked in the morning sunshine. Her eyes were still not fully accustomed to the bright daylight after her captivity in the darkness.

She had been afraid at first when the police found her that it was him . . . that he had returned from his visit to the shops.

Before he left her, he manacled her to the iron post with the handcuffs, and warned her not to move or call out. He said he had placed explosives around her prison which could be set off by any loud noise. She had not known whether to believe him or not, but she had been too afraid to take any chances.

'Standard issue police handcuffs,' they had told her as they released her. She had been trembling so much it had taken them several attempts to fit the key in the lock and turn it. She had only learned later in the car, once she was safe, that they had been terrified that the place really was booby-trapped—that they might all have been killed.

They had taken her away from her prison very quickly, but not quickly enough to prevent her from seeing the tomb-like nature of the lair Dennis Phillips had held her captive in. Her legs, weak and stiff with cramp, had almost buckled beneath her. She shuddered.

But right now Dennis Phillips was the last person she wanted to think about.

Through the car window she saw Jay looking at her. Her heart started to thud so heavily that it made her feel dizzy. Jay was here . . . Jay was waiting for her.

The door of Bram's house opened. Her parents came hurrying out, her mother running towards her, followed by her father. Taylor and Bram were behind them. She searched anxiously past them, looking for Jay. She could see him standing in the doorway, apart from everyone else. As she looked at him, he looked away from her.

Jay frowned as he drew back inside the house. Fate was being hugged tightly by her mother while her father looked on with tears in his eyes. Bram and Taylor were standing close to them. Caroline was laughing and crying at the same time as she said Fate's name over and over again.

Fate was laughing shakily too, as she reassured them all that she was all right.

She had barely looked at Jay, just a brief glance before turning away from him, before turning her back on him. But then what had he expected?

And wasn't it, after all, better this way...? Safer?

He was afraid of his own emotions, he recognised bleakly. Afraid of the pain they caused him. Afraid, too, of their depth and intensity.

'I don't hate you,' Taylor had told him. 'But I *do* fear you.'

Now he, too, shared that fear.

The police inspector was ushering everyone inside the house. Jay stood to one side to let them in. No one looked at him or spoke to him. It was as though he didn't exist...as though he had no place here among them, as though he were an outsider, an alien...

Sombrely he watched them; watched as everyone in turn embraced Fate, as she hugged them back, as their tears and laughter mingled. The room was filled with the exultation of her release and her safety; the pain it had previously held was banished.

It was Fate who noticed first that Jay wasn't there. She asked anxiously, 'Where's Jay gone?'

None of them could answer her. They had all been too preoccupied with her safe return to notice.

It was easy enough for Jay to slip inside the perimeter fence. The police had made a large hole in it when they had broken in to rescue Fate.

Dennis Phillips had been apprehended on his way back from the supermarket and taken immediately to the nearest police station to be charged. Jay found the place where he had held Fate without too much difficulty. Knowing what he did about the man, having learnt what Taylor had told the police, he easily recognised the pile of rubble in one corner of the otherwise empty site for what it was.

His stomach heaved as he eased himself down through the narrow aperture to the darkness beneath it. Dennis Phillips was obviously considerably smaller than he was. The burrow was lined with tarpaulin. It felt cold and damp. Even with the torch he had brought with him from his car, Jay could feel the prickle of atavistic fear shivering over his skin.

Starkly he acknowledged that he doubted that he could have survived two hours of captivity in such a space without going mad, never mind two days. He touched the sleeping bag where Fate had lain, the metal pole to which she had been chained, and a deep shudder ran through his body.

When he stepped back out into the sunlight, his face was wet with tears.

Epilogue

'You know that Fate's coming home, don't you?'

Jay rescued his two-and-a-half-year-old brother, Thomas, from the grasp of Lara, Plum's younger but decidedly more aggressive two-year-old daughter, before turning his head to reply. 'Taylor has mentioned it,' he agreed calmly.

Plum grimaced to herself as she heaved her pregnant bulk in the direction of her now screaming child. Who would have thought Jay of all people could change so much? she thought. To look at him now, to watch him with Taylor and Bram's two children, no one who had known him before could ever imagine how he used to be.

It was no secret that he had undergone analysis and counselling after Taylor and Bram's marriage. Plum had been too caught up in her own affairs at the time to pay much attention to what was going on, but she had heard about it through her mother later.

Jay put Thomas down, having soothed his dented male pride, and held out his arms to Lara. Little minx, Plum reflected, watching Lara bat her eyelashes coquettishly at Jay and coo in feminine appreciation of the attention he was giving her.

Plum had never imagined she would see the day when Jay would willingly allow assorted toddlers to crawl all over him, but he did—and with every evidence of enjoyment.

Plum had been rendered speechless on the occasion of Thomas's last birthday party, when she had arrived with a friend to collect Lara and heard the friend marvelling at Jay's 'way' with children, as she asked enviously which child was his and where his wife was.

'Come on, Lara, time to go home,' she announced now, puffing slightly as she walked towards Jay to take her out of his arms.

She felt enormous with this second pregnancy, and neither she nor Gil had been surprised to be told she was carrying twins. They were due in two weeks' time, six months after Taylor and Bram's second child.

Helena had been disconcerted when she heard her new grandchild was to be grandchildren. 'It's all right, Mother,' Plum had told her mischievously. 'They both have the same father, you know.' Of course, Helena had disapproved of the teasing comment.

'I'll carry Lara out to the car for you,' Jay offered now, grinning as Thomas bellowed his protest at being left behind by his adored elder brother.

'Come on then,' Jay told the child, and waited for him to catch up.

Plum could still remember how her mother had disapproved the first time Taylor and Bram had gone away together, leaving Thomas, then only an eight-months-old baby, with Jay. 'I know Bram has never wanted to see any wrong in Jay, but you'd think Taylor would have more sense,' Helena had said.

Plum had been staying with her mother at the time, and had willingly agreed to her suggestion that they drop in for a visit while Bram and Taylor were away. She had been shocked to see how thin and gaunt Jay was; she hadn't seen him since her own wedding. But, to her astonishment, he had seemed perfectly at ease, talking quite openly about the benefits a period of self-examination had brought to his life.

What had amazed her even more, though, was the way Jay responded to his baby half-brother—and the way Thomas responded to him; to see such a deep bond of love between a child and a man—and such a man with such a child. She, like her mother, had been so sure that Jay would hate and resent this child. The sight had made her feel so emotional that, as she told Gil later, she had made a complete fool of herself by bursting into tears and having Jay sympathise with her for suffering post-baby blues.

'You wouldn't believe it, Gil,' she had told her husband. 'He was so gentle with Thomas, so loving...so caring...it was like...'

'Like he was Thomas's father?' Gil had suggested.

But Plum had instantly and instinctively denied that. 'No . . . not like that at all. . . . It was as if . . . as if there was a special closeness between them . . . a special bond. I can't explain it properly, but you could just tell how much Jay loved Thomas and how much Thomas loved Jay. They were . . . they were proper brothers, if you know what I mean. . . .'

She hadn't been able to put into words the extraordinary feeling she had experienced, but what she did know was that Jay had somehow become a man—*the* man whom all children loved and who loved all of them. But none so much or so specially as Thomas.

After a few drinks at Thomas's christening party, she had asked Jay to explain. He had looked at her and told her quietly, 'Perhaps because he is my salvation. As I shall be his, if ever he needs me to be—which I hope he won't.' She hadn't really understood what he was saying, either then or now, but then Jay had always been very deep.

He was into his thirties now and still unmarried. Helena had commented dryly more than once that she doubted any woman would be fool enough to marry him.

Plum had disagreed, of course. But since her marriage to Gil, she found it much easier to understand why her mother was the way she was, and even, sometimes, to feel sorry for her.

Of course, Jay could find a woman to marry him if he wanted to. *A* woman perhaps, but not *the* woman. Plum looked sideways at him. He might have lost that hard brilliance which had once made him glitter like a multi-faceted diamond, all sharp light prisms and cutting brilliant edges, but he was still one of— if not *the*—most completely male and physically sexy man she had ever set eyes on.

Seeing Jay handling a small child or a baby was to have one's insides turn to instant female mush; even if, like Plum, one was totally immune to him and blissfully and completely in love with Gil.

She had seen Jay with Fate at her own coming-of-age ball and hadn't been surprised to hear both that he had proposed to Fate shortly after that awful time when she was kidnapped, and that she had turned him down.

'Give Taylor and Bram my love when they get back,' she reminded Jay now as he strapped Lara into her car seat. 'I'm going home tomorrow.' She gave a small giggle. 'Gil says he doesn't want a repeat performance of Lara's birth with these two.' She patted her stomach.

Plum had gone into labour with her firstborn midway through her journey home from her mother's and Lara had been born in the ambulance taking her to hospital, parked in an emergency stopping area just off the motorway.

Lara blew doting kisses in Jay's direction as he eased himself out of the car.

'Drive carefully,' Jay admonished Plum as he opened her car door for her. 'Remember that's my goddaughter you've got in there with you.'

Plum pulled a face at him. She still wasn't quite sure why she had suddenly changed her mind about asking Bram to be Lara's godfather and asked Jay instead. But like marrying Gil, it was one of the best decisions she had ever made.

Jay waited until Plum's car was out of sight before scooping Thomas into his arms and carrying him back to the house.

Taylor and Bram were attending an inauguration ceremony for a young, disabled graduate whose university course had been made possible by one of their specially adapted computer programs.

He and Bram still sparred occasionally, Bram's philanthropy opposed to Jay's dedication to the cut-and-thrust of commercial business. But Bram had to admit that Jay was making an international success of the company signed over to him, and the long-fought-over Japanese deal had brought growth and additional security for all concerned.

'Someone has to keep the company going until he grows up,' he had told his father at Christmas as he had relieved Taylor of Thomas's weight.

Only Bram and Taylor were privy to the full details of the metamorphosis Jay had undergone during therapy. It had been Taylor who told him about Kingspeace, the remote centre which offered itself as a retreat to those in need of voluntary temporary withdrawal from the outside world. Rather dubious at first, Jay had made arrangements to visit the place. Oddly enough, the very things which he suspected would put most people off it were what had appealed to him the most—its isolation, its separation from the rest of the world. He needed to put some distance between himself and the unhappy memories in London.

Jay smiled apologetically at Thomas. The child had just reacted noisily to the sudden tightening of Jay's grip when he thought about that traumatic time.

Dennis Phillips's case had never come to trial after all. A fight had broken out among prisoners on remand in the police cells where Dennis was being held. Dennis had been pushed to the floor and had cracked his head against a corner stone.

Death must have been almost instantaneous, the coroner had decided, acknowledging that though the accident had been unfortunate, it was the fault of no individual, just the result of unavoidable overcrowding of the cells.

It had been left to Taylor to say what the others were all thinking when she announced bravely that she was glad he was dead.

Fate had been working abroad at the time. She had left the country three days after the Christmas following her kidnapping . . . three days after rejecting Jay's marriage proposal.

And he hadn't seen her since.

Fate . . . He might not have seen her, but he had certainly thought about her. But there was no point in constantly looking back into the past, wishing that things were different.

The old Jay, the Jay he hoped he had left behind, released himself from, would have demanded that Fate note the changes in him, might even have tried to use them to manipulate her, by telling her that she was the cause of them. But for the new Jay— the Jay he did not believe he was yet but hoped he would one day become—it was enough that *he* was aware of the changes within him, that *he* could find a measure of peace and solace in knowing how much he had changed and why.

A tug on the collar of his shirt and a hopefully lisped 'biscuits' in his ear reminded him of more prosaic concerns.

'No biscuits,' he told Thomas firmly. He knew the rules and so did his crestfallen half-brother. 'Tea and then bedtime.'

'Story?' Thomas pleaded. 'You read me . . . '

'We'll see,' Jay responded in a mock stern manner.

The baby, Charlotte, was lying gurgling in her pram, the big old-fashioned sort with a high curved body and bouncy wheels. Jay had carefully turned it round so that she was out of the direct sunlight, before walking Plum to her car. Securing Thomas firmly with one arm, Jay wheeled the pram towards the house. The baby smiled up at him, blinking her eyes, which he found achingly familiar.

'She's got Fate's eyes,' Caroline had commented the first time she had seen her, and Jay had noticed the quick, protective look Taylor had sent him.

There was no going back, he knew that. He was the one, after all, who had destroyed Fate's love for him, and in doing so, almost destroyed her as well. The man he now was might suffer in the knowledge of what he had lost, far more than the man he had been ever could have done, but there were compensations, other kinds of love, and he was holding one of them in his arms right now.

'Biscuits,' Thomas repeated winsomely as Jay opened the back door and pushed the pram into the huge old-fashioned kitchen, which Taylor had made the warm heart of her new home.

The large, run-down Cambridgeshire house, which Bram and Taylor had bought three years earlier, had now been restored to its original Georgian elegance, plaster ceilings repaired and, where necessary, replaced, fireplaces and panelling restored, country fairs and antique shops scoured for furniture and 'stuff,' as Taylor laughingly called the pictures, china and silver with which she had ornamented the old house. When an enticingly tempting period piece could not be found, Taylor had commissioned young craftsmen to make new pieces for her. The result was a home, one which breathed warmth and happiness, a wonderful harmony of old and new which soothed and restored.

The ramshackle collection of stables and outbuildings had been restored to provide Bram and Taylor with the space from which to run their new business venture, which had become so successful that, increasingly, they were asked to travel abroad to lecture on their work and what they had achieved. Taylor, who refused to have a full-time nanny for the children, tried to time their trips so that Jay was free to stand in for them when they were gone.

So, Fate was coming back. Jay pondered on Plum's earlier remark. Since Fate worked for Taylor and Bram, she would know that they were currently away from home, which meant, thankfully, that she was scarcely likely to turn up at the house until after he had gone.

As he settled Charlotte in her high chair and recklessly promised Thomas not one, but two bedtime stories, he mentally ran through his upcoming business commitments. If necessary, he could bring forward a couple of overseas trips to ensure that his departure coincided with Fate's arrival.

'Open wide,' he instructed Charlotte, deftly miming the movement himself before spooning the mushy pulp he had just heated up for her which, if her wide, toothless grin was anything to go by, she was thoroughly enjoying.

Fate had spent the past eight weeks taking her turn driving the large camper that her parents had hired for their touring holiday of Australia. Now the small Ford she had rented from Hertz seemed tiny. Fate grimaced a little as she curled herself in behind the driving wheel.

Predictably, it had been raining when her plane touched down at Heathrow. It perhaps hadn't been such a good idea, after all, to come straight from an early Australian summer to the beginning of a wet British winter. But there had been things she needed to discuss with Bram and Taylor and she hadn't seen Charlotte since she'd just been born.

Besides, she had wanted to come home. Seeing her parents relive their youth by means of their long-planned-for extended holiday in Australia; watching them reaffirm their love for each other had awoken within her a restlessness, an uncertainty, a vague feeling that something was missing in her life—or someone.

She knew she was fortunate to have her family, her good friends and a wonderful job . . . even if she had initially been dubious about the latter. In fact, she had been angry with Taylor for suggesting that she work for her and Bram, help them establish a network of universities in both America and the Antipodes which would offer places to those would-be students who, because of some disability, had previously been unable to take such courses.

'A sinecure,' she had scoffed when Taylor had first told her about the job. 'I've been kidnapped, Taylor, and while it might have affected me emotionally, it hasn't damaged my intellect. I do not need you or anyone else to feel sorry for me, to pity me and make allowances for me or give me opportunities I haven't earned. I *am* still perfectly capable of functioning. I *can* still find myself a job.'

'Of course,' Taylor had agreed crisply. 'But I'm afraid you're making us seem far more altruistic than we actually are, Fate. The reason we want you is not for your sake, but for ours.

'We need someone who shares our beliefs, our aims, our commitment to the future, to what we're trying to achieve. I, *we*, believe that you are that someone. It won't be easy and it certainly won't be any sinecure. We've got to go out there and prove ourselves, both to the students who we hope will use our programs and the universities we hope will accept our students. We've no history to sell ourselves on, no facts and figures to support us, only our own belief that it can be done.'

It had been several months since her kidnap trauma and Fate had still been edgy and irritable, angry both at herself and the rest of the world for what had happened to her. And as though that hadn't been enough, Jay had chosen that Christmas to reinforce everything she already felt about herself by proposing to her. She had hated him for that, for humiliating her with his pity and offering it to her as a counterfeit form of the love he could never give her.

And so she had taken the job, seeing it as a means of escape from all the things she no longer had the strength to fight. It had drained and exhausted her more than she wanted to admit, to be surrounded by people so concerned and anxious for her, so obviously behaving as though they had to walk on egg shells around her. The job would provide an escape from their smothering concern into a more robust atmosphere where people did not feel they had to weigh their every word, their every thought, in order to protect her.

Initially, she had agreed to work for Taylor and Bram for six months. She had now been with them for close on three years. She loved her work and was justifiably proud of what she had achieved.

The first students accepted reluctantly sometimes by the universities that took them on, were now approaching the end of their courses. All of them, according to their tutors, were destined to achieve outstanding degrees. Fate knew that Bram and Taylor planned to employ several of them, needing their skills and experience to expand their growing business. The company's reputation had spread by word of mouth. Universities now tentatively sought Fate out to enquire about the program and other computer-based aids the company produced to help disadvantaged students.

At Bristol University a very senior and magnetic lecturer had made it plain to Fate that he was falling in love with her and wanted her to play a permanent role in his life. She had liked him, admired him, known that intellectually they were well matched. But she hadn't desired him. She had turned him down, and added another reason to her already long list of reasons why she should keep Jay very firmly out of her life.

And so she drove east towards Cambridgeshire and Taylor and Bram, firmly ignoring the temptation of the signs indicating London. Jay was in London, and wherever Jay was was where she did not want to be.

Jay had just stepped out of the shower when he heard the front doorbell ring.

Frowning, he pulled on a robe, ignoring his damp skin. The house was too far off the beaten track for casual callers, and so far as he knew, Bram and Taylor were not expecting any visitors, which meant . . . which meant that it was probably the vicar's wife canvassing Taylor's support for one of her charities, or, more likely, Plum, having returned after losing her way or mislaying some vital item. As he passed Thomas's half-open bedroom door, Jay could hear the familiar soft whiffling sounds his half-brother made in his sleep. He paused, and then continued on his way downstairs.

* * *

'Hi, I got the opportunity of a seat on an earlier flight and so I took it and here I am, and . . .'

Fate's voice faltered into shocked silence as she stared at Jay and he looked back at her.

Had he been ill? she wondered shakily. He looked thinner than she remembered, his face paler, his flesh stretched tightly against his bones, giving him the look of a satyr turned angel; a look which made him more rather than less explosively male.

'Where's Taylor . . . and Bram . . . ?' she asked as she stepped into the hall, firmly ignoring the fast rocking trip of her heart and the sudden effort it took to breathe normally.

'They aren't here. They're attending Neil Walters's ceremony, and then they're having a couple of days away together.'

Fate flushed. 'But that's next week.' She would never have come up here if she'd known that Taylor and Bram were going to be away.

She knew that Jay always stood in for them and looked after the children in their absence; she had had enough letters from Taylor extolling his virtues as a devoted and doting elder brother to his two small half-siblings.

Now he was bound to think that she had come here deliberately knowing that he would be here. She looked defensively towards him, but it was too dark in the shadowy panelled hallway for her to read his expression.

Uncertainly, she glanced back towards her car, wondering whether to get back in it and find herself a hotel. But she was already shivering in the unexpectedly sharp breeze that felt cold after Sydney's warmth, and Jay was frowning at her as she hovered just inside the doorway. If she left now, he would think she was running away, behaving like a child. Taking a deep breath, she stepped past him, realising for the first time what he was wearing, or rather, what he was not.

She could feel her skin start to flush—a hot burn of colour crawling betrayingly through her body.

Every time she saw him or even thought about him, it was the same. She had hoped that once she was away from him things would be different, that she would be able to put behind her her unwanted legacy of pain and anger.

'Why don't you tell him how you feel?' her mother had suggested gently, when Fate had unwittingly revealed to her how deeply her emotions still ran towards him.

It wasn't that Fate blamed Jay for what had happened to her. It was just that the pain and fear she had suffered, the anger she had been unable to express at the time of her kidnapping were somehow all tied up, in some inexplicable way, with her feelings towards him.

Or was it more simply that she had loved him and he had rejected her and because of that . . . ?

'Don't let me keep you,' she heard herself saying tersely, with a cool glance towards him.

'You're very on edge. Why? Surely it can't be the sight of me in a bathrobe. After all, you've already made it more than plain that you don't have any need or desire for what's underneath it. Or have you changed your mind?'

Jay knew that he was doing and saying completely the wrong thing, that he was behaving every bit as boorishly as the old Jay would have done, but he didn't seem able to help himself. She seemed to bring it out in him, with the disdainful way she was looking at him, the contemptuous curl of her mouth...that same mouth which he had once kissed into wanton submission . . . that same mouth which had once adored every inch of his skin, his body; that same mouth which he still . . .

She had changed. She was a woman now, not a girl, he reminded himself—the urchin crop replaced by a smooth, elegant silky bob, the worn jeans by a tailored Armani suit and a soft silk shirt. In the dim light of the hallway he could see the gleam of her plain gold earrings, their rough unpolished texture matching that of the bangle on her wrist. Her nails were polished, her face expertly made up.

She looked elegant and sophisticated, immaculate, untouchable.

Jay cursed himself and his body under his breath as he turned away from her, knowing full well exactly how she would feel about the thoughts running riot through his head. There was no way she would share his body's rebellious pleasure at images of her naked beneath him, her body sleek with sweat, sated, satisfied, her eyes heavy with that blissful look of pleasure he could remember so well, her mouth soft and swollen from his kisses, her hair tangled, tousled, soft against his skin.

'When will Bram and Taylor be back?'

'The day after tomorrow.' His eyes dared her to refuse to stay, to say what she was so obviously longing to say and to reject him as she had already done, as she always would do now.

'There's a bed made up in the guest room if you want it,' he began.

Fate interrupted him, her face flushing with anger as she told him fiercely, 'Well, I certainly shan't be asking to share yours.'

Some wounds never heal. Some wounds go on surprising and shocking by the intensity of the pain they can still inflict. Some wounds go on for ever, and ever.

'No, I don't suppose you will,' Jay agreed.

He sounded tired, and something else as well, Fate realised. But she wasn't in any mood to analyze what it was, especially after the betraying and stupidly childish comment she had made.

She put down the overnight case she had brought in from the car and shrugged her shoulders, saying 'Well, now that I'm here, I suppose I might as well stay.'

Jay picked up the case, leaving her with no alternative but to follow him as he headed for the stairs.

Two of the bedroom doors stood slightly ajar, one of them the children's, she recognised as she looked in and saw the cot. The other— Her body stiffened as she glanced inside. The light was on and she could see the unmade, rumpled bed and the pair of discarded and very feminine briefs that lay on the floor.

Jay had obviously had a woman here. Had quite obviously made love to her here on that bed. Made love to her ... Jay didn't know what those words meant. All Jay knew was how to give a woman sexual pleasure and how to hurt her unbearably and emotionally at the same time, how to give himself sexually as he withheld himself in every other way, how to ...

'They're Plum's.'

Fate's eyes widened as she realised what Jay was saying, both her shock and her anger flashing through her eyes as she focused on him.

'No. I have not been to bed with her, nor have I ever, nor am I likely ever to have any wish to do so,' he explained quietly.

'Plum is very heavily pregnant with twins. The reason for the rumpled bed is that she had a rest. The reason for the discarded underwear . . . ' He gave a small shrug. 'You're probably better able to supply that than I am. . . . '

It would be totally like Plum to decide to change her under-wear and then to forget to take her discarded briefs with her, Fate admitted. But the small incident had left her feeling raw and vulnerable, angrily aware of the confusing and conflicting emo-tions the thought of Jay making love to someone else had caused her.

She tried to tell herself it was because he was here to look after the children, not ignore them while he spent his time in bed with one of his women, but she knew that her excuses weren't really convincing.

'This room's empty,' Jay told her, pushing open a bedroom door, 'and it has the added advantage of being at the opposite end of the house to mine.' He added sarcastically, 'An advan-tage from your point of view, at least.'

What had he meant by that final comment? Fate wondered as she said good-night to him and firmly closed her bedroom door. Surely not that he still wanted her. Her heart started to beat uncomfortably fast. What if he did . . . why should that affect her . . . ? She was over him completely now. Completely and for ever.

Fate frowned as she walked into the empty kitchen. Where were Jay and the children? She had heard them earlier.

It was past nine o'clock and she had slept later than she had intended—out of tiredness or cowardice? Last night she had been too shocked and too jet-lagged to do anything other than reg-ister her body's unwanted reaction to Jay's unanticipated pres-ence.

This morning . . . She couldn't stay here, of course. It was im-possible. But if she left . . . Her frown deepened as she walked into the morning room and saw Jay through the window. He was carrying the baby on one arm and holding Thomas by the hand as they walked over the dew-damp grass towards the ornamen-tal lake, which was a particularly pretty feature of the house's extensive gardens.

When Thomas was born, Bram had wanted to have the lake filled in but Taylor had disagreed. 'If we remove every slightest danger from his life, how is he going to be able to recognise it later on when he needs to be able to do so? It's up to us to protect him from the danger while he's too young to recognise it for himself, and just as soon as we can we'll teach him to swim, him and the others,' she had added mischievously.

And so Taylor had had her way and the lake had remained, a tranquil, pretty sight under the morning's bright sunshine. Only Thomas could not yet swim, and Jay was releasing his grasp of the little boy's hand and allowing him to run towards the small jetty which projected into the water. Thomas still wasn't completely steady on his feet . . . If he should trip and fall . . .

Quickly, Fate opened the breakfast room's French windows and stepped through them, running across the grass.

Jay had walked onto the jetty behind Thomas. The little boy seemed perilously close to the edge. Fate felt her heart leap into her mouth as Jay reached towards him. Everyone knew how much Bram adored Thomas. Jay was bound to have contrasted Thomas's birth and Bram's presence in his life with Jay's own birth and childhood.

She let out a small audible gasp as Jay suddenly picked Thomas up, holding him so that they were face to face with each other.

She couldn't see Jay's face, for he had his back to her, but she could see Thomas's, and the love and wonder on it as he reached towards Jay, touching him with his still pudgy baby fingers, kissing him.

Fate felt a huge lump come into her throat as Jay bent his head over the toddler's. She could see the exposed, oddly vulnerable nape of his neck just where the thick darkness of his hair ended and the collar of his shirt began.

She could see the protective way Jay's arm tightened round his half-brother, feel the emotion with which he returned the little boy's kisses.

On the other arm Charlotte wailed her protest at being excluded from this scene of mutual love, tugging impatiently on Jay's hair.

Jay laughed as he turned his head to look at her, the intense emotion of the earlier scene lifting. She should not be here watching them, Fate acknowledged. They shared something intensely personal and special, these two who shared the same blood, who were brothers and yet who . . .

And she felt sickly ashamed of her own earlier fear that Jay might be so jealous of Thomas that he would wish to hurt him.

She remembered how, after Thomas was born, she had actually asked Taylor if it was wise to let Jay get so close to the baby.

'But I trust him,' Taylor had told her. 'Someone has to. . . .'

'But with Thomas . . . your child,' Fate had protested, ignoring the look Taylor was giving her. It was no secret to her aunt that while Fate felt not the least degree of bitterness or resentment about the role Taylor had played in bringing Dennis Phillips into her life, there was still a part of her that *did* blame Jay. She herself knew that it was illogical, but what could she do? That was how she felt.

'What better way can there be to show Jay that I do trust him, after all,' Taylor continued. 'He has worked hard for this, Fate. All his life, he's been told in one way or another that he isn't worthy of being trusted, of being loved. He's working hard to prove to us and to prove to himself that that isn't true, and now it's our turn to show him that we believe him.'

'And Bram agrees?' Fate had queried.

'Bram agrees that, in this instance, the choice . . . the decision rests with me.'

'But after all, he did try and split you and Bram up. . . You said yourself that you felt intimidated by him, by his possessiveness towards Bram.'

'Yes, I know. But that was the old Jay. The new Jay isn't like that.'

'A leopard doesn't change its spots.'

'No?' Taylor had looked thoughtfully at her. 'A leopard *can* change its spots, given a different habitat, a different lifestyle . . . and enough time. Its spots are only camouflage, after all.'

'And its killer instinct . . .'

'It hunts to eat, not to maim. As Jay has come to understand and accept that Bram has always loved him and that my relationship with Bram cannot and will not prejudice that love, so his desire—his need—to control Bram's love and keep it all for himself has been vanquished.'

'He's over thirty years old and he's an intelligent man. If he had really wanted to do so, he could have taught himself that much before.' Fate had interjected.

'Yes. If he'd really wanted to do so. That's the difference, you see, Fate. He couldn't do it by himself. He had to wait for something to happen which was so traumatic that it pushed him into taking stock of himself and his life, of understanding what he was doing to himself and others, of being ready to let go of his own fear.'

'Something so traumatic . . . you mean Bram falling in love with you?'

'No,' Taylor had told her steadily, 'I mean *Jay* falling in love with *you*.'

'He told you that?' She had laughed bitterly. 'Jay never loved me . . . he isn't capable of loving me or anyone else.'

And up until now she had truly believed that. But it wasn't true. She had just seen for herself how much love Jay was capable of feeling and how openly and unaffectedly he could express it.

She started to turn away, intending to head back to the house, but Thomas had already seen her. Jay turned round and looked at her.

'I saw you from the house,' she told him awkwardly, 'and I thought . . . ' She stopped uncomfortably, knowing he wouldn't believe her if she tried to pretend and lie that she had simply come out to join them. Already she could see him glancing from her to the jetty and back again.

'I . . . I was afraid that Thomas might fall in.'

'Or that I might push him in,' Jay supplied quietly for her.

Fate looked away from him, unable to meet his eyes.

Damn him, why the hell should he make her feel guilty when . . .

'You never wanted your father to marry Taylor,' Fate defended herself fiercely. 'You . . . '

'No, I didn't,' Jay agreed. 'But people change, Fate. You should know that. After all, *once* you loved me.'

As though the children could sense the darkness and pain of the adult emotions, unexpressed verbally but still there between them, Charlotte started to grizzle while Thomas complained that he was hungry and wanted to go inside.

As Jay strode past her, still holding the children, Fate half raised her hand to touch his arm and stop him, and then checked herself.

What good would it do . . . ? What was there, after all, for her to say? What was there for either of them to say, now?

Two days later, relating the incident to Taylor, Fate flushed as she saw the way her aunt was looking at her.

'It was what anyone would have thought,' she protested defensively.

'No, Fate,' Taylor corrected her gently. 'Jay loves Thomas and Thomas loves him. *They* have a bond between them which is stronger in many ways than the bond between Thomas and us, his parents.

'Jay told me once that he felt that in some special way Thomas's birth gave rise to his own rebirth and that the two of them are growing and learning together—that in Thomas he sees himself as a child, but wiped free of the pain and darkness of his own childhood. And that just as Thomas's gift to him is his uncritical, accepting love, so his to Thomas will be to make sure that his childhood is never shadowed or made unhappy in the way that his once was. He wants Thomas never to know what it means to feel unloved or unwanted. He wants Thomas *always* to know that whatever else happens in his life, he will have Jay to turn to.

'One day Jay is going to want children of his own and when he does . . . How long are you going to go on punishing him, Fate? Until you see him married to someone else? Until you see her bearing his children? Until you see him looking at them with the same love in his eyes he has for Thomas and Charlotte, and at her with the love he once felt for you?

'And why? What is it you want from him? What penance? What—'

'Nothing. I want nothing from him,' Fate interrupted her angrily.

'Liar,' Taylor contradicted her softly. 'You still love him, Fate. I know that and so do you and he still loves you....'

'Still . . .' Fate laughed bitterly. 'You once said that Jay loved me but Jay never loved me. Never. Oh yes, he asked me to marry him . . . out of remorse and guilt . . . shocked into it by what had happened to me, because he thought I would be too damaged to rebuild my life. But he was wrong, and the last thing I want or need is his pity. Jay never loved me.'

'Yes, he did,' Taylor told her quietly. 'He loved you before Dennis kidnapped you. He was just too afraid to admit it.'

'He told you that, did he?' Fate derided.

'In a sense, yes.' Steadily, Taylor proceeded to tell her about the night Jay had had his bad dream; the night she had heard him crying out in his sleep and, on instinct and impulse, gone to him to find him deeply asleep and reliving the misery of his lonely childhood and his mother's death, crying out for her. And then, the next morning, as Taylor and he had left the church and they had talked, he had confided in her, albeit reluctantly, but honestly, and told her about his love for Fate, about his fear of allowing himself to love her in case she rejected him, about his need for her and his anguish over what had happened to her.

'You're lying, making it up,' Fate insisted when Taylor had finished. But she knew that she wasn't.

'No,' Taylor denied.

'But why has he never told me . . . said something?'

'Perhaps because he didn't think you would be prepared to listen or want to hear what he had to say. When you turned down his proposal, you told him that there were no circumstances, no circumstances at all, under which you would want to marry him. When you said that, it wasn't just Jay you were rejecting, Fate. You were rejecting his love as well.

'He thinks you still blame him for what happened. I believe that, subconsciously, you are allowing him to believe that as a means of punishing him because you believe he didn't return your love.

'It's your choice to decide what has the greater value in your life—Jay or your pride. No one else can make it for you.

'We had a card from your parents this morning,' she added, changing the subject. 'They're obviously thoroughly enjoying themselves.'

Next year Caroline and Oliver would have been married for twenty-five years.... Twenty-five years and they still loved each other as much as ever, more in some ways.... What would she be doing in twenty-five years, and with whom?

'What's Jay's address?' she asked Taylor abruptly. She knew that he had sold his apartment and bought a small house in Richmond, overlooking the river.

'He likes being near the river,' Taylor had told her when she expressed her surprise at this change of habitat. She gave Fate his address, but warned her, 'I doubt very much that you'll find him there.

'You hurt him very badly, Fate, by thinking that he might endanger the children. Oh yes, he told me about it,' she added dryly when she saw the surprised look Fate was giving her.

'He needed to hear me say that I didn't share your fears,' she explained. 'Outwardly, he might seem the same old inviolate, impregnable, enigmatic Jay, but inwardly he's still very fragile, very unsure of himself and how far he can trust himself, how far others trust him.'

'What . . . what did you say to him?' Fate wanted to know.

'I told him that it was high time he started giving Thomas swimming lessons. He's the only one Thomas will allow to take him into the water. Bram was mortified when we all went to Cyprus earlier this year, because Thomas flatly refused to go into · the pool with his father, only with Jay.

'I think he's probably gone back to Kingspeace. He still does go occasionally when he feels the need. An awful lot of high-flying executives are starting to take advantage of that kind of retreat to recharge their batteries.'

'Yes, I know, but Jay. . . Where exactly is this place?'

As Fate drove north she wondered what on earth she was doing—what, but not why. Oh, no, never why.

To love someone the way she loved Jay was to love him for ever.

She found the centre easily enough, an untidy ramble of buildings originally built by the Benedictine monks, which straddled and guarded the approach to the fertile plains which lay beyond it.

Monks had come here with the first wave of Christianity, and the order had held the land through many vicissitudes and misfortunes. Acts of great cruelty had been performed within its walls as well as acts of great nobility and love—a Prior decapitated at his own high table by the servants of a jealous lord, an Abbot whose reign of terror and cruelty was still remembered in the order's history. And yet the air that surrounded the place, the atmosphere which saturated it, was one of great peace and wisdom, Fate sensed as she parked her car and climbed out.

A polite receptionist informed Fate that she would find Jay in the northern cloister, where a group were repairing the walls, and gave her directions.

She saw him before he saw her. He was working on a damaged section of shale wall, carefully matching the space he was repairing to the pieces of shale to one side of him before slotting them into place, the whole of his concentration given to his self-imposed task.

It made her heart ache to recognise that the jeans he was wearing were slightly loose on him and that his exposed forearms, while still as strongly muscular as she remembered, were somehow slightly less full than they had been.

Her long, anxious, uncertain drive north and the tension she had brought with her had somehow dissipated in the calming atmosphere of the monastery gardens. Up above her the northern sky was a pale blue and the grass within the cloister garden a rich, soft green. The scent of the growing herbs and flowers was soothing and healing.

Her sense of urgency left her. It was enough just to stand and watch, to absorb each and every tiny detail of her surroundings and the man she had come to see.

And, as she did so, Fate was slowly filled with a sense of deep and powerful love, of knowledge and hope, of sureness and faith.

It filled her like the warmth of the sun, enriching and enfolding her, empowering her, freeing her. It was, she understood intuitively, a benediction and a gift.

Taking a deep breath she started to walk towards Jay. When he turned round she was ready for him, keeping the six-foot distance between them but looking straight into his eyes as she said steadily, 'That proposal of marriage you made me, Jay. If it still stands, and I hope it does, the answer is yes. And even if it doesn't...' She kept her head held high and refused to be daunted by his unreadable expression.

'Even if it doesn't, that doesn't stop *me* loving you. Nothing can do that. Nothing has and nothing ever will. But I want my love for you to be a gift, not a burden. I want—'

Abruptly she stopped speaking, her words cut off as Jay closed the distance between them and took hold of her, kissing her with such slow, sweet, savage passion that her eyes filled with tears and she clung to him, forgetting all the other things she had meant to say and telling him instead, in the same way that he was telling her that she was his, that he was loved, that anything else . . . everything else could wait.

He took her to a small country inn and booked them into a room with a huge old-fashioned bed, piled high with soft, immaculate white linen bedding and feather pillows that melted into nothing.

While she lay against them, he undressed her with slow, careful fingers that trembled betrayingly when he touched her. Her skin was warmed first by the late-afternoon sun pouring through the tiny latticed windows, and then by the tender adoration of his mouth as he kissed and caressed her slowly, everywhere from the tips of her pink toes to the top of her ears. He would have done so again if she hadn't held him to her and fastened her mouth hungrily on his, telling him between urgent kisses how much she needed him, how much she wanted him . . . how much she ached for him.

Her laughter darkened her eyes as she reminded him of how he had once told her that he would make her beg for his lovemaking.

'I'm ready to beg now,' she whispered to him, shuddering as his hand cupped her breast and she felt the warmth of his breath against its hard tip.

His fingertips against her mouth silenced her. The look in his eyes as he moved so that he could look down into hers was sombre with pain and regret. 'Do you think I haven't wished those words unsaid a hundred, thousand times?' he asked her. 'Those and others . . .'

She knew he was referring to his expressed belief that Taylor had been her mother, words overheard by Dennis Phillips and fuelling Phillips's delusion. Now it was her turn to silence Jay as her fingertips touched his lips and were then slowly and deliciously caressed by them.

'I understand more than you think. You could not let go of your . . . your fear of losing your father's love. . . . I would not let go of my need to blame you for . . . for what happened to me. But now . . . now both of us have learned that we can let go of those things. Both of us are here together where we can release the past and go forward together into the future . . . our future. Here in this place now, we *can* begin again *if* we choose. We can begin. . . .'

'I choose,' Jay told her emotionally as he cupped her face and bent his head to kiss her.

'And so do I,' Fate responded simply, her words like his a private and deeply felt vow of love. She opened her mouth beneath his and wrapped her arms around him, as she would later enfold him with her body, with it and within it, holding him, loving him, being held and loved by him in return. Together they would complete a perfect circle of love, unbroken and unbreakable, a circle of love . . . a circle of life, for the rest of their lives. For ever and always.